A Lovely Pair

"Very entertaining read."

....*...son*, Actor.

"A jolly decent page-turner, it certainly kept my attention."

.........*Dave Day, The Golden Lion Group.*

"Stephanie M was the easiest Author I have ever had the pleasure to work with. Good Luck."

.................*Mark Tulley, Gemini Press.*

"I didn't realise she was such a talented writer."

.........*Mike Holland, Philanthropist.*

"She definitely gets what The Brighton Knocker Boys were all about, and does us all proud, cheers Steph."

.................*Frankie Slimtone, Local Legend.*

"I'm proud to be one of the few, to know the really true, I.D. of Stephanie. Ooh, I'm a poet and didn't know it"

.........*Derek Le- Warde, No longer on the Knocker.*

A Lovely Pair of Knockers

Also by Stephanie Marchant
'Brighton's Knockers'

All Rights Reserved First Published 2016
'A Lovely Pair of Knockers'

Self Published by Brighton's Knockers

© Stephanie Marchant 2016
ISBN NUMBER 978-1-78280-943-2

Illustrations by Jo Jo Cusack

Printed in Great Britain by
Mark Tulley @ Gemini Print Ltd,
Shoreham-by-Sea, West Sussex

A Lovely Pair of Knockers

My Most Sincere Thanks To:

All of Brighton's Honest Antique Dealers

Still alive or Long since Dead

All Three of 'em!

One Came To Light Since The Last Book.

This book is dedicated to my Dad.
After All, Family is Everything.

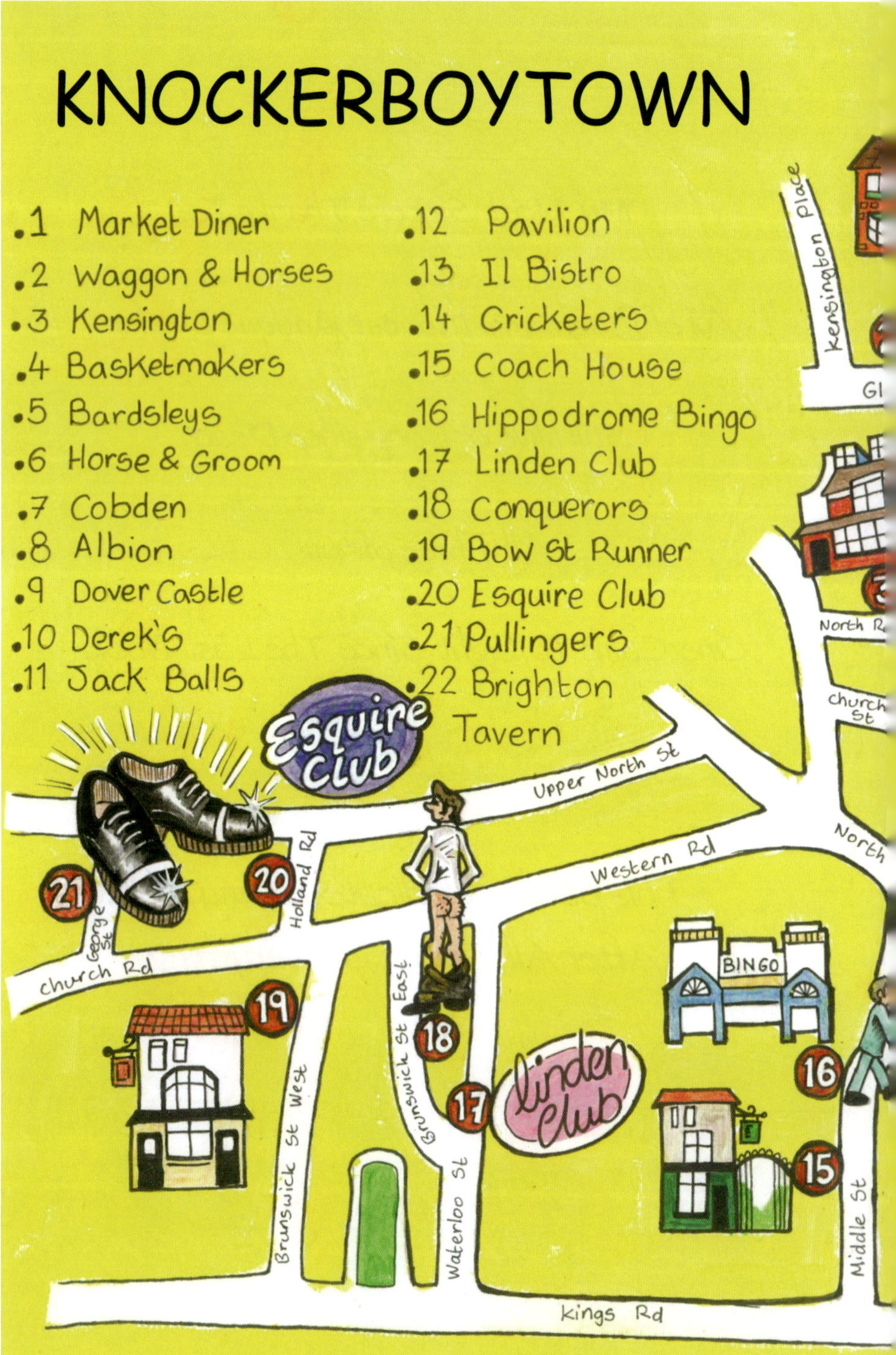
KNOCKERBOYTOWN
1 Market Diner
2 Waggon & Horses
3 Kensington
4 Basketmakers
5 Bardsleys
6 Horse & Groom
7 Cobden
8 Albion
9 Dover Castle
10 Derek's
11 Jack Balls
12 Pavilion
13 Il Bistro
14 Cricketers
15 Coach House
16 Hippodrome Bingo
17 Linden Club
18 Conquerors
19 Bow St Runner
20 Esquire Club
21 Pullingers
22 Brighton Tavern
Kensington Place
Esquire Club
Upper North St
Western Rd
Holland Rd
George St
Church Rd
Brunswick St West
Brunswick St East
Waterloo St
BINGO
linden club
Middle St
Kings Rd
21
20
19
18
17
16
15

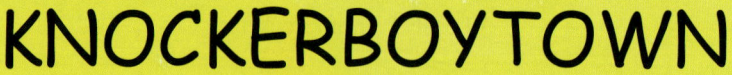

A Lovely Pair of Knockers

CONTENTS

PREFACE.

1. Let's Get the Party Started!
2. Onwards and Upwards.
3. Just An Old Fashioned Love Story.
4. The War and More.
5. Was It Really Worth That Much?
6. The Proposition.
7. A Turn of Events.
8. It's Just Not Cricket…….It's Baseball.
9. The Forest Row Coup.
10. Plans Into Actions.
11. The Partner.
12. Now Where Was I?
13. Getting It Together.
14. Sealing The Deal.
15. Revealing The Prize.
16. Let The Games Commence.
17. The Carve Up.

18. Dotting the Eyes and Crossing the Teas.
19. Let's Do Lunch.
20. Time On Your Hands.
21. The Outcome of The Forest Coup.
22. Life Goes On and All That.
23. A Day At The Races.
24. Frankie's Story.
25. The Double Act.
26. The Longest Day.
27. The Longest Day Part II.
28. The Longest Day Part III.
29. The Longest Day Part IV.
30. Adios Amigos.
31. The Golden Rules.
32. Making The Best of A Bad Job.
33. Wake Up and Smell The Coffee.
34. A Weekend To Remember.
35. All in a Weeks Work.
36. Settling The Score.

EPILOGUE

GLOSSARY

A Lovely Pair of Knockers

PREFACE.

First things first. As this is a sequel to Brighton's Knockers, it's only fair to fill you in on how it all began. This will not however, detract from your enjoyment of this edition. Although I am integral to some of the events covered, it is not really about me, but a depiction of the exploits of some very entertaining fellows from Brighton who started up the Knocking Game in the 60's.

A chance meeting in 1986 led to my integration into this loveable bunch of rascals. Upon the demise of one of the main protagonists, who provided many of the tales contained in the first Book. It became necessary for me to integrate deeper within this tight knit community in able to continue with my project.

The catalogues of stories were kept safely under lock and key till October 2014, quite simply to protect all those involved. I had also promised my Dad that nothing would come to light while he was still alive. It would not have gone down very well to shop your own Father, now would it?

He is no longer with us, and although many others mentioned are also in the ground or had their ashes scattered, no individual or partnerships can be implicated or deemed responsible for any of the incidents mentioned.

Some Brighton folk may think they recognise certain characters or chain of events, and feel they know differently, but who's to say who's right or wrong?

Not me, that's for sure, and I'm the one who wrote it!

I should forewarn you at this time, of the continuous use of colourful language, by these characters. To remove the language completely, would detract from the way these guys talk to, and about each other, would not do the stories justice, and would therefore take things completely out of context. But I took on board a small piece of advice, let's call it constructive criticism, and so have replaced one particular word with something else, in a way I hope you will find suitable and amusing.

Of course some situations do in fact require more of an actual interpretation and therefore the true word needs to be spoken. For

1

the same reason, as it can be replaced with a softer voice sometimes, on other occasions it rightly deserves to be included loud and proud. The point is then made in the graphic manner with which it was intended.

The book does not however, contain any racist, sexist or homophobic rhetoric. Although prevalent at the time, I deemed it irrelevant and unnecessary to include. It neither hinders nor enhances any of the stories, experiences, or even alleged occurrences referred to in this book.

The tales flicker back and forth in time with one particular chain of events beginning before World War II, to the present day. Covering in total, nearly six decades, of what sometimes could be referred to as mischievous, totally innocent, or even unscrupulous behaviour, by all those concerned. My own storytelling ability and initiative, I trust only embraces the whole experience.

Somehow or other, all things and beings have a form of connection. If you have ever heard someone remark "I bet that piece of furniture (car, house or room) could tell a few stories," well this is the book to read to hear about those stories, in what I hope you find to be an entertaining and amusing way.

*

The Glossary is merely there for reference purposes. So if you come across a word or phrase that makes no sense whatsoever it is explained in layman's terms for quick and sharp understanding. Some of the words or description of items are in terminology of those involved only. They would not be common knowledge at any Oxford or Cambridge University College, for example. So don't wait for the next Pub Quiz to ask 'Know it all Nigel', 'cause the chances are he won't have a 'Danny' what you are talking about.

Point Taken. Just flick to the back anytime you like.

There should also have been a complimentary postcard/bookmarker included in your purchase price. So just stick it somewhere amongst the back pages, and Glossary reference is attained at a simple flick of the wrist.

A Lovely Pair of Knockers

Sycophants and proof readers read no further, as there are multiple idiosyncrasies in the following pages, but they are all there for a reason. Your expertise is therefore not required, welcomed or given any respect whatsoever.

It is said that good written English should not contain the same word more than twice in the same sentence, but with these people they could quite easily call you a soppy twat five times in one rant. So how would that pan out? I also, tend to repeat myself a bit as well, but there you go!

A very well educated and close friend of mine, Alan Constable, helped, free of charge, with proof reading of another project of mine years ago, pointing out that proper written English should never begin a sentence with And, But or However. But, however, modern English has taken a turn for the worse these days. And so is no longer applicable. Sorry Alan.

It is only fair also, to point out, that this is merely a recollection of things gone by, so simply treat it more like a Pub conversation rather than God given rights or set in stone. Get involved with the characters and guess what their next move might be.

This will only be possible of course, if I have described their character sufficiently enough for you to come to the right conclusion, use your own imagination. Any locals that have been named specifically have given their full consent, and have been only too pleased to contribute. Two main characters are predominant but all the 'Big Brighton Families' who got the game going in the first place are all well represented.

New York City was said to be run by the Five Families, Brighton has the same notoriety, at least in the Knockin' Game anyway. I've done my homework just as diligently as they did theirs, so there's no problem there. See what I mean about repeating the same word in one sentence.

*

There are a few events mentioned which are historical facts, and all have been fully researched for validity. This was wise advice from another local, very popular and successful Author. But please remember that my due diligence also has been tried and tested over the years and I come with the back up of Brighton's Knocker Boys. They gave me first hand knowledge and who could possibly doubt their integrity?

One last thing. At times it may seem I have gone off at a tangent or lost the thread, another little habit picked up from Brighton's Knocker Boys. But please be patient and stick with it, it'll be worth it in the end.

That sounds like I am criticising my own work a little bit, doesn't it?

The only reason I mention it, is because when you do have to put the book down at some stage, you may be a little confused where you left off. Not everybody can sit in their shop, office or on the Beach, even on one of the upper decks of a Cruise Ship for that matter, and have the pleasure of reading it all in one go.

This is unlikely though as I did get carried away when writing and despite Proof Reader and Editor's attempts to convince me it should have been two books, I dug my four-inch heels in and simply made it a bigger book. The first book contained nearly 74,000 words, this edition has over 126,000. Hence, I would like to think, much better value for money.

One other thing, I love to include puns, slip in Film and Song Titles, also Groups as a bit of fun. See how many you notice.

Good luck with that one!

I sincerely hope you enjoy reading as much as I did writing. Love always SM.

stephaniemarchant123@yahoo.com

*

A Lovely Pair of Knockers

1. Let's Get The Party Started.

I was not born with a Silver Spoon in my mouth by any means. You could say, more of a Golden Toothpick, tackier I know, but what can a newborn baby do about their circumstances?

My dad Robert was a self-made millionaire, a few times over, albeit under dubious circumstances. But I never ever saw him hurt anyone, and only witnessed him lose his temper once, and this was only expressed in a verbal manner. His face did go a kind of purple colour, eyes bulged like Marty Feldman and chest puffed out like a prized carrier pigeon. Comically enough, it was with reference to the subject of this book that triggered this reaction, still, it's only a laugh anyway, is it not?

I was, as I say, born with certain privileges, but money can't buy you everything. I did unfortunately grow up without a Mother, so it wasn't all joy and splendour. I feel sympathy when a friend or associate mourns the death of a parent, but as in my situation, you can't miss what you never had. She had died in a tragic boating accident when I was only two years old, and still in a pram.

Dad obviously did his best, with Private Education etc, etc, but I was hardly a star academic pupil. I was, what you might call, a student of life. Not all these establishments complied with my train of thought, and it was slightly embarrassing coming home halfway through a term, with all my belongings packed, and a refund of the fees. With, 'Attendance No Longer Welcome At This Establishment' plastered along the top of the envelope. We managed though and I loved him dearly.

He always said I was a proper little Minx, affectionately nicknaming me "Minnie", something that I accepted in the loving way in which it was meant, my closest friends all tag me the same.

He once proudly remarked, "You can pay for school, but you can't buy class. You have it in abundance." Then kissed me softly on the cheek.

*

These stories came into being, when I moved from Surrey to Brighton to attend University on a Journalism course. I happened to come across an interesting character, who had an abundance of tales, about himself and many other Brightonian chaps, who were 'On The Knocker.'

Georgie Balcock was his name. He and many of his friends plied their trade going around knocking on doors and asking if there was any unused or unwanted stuff in the house. They would then proceed to purchase all or anything once they 'Were In.' This could be anything from the dinner table and chairs, ornaments and the cabinets they were in, to old heirlooms, paintings or even garden furniture.

On occasion, they would be targeting one specific piece that caught their eye. So would offer exorbitant sums for worthless things, in order to include something else, 'The Prize', for an amount less than it's true worth.

Some of these dealers could be deemed unscrupulous, but the householder had probably inherited everything in the first place. Even though they may not be aware they were being sold short, they hadn't paid for it in the first place.

I don't consider myself a prude or a pompous prat; we all have our dark side. Once finding myself drawn into the world of Brighton's Knocker Boys, I was fascinated, and felt a strong allegiance to all of them. Still do for that matter.

When my first contact with these guys passed away, on a most memorable night at the Il Bistro Mediterranean Restaurant in Little Market Street in Brighton's Lanes, one Georgie Balcock. The funeral was to become a landmark in my life, very memorable indeed. Whilst chatting with someone, Joker Smythe, it became apparent that the love of Georgie's life had died many years before, and he had never really recovered from the event.

Being a nosy cow, I couldn't leave it. My instincts told me to slow down, but I paid no heed. It eventually came out, that Georgie had been in the South of France with my Mum of all people, who had temporarily left my Dad and I, when the accident occurred.

I was absolutely devastated as you can imagine. My saving grace was my trusted friend and companion Grace. She had been a friend of Mum's and married to Dad's best friend and business partner. When I moved to Hanover Crescent, Brighton, it suited everyone for Grace to live in the lower ground floor self-contained flat in the same building. She helped show me how to look after a place and we bonded. She became, I suppose, the mother I never had.

Needless to say, the confrontation with my Father was harrowing. Yet with the advice from Grace and another close friend Tracey, I managed to contain my anger and resentment at having been lied to all my life.

It turned out to be equally distressing for my Dad. When the tragedy had happened he had been to hell and back. Thinking only of how to protect me, and do the very best he could, raising a child on his own. He also wanted to kill the rat that had taken his beloved wife, and robbed his daughter of a Mother. I told him he couldn't have done such a bad job, he cried, I cried, we both cried. Grace started crying, Tracey joined in, and we had to phone a plumber because there was a leak in the kitchen. Not really, it just seemed that all the tears were flooding the place.

Once, all was said and done, we made a plan. Never to keep secrets from one another, never ever again. Dad revealed that he had set out to ruin all of Brighton's Knocker Boys, once he found out about Mum running off with one of their crowd.

We all found it slightly ironic in a sinister kind of way, that it would turn out to be, at the very root of all the trouble, Georgie Balcock of all people. The Knocker Boy I had met and befriended. It was his stories that led to my interest in writing about their exploits.

Now, as well, my Father was about to reveal his part in the tales. A much, much, much bigger part than would ever be thought possible.

Later that same evening my pregnancy test came back positive again. It was my third positive result, talk about living in denial. Guess what? Surprise surprise, I didn't tell anyone.

*

This was late 1986, I was only 20, but on that very same day I was drafted into the Family business, at my request. This at the time was mainly dedicated to property development and management. Also revealed on the same day was a hoard of old furniture, and some very classy Antiques. Dad had stored it all in a warehouse he had acquired out at Shoreham Airport.

One of my first assignments was to find a way of selling it all off without bringing any undue attention. My first reaction was to go to auction, to achieve the best price. This got the thumbs down from Dad.

Then I was inclined to go to one of my associates in the business, who I had met in the recent months. Thumbs down again. Although the hatchet was buried as far as 'revenge on the knockers', was concerned, there was no need to give someone else the Lion's share, was Dad's opinion. I could offer no reasonable argument there.

"Okay then," I announced one evening, "Seeing as you have seen fit to veto all my ideas so far. How about this one? We buy our own shop, with storage space, and sell directly to the public. We must surely get the best price then?"

Dad replied in a contained and serene fashion,

"But sweetheart, you are forgetting that a lot of that stuff is stolen. The filth will be on you like a ton of bricks. Why do you think I have still kept hold of it all?"

"Well," I began. "I am not bloody stupid, and I do realise that. But don't you think that a lot of that gear is long forgotten? The victims have all been paid out on their insurance. Unless something is guaranteed to be a one-off, and worth a fortune, I don't see the problem."

It was always a good idea to pose a question, then include the solution when dealing with my Father. A trait I had picked up from him in the first place, and it niggled him when on the receiving end of his own tactics. Role reversal is a sure way to gain the upper edge, in multiple situations, and this particular scenario was certainly one of them, in my opinion.

*

Any dispute, with a trades-person or even shopkeeper, over money, "What would you do, if you were in my position? You would *question it undoubtedly," being a classic example, or "Would you pay all that extra without question? Of course you wouldn't."*

*

He succumbed. For the time being anyway.

I still had to get my thinking cap on, and in my present condition, was fully aware the ball needed to get rolling sooner rather than later, or I would miss my chance.

One morning, I was up at Churchill Square, Shopping Centre, and bumped into a girl from my time at University. I couldn't remember her name at first, so blatantly asked her.

"I am so glad you were honest," said a relieved Poppy, "I wasn't sure of yours either." How could I be offended at that?

We agreed to pop into British Home Stores for a quick coffee and a catch up. She was happy to see me and was thrilled at a recent job opportunity. She had been given a position at Liberty's of London as a window dresser. It was all very exciting. Poppy had been given an assignment for a whole window display, at the side of the store, and needed to come up with her own original concept in two days, this deadline posed a bit of a problem for her.

"One minute I am on top of the world, and now I am in the depths of despair, this window is huge and I haven't got a clue what to do," it was a bit dramatic, admittedly, but I spontaneously saw an angle.

"What if I can help you with an idea," I ventured, "How about, a whole window, with evenly measured shelves, filled with old metal sewing machines. Indicating that everything in the store is hand made, on the premises, so to speak."

Poppy looked amazed, "Well, I can see where you are coming from, but where the hell would I get the machines in such a short time and what the blazes would it cost. I only have a budget of £2,000."

"Well, for starters, you get the maintenance department to fit the shelves. Glass would probably be the best to use, so people can see into the shop, they are bound to have plenty of glass shelves in storage, surely, don't you think?" Poppy nodded, becoming enthralled.

"As for the sewing machines. I happen to know someone who could, quite possibly lay their hands on quite a few, and may well be able to help us out with that one." All of a sudden this is a joint enterprise and she didn't even flinch.

"Do you really think that it's possible Steph? When can we find out?"

"The best thing to do Pops, is go straight back to your office or workshop, and do some kind of design, blueprint or whatever you call it. What I will do is locate the machines, check out their suitability, and negotiate a price. You run the idea past your bosses and we can meet this evening and see how we are situated. Whaddayassay?"

"Sounds terrific, Steph, let me get your number, and here is my card, call me any time you like. Dinner is on me. Bye, bye now."

As we both stood up we kissed each other on the cheek and went our separate ways. She certainly had a click in her heels did Poppy, in fact she nearly fell over as she went up the escalator, she was so excited.

Back at the warehouse I convinced my Dad that all the sewing machines could easily be detached from their tables if applicable, at no cost.

"Stephanie, I have told you time and time again, nobody is interested in these relics. They have to be seen in working order before anyone will even think about it, and they are so bloody awkward to transport what with the tables an' all."

"You, haven't listened to a single word I have said, have you?" Giving him no chance to answer, "I don't care if they work or not, it doesn't matter what make they are either. Singer, Jones, Vesta or Empress. All we need to do is dust 'em off, and send 'em off. Now how much do you want for them? I make it 225 machines in all. Come on, how much?"

"Well, it's hard to say really," he ventured cagily.

"Why is that then, have you suddenly lost the use of your wagging tongue or something?"

"Don't start getting saucy with me young lady."

"Well just answer the bloody question then. How much?"
"Well years ago,"

A Lovely Pair of Knockers

"Come on Dad, don't start giving me all that old nonsense, how much? Do you need to phone a friend or what?"

"Alright, alright. They used to scrap for 10/6 each. Brand new they woz about, ooh I don't know. I'm sorry, I really don't know. Alright then, what will you offer me for the whole lot?"

We had finally got there. Now was the time to play the ace. "Well, like you say, nobody really wants them. And then of course, we don't know if they are all in working order or not. Someone has got to be paid to undo all those screws. The tables are not worth diddly once the machine is gone, but we might be able to work something out."

"Tell you what I'll do. I shall speak to a prospective buyer this evening and call you in the morning with a one off offer. How does that grab you?"

He was a bit miffed, but I could see he saw the funny side of all the haggling, and still not an offer on the table. I would not mention a price till he asked for one.

On the journey back into Brighton he came clean,

"You know what Stephanie my darling, you are absolutely right. I have been holding onto all that stuff for far too long. Due to the circumstances, I suppose. I was not really hanging onto it all for sentimental reasons, just became a bit attached to the rhyme and reason, that's all. It's served its purpose now, so let me, let it be."

"You can do what the hell you like with all the poxy sewing machines. If you make any money, good luck to you. I will just be glad to see the back of em'. Whatever you make, donate 10% at that little charity event next week, you know, buy something in the auction. How does that sound?"

As we pulled up outside my house I said:

"Fantastic Dad, I'll be looking forward to it. Oh, and by the way, I'm pregnant".

Before he could say anything I hopped out of the car and scarpered indoors.

*

2. Onwards and Upwards.

Upon entering my place I quickly looked out the window, and as expected, saw my Dad was parking up. Fortunately I did have some wine in the fridge, so poured myself a glass and settled down on the couch. Not even bothering to switch the telly on.

Four minutes later came the knock at the door, both Dad and Grace were standing there beaming.

A heavy discussion ensued but everything was covered and some vague plan was made. Dad felt it might be a good time to look for somewhere else to live. Private schools in Hove were reputedly much better equipped for the younger children's education. Also they would be raised in a nicer environment. I questioned about how he had all of a sudden, an educated awareness of such things.

He simply shrugged it off, in a dismissive manner, as if to say 'well someone in the family has got to know these things', so I pressed the issue no further. Grace actually agreed, and she would only do this if she did indeed, genuinely feel the same way.

We all agreed there was no doubt as to who the Father was, but he had recently departed to begin a new life in the U.S.A. unaware of my condition of course. I was adamant he should not be contacted or at least for the time being, have any involvement in proceedings.

Dad, bless his heart, did make a half-hearted attempt to change my opinion, but could clearly see I had not made this decision lightly. The only thing they were jointly pleased about, was the fact they were the first to know.

In this day and age, the plight of a single mother was nothing compared to forty or thirty years ago. In my case money and family support was certainly not going to be an issue. I still consider myself extremely lucky, compared to the many single parents out there, that do not have the benefit of that all-important cushion.

I met with Poppy that evening in The Cricketer's, Black Lion Street. She only had good news. Her idea had been met with great enthusiasm. She admitted, straight away, that she had proposed the concept as her own original idea, and not revealed it was a collaboration. I accepted this as a given, she got the job in the first place because it was her responsibility to bring fresh creativity. How she achieved this was her business.

It all hinged on how this could become a reality, and that was where I came in. She felt a tinge of guilt, but I reassured her this feeling would soon fade,

"Business is business," I said, "Don't you worry about me. Now, how does the budget look? I may well be able to help on that aspect."

Question. Then answer yourself. Playing the part once more.

"Well, that was the one awkward point of the whole thing," she began, "One of the other members of our department mentioned that he knew of an old fur factory that had recently gone out of business, and that they could very possibly get a load of machines from them, as they were going into liquidation. I asked him to get a costing. I could hardly ignore someone who has been with the company for thirty years, what with me being new and this being my first assignment. Sorry Steph, will this be a problem?"

I was certainly not impressed, but not about to be thwarted. "Don't you worry Poppy darling. Just make sure, that when he comes back with an estimate you mention all these machine makers names that must be represented, or their may well be legal implications."

Passing her a list of all the prestigious makes, that I had noted we had in stock at the warehouse, I didn't have a clue, but it looked very professional.

"May I just add Poppy? That if those other machines are from a Furrier, I guarantee you that the source will be of the Jewish fraternity. They don't give away ice in winter, and you can bet your bottom dollar, they will try to infer that they are doing you and your company a favour, by letting you have the machines. Whether they are out of business or not, the price is not going to be cheap."

"Oh that's grand, Stephanie. Now do come along I have reserved a table next door in the Restaurant, or we can just eat here at this table, if you like, I hear the steak is good."

We had a lovely meal with a nice South African Shiraz, and my Tia-Maria Calypso coffee finished things off nicely. We had not been

A Lovely Pair of Knockers

close at University but somehow had a sudden unique bonding. There was an unspoken trust between us. I told her I was pregnant, and was then overcome with guilt, as I had not even told my best friend Tracey it was definite yet.

It was left till 3:30 pm the next day, to check on the latest with the machines, but I assured her that the two thousand should be enough for 225 pristine machines. Poppy ordered two Taxis, as she was off to Hove.

I had decided to tell Tracey of my new condition. Tracey was pleased for me and everything was all sorted and taken care of. She had recently visited relatives in California and told me about this American tradition of 'Baby Showers', and how we should start it in England. This all sounded quite exciting, so I readily agreed. Then we went into all the Old Godmother business and all that.

Tracey stayed till about 2:00 am, and then decided to crash in the spare room, easier to get to work at American Express from my place.

Poppy called me at home, at 12:30 the next day, sounding hysterical. I managed to calm her down and arranged to meet at Hove Place, 1st Avenue at 1:30. She looked in a terrible state and had obviously been crying. She then began to explain the morning's events.

The upshot was this Maurice herbert, had a brother in the fur trade, hence the source of the machines. At the morning meeting he had revealed his own version of Poppy's design. He had halved the number of shelves and pre-ordered 100 machines at £30 each.

This proposal had been given a preliminary confirmation by one of the Director's. With whom Poppy had no chance of meeting and being able to explain it was her idea and had plans of her own already in place.

We had a couple of nice sandwiches with our drinks while I considered the matter. Thinking and plotting all the while. This was all out war as far as I was concerned. Irrelative of my gain or loss, it was most definitely imperative Poppy should not suffer because of my interference.

"Right then," I began, "Think about this before you answer. Are you prepared to let me intervene and take care of this for you?

Remember it is totally up to you, it is your decision. I am confident I can resolve this situation and turn it right around in your favour. As long as you can trust me, and I know you do. Do you want me to sort this out?" She nodded like a child eager for ice cream and jelly. "Right then, you just sit tight my dear little Poppy. We'll show that scheister Maurice, how you really play the game."

I indicated to the Manager Richard that I needed a word, and after a quick chat, had him on board. The telephone booth there had a reasonable bit of privacy, so was ideal for the three of us to carry out the first part of my plan. Not that I knew what the second or third parts were yet.

Having dialled the number for Head of Design at the HQ for Liberty's. I spoke with a secretary and asked to speak as a matter of urgency to the Director involved with the new window at the Liberty's of London store, next door to The London Palladium.

She obviously tried her hardest to avoid putting the call through, but after requesting her name, for further reference, when this matter went to legal proceedings, she put me through. I then passed the phone to Richard. When the phone was answered he questioned the recipient immediately in an abrupt manner as instructed.

"Is that Sir Percy?"

"Why, yes of course it is, to whom am I speaking?"

"Don't you worry about that sir, please hold while I put your call through. May I also caution you at this time that this call is being recorded and anything you say during the following conversation with Miss Marchant, will be available to all relevant departments and concerned parties. Thank-you sir I shall put you through now."

He covered the mouthpiece, tapped it twice then passed it to me, whilst smiling all the while.

"Hello, is that Sir Percy? Okay, thank-you for getting back to me so soon. I do not have much time to waste on this ridiculous situation, but let me fill you in on the facts as I see them at the present time. If you continue, with this preposterous proposal of this man Maurice Cohen, you will find yourself on the skids with all the yids."

"They have managed to throw away a perfectly functional industry, the Fur Trade, employing nearly eighteen thousand people across the country, with their greedy and selfish attitude. Now this is not the direct issue, but, why on earth would you, yes you Sir Percy, and please don't interrupt me Sir."

"Why would you for the love of god, agree to pay £3,000 for a load of useless and ineffectual machines that have no bearing or recognition to the general public. Do you not realise that the aforementioned sewing machines, used in the fur industry are in fact over-locking machines. They have two cogs or spindles, however you wish to describe them, between which the fur hide is placed and then sewn together."

"These machines have no resemblance to the household sewing machines that would be recognisable to our targeted customer. The young lady that placed a preliminary reservation on the goods concerned, has been treated in the most diabolical fashion."

"A good friend of mine at The Evening News may well be interested in this story but I am confident that will not be necessary, now will it Sir Percy? I thought not. You know it makes sense."

"My personal opinion on the matter, for you, Sir Percy is this. Simply to take another look at the first proposal, and agree that it is in the best interest of The Company, and all concerned, to go with the first blueprint. By all means converse with the other heads of advertising and senior partners, but I am confident you will come to the right conclusion."

"I will leave my personal details with your secretary and look forward to your decision. I do realise of course Sir Percy that the responsibility of the success, or failure, is all on your shoulders, yours alone, and will abide with your wishes as you see fit. Do you have any questions or require any other relevant details sir?"

This tirade had come over me on the spur of the moment and my adrenaline was pumping through me as if on some form of drip-feeding apparatus.

There was a brief silence at the other end, and both Poppy and Richard alike were holding their hands over their mouths to prevent exploding.

"Well, I think this matter may need some reconsideration by the sounds of it. What did you say your name was again my dear?"
"It's Miss Stephanie Marchant, Sir Percy. Of Marchant and Marchant

A Lovely Pair of Knockers

Holdings Limited. We are a very well established shipping company, on the South Coast, with a strong reputation to protect, and so you can understand my concern in such disturbing circumstances."

"I need not bother you any further on the details. Please hold one moment I have a very important call on the other line………. Sorry about that, but I have a transatlantic caller on the other line. Can I entrust you to deal with all this messy business Sir Percy? Great, you have a nice afternoon and maybe we will catch up sometime in the near future. Perhaps even the unveiling of this great window dressing idea, by, oh yes, I think her name is Poppy. Thank- you."

Then I hung up before he could stutter another word.

Poppy was exuberant and jumped up and down with glee. Richard congratulated me on the first part of the plan, then offered us both a drink. Knowing he couldn't give drinks away I declined but he insisted and brought them over anyway.

It's tough sometimes working behind a bar and putting your own money in the till. Still he was a good bar manager, a dead ringer for John Conteh, that great boxer from Liverpool, and was paid top dollar by Dave Day who was still in charge of The Golden Lion Group at the time.

There were now a few Pubs under his guidance. Not always the cheapest, but always the cleanest, with competent and knowledgeable staff. It's not just the food and drink you have to be aware of, but the customer's likes and dislikes also.

We had a few more drinks then decided to call it a night. Poppy then revealed she was not ready to go home. Her boyfriend was not too supportive when it came to these situations, and her parents still wanted her to be a teacher. I suggested she came back with me and I'd introduce her to Grace and my other reliable friend, a well-chilled bottle of Chablis.

Grace was up for it, Tracey also popped round and we all had a lovely night. Poppy stayed in the spare room and although a bit groggy in the morning, soon perked up after a fresh coffee and Danish Pastries.

"How on earth did you manage to go out and get such lovely fresh fruit pastries at this time of the day?" she enquired.

I just smiled, pointed to the flat below and whispered,

"There is such a thing as a Fairy Godmother you know. Good luck, today, we will all be thinking of you."

I was looking forward to a lazy day, but at 1:30 the phone rang, and Poppy sounded ecstatic.

"Please, please meet me at 4:10 at Brighton Station, bring Grace if she can make it."

We were both waiting for her at platform 6, but nearly missed her entirely. She was a complete transformation from the ex-Uni pal I had met with a few days earlier. Not only did she now carry herself like a Fashion Magazine Editor, she really did look three inches taller.

Greeting us with an exhilarating smile that literally electrified the place, she indicated to jump straight in a cab. She confidently instructed the driver to Hove Place, then looked at us both to make sure this was okay, 'Why not', we both answered without a word being uttered.

Poppy composed herself beyond her years and managed not to say too much on the short journey to First Avenue. We took a table at the rear and Poppy, relieved to see Richard, requested a bottle of their best Champagne and four glasses. He frowned as to the number of glasses and she simply indicated that he could have at least one glass surely? He concurred.

She began, "Well, you would never believe in a million years what has happened to me today. You know how much I was dreading the meeting. Miss Hepworth did her best to comfort me, but I was a bag of nerves. That creepy Mr Cohen was looking all smug and pleased with himself. There I was thinking it was all ended before it got started, when we were all summoned to the Grand Boardroom.

As we entered we were guided to our seats, I was next to the top. All the Director's came in afterwards, and Sir Percy was head of the table next to me. He asked if I was Poppy, when I said yes he tapped me gently on the shoulder, winked and said hello. It was then indicated for his Personal Assistant to read a memo."

She then reached in her oversized handbag and removed some A4 sheets of paper from an embossed envelope,

"This is the exact statement, I knew I wouldn't be able to remember it all so I asked for a copy. He spoke in a really posh accent so it came across deadly serious too. A bit like Basil Fawlty he was. This was what it said:

> 'It has come to our attention, that contrary to company policy, some extremely unfavourable procedures have been conducted within the Advertising and Display Departments.
> It appears that a new, and therefore junior, member of staff. Was tasked with creating a new and yet exciting visionary window display for our Liberty's of London Flagship Store, next to The London Palladium.
> It follows that the task was completed within the time allotted. Also, pending authorisation and contract negotiation, within budget.
> It has now also come to our attention, that a senior member of staff, took it upon themselves, for whatever reason, to redesign the first presentation, and 'Make – A – Better – Job – Of - It'.
> After further investigation, and confidential information received from an outside party, without prejudice. It appears that the new and revised structure is not only much more expensive, it does not comply with the remit of the original requirements.
> Furthermore, it has been discovered that, not only does this have no bearing with the aforementioned remit, it will have no presence or familiarity with our targeted clientele.
> If this were not scandalous enough, it appears that there is a conflict of interest. Which has brought further discomfort amongst the Members of the Board.
> Not only has this senior member of staff apparently gone way above their station, the main benefactor of a huge sum of money is indeed a Family member, contrary to company policy.
> As a result of this extremely distasteful and totally unacceptable behaviour. It is therefore, with much regret, that the contract between Liberty's of London and Mr Maurice Cohen is terminated immediately.

Due to his long-standing relationship within the company, we agree to honour his pension. Although doubt is cast upon the honour with which he has conducted himself over the years.
The publicity could do the company no good so we choose to turn the other cheek.
Please escort Mr Cohen from the building, forthwith.
Due to this unexpected turn of events, radical changes are to be made.
It has also regrettably come to our attention, that despite some awful behaviour and ill treatment, by her colleague. Miss Poppy Perkins, has conducted herself in the most gracious manner, befitting a trusted and loyal member of staff.
A trait that has not gone unnoticed, and is to be admired by all those in her midst. It also therefore should not go unrewarded, in our humble opinion.
We herby announce, with the greatest of pleasure, that Miss Perkins is the newly appointed Head of the Displays Department. Congratulations.
She is without doubt the youngest Head of Department in the history of the company.
We would also like to take this opportunity to point out, at this stage, that it is of no detriment to Miss Hepworth. Who should, as a rule of thumb, be next in line, but under these exceptional circumstances we hope she fully understands.
The company will only grow stronger with new blood such as Miss Perkins, and we intend to keep up with appearances.
With reference to the case at hand, it has been decided by the Board, by a unanimous decision, that the design by Miss Perkins will be moved to the front of the store, and after due course will then be re-constructed in other stores in other parts of the country.
The budget also, has now been doubled. Instead of that scoundrels three thousand pounds, six will be allotted to this project, with our blessing.
This will also ensure a continued respectful relationship is retained with our shop fitters and suppliers. Well done everyone.'

Even I didn't know what to say. Grace hugged Poppy like she was her own child. Then they looked at me in a funny way,

"What's up," I asked. They were both crying now, and didn't know I was so sentimental. I had been sobbing evidently, half way through it all, and my make up was an absolute mess. We were all thrilled, and the champagne flowed.

Poppy declared that she would make sure the window display would be absolutely perfect, then a look of panic came over her face, "Oh my God, I never even asked. What happened about the bloke you thought might be able to help? Still it doesn't matter so much now, we've got plenty of cash flow to cover it now anyway. It's just the time factor, any chance he can help Steph?"

I raised my glass to toast the pair of them,

"It's in the bag Poppy, absolutely in the bag my lovely. Don't you worry your pretty little head. It's all sorted. They can be delivered on Sunday afternoon. There won't be so much traffic, I will follow the delivery up myself, with you by my side, and we'll oversee everything and conquer the world."

"Fantastic, we can give the bloke extra now. Let's call it five thousand and you have the extra grand for doing all the real work. It's all been down to you anyway from the very start. I am so glad I took a chance on saying hello to someone, even though I couldn't remember your name. Cheers Stephanie Marchant, my hero and friend forever."

The fact that without even thinking, she automatically wanted me to have the spoils and monetary reward was very heart-warming. My instincts of trust had not failed me. Knocker Boy instinct they call it.

My turn now to tickle the senses,

"Well I am afraid that won't be possible Poppy. You see, that would be tantamount to conflict of interest. If someone were to find out it was a friend who supplied the sewing machines and benefited from the sale, you'd be in the same boat as old greedy bollocks Maurice."

"You could, however, make a charitable donation of one thousand pounds, in the name of Liberty's of London, courtesy of Miss Polly Perkins, Head of Window Displays."

"We happen to have such an occasion next week, a dear friend of mine Mike Holland, a local Businessman has organised it and you can be my guest of honour. Befitting a girl of your calibre and position. Whaddayasay?"

We laughed some more, but another added bonus was that Poppy was now more than happy to go home that night and tell everyone at home, about her day.

Four thousand pounds was gratefully received by Marchant & Marchant Holdings accordingly. We had a great night at The Grand Hotel the following week. Poppy presented the charity with a cheque for £1,000, with the compliments of Liberty's of London, signed by Sir Percy himself. I purchased a painting by Chris Ellison, renowned local actor and artist with his own unique and original style, for four hundred pounds, in the auction.

Dad remarked proudly whilst raising his glass of wine,

"I said ten percent of the sale, not the whole jolly lot." I smiled knowingly, Poppy and Grace both raised their glasses and toasted me, it felt really good. Not so good in the morning though, so it was clearly time to knock the alcohol on the head. Something below was making its presence felt.

I did joyfully attend the opening of Poppy's window display; a couple of weeks later and it was a sensational success. She advised I would always be welcome to help with creative input anytime I liked. But she knew where my loyalties lay, and never expected me to take her up on it for a minute. She had also come in one thousand pounds under budget.

On top of that she was credited for attaining some much appreciated good publicity, for Liberty's. She was hailed as a great asset to the company and eventually became the first non-family member to be elected onto the board.

She recommended that Miss Hepworth be recognised for her services to the company and arranged for a private pension fund in her honour. Miss Hepworth went on to have her own range of clothing, and when asked, credited it all to a young Polly Perkins, who had inspired her. Dorothy Perkins also had quite an impact on the fashion industry, any relation do you think?

A Lovely Pair of Knockers

There ended up being 225 sewing machines in the display. Singer, Jones, Empress, Frister & Rossman, Serata M, Vesta, Davis, and Universal were all represented.

If you were to check out a lovely ladies fashion store, All Saints of Spitafields, in East Street, Brighton, you could witness for yourself what such a display would look like. They only have 200, 8 shelves high by 25 long, stretching out over the whole side window, but you'll get the idea. The side window was the original destination for the Liberty's of London Store, funny that.

*

What's all this got to do with Brighton's Knockers I hear you ask?

Well quite simply, before I met Georgie Balcock, on that fateful night outside that sleazy, All Night Diner. I was destined for a run of the mill life myself. Starting a mediocre career, looking forward to an equally mediocre existence. With even less ambition, than most. I would have been waiting, in anticipation of meeting Mr Right, who eludes us all; no matter how far and wide we search.

But Now. With all the vibrant characters I had met over a period of just about only five months, and heard of the most fascinating and unimaginable circumstances. I truly believed that absolutely anything was possible. And with a bit of guile, cunning and unadulterated cheek, you could achieve the impossible.

I could never have imagined myself even contemplating such antics as I had over the last couple of days for instance. Now though, armed with the knowledge of how supposedly uneducated youngsters, by simply using other people's greedy inclinations, were more than capable of manipulating any given circumstances to evolve in their favour, and come out on top against all the odds.

All the stunts and slippery tactics I had pulled were all down to the likes of Frankie Slimtone, Barry 'The Buzz' Bubball, Phil Decanter, Bingo, Giles Capshaw and Murphy McCuigan. The Collins Crew, Nearly, Drawers, Missin and Bowels brothers, all had their parts to play. Plus all the other comical characters who had crossed my path in such a short yet influential time in my life.

A Lovely Pair of Knockers

*

My previous work explained how the 'Knocker Game' got started. But that only applied to a small group, Georgie Balcock and The Nearly's. Helped most fortuitously with the guidance of a renowned dealer Tommy Barnes.

Of course there are many other versions of how 'Brighton's Knockers' got started. Coco Collins with Brother Bertie and their little crew, all enjoyed peddling their wares on Brighton Beach. The classic 'Eachy Peachy Sixpence Eachy' was first announced by this little gang. Along with 'Choc Ice, Choc Ice,' and get 'Yer Muvver a Mivvi,' were all very popular cries.

The ice creams were usually pilfered in a professional manner by tempting the shopkeeper to check the out-the-back freezer and they were willing to buy in bulk. The only thing was, they would nick everything in the cooler and scarper. Not being dummies, they would cry desperation stakes later and return with the appropriate funds. You can now guess where the saying, 'Yeah I Should Coco!' comes from.

All the boy's back in those days had a 'Pedlar's License', but even to this day it does not allow anyone, in possession of a License, to sell perishable goods. So basically they were all flaunting this rule on a regular basis with whatever goods they had purloined for the day.

The other Restrictive Rule was that they should be constantly on the move, adhered to on the beach but forgotten when plotted up with a barrow loaded with fruit and Veg. The License of today stipulates quite clearly that the seller is not allowed to just go ten yards up the road when told to move on, and only non-perishables can be sold, no change there then!

Others claim it is down to the fact that the new lightweight sewing machines, by Singer, were to blame. As now, all the old ones that weighed a ton, were right good for scrap and henceforth had to be eradicated from every single gaff they could get in.

As it was very rare for the Lady of the house to be helped with any chores in the household by the old man, they jumped at the chance, usually with the promise of a blinding discount at the nearest department store to have a modern sewing machine in stock. These would have included locally, Hanningtons, Hills of Hove and Debenhams back in the day. In those times each different Town would have it's own long running Family business which operated stores of 'Grace Brothers, Are You Being Served' stature.

*

    Myths and legends get mixed up easily enough. Mainly because they go back so far, so that no one can clarify or verify the real truth. The following tales are all real life events. But how they all come together and have connections going back over fifty years is incredible.
Even by Brighton Knocker Boy's standards.
    Lot's of them tell of unbelievable exploits, but on getting to know a lot of them personally, I have had to come to the conclusion that nothing is impossible.
    The money itself is one of the most remarkable aspects. A four-drawer commode worth £500 in 1972, can't be given away in a charity shop today, and invariably ends up over 'The Tip'. Some glassware worth maybe £275 in 1975, is smashed and thrown in the bin, unless it just happens to appeal to someone, and yet it has no intrinsic value.
    Only paintings of renowned artists retain any true value. In that case though, the owner is aware of the value anyway. Modern prints cost more than an oil painting by a nobody, but still, nobody wants it.
    Obviously pieces of furniture by Chippendale, and period pieces of Historical significance are still worth a lot, but are few and far between. Joe public is also too well educated. Merely another blight on the landscape, sole responsibility of television. Quite a few dealers have resorted to spilling the beans on the game, simply because they themselves can no longer pull the wool over people's eyes. A case of can't beat 'em join 'em.
    You do now have the opportunity to experience first hand, some of the most incredible exploits imaginable. Nobody gets hurt much, a bit of pride maybe, but that doesn't really count. Does it?
    You be the judge on that one.

3. Just An Old Fashioned Love Story.

Now although the following chapters are basically four different stories, yet all on the same subject. I have heard all four sides of the events that took place, from the relevant parties themselves, many times. So rather than tell it through their lips you can get it straight from mine. It's nowhere near as complicated as it sounds so relax and let the stories flow till they come together, beyond belief.

*

Edward and Edwina were brother and sister born ten months apart in 1947. It was the homecoming of their Father from the War that led to such close proximity. Not believing his luck at surviving Dunkirk, D-Day Landings and The Battle of El Allemagne. Big burly Ted with his uncontrollable mop of wiry Ginger hair, had not stopped loving his wife Emily, literally, since he had been de-mobbed.

With his bright red bulbous nose and huge sticky out ears that Dumbo would be proud of. Emily often worried that the children might suffer unfair taunting at school if they should inherit some of his 'charms' when they came into the world.

She need not have fretted; her genes were apparently much stronger than her husbands, and neither of them had any of his exaggerated characteristics. Neither either, had assumed that jolly and infectious demeanour that he carried with him at all times.

It was a mystery to some folks how she had ever dated the six foot four-inch Irish navvy in the first place. He never once thought twice about it. From the very first moment he had laid eyes on the delicate little flower behind that Sweet Shop counter in Burgess Hill. He had thought of nothing else but how to win her over.

Their courtship had been quite interesting to say the least. He had begun to come into the Corner Shop at precisely 4:55 pm every day. Except Wednesdays of course as it was early closing, and Sundays obviously. Those two days were the Bain of his life for nearly two months.

A Lovely Pair of Knockers

Each time he would request a quarter of sugared almonds, they were the most expensive sweets in the place and took pride of place on the top shelf. This meant she had to fetch the small set of steps to retrieve them. Measure out the four ounces on the scales, pour them carefully into a small white paper bag twist it shut then replace the jar to its rightful place. The same process was followed for the next selection, which on alternate days would be either some Basset's Liquorice All-Sorts or Callard & Bowser Liquorice Toffee. The toffee had a very sweet/buttery flavour and creamy texture, which were individually wrapped in Silver and Black paper and were rectangular in shape. Along with the Evening Argus, twenty Players Cigarettes and a box of Swan Vesta matches.

He would then offer Emily a sugared Almond, she accepted the sweet, which made her giggle, and which never failed to arouse Ted. He would then rush out of the store embarrassed and light up a cigarette as soon as he got round the corner. At just after five, having been delayed by the last customer, Ted. She would then close the shop and begin her short walk home. Knowing full well that that hulk of an Irishman would soon be coming her way and bid her a nice evening.

On one particular evening though he did not come into the shop and she felt an awesome feeling of loss or regret. This made her feel uneasy and she was uncertain why she should feel this way. The Man was quite clearly totally unacceptable as a suitor to a Girl of her standing.

It was drizzling a bit as she locked the shop door and this now added to her agitation. Then as she turned a corner, there he was, bold as brass. In a Grey Pin Striped Double Breasted Suit, Trilby Hat, white shirt and grey tie, what looked like brand new shoes, a Grey mackintosh with an Umbrella in one hand and a wonderful bouquet of flowers in the other.

"Good evening Emily. I wonder if I might walk you home this evening?" Ted had practised this manoeuvre and speech over and over again in his head and in the mirror at his digs in Town. The moment, however did not go as planned.

All of a sudden there was a crack of thunder and the heavens opened. With hailstones the size of marbles raining down like bullets from a Japanese kamikaze airplane. Emily's instinctive reaction was to throw herself at him and take refuge under the brolly. She had never felt so safe in all her life, so when he looked down at her and said,

"I'll take that as a yes then, shall I?"

She comfortably replied, "You may."

The rest was plain sailing really. They enjoyed visits to the local picture house. The Orion, in Cyprus Road, which had opened in 1928, squeezing each other's hands anxiously whenever that tyrant Adolf Hitler was on the Pathe News. Ted's actual favourite part of the evening was standing in the queue. Never too early, not too late, this would always ensure a perfect date, he often mentioned when collecting her.

He would be standing there in the queue, like a strutting peacock, her arm linked through his, with him knowing she was the prettiest Girl in the line. They never rushed out at the end of the programme either. He would make a fuss of putting her coat on and that she had her gloves and handbag all prim and proper before venturing out into the night.

They had seen Gone With The Wind three times, The Wizard of Oz twice and Ted's favourite The Four Feathers three times also. The Hunchback of Notre Dame starring Charles Laughton had scared Emily a bit and they enjoyed Gary Cooper in Beau Geste. James Stewart entertained with Jean Arthur in Mr Smith goes to Washington. He then visited the infamous Last Chance Saloon, in the pioneer town of Bottleneck alongside Marlene Dietrich, in Destry Rides Again. Their favourite actor of the year though was Errol Flynn. He cleaned up Dodge City whilst trying to woo Olivia De Havilland and had worse luck still with Bette Davis in the Private Lives of Elizabeth and Essex.

Sundays now became Ted's favourite day of the week, as Emily allowed him to take her for walks in the countryside. Followed by a Cream Tea at one of the many Tea Rooms that adorned the Countryside in those days.

They had the most fantastic day once in the summer when deciding to go Strawberry picking. Hurling large juicy Strawberries at one another, then feeding themselves to each other whilst laying on their backs in the sunshine was both exhilarating and sensuous.

A Lovely Pair of Knockers

Things got a little heated that afternoon, but Ted was certainly an honourable man, and Emily was not someone he could possibly dream of dishonouring. Therefore it was in fact that very same evening, whilst queuing at the Cinema that he proposed to her and she readily accepted. There were smiles all round by the people within earshot.

"Not the most romantic place to ask the most important question," apologised Ted later. Emily patted his arm and advised, "I wouldn't have it any other way my darling."

They made plans to go into Brighton the following weekend to pick out her engagement ring. Ted explained, in his own imminent way, that such an important event should be carried out in earnest, as a couple. What if he picked something out that was not to her taste, a dreadful mistake. She would still have to wear it for the rest of her life and that just wouldn't be fair, now would it? How could she resist such an unselfish gesture?

They ventured into Walter Bull's in Ship Street, one of the most prestigious Jewellers in The Lanes. As they entered, an elderly gentleman, unbeknown to them, Walter Bull himself. The glow of true love about them, he instinctively picked up upon, and knew they were to be the recipients of today's special deal. After the usual ritual of trays adorned with of run of the mill modern rings, with no character. He guided them to the second hand department, a small-enclosed room at the rear of the shop, which he alone had access to.

He revealed a recent acquisition personally overseen by himself. A Jewish family, recently escaped from Hitler's abominable threats of invasion and sub sequential regime of their homeland Poland. They were not particularly wealthy or desperate. Merely using some of their more valuable items to good use.

In this particular transaction, the money received for the ring and a few other well-selected items of value, secured a deposit for a property in Hova Villas. They were then able to get a small mortgage, so everyone was happy.

Years later, when their children having grown up in a safe environment and flown the nest, Mr and Mrs Goldberg converted the property into five flats. They decided to live in the basement themselves and survived comfortably on the income of the other four flats, that were rented out to the council.

This was common practise in the day, it guaranteed the rent for a start and meant that it was not their responsibility to chase up any late payments from the tenants. Anyway, back to the story.

He pointed out a lovely Two Diamonds on a Twist design. It was Victorian, with a high platinum shank. Each diamond a three quarter carat of a relatively high clarity, it looked made to measure. Ted agreed it was the loveliest of rings but may well have slipped his notice had he been left to his own devices. It befitted a princess and her slender fingers looked amazing when she tried it on, perfect fit!

It was short-lived however, as although Ted was earning a decent wage the cost of this particular ring was beyond his wallet. Relevant paperwork was filled in and weekly payments of three pounds seven and six would now be his sole responsibility. The deposit of thirty-eight pounds and ten shillings was handed over without a second thought. This was the ring they had come to buy. Ted mentioned he might try and get a bit of overtime to pay it off sooner than the eight weeks required.

"The sooner we get that little beauty on your finger the sooner we can order our wedding rings," he stated. It was a statement he intended to carry out and true to his word within seven weeks the balance had been paid in full. The ring was collected when the last payment was made, and duly slipped on her finger for the rest of her life. He had had to sacrifice a couple of Sundays to achieve his goal, but one of them had been a rainy day anyway, he had consoled himself.

Neither one of them ever mentioned that she probably had the most valuable ring in town, but it was inconsequential. No money could equal the pride with which she wore that ring. It had finally come to sixty-two pounds, two and six. If it had only been four pounds three and tuppence it would not have mattered.

Her parents were not particularly impressed when they first met the young Man their daughter had spoken fondly of. It was probably the shock of such a huge Ginger Haired Giant arriving on their doorstep. By appointment of course, one Saturday evening, before asking for their daughter's hand in marriage.

A Lovely Pair of Knockers

Emily had neglected to inform them of his stature, but in her defence she no longer noticed the fact that he was a good one foot one inch taller than she. They could hardly refuse, they knew she was smitten, and there did not seem to be any harm in the Jolly Ginger Giant, as they nicknamed him privately.

The threat of War was imminent and Ted had already mentioned he would not be found wanting if the country needed him. They had made tentative plans for a Church Wedding in Ditchling. Those plans were scuppered when Ted got his call-up papers, just before Christmas, 1939.

When he told her the news, Emily simply remarked,

"Well, we cannot have you going off to War without a wedding ring on your finger. I will call the Vicar and make all the necessary arrangements." Ted did not even bother to reply, just hugged and kissed her.

He was then dispatched to go visit Walter Bull's and pick the wedding rings out. Unbeknown to him, the same gentleman had already been contacted by telephone, and was waiting for Ted as he entered.

He merely ushered him into the same small room and presented him with the required items. Ted handed over seven pounds twelve and six for the pair of matching platinum wedding rings. This may sound like a lot of money for the time, but Ted had loads of finger to cover, and a thin wiry thing was not acceptable, to Emily.

'A proper ring for a proper man', was her view.

A receipt, along with the rings was inserted in a pretty little velvet-padded box, along with a card, congratulating them both and best wishes for a lovely wedding day. When Ted revealed the rings, there was also a crisp five pound note folded inside the receipt, on a small note was written, 'Paid in full. Five pounds change enclosed'. They smiled at each other and vowed to always visit the same shop when any similar commemorative occasions appertained.

They still managed to take their vows in the Ditchling Church, but it was a much smaller affair than previously hoped for.

The wedding night was everything both Ted and Emily expected. Very little alcohol had been consumed by either of them as they could not wait to get into each other's arms in the bedroom. Both were very happy in the morning, but fully aware they would only get to spend one more night of matrimony before Ted was packed off.

*

4. The War and More.

She waved him off at the Station with the bravest of faces she could muster. That bloody Army lot had better take care of my Ted she thought. They've already made an enemy of me by cutting off those beautiful Goldie locks of his.

She had visited him in Hospital after that dreadful business at Dunkirk but there was no holding him back, and he was back off across the channel before she knew it, on some D-Day exercise or something.

Then he had been shipped out to Africa to sort out some renegade German General called Rommel, and Monty needed good blokes like Ted to get things sorted. It had all become very confusing and where or when he had been at any given time had gotten lost in translation.

You just wait till we get the bloody vote she found herself thinking.

*

She had questioned him on his job aspirations and prospective employment opportunities on his return, but all he could do was get her back into bed and tell her there were more important things to take care of.

"For the time being we've a duty to repopulate this fine country of ours. I've risked life and limb and am now prepared to do my bit back home, I suggest you do the same Emms."

It just wasn't what she had expected. They were married after all and it was part of married life, but somehow the ritual of lovemaking had become something of a chore. That magical sparkle had dimmed a bit in Ted but she was sure it would soon return. He had after all seen quite a bit of action these last six years. She had it quite good really, as once the two children were born things slackened in that department on his part. Most families of the time averaged seven or eight children. Nowadays warmly referred to as the 'Baby Boomers'.

There was one thing that cheered them both up equally, in 1946, it was the Christmas Film. Frank Capra's, It's A Wonderful Life, with James Stewart and Donna Reed, was fantastic. They saw it four times, and it was to remain their family favourite forever. Mind you it's generally regarded as everyone's favourite Christmas Film to this day. So they couldn't have been bad judges after all.

Ted tried his hand at a few low key Building industry trades, once he got his act together, and went back to work. There was obviously plenty of work available but it depressed him a bit, reminding him so much of his recent experiences.

Then one Monday morning after a cup of tea, in what can only be regarded as a Eureka moment, his eyes lit up and he announced he had decided to join the Police Force. Emily saw no reason to object and Ted began proceedings accordingly. Over the next few days the necessary forms were delivered, filled out and sent off.

This miraculously, also bought back to life that 'Devil May Care' attitude of his character. So Emily now saw a brighter future ahead. Ted also noticed a new vigour from his wife in the bedroom department, so things were looking all fine and dandy once more. With his war record he was accepted immediately on principal, and skated through the training.

The tiny piece of shrapnel still in his right leg would play up a bit in the wintertime, but of no consequence to his physical capability. It did peeve him somewhat when people mentioned that it would always give him 'something to talk about'. Yet he hid very well the fact that he was seething inside for their lack of sentiment or understanding of what so many had sacrificed to ensure the safety and security of the Country.

At his passing out ceremony though, an experienced senior officer did mention to him that he would probably be referred to as the 'Carrot Top Copper'.

To which Ted replied, with a wry knowing smile on his face,

"If that's the worst thing to expect, it'll be a doddle Inspector Waddle."

A Lovely Pair of Knockers

He took up his post as Sergeant in the spring of 1949 at Forest Row in East Sussex. It draws its name from the close proximity of Ashdown Forest a Royal Hunting Park first enclosed in the 13th Century. Just three miles South of East Grinstead. It had rail links with Tunbridge Wells so was well connected at the time. It was closed in 1967 due to cut backs, you can thank Richard Beeching, British Railways Chairman at the time, for that decision.

A tidy little Village of a few thousand inhabitants in that period, with no crime rate to speak of. The position included a four bed roomed detached property, front and back gardens mind you, with a separate space to build a garage if required. It also had unusually large gables, which meant there was a humongous loft space. In modern times this would appeal to D.I.Y. enthusiasts to extend into a room or two in the roof, but not in them days.

At the time the Bobby's allotted form of transport was the bicycle. Ted was a forward thinker and included the extra bit of land on the side when he found out that he had an option to buy, at an extremely reduced market price, if he accepted the post for a minimum of ten years.

"But what if we don't like it here, in say three or four years' time," had declared Emily.

"If I have not sorted out every single family in this wee village, my lovely, within two years and six months. Well, I'll eat my helmet without even putting salt n' vinegar on it. Don't you worry my little sweetheart, this place will suit this little family good and proper."

He wasn't wrong either. There was still no trouble to speak of during the next three years and by her own admission, Emily could not be more content. Ted was on the School Board, which guaranteed the children the best available education in the surrounding area. She was now Vice Chairwoman at the WI. Despite being one of the youngest members and with young children to look after also, she found her time was taken up in a fulfilling way.

In the third Summer Ted decided to give the exterior a spruce up. Eric at the hardware store had assured him of a good discount on paint, but when it came to it there was a downside. The only paint available at 'mates rates' was a decidedly ugly shade of green. This of course could only appeal to someone of Ted's sick sense of humour and he readily agreed to pay two bob a tin for the exterior paint required.

Once finished he declared magnanimously,

"Now they can all call me 'Ted of Green Gables' and they won't be wrong." Emily who was well aware of the various nicknames her husband had acquired over the first couple of years was inspired by the whole affair. Declaring at a WI meeting that her house would now be referred to as 'The Green Gables'.

A suitable plaque was soon acquired. Emily designed it herself and lovingly coated it with three layers of specially ordered yacht lacquer, which gave it a marvellous luminous shine. When presented with it, one Sunday morning Ted was duly impressed. But to Emily's horror he promptly went to the recently assembled asbestos and wooden garage and reappeared with a club hammer and two rusty looking six inch cut nails. He marched up to one of the apple trees at the side of the small driveway and smashed a nail straight through the middle of the plaque. Then leaned back arms folded and admired with a great big grin across his bright red face at his handiwork. Emily had winced at the vicious strike, and then just raised her eyebrows in surrender as he wandered off down to the Pub.

*

5. Was It Really Worth That Much?

A normal honest to goodness family, by all accounts.
Ted was a good copper.
A hard yet fair copper undoubtedly.
He always got his man.
He played by the rules. His that is.
An honest copper he was not.

One of the main reasons for such a low crime rate, in the area, was due to the fact that Sergeant Ted always diligently pursued any reported burglaries.

He also moonlighted as an Insurance Salesman for the local Co-Operative Society. He always made sure that any unfortunate victims of a break-in were fully covered. Miraculously a cover note materialised that had not been filed, due to the heavy workload you understand. Once such an occurrence had befallen the said claimant.

Quite often he had managed to convince the household to take out a minimal policy against breakage or damage to sentimental items, just in case, you never know. With the crime rate being so low in the area the premium for theft was at the National minimum rate.

He always left a couple of spare lines blank on the contents list. This made sense, as other items may be purchased or acquired between taking out a policy and a claim. He took great care, never to estimate the total worth of a potential claim. Always using his own fountain pen so that any later additions would go unnoticed. The last thing one needed was some jobs worth at Head Office noticing any indiscretions.

On many an occasion, the recipients of a cheque from the Insurance Company would contact Ted, or discreetly corner him in the Pub, to query the amount received.

"Was it really worth that much?" was the most common remark.

He always strictly instructed clients never to call Head Office. They were far too busy, and it might reflect on Ted's position, insinuating he couldn't handle the workload. Now, they would not want that would they, and he was more than capable of sorting out any problems on their behalf.

"Don't you worry about that," would reassure Ted "Everybody has to have their day you know. You have been through a terrible ordeal and have surely suffered enough. I felt it my duty to ensure you were compensated sufficiently for this unfortunate and ghastly experience."

On replacing the telephone, or departing from the crime scene venue, he would mutter to himself under his breath,

"Terrible experience they have suffered, they don't know the half of it. Them poor unfortunate Yanks dropping like flies all around me, and the only inkling of hope I ever got coming was them two likely lads, Jimmy and Johnny, who wanna know where the three of us can hide in safety."

He'd been caught in the leg at Dunkirk, so they had gotten under both his arms and dragged him into a tiny bunker built for two. Huddled together like suckling pigs, the three of them had managed to gain a short reprieve from the onslaught. Then, smacking himself on his leg, he would say to himself, "They saved my life that day and I'm the only one who made it home."

Upon his return home from the War, even before seeing his beloved wife Emily. He had visited East London, which was of course nothing short of a bombsite. He managed to track down the wife of one of the Cockneys that had rescued him and met the son Bobby. He gave the little nipper half-a-crown, his address, and promised he would always be there for him if he needed help of any kind.

A scrawny scruffy snotty nosed little kid, but what would you expect, who insisted he also meet his best mate next door, Barney. He was the son of the other mucker who had seen him to safety, but a different kettle of fish entirely. Looking a whole lot tougher and stronger than his pal despite the pitiful rations they existed on. He only got a shilling but Ted promised him the same applied if he ever needed anything, knowing full well the two would share the spoils.

The War had certainly took its toll on this area of London, 555 killed and 400 seriously injured, and they would have been serious too. They had also suffered the biggest single event tragedy and civilian disaster in England during the War years.

On March 3rd 1943 at 8:27pm the unopened Bethnal Green Tube Station was crowded with families due to an air raid siren at 8:17, one of ten that day. There was a sudden panic coinciding with the sound of an anti-aircraft battery (possibly the recently installed Z battery) being fired at nearby Victoria Park. In the wet dark and dank conditions the crowd was surging forward towards the shelter when a woman tripped on the stairs, causing many others to fall. Within a few seconds 300 people were crushed into the tiny stairwell, resulting in 173 deaths.

Although a report was filed by Eric Linden of the Daily Mail who witnessed it, the story never ran. It was reported instead that there had been a direct hit by a German bomb. The results of the official investigation were not released until 1946. There is now a plaque at the entrance, which commemorates it as the worst civilian disaster of World War II. There is a unique memorial, which was added in 2014, but funds are still required to finish the project to the full satisfaction of those concerned. It is entitled 'Stairway to Heaven'.

Bob and Barney were there that day but never mentioned it.

*

Ted reflected as he made his way home that day. That they, them little urchins Dad's, had gone back for others in the same plight as himself , saved quite a few more fellow soldiers but never made it back themselves. He swore then he would make their heroics worthwhile, and their lives not be wasted fruitlessly.

He thought to himself he had seen the last of them when he sent a short note to the old address near Victoria Park, Bethnal Green that he had taken up the position of Sergeant at Forest Row, East Sussex.

6. The Proposition.

Two years into the job and the same pair of young whipper-snappers turned up, out of the blue, at The Village Inn, now known as The Swan.

Young and fresh with all the vigour of their Father's before them he could not resist their fervour and enthusiasm. He felt compelled to hear them out and surprised himself when he concurred with their proposal, albeit early days and all that. The superior intelligence and concise planning, however, that lay behind their intentions would be criminal to ignore. Absolute pun intended!

I did warn in the preface that you might wonder where things are headed but please be patient, it'll be worth it soon enough.

They had convinced him that on his present wage of Five Pounds Ten and Six a week, for, on average fifty hours, it was unlikely he'd be retiring to the seaside any time soon. He could not disagree.

More likely have to run a Bed & Breakfast and keep/continue looking after ungrateful sods/bastards who didn't have a clue about all that had been sacrificed for them so they could still have their liberty.

"For Christ's sake Ted, our Dad's made the supreme gesture, and you, yeah you, told us. That if there was ever anything you could do to make it up to us you would give it your all. Now here's your chance mate, to make good your promise and honour your word, to us and to our Dad's. You will also benefit considerably yourself of course. Whaddayasay?"

It was emotional blackmail for sure. But what could he do?

Well, he could have told the pair of 'em to bugger off back to London and don't ever come back I suppose. But he didn't.

And he certainly never told the missus about it.

This is what we have in mind, they began to explain, although it was Bob who did most of the talking. Upon receipt of a little inside information they intended to visit the surrounding areas from time to time and relieve the inhabitants of some of their more valuable and saleable items.

Making a point in mentioning, that, at this point we would like to categorically assure you that nobody will ever come to any physical harm. Nor will they suffer any traumatic experience that they don't get over in a short period of time. All said and done however, we cannot 100% guarantee it.

Therefore we do not expect to be held responsible for any unexpected events that may be deemed in connection with the loss of aforementioned goods. In other words, if someone should suffer extreme grief or anxiety at the loss of an old oil painting, how could anyone have foreseen or predicted such an exaggerated reaction. Are we clear on that matter?

Ted nodded waiting for the next instalment of proposed actions.

Then with a mocking yet sinister smile young Barney pipes up and explains in a most mischievous manner. That if, for instance it was common knowledge that the guard dog, which needed to be neutralised, was more a member of the family, then, well, they wouldn't poison it!

They both laughed together at this point and Ted realised they were getting him at it. They had no intention of poisoning any pets, but were also ensuring that they should be privy to any and all relevant information regarding the proposed job at hand. Enough said on that matter.

If ever the subject was broached again, none of them care to remember, rightly or wrongly. There was of course a moral high ground being established here, and they were not intending to cross any boundaries that should be drawn, and therefore be respected.

Next came the divvy-up and solutions to any retribution or awkward circumstances after the event. They had certainly done their homework and seemed to have covered every angle. But Ted, as I said, was a good copper, and was waiting for his moment when he could scupper all their plans and reveal where it would all go wrong.

That moment never came.

They were only about 15, but certainly had their little heads firmly screwed on and were not taking anything lightly. So Ted at this stage decided to take them all the more seriously. What had begun as a curiosity from his point of view, was now developing into a major undertaking on his part and the realisation that he was to be an all-important contributor.

Realising that they now had his undivided attention they continued, by revealing more of their 'no stone unturned' approach to business and research, but also how it would benefit him.

Now, we know you can't be seen to have excess monies going into your bank account, you have enough problems now with the commissions you get from the Co-Op. You don't gamble, so the extra readies are not really going to be your sole desire, we reckon. After each job we will select a fine piece or two from the haul and save it for you until an appropriate time of delivery or collection at your convenience. We need not explain that discretion will be paramount at all times.

We understand you have a spare bedroom that has Access leading up to a huge attic, so suggest you make some excuse about a new hobby or something and so the stuff can be stored discreetly, safely and securely.

Indignantly Ted jumped in at this stage, accusing them both,

"Hold on a bleedin' minute, you two. Have you already been into my house you little bastards?"

"Nah, nah, nah. Don't worry about that. We saw that although all these houses are offset from the road they are all the same design. So we investigated number seven which is empty. As a rule the loft access is in the hallway but we figured if it was in the smallest room there, it was probably the same in your drum."

Ted confessed he was very impressed with their due diligence, and military style planning and execution. (He was also quite intrigued as to how the hell they had such an incredible vocabulary, but he didn't mention it at the time.) So he was prepared to give it a go. On the proviso that if he felt that at anytime his position might be compromised he was well within his rights to withdraw from any further involvement with them.

This they agreed was only sensible and accepted his conditions wholeheartedly. They shook hands, then had a nice little drink, once of course Ted had assured the landlord there would be no problems renewing his license next month.

"They just look young," was all he needed to say.

A Lovely Pair of Knockers

He immediately set about his side of the bargain by informing Emily he had decided to start collecting a few bits of memorabilia, possibly various artefacts or whatever might take his fancy. She paid no attention whatsoever, there was an afternoon Tea Dance to finalise at the Village Hall this weekend for Christ's sake.

Funnily enough, just a few weeks later, at about 7:30 am he interrupted a couple of likely lads who were in the middle of helping themselves to a load of old used floorboards at Bert's Timber Yard. They were the Fletcher boys; Norm and Stanley, just released from prison so could easily be traced through their parole officer, if deemed necessary by the local constabulary. They were in fact habitual career criminals, so therefore regarded arrest followed by inevitable incarceration as an occupational hazard.

Now, some won't say 'Boo To A Goose', but, if you say 'BOO' to someone who had spent more than a year in the trenches, during the First World War the chances are they would flinch, cower away and seek refuge in the nearest dark corner. Bert was one of those and they knew it, the pair of bullying little shits.

Anyway, Bert came back to life as soon as the Sergeant arrived on the scene. Ted had already pulled the Gates together and advised Bert things were in hand by a simple index finger over his lips. He was not one to be messed with under such circumstances.

A distant cousin of the terrible twins, as they were referred to, had spent three months in hospital when he mistakenly ran at Ted during a domestic dispute. An incident from which he should clearly have ran away from instead. It was a fair cop.

A short consultation with Bert, who advised it was a load of old crap as far as he was concerned, and not worth ten bob.

"How shall we deal with this then Bert," was Ted's opening gambit. Certainly not relishing the idea of ridiculous amounts of paperwork, another needless blot on the crime figures. With the full knowledge that neither one of these faces was likely to show up in court if the matter were to be pursued further. He slipped Bert a ten bob note and suggested something in his ear to which Bert hastily agreed.

"Don't even bother unloading that timber lads, just follow me," beckoning again with his finger. Straight round to his place and he fancied there was more than enough to deck the whole of the attic.

"Unload the evidence here at H.Q. if you don't mind." He instructed "I'll just put the kettle on for a cuppa, then we will take down all your details while I decide what to do with the pair of you."

True to form they unloaded the floorboards nice and neatly while he busied himself in the kitchen, watching them through the window all the while. Then he gestured with a nod of his head, for them to clear off in no uncertain terms and they couldn't believe their luck.

They slipped into the truck and bolted, never to be seen again. Smiling to himself as he watched them speed off down the lane. Ted looked at his watch, 8:00 am; he had had a good start to the day. He celebrated by enjoying a nice bowl of porridge.

His little experience in the building trade after the war paid huge dividends. Ensuring his little electrical knowledge lit the place up nicely and the carpentry side was a doddle. There was plenty enough timber to deck the loft and with the excess he made a sturdy pull down ladder through the now enlarged hatch. Very nice indeed he complimented himself, the boys would be proud.

'The best laid plans turn to shit', was a common phrase of the times, but young Bob and Barney were as good as their word. At regular intervals there would be a delivery of some sorts that required Ted's signature and a veritable array of all sorts of treasures were piling up in the loft and spare room.

There was a lean period between 1955-57 when the lads were doing their National Service, but as soon as they were out they paid him a courtesy visit. During this time he had even managed to catalogue a number of places of interest that would prove to be quite profitable for all concerned.

Bob and Barney had discussed this improper liaison many times with each other but always came to the same conclusion. Ted was lacking in one of the sacred vices. GREED, the one that would get you all in trouble in the end, so everything was good.

7. A Turn of Events.

Autumn 1958 saw a slight change in circumstances, it seemed they had made the acquaintance of a new source of information. The jobs were much more lucrative, but took a lot more planning and they were obliged to give priority to the new associate when the situation arose.

He would still benefit from these jobs anyway, he was part of the team. Their relationship was by no means over and they would keep in touch whenever in the neighbourhood. Alternative measures were in the pipeline anyway so rest assured everything was in place for operations to continue.

*

They turned up in long Brown coats themselves to make an especially nice personal delivery in July 1963, he remembered it well. It was quite comical really. He was extremely busy overseeing security with the American Special Services in the area. As President John F. Kennedy was attending a service at The Our Lady of the Forest Church.

This other matter, however, also needed his immediate attention, "So please excuse me for twenty minutes or so," he had requested the Special Agent who was now scratching his head in amazement. JFK was in a series of discussions with Harold Macmillan who lived nearby in Birch Grove. A plaque is still there commemorating the event, which is all the more poignant as it was placed there at Freshfield Hall in 1964.

One of the C.I.A. operatives, got a bit suspicious, but upon observing the delivery of a nice looking desk, filing cabinet and two chairs, was satisfied nothing was amiss. Simply an eccentric English Bobby unaware of the importance of, The President of The United States of America.

Even more poignant was the fact that Bob and Barney made this delivery to cover themselves. This gave them a 100% alibi as to their whereabouts at this period. They were both aware that the biggest and most infamous crime of the century had already been placed in motion. The Great Train Robbery occurred in August 1963.

Resulting evidence provided by the police, insinuated that all the perpetrators were present at the farmhouse involved, for at least three weeks prior to the deed. This gave our two latter day heroes absolution, and an ironclad alibi.

By the Policeman, that was in sole charge of security whilst The President of the United States of America was visiting England, talking to the Prime Minister. Touché.

*

Unbeknown to Ted the 'Two Little Boys' as he called them, had now built up a nice tight little crew so were also accepting their own dividends from similar pieces of work all over the South of England. Now also delegating or sub-contracting certain jobs if they felt it was warranted. They were very picky mind you, and only after serious vetting and having been severely tested would anyone be invited to join the firm.

Most of them had made their acquaintance in the Army, so due rank and file was immediately in place, and everybody knew to follow orders implicitly.

There was even a former Sergeant from Southend and his mate a Lance Corporal who managed to get in touch. A bit older than the boys, they were actually cousins but had both signed up for a couple of extra years after their National Service. The call of public life had beckoned them, but, once relieved of duty, the promised work never materialised and they had become slightly despondent.

They felt the two little cockneys, Bob and Barney, could be trusted so had endeavoured to track them down. They joined up with 'The Bethnal Green Berets' as they now referred to themselves, and never looked back, just over their shoulders from time to time.

*

Anyway, by this time, the attic was crammed to the rafters and the spare bedroom converted to an office. When he had mentioned he

A Lovely Pair of Knockers

was in the market for a new desk the boy's had managed to secure an amazing looking piece of furniture. This was the delivery that coincided with the J.F.K. visit. The pair of Regency Bergeres that came with it looked splendid but only one of the chairs was ever used in this office.

The matching filing cabinet, which must have been a commissioned piece, so was very rare, would prove to be worth more than it's weight in gold.

He knew they probably already had it in stock but gladly accepted it as his share of a warehouse job, he'd put them onto. The office was his pride and joy, but as with all 'Pirates Treasure' it was just a shame he was unable to share it with anyone.

They had advised Ted that after about 4-5 years most things could be sold off by putting in auctions up North or down the West Country, but private buyers would always pay more and was less likely to attract any attention.

But Ted by now had become a bit of a hoarder.

His wife had become slightly curious how he could spend more than an hour at a time just 'logging' his stock, as he referred to it. She had once, ventured into his office, seeing the steps lowered she had innocently popped her head through the hatch. Merely to tell him tea was ready, and was shocked to the bones by his reaction. He'd never so much as raised his voice to her before, but this time he practically chased her down the stairs demanding what the hell did she think she was doing.

She never ever even ventured through the spare room door again, not for the rest of her life. She told the children of this uncharacteristic outburst by their Father, swearing them to secrecy. Then asked them to promise never to make the same mistake. They were not particularly curious individuals, like you or me, and readily agreed never to venture into that vicinity. They never ever broke their promise either.

*

Thank-you my dear reader, for now we come to the crux of the matter and your due diligence and patience is to be rewarded.

What has all this got to do with Edward and Edwina?

In October of 1969 Ted was taking his last 'look in' at The Swan. He now had the use of a Panda Car these days (Morris Minors were the chosen vehicle of the time) but on Saturdays he liked to stick to his old routine. This of course, also justified the five or six pints he would customarily consume by about nine o'clock. On his way home as he turned onto the High Street from the Pub Car Park, a car took an unexpected left turn, one can only assume, knocked him off his bike and instantly killed him on the spot, Stone Dead. That was the coroner's decision anyway. There were no witnesses and after three agonising months nobody had come forward with any further information to offer any other explanation.

The whole Town grieved for Ted. He would be sorely missed for sure.

Emily, unfortunately, but not surprisingly, went into a comatose state from which she never recovered. The Doctor's described it as a kind of advanced state of Alzheimer's disease, which had recently been linked and subsequently diagnosed in some of the soldiers from the Great War. At the time they had referred to it as shell shock.

Trauma being the decisive factor in most cases, therefore not particularly exceptional in Emily's case due to the recent events. She was not able to hold a sensible conversation with a single soul after the day of the funeral. With their Mother registered as incapable of due sensibility, at 23 and 24 years of age respectively the two children inherited everything without prejudice.

But why wouldn't they?

They were advised by the local health authority to place her in a most reputable health asylum, where her best interests would be met.

They were still kids at heart, what were they supposed to do? Their Dad had been a war hero, long serving Policeman and pillar of society, whilst Mum had served the local community in more ways than most. All the members of the WI agreed it was a terrible shame.

They asked each other numerous questions and could not perceive what the future held for either of them. They had not really used foul language before but found themselves slightly more relaxed

A Lovely Pair of Knockers

when expressing themselves more fervently than when their parents were alive and well.

'What the bloody hell are we gonna do?'

It was only a house after all. They had lived here for most of their lives for sure. But what did it all mean? What were they to do with themselves? They were lost.

They had a local Estate Agent give the place a once over and he valued the property at £27-28,000 this of course now included an adjacent plot of land approx one third of an acre. It was slightly overgrown and had no meaningful use, and, well Ted just hadn't got around to making any solid plans with what to do with it. It had been offered to him for £150 and he simply couldn't resist the opportunity.

"A householder and a landowner I am this day," he had declared down the Pub one Sunday lunchtime.

"That's handy that is Ted," had quipped Marjorie, the Landlord's wife, "You can grow a lovely variety of vegetables on that patch and I'll give you a discount on Sunday Lunch. Then in the summer get a cushty little greenhouse sorted and I'll do a deal with you on all the salad stuff. How does that sound?" they all laughed and joked about numerous other uses for the plot that afternoon, but, alas he just didn't' get around to it.

Sorry about that went off on a tangent, back to Edward and Edwina!

Neither had had any particular meaningful relationships. Edward and his father had not spoken much since his medical failure for the Army. Ted was angry, but you can't really blame someone for having flat feet, surely?

Edwina had tried the WI, at her Mother's request, but just didn't really get it. This of course strained her relationship with Mother. All four had practically lived separate lives under the one roof for five years. Apart from Church on Sundays, which was obligatory. They were not particularly religious, it was simply expected. Ted sometimes could not be bothered and had a bit of a niggle in the old war wound which fortunately eased off around five to twelve when the Pub opened. Hardly excuse enough to banish him to hell for all eternity.

So, neither of them had any great sentimental attachment to the place and agreed amicably that probably the best plan of action was to just sell everything and go their separate ways. Always keeping in touch of course.

Edwina could care less for her job at the Library and as far as Edward was concerned his position in the Men's outfitters at a local department store was a dead-end job anyway.

The house did not seem to pose any problems, and the estate agent had suggested the extra land would be a bonus if included in the asking price. But what to do with all this bloody furniture and God knows what else that's upstairs. None of it was to their taste. They hadn't had any input whatsoever into any of the things that gave this place it's identity, or lack of it for that matter. The only thing either of them could remember having a say in, was the wallpaper in their bedrooms. So, needless to say, they had no real roots to speak of, or sentimental strings attached, that so often stopped folks from moving on with life after such a loss.

They both agreed though that they suddenly felt free.

Although they both loved Mother and Father of course, the annual trip to The Isle of Wight, usually Pontin's Little Canada Holiday Camp, could hardly be the highlight of one's life, surely?

As they had got a bit older this too had become a bit of a chore.

Edward after all had won the Donkey Derby one year, but due to work commitments Father was unable to take him to the National Finals in Blackpool. The pair had also won the Fancy Dress couples category another year dressed as Sonny and Cher. They did however still sing the memorable grace at Christmas as homage to those times, it goes like this;

Always Eat When You Are Hungry
Always Drink When You Are Dry
Always Wash When You Are Dirty
Don't Stop Breathing Or You'll Die......holding the last note for as long as possible.... aaaaaaaaaaahh.....men!

The Bluecoats were fun, but it was all kids stuff really. At least they didn't have to suffer with camping like some of their schoolmates. Now that really did sound like a waste of a week.

A Lovely Pair of Knockers

The pair of them were pondering their predicament one Monday morning, when all of a sudden there is an unexpected Knock on the door. It was about 10:30 am but that for sure is irrelevant, the actual time anyway.

Edward answered the door and was greeted by a bright young fellow in possession of a most welcoming grin, with which he would like to take you in. He introduced himself as Frankie. He happened to be in the neighbourhood in search of a young Vicar wishing to sell his household goods before trekking off to Africa and setting up a missionary in the name of Jesus.

Somehow or other the address had been misplaced and could they help. Funds had been secured from the highest order and if he didn't manage to locate said Vicar and make some sort of deal this very day it was highly likely his recently appointed position of area purchasing manager in the name of the Church was in serious jeopardy. 'Dire Straits' was the terminology used. But Edward was so overcome with excitement he failed to remember.

How somebody could explain so much in such a short space of time beggars' belief, but this little knocker had been taught by the best and this was going to be his day.

"Please come in," said Ed, "This is not the actual place you are looking for, but my sister and I have been discussing our future plans, and, If. If being the operative word or phrase, you understand. You might be able to help us with our predicament. Then we may well be in the market to have some sort of deal with you ourselves today."

"That sounds positively fine and dandy," answered the young chap, and he followed him straight in.

Now, this kind of welcome to any Knocker Boy, could be compared a bit like some attractive young lad saying to some old poufter, "Why don't I just take my trousers down and let you do whatever you like?"

Needless to say, this particular visitor simply continued to smile like a sunflower and followed him through the spacious hallway.

Remarking as he walked confidently behind his prey,

"Well thank-you very much Sir. Let me see what you no longer have use of. Make you an honest yet generous offer and we'll take it from there. Whaddayasay?"

A Lovely Pair of Knockers

"Edwina," cried Edward, "Put the kettle on please luv, we have a visitor, and it seems our prayers have been answered. The Lord has sent us a true redeemer who may be the answer to all our prayers."

"Of course Brother dear, what is the Gentleman's name?" She replied.

"Sorry Sir, did you mention your name?"

"It's Frankie, Frankie Slimtone, glad to make your acquaintance."

So begins the greatest 'Haggerty' of all time, I don't care what anybody says! With my inside knowledge from all four different angles you can rest assured this is without doubt the best ever.

It could have been any one of the newly established gangs of 'Brighton's Knockers'. A newly formed Double Act or even a recently collaborated team. It just happened to be the one and only Frankie Slimtone. The star of this and many more tales to come!

*

8. It's Just Not Cricket........It's Baseball.

This was the sort of greeting of yester-year. Not as uncommon as some might think, but anyone who started knocking doors post 1990 would refer to such a greeting as mythical.

Still, Frankie had to take a deep breath as he was led through to the morning room. The side table he had just passed surely could not be what he thought it was. George III satinwood and giltwood, the top banded with rosewood and tulipwood with an inappropriate Louis XVI ormolu mounted mantel clock upon it. If they were to go out the door today it would save any further work this week. He reckoned around the £15,000 mark for the two.

Calm down Frankie boy, calm down, he said to himself. This could be a little old pools win if you play your cards right. Then, as he entered the room, as if by magic, was the most stunning card table he had ever seen. Later to be confirmed as George II walnut and fruitwood in the manner of Benjamin Goodison. Panelled frieze and sides, concertina action, with hinges stamped S. Johnson. Even at the salerooms such a magnificent piece he had never witnessed. In excess of £20,000 on a bad day in the rooms, but if two punters fancied it, and went head to head, it could make 25.

"She'll just be a minute Frankie. Please, take a seat. I hope you don't mind waiting. I think it's best we all speak together so we don't get our wires crossed, is that okay?" Edward politely explained.

"Of course, of course Ed. I think I can safely say I am here for the day, okay? Would you believe it, I'm a poet and didn't know it." Then laughed aloud at his own little anecdote.

He hadn't a clue that morning when he'd got dressed, what was in store for him and his new partner today and coming months.

Frankie Slimtone actually fitted the name perfectly. He had a slim lean body with matchstick legs and bony knees. He had a rugged look about him sometimes, but that being more of a Charlton Hestonesque Arabic Nomad, his features were strong. Straight nose, sparkling hazel eyes slightly high cheekbones and full lips covering Hollywood style shiny white teeth that seemed to glisten on a sunny day.

Although dressed immaculately at all times his one failing feature was his thick jet-black hair that had a mind of its own. Brylcream was his best friend and ally, but it just still didn't quite do the trick. So he resorted to always carrying a metal comb in his top pocket, as a back up. Always have a back-up plan.

This had once been deemed an offensive weapon, at a magistrate's appearance by some soppy little clerk of the court. He had gotten involved in one of those altercations with some rockers from London on the seafront one Bank Holiday in 1965. This had earned him an extra two pound seven and six to his original fine of three pounds ten shillings. Absolute diabolical liberty!

Today he was in his brand spanking new navy blue mohair suit. Picked up from Bernard Luper's in Trafalgar Street on Saturday morning. He'd felt the bee's knees that night up at the Regent Dance Hall, and he hadn't gone unnoticed.

To complement the new whistle he'd selected a freshly pressed white shirt, silk purple tie with pink spots and his lucky horseshoe cufflinks.

It was also the first day at work with his recently acquired Two Tone Blue leather loafers that really stole the show. Young Barry, a kid that hung around at Pullingers, George Street, Brighton, had enquired why he didn't have some 'Special Shoes', to 'Stand Out From the Crowd', as he put it. It would be a few years yet, 1979 in fact, but this young kid would one day end up running the high quality shoe and repair shop.

Frankie was sold on the idea, and had some custom made from James Taylor & Son, at 4 Paddington Street (nr Baker Street), London. The £115 he had paid was one of the most exorbitant purchases of his life but he had justified it to himself, and anyone who enquired. By explaining that your feet were precious and he spent most of his time on them.

'So they should be respected and treated accordingly'. Some called him a flash git, but nobody could deny that they were truly a blindin' pair of four by two's!

Not bad, not bad at all, he'd said to himself in the mirror that morning.

A Lovely Pair of Knockers

His Mum had always said he was too pretty to be a boy but there was nothing girlie about his demeanour. He had more fights than most at the St Luke's infant school which he attended and even more at the Juniors once they combined with Queen's Park. He dreaded any time Mum found it necessary to bring out the photo album. She had thought he looked so cute in the matching knitted shorts and cardigan outfits she had bought in Belgium for him when he was a toddler. He always cringed and went as red as a beetroot on such occasions.

Frankie had heard it through the grapevine that the local plod had 'karked it' in Forest Row and the missus taken away to the funny farm by the men in white coats. Good riddance an' all.

So the area was going through a transitional period. The coast was clear and everything ripe for the picking.

It was common knowledge that 'The Carrot' was a devious bastard and there was half a chance that there may well be a few selected items stashed away up in the attic that may have dubious origins. He'd overheard in The Linden Club that if someone were fortunate enough to gain access, they might well have a little tickle. Why wait? He had thought to himself, and I think I will invite that little toe-rag Barry Bubball on this one, and see what he's really made of.

As always, as he approached the front door he took a long deep breath and was ready for the worst. Which was of course something like 'Sod off you thieving little git we've had your type around here before'. Yet also alert and equally prepared for the dream greeting, 'How nice of you to call, won't you please come in'.

Today it was to be the latter. Served right up on a silver platter!

"Would you like a biscuit or two?" asked Edward. "Sure, sure. I am in no hurry now that I am in your safe capable hands Ed" came the reply. "I shall make all the relevant phone calls to the diocese once we have taken care of this situation. Don't you worry yourself about a thing me old cocker sparrer."

Edwina arrived with the tea and biscuits and momentarily there was a furtive air of anticipation in the room, but was quickly expunged with Frankie's concern for their well-being and expectancy.

Pleasantries were exchanged and then they felt compelled to make Frankie aware of the predicament they had found themselves in. It was only fair to inform him of their recent upheaval and desire to move on. Visiting Mother had just become more and more stressful at every visit. Even the Doctor's had warned that their visits did nothing to help Emily's condition, and sometimes resulted in her being more confused than ever when they left.

Then he went for the jugular.

"So, pray tell, what is it that you are both looking to do. I realise as Brother and Sister you wish to take new steps, but do you really want to go your separate ways. After all, all you've got is each other at the moment. Family is very important you know."

He'd already clocked the couple of framed newspaper clippings in the hallway. So continued in a concerned tone of voice, "You never know what you've got till it's gone, my old Gran used to say. Then of course my Grandfather died at Dunkirk."

"Oh my word," cried Edwina, glaring at her brother in astonishment, "Our Father Ted was also at Dunkirk." JACKPOT!

"Oh I am so sorry," said Frankie, "I didn't mean to upset you."

"No, no of course not," she apologised. "No not at all, quite the opposite, our Father was one of the lucky ones. Rescued by a couple of brave Cockney lads, he made it home and lived to fight another day. They sadly did not."

Frankie then made a gesture with both hands and then covered his face. Apologising for his behaviour he said,

"Sorry, I shouldn't burden strangers with such emotional outbursts, please forgive me. It's just that, well, it goes oh so quiet in our house whenever that subject arises."

"There there," comforted Edwina as she moved over to the couch next to Frankie and put her arm over his shoulders.

Now, many others, finding themselves in this position would have just taken a closer look at the things around them, but Frankie was suddenly conscious of something much more fruitious developing, even at this early stage.

"Get into their nuts my son. Once you've got into their head and the trust is set in stone, you can have anything you like. And the

A Lovely Pair of Knockers

best thing is, they thank-you for it afterwards." Pearls of wisdom from Vince Nearly his mentor, who had introduced him to this profession just three years ago.

This could be the one, he thought to himself. Let's look at the bigger picture my old son. Take in the landscape, be patient, look all around you and then, only then will you make your move, like the Master Chess player you are destined to be.

Straightening up and loosening his tie slightly, Frankie went into action.

"Now," much louder than necessary but in an extremely assertive manner, "Now, let's not get soppy or impractical. Back to the more important situation at hand. The pair of you. Which is my main concern at this present time. Let's say, for the sake of an argument. I am not only able to help you both with the contents of the house, presumably the garage as well?"

They both eagerly smiled and nodded like school children who'd been asked if they fancied an ice-cream sundae instead of a lolly.

"From what I have seen so far, I can safely say, I will be able to help. (Long pause) Most things seem or appear to be in reasonable condition. (Short pause) But in a case such as this there are many items that have no intrinsic value. When this occurs I have a tried and tested system that invariably suits all those concerned, but you must both be made well aware of my intentions. So as not to upset the apple cart at a later date, is that clear?"

Not having a clue what the hell he was talking about they both nodded in affirmation anyway, they both liked him and trusted him already. What could go wrong? Things were shaping up nicely and the pair of them looked like getting on with their lives sooner than expected.

Frankie, carrying on in the same authoritative tone,

"I mention this purely on the understanding that if, by some miraculous coincidence you were to notice the sideboard against the wall there," gesticulating to said piece with the over used index finger, "In a children's home or some other establishment that provided safe haven for the more vulnerable in our society. War veterans for instance. Would either of you be offended?"

By this time they were both perplexed and transfixed by his mesmerising tone. In what seemed to appear a hypnotic trance, the pair of them agreed that no such situation would arise if Frankie were able to help them.

Edward interjected, "If it were the case, that you find yourself in a position to do as you propose Frankie. Surely it would be nothing short of abominable behaviour on either of our parts to feel anything other than extreme gratitude towards you. Don't you agree Edwina?"

"Of course Edward, of course."

FIRST STRIKE! Thought Frankie.

"So, where were you thinking to relocate then?" Frankie asked, changing tack.

"Well," answered Edwina, now feeling much more comfortable with this extremely polite and respectable young man. She had actually felt a slight tingle in her lower regions when he had mentioned his charitable persuasions, and after all, this was turning into a very interesting day.

"We are both drawn to the South Coast. Eastbourne, Brighton or perhaps Worthing."

"All three are nice places I agree," replied Frankie.

"But to be fair, you are both bright young things with the world at your feet and are supposed to be starting a new life, not finishing an old one. Eastbourne and Worthing both have Piers granted. They are also referred to as God's waiting rooms, did you know? But," then raising his hand and voice simultaneously whilst pointing his index finger to the seemingly endless sky, repeated, "But, in the middle of those two, not only has Brighton got two Piers and plenty of job opportunities. It's also got me, coz that's where I live."

The two Eds stared at each other and when they referred their gaze back into Frankie's direction, it was as if wedding vows had been exchanged.

STRIKE TWO!

A Lovely Pair of Knockers

Now in full flow, he reeled them in yet further.

"It's my home town, born and bred, and if anyone is worth knowing, I'm on first names terms with them, mostly anyway. If not, my close friend, also Brighton born and bred Barry Bubball, does for sure. That's the poet coming out in me again, sorry 'bout that."

"Please don't apologise so much," reassured Edwina who was becoming more and more attracted to Frankie as things progressed.

"I know the first name terms bit sounds a bit weird, but an exceptionally close and valued acquaintance of mine, Lady Hughes, happens to be a Director of the finest Department store in Town, Hanningtons. By way of a simple introduction, Edward here could comfortably be head of his own department by Easter."

Talk about the corporate ladder he thought to himself.

"If on the other hand, you fancy commuting, but I don't personally recommend it. Her fine husband, Sir Jack Hughes, holds a position on the board of Selfridges and a similar arrangement could be sorted out up in Oxford Street with no fuss whatsoever. They reside in a fine house just outside Brighton in a quaint little village called Rottingdean."

"I visit their home, The Challoners, from time to time but never miss a Christmas Eve. We have mince pies and eggnog accompanied by the Salvation Army Choir providing Christmas Carols. I'm not in the Sally mind you, just make a little donation at that time of year. You know, there is always someone worse off than yourself and all that, if you can't help folks at Christmas what kind of a person are you?"

Edwina was beginning to melt at this stage and Frankie knew it. Edward was starting to feel a little uncomfortable at the way his sister was staring at their guest so he attempted to switch the conversation back to the case at hand. Didn't get a look in. There was no stopping Frankie now.

"My numerous contacts at the council make me confident in ensuring a position at the Library would be simple enough to arrange for Edwina. But, pardon me for saying Edwina, I feel you should be a bit more 'Out there', and with such an array of beautiful stores to choose from, let's just say, I think you can do much better for yourself.

But of course, (pause) it's entirely up to you". Edwina was now beaming, inwardly and outwardly.

The pair of them stared at Frankie, holding their teacups in their right hand, six inches above the saucers in their left. Unable to so much as blink and mouth's agape.

STRIKE THREE………………….. AND YER' OUT !!

*

9. The Forest Row Coup.

"Well Frankie," began Edward, "You seem to have planned our future for us in just half an hour. But how can any of this be possible?"

Looking across at his sister who had now manoeuvred herself back into the walnut winged armchair. Georgian, upholstered in floral moquette, on cabriole legs and pad feet. Re-railed and with a good professional clean easy worth two bags.

"Well Edward, It's like this," explained Frankie.

"If I hadn't knocked on your door forty five minutes ago, it wouldn't be would it? It's fate me old mate. Of course it's entirely up to you two how you wish to develop our relationship. For the time being why don't one of you, or both if you so wish, show me around the house. Then I should be able to get a better idea on what you are sitting on, and the kind of finances you are likely to have at your disposal once we are all done and dusted."

"Gladly," said Edwina. "Perhaps you may be able to stay for lunch once you have gone about your business Frankie."

"Delightful" came the reply.

Even Frankie couldn't believe his eyes or ears as they traipsed from one room to the other. All the while neither of the two Eds having any emotion or reaction to any of the figures he was quoting, which were gradually becoming less generous as they went.

It did get a little precarious though in the Dining Room when he mentioned that strangely enough when it came to large pieces such as the mid-Georgian mahogany bookcase, it was usually the things on display or in the drawers and cupboards that fetched more than the furniture itself. They looked despondent, and for a moment he thought he saw a glimmer of doubt in their eyes, and he may be losing them.

"Mind you, it's still worth two hundred and fifty quid of anyone's Money." He slipped in. They gasped and said in synchronicity "Is it really worth that much?" Back hooked on the line. Phew! Close one. It would later fetch £8,000 at auction.

It took longer than he thought, but Frankie was doing a thorough job and noting everything down in a more professional manner than ever before. His only cause for concern was that neither of them chose to express any exception of selling one single thing. Every single time someone says take the lot, there are always a few bits they won't let go of, usually the best bits purely by coincidence. The one coin or stamp in a collection for instance that is worth the rest of it, on it' own.

But these two, not a bit of it. They were nearly done when Edwina announced lunch was almost ready, and they could sort upstairs and the Garage afterwards, as it would only take half an hour or so.

Whilst they were waiting in the Dining Room, Frankie asked Edward what he might find upstairs. Once he heard how Father had practically banished all and sundry from the spare room and the attic he just had to his excuse himself for a moment and visit the Bathroom upstairs. This in itself was quite the luxury, most of his pals still had an outside toilet back in Brighton. He popped his head into the kitchen and mentioned it to Edwina and she confirmed that she too had not entered the spare room, not even since Father's passing.

The door was locked, but he soon located a key. Moving a hall chair, it was above the door on the small ledge provided by the heavyset frames of the time. Upon entering the spare room, then switching the light on after sticking his head up in the loft it was now Frankie's turn to fall into a catatonic state. As white as a Hospital sheet he just about managed to negotiate the stairs and sit down. His complexion had changed, the blood had drained from his face and his ashen state was beyond all or any comprehension.

Lunch was served in an unexpected silence. He spilt his minestrone soup down his shirt, resembling a stroke victim. Pinged a boiled potato into the air, whilst demolishing the chicken Kiev, and garden peas were strewn all over the tablecloth. The arctic roll just melted on the plate and he scalded his tongue on the coffee despite being warned it was freshly brewed.

There was a short interruption during lunch when an associate of Frankie's knocked the door and enquired if they had seen his friend Frankie. As he seemed in such disarray Edward was hesitant at first, but Frankie appeared to snap out of it when told he was needed at the door. He gave Barry a cockle and told him to pick up as many leaflets as he could after a pub lunch. Then just wait in the motor by the

Garage on the green until he came to him and not interrupt again please. That suited Barry just fine.

They thought he had seen a ghost and maybe that was why Mother had warned them never to venture into that room.

Poor Frankie, he never seemed himself again for the rest of the day. He cunningly followed their parent's lead when he told them both to keep the promise made to their Mother, and not to follow him when he went back to 'That Room'. It took a while but he persevered.

The other three bedrooms took all of ten minutes. The Garage also took much longer than expected but eventually Frankie came back in at 4:00pm and sat down with them both for afternoon tea.

His opening gambit was simple, blunt and to the point,

"How much did that rascal of an Estate Agent value the property at, if you don't mind me asking?"

"Certainly," replied Edward.

"It was in the region of £28,000."

"Including the extra piece of land that lies adjacent of course, did we mention that," added Edwina.

Frankie just gulped.

"So that's about £13,000 each after expenses costs etc."

"Correct, plus of course he was prepared to clear all the furniture free of charge."

Frankie could never remember which one of them came out with that particular line.

"Okay, okay, well that is a nice little sum to start the rest of your life with, I do agree." Shaking the all too familiar raised index finger, "But, if you can both trust me, and I know you do. Here is my proposal."

"There are a few items that I know I can place with customers immediately. I will pay you for whatever I take on post-dated cheques, if that is agreeable. Not only does this provide evidence of the date taken it also shows the value of the pieces removed, that way we can all be aware of what has gone and what has not. Obviously all your personal belongings will be separated, but from what I can tell that's all in your own rooms anyway, so that won't cause any problems."

"This is what I propose," index finger, eyebrows and voice well raised, then in a more seductive and Mother Teresa tone, he continued, "I would like to buy the house with the piece of land of course, but at my honest and dignified true market value. This will include all the contents of course, but you won't have to worry about any of that because for the time being it will all stay where it is, so of no concern to either of you."

The two Eds were nodding and smiling as one, as this all seemed agreeable, so they just waited with baited breath for his price.

Frankie hesitated for a moment, then said "How does sixty, yes sixty thousand pounds, six-zero-zero-zero-zero thousand pounds sound to you both?"

They were both now in a state of shock. Not believing his ears Edward said, "Would you mind repeating yourself Frankie."

"Of course. I will buy the house lock, stock and barrel for a total of £60,000, on top of that, I will cover all legal expenses. (This was an instantaneous thought from God knows where, bit of a risky call but would surely seal the deal) Which means instead of the paltry thirteen grand each you would get from that cad of an Estate Agent, you will both receive thirty thousand pounds apiece."

"That, I am quite confident, will set you both up quite nicely in Brighton. (Not giving them anytime whatsoever to reply or think) I have, as I am sure you are both now aware, many friends in town. Amongst them, some are Estate Agents and Property Developers."

"I have no qualms in stating categorically that you will both be able to purchase, completely outright, a comfortable flat in the nicest part of Brighton or Hove. Or, a terraced property to your liking in the area of your choice. If you decided to branch out a little further to say Saltdean, Peacehaven or Patcham, you may get a little more for your Money."

"Wherever you decide to begin the rest of your life, you will both also still have a tidy sum in the Bank into the bargain. As I have said all along, it is entirely up to you. Whaddayasay?"

Raising his hand in the air, he announced like an MOC,

"All those in favour, say aye". The two Eds copied his motion and said "Aye", he shook Edward's hand, but Edwina could hold back no more, and hugged him closely, whispering in his ear,

"Is it really worth that much?" Nearly, he mimed.

They were both now quite delirious and Edwina's hands were shaking as she attempted to pour some more tea. Edward tried to steady her but he was in the same predicament. Frankie now sat there like a newly crowned king, surveying his subjects, then continued.

"At this stage, I have only one stipulation." He felt anything short of suicide would be amicable at this stage.

"Please do not discuss this proposed arrangement with anybody for the time being. Jealousy is a terrible thing and people will for sure start to ask for Money, favours or whatever, and believe me, nobody can be trusted once there is this kind of Money floating about. Always remember it is yours and yours alone. I am your friend, and come tomorrow I shall return with all the appropriate paperwork to set things in motion."

"Let's say about eleven o'clock, not too early, not too late. I will also arrange the transportation of the few things I can place in a new home quickly, as mentioned, for which I will give you receipts. I will also, as a gesture of goodwill and good faith pay a deposit of £2,000 cash. That's £1,000 each to help you both adjust to your newfound wealth. See it as a bit of playing about Money."

Neither of them had ever had more than £75 in their relevant Bank accounts to this date, so you can imagine how elated they were feeling. Sensing that the pair of them were pretty dumbstruck by the whole affair, and basically in a state of shock, he slipped in the official confirmation of such an arrangement, by simply adding, "You can give me all your Solicitor's details now. Relevant names and addresses obviously, and this will be passed onto my Lawyer to draw up the papers first thing in the morning."

Then with a slightly over-exuberant holler that he couldn't quite contain, "Let's get this show on the road!"

Then calmed down like having taken an instant sedative, adding quietly and reassuringly in a confidential whisper,

"Of course my man can deal with it all if you like, all at my expense as I said earlier, but remember, as always, it's entirely up to you."

He then lingered awkwardly, awaiting their response. It didn't take too long, but felt like an eternity all the same. With an agreeable nod from Edwina, Edward ushered Frankie back into the study to provide what they thought would be all the relevant details needed to proceed with the paperwork.

"Maybe I could help you with the washing-up whilst yer bruvver' takes care of the boring stuff, Edwina?" asked Frankie.

"Don't be ridiculous Frankie," she replied warmly, "You just explain to him what it is you need and then we can have a nice cup of tea before you make your way home. You do look ever so tired and it doesn't look like things are going to get any easier over the next few weeks."

Don't you worry your pretty little head about that my little treacle, he said to himself.

As they bade him farewell at the door, Frankie had to compose himself and restrain from jumping in the air and clicking his heels in Fred Astaire mode. He most certainly had the energy and reason for it.

Unaware that the two Eds were only too pleased to see him off, as they too were in a similar frame of mind. As soon as they shut the door behind him and witnessed him walk down the drive, they hugged one another like two star-crossed lovers. Their boat had just come in.

Whilst opening an old bottle of champagne, reserved for some celebration that had never arrived, they promised each other not to mess up this golden opportunity that had somehow come out of nowhere. With the Good Lord's blessing for sure.

*

10. Plans Into Actions.

It was twilight as he walked towards the Village Green, but in all honesty Frankie was still in a bit of a daze himself. The downstairs contents alone would easily take care of the price he had offered for the house, and some.
But upstairs, that was just simply incredible.
The desk in the office was something to behold, the matching filing cabinet must surely have been custom made to match and so had to be a one-off and increase the value tremendously when sold as a pair. Even he felt that it would be criminal to break up. Resembling splitting a family at a slave sale, but if it would compromise or hinder a legitimate sale then it would have to be done. Of all the things he had witnessed upstairs, even in that relatively short space of time, it was his favourite.

It was a Regency ormolu-mounted mahogany and ebonised Carlton House desk, with leather-lined easel slide, 3 drawers with twin Dolphin handles, 57in (145cm). Fetching £85,000 in 1987 when he eventually sold it. The temptation to remove the gold wristwatch and nice looking pocket watch was beyond even Frankie's moral standards. They would surely be worth the risk, who knows what might happen tomorrow, being the justification. The matching filing cabinet was disappointing when the forced split sale was arranged by Sotheby's, with a final price of £42,000. He always reckoned there was a bit of insider trading involved, but at the time his hands were tied, literally.

The rug in front of the desk was definitely an Agra, worth £3,500 easy. The tapestries on the walls took his breath away, but the thing that made it all so surreal was the fact that if a couple of the items were genuine then the chances were, everything else was. It stands to reason, he assured himself. Talk about Aladdin's cave, this was more like the cave of Ali Baba and His Forty Fucking Thieves.
He found Barry snoozing in the motor and woke him up with a shove. His breath smelt of stale booze, and there was definitely the

aroma of one of his funny cigarettes in the air, but what difference, he had been hanging around for five hours. When he came to, Barry obviously enquired as to the success of the call.

"Well, I'll tell you this much," declared Frankie, "We have got our hands full with this one, full of money my old son. It's gonna be a Haggerty with a plus. Coz we're having the drum and a brass band to boot this time matey."

Not believing it for a second Barry just quipped,

"Ah, you're taking the piss. You've been in there all afternoon getting your end away you crafty rascal. I don't appreciate driving all this way and hanging around all afternoon while you're having a Donald. Still I picked up most of the flyers, bought a couple of bits that should cover the X's and won a tenner on the gee-gees, so not such a bad day after all's said and done."

Frankie couldn't bring himself to reveal the real graft done that day, so left it for ten minutes or so. His head was still spinning, going ten to the dozen and trying to figure out how he was going to get things under way for the next morning.

As they were cruising through Haywards Heath, Frankie came back to earth a bit and informed Barry they still had things to take care of this day.

"Right then, what we need to do is this. Get back to Brighton sharpish. So I wanna go over Ditchling Beacon way on the way home. We've got a few things and people to find tonight and I'm not taking any chances on leaving it till the morning. Straight to Tommy Barnes Yard, and if it's closed, everywhere and anywhere until we find him."

Barry winced, "Aaw, I promised that Eileen who works behind the jump in The Basketmakers I'd take her to the flicks tonight. Go and see that special late showing of Butch Cassidy & The Sundance Kid, you know, wiv Paul Newman and Robert Redford. Can't we leave it till tomorrow?"

"Certainly," answered Frankie, "I'll just get someone else to drive me about and you just take the rest of the week off, enjoy yourself mate."

Sensing he may be making a grave mistake Barry made a quick retraction and perked up a bit.

"Nah, it's alright, that film's supposed to be one of the best mate and it'll be back at the Astoria anyway later in the year. If not we'll catch it at The Classic in Western Road or ABC in East Street when the time is right. Anyway business is business and you've obviously found one by the sounds of it. We'll just pop in and let her know we have other important business to take care of. You know, before she gets all made up an all that, okay?"

"Sure mate, wise move my son, wise move. Now, put that right foot of yours down and get us to where we're going. Lively, come on lively!"

The rest of the journey was nice and smooth, with Frankie smiling to himself all the way. Any attempt to gain any further relevant information or details fell on deaf ears so Barry drove into town as instructed. Frankie looked in the mirror and straightened his tie. There was indeed still some serious business to attend to this evening and he wanted to look sharp.

*

11. The Partner.

His present partner on the other hand was of course quite the opposite. He could have a bespoke suit from Saville Row, or pick something off the rail in Jack Balls down Edward Street and still look like he he'd been dragged through a hedge backwards. On the other hand his wispy blond hair was always in pristine condition, but, he had a terrible habit of running his fingers through it all the bloody time, causing it to look a bit greasy, so that too did nothing to help his presentation.

Today it was black suit, white shirt, and black tie, like sweet Gene Vincent. He also had the appropriate black brogues from Pullingers just opposite Silvers Clothing on the corner, where he got most of his suits. But there was something about Barry that made him shine, and if you'd never even met him he could be your long lost best friend within ten minutes.

Seriously overweight, baggy puppy-dog eyes and podgy fingers all brought together the package that was Barry Bubball.

Unlike his present compadre (as he liked to refer to any of the many people he worked with, on a rota basis) he had more than just a couple of vices.

In fact he had nearly all of them.

He was greedy, with both Money and food. He was a heavy gambler when he had the Money. He would have his last ten-bob on the favourite at Ripon Races confidently, even if the Gas metre was running low. The sloth bit we've already covered, but why he even bothered putting on a clean shirt, Frankie would exclaim in sheer desperation, was beyond belief.

You could bet your bottom dollar some baked beans or an angry tomato would surely adorn his attire after the statutory breakfast that he insisted was necessary, to ensure a decent day's collar. And that shirt, why oh why, will it not stay tucked into his trousers like anybody else's?

"I can't help it can I?" would always be his defence. The same applied to his shoelaces; maybe he just never tied them in the first place.

He could never be faithful to women for more than a fortnight, if something else were to come along. Strangely enough in this department he was a bit of a magnet when it came to the fairer sex.

He lied a lot and was not particularly trustworthy.

Not only did he enjoy drinking alcohol at every given opportunity, he also indulged in smoking pot with some of his old hippie friends. The Virgin record store at the Clock Tower being the easiest place to score on a Saturday morning. Tablets were not Taboo and he nearly always had a gram or two of 'Hurry Up' on his person.

He always had his wits about him though and never got done for possession of banned substances. One copper was said to have referred to him as 'Sharp as a tack and twice as nasty'.

He dabbled in Cocaine a bit, but only on special occasions. Christmas, Bank Holidays, Weddings, Funerals, Christenings, Race meetings, The Dogs or Bingo. If there was ever a week in the year that did not involve one of those you're welcome to it. This earnt him the nickname 'The Buzz' as he was buzzing around all the time all over the place.

So all said and done he had all the right credentials to have a successful career on The Knocker, without question. He certainly lived life to the full did Barry, but will he get past fifty. Keep reading and we'll see.

Did I mention he was also a chain smoker?

Didn't really need to did I?

Needless to say though, despite being one of the most notorious and successful people to work 'On The Door', he never seemed to have a great deal of Money for very long. He was a spender. Shirley Bassey sang his favourite songs and he met her on more than one occasion. Often after a show.

Barry was to become a bit of a legend. He once presented himself at John Street nick at 11:55 pm one Monday and asked for a key to his room. The desk Sergeant replied quite curtly,

"This is not your personal Hotel Bubball, you have been a bleedin' pest all weekend. Piss off!"

To wit Barry undid his flies and urinated all over the reception area. The Sergeant tried to stop him but The Buzz side-stepped him, did a quick Ali shuffle and sucker punched him right on the back of the crust. Then managed to slap him round the ear'ole for good measure.

This earned him a record fourth night on the trot in the cells. Only this time the following morning it came with a £95 fine plus £15 costs and a year's probation for being a Public Nuisance and assaulting a Police Officer trying to go about his duty. Defending himself as usual, he then declared, with the most innocent of faces,

"I was only doing what he told met to do. He said piss off so I did. What's all the bloody fuss about?"

"Make that another twenty pounds for insolence" replied the lead Magistrate. He calmed down a bit, for a while anyway, after that episode.

In those days minor infractions would go unpunished but that scenario was a bit special, even for The Buzz. Friday night he had been at the Blue House, which was a regular haunt for The Knocker Boy's, especially if they'd had a good week, as this was the place to broadcast it.

Barry had done a bit of work with one of the Missin brothers and there was a dispute on the carve-up. Not unusual of course, but on this occasion Timmy Missin thought he had been tucked up and he really didn't like it when the shoe was on the other foot.

It had ended when it finally came to blows with Barry suffering quite a bad cut above his right eye, from a very solid left-hander. He didn't want to, but the landlord Harry insisted he go to the hospital and get it stitched up, or risk a nasty Mars Bar as a result. Good sound advice, even promising one of the regulars with ten pounds credit behind the Bar if he made sure Barry attended the A&E at the Sussex County in Eastern Road.

Barry was stitched up in record time and thought he might still make last orders as they left. But fate would have it that Timmy Missin was just on his way in with one of his brothers, as his left hand was severely swollen and probably broken. Feeling hard done by and that it was that Barry Bubball's entire fault he picked up a lump of wood and started chasing Barry around the Car Park.

He hadn't noticed the Police Car parked in a corner and the two officers had no choice but to interfere. The biggest of the Missin brothers Timmy wouldn't shirk from a fight with anyone in those days and so inevitably all four ended up in the back of a Black Maria within 20 minutes and escorted to the station.

There was a relief duty Sergeant that night that just took the Coppers word for it that it was just a storm in a teacup and let them calm down in the cells till morning.

When they were turfed out at 6:30 am, so no Breakfast had to be provided, they all shook hands and decided to go to The Big Northern for a 'Livener' followed by breakfast at the Market Cafe. Barry paid and all was forgiven, the poor sod who had accompanied him to the Hospital commented that Harry had better cough up with that tenner credit at The Blue House tonight or I'm gonna have the right hump.

Then Barry made his way over to Upper Gardner Street market where a lot of the boys would be trying to sell their leftovers to the general public, and it was very likely he might be able to get a drink in the Brighton Tavern on the sly. Just to get the day going of course.

On the Saturday he had gone to the Dogs in Hove, had a good night and decided to pop into Hove Casino. Whilst waiting for a Taxi he saw a fellow steaming into his missus in a nasty manner. He knew he should keep out of domestics but this was looking a bit dodgy, so he intervened.

As he did so the wife turned straight on him crying,

"Don't you touch my old man you nosy git, it was all my fault anyway so mind yer own business."

"Fuck the pair of you then." said Barry and walked off, flagging down a Cab at the Bus stop, at the top of Sackville Road.

He was holding his own at the Roulette two hours later when he had a tap on the shoulder from a familiar face. Detective Sergeant Percy Whinger was not a happy man.

"Now Barry," he began once they had found a quiet corner,

"I don't know the full score yet. But we have an eyewitness that places you outside the Dog Stadium at the time of a serious incident. The Taxi Driver, who brought you here earlier, confirms that you told him you had been involved in an altercation with a couple. Is that correct?"

"Yeah but it was nothing to do with me and the bird told me to piss-off and mind me own business, sod 'em."

"Well, it's not as simple as that me old sunshine. Are you gonna come down the Station peacefully or what?" said Whingie Percy Plod.

Barry made the wrong choice, refusing to go, and was subsequently charged with Resisting Arrest and Preventing a Police Officer going about his duty. Again.

The couple had continued their argument and the woman was now in intensive care with serious head injuries, and the man blinded in one eye with a stiletto heel. At the station Barry made his statement as per what had taken place, adding that if they thought it was his stiletto heel that had been embedded in the bloke's face they must be more stupid than he thought.

Fortunately at 6:00 am the duty Sergeant let Barry out confirming that the Man had come to and made a full confession with regards to the assault, so Barry was free to go. Relieved at this news Barry just asked the Sarge if he really thought he was guilty.

"Sorry Barry, no of course I didn't. Neither did the C.I.D. but they had to follow protocol, you know how it is. It's a good job the bastard coughed up though cos' at the moment it don't look good for the girl and may well end up as a manslaughter or even a murder charge. Think yourself lucky."

"Oh don't worry Sarge, lucky is my middle name," and off Barry went once again. This time he had to go home, as there were not too many options in those days for early Sunday's. He had another couple of hour's kip. Got up had a shower and got dressed up in his Sunday best.

The Sunday was a different kettle of fish. It was, by his own admission, entirely his own fault. Deciding to stay out of the limelight and keep his head low Barry had ventured out into Hove. The Freemasons, The Wick and The Albion were all paid a visit, and then he decided to have something to eat down Preston Street.

The Vineyard was open and George The Greek was always a good host. For some unknown reason however, despite enjoying a nice lamb shank dinner and a couple of Irish Coffees. Barry disputed the bill and refused to pay.

A Lovely Pair of Knockers

George had often let things like this go and allow the punter to return the next day and settle the bill, but Barry was being obnoxious and rude to both George's missus and Daughter. George had also dropped about £400 at the Casino the night before, so wasn't in the best of moods. This behaviour would harm his business on a day like today, so reluctantly he was forced to call the Police.

The two officers tried to reason with him but he just wasn't playing ball so they arrested him. Back at the Station when his pockets were emptied Barry had £285 on him, so felt a bit of a plum. He swore blind that he would settle the bill first thing Monday and confirm this at the Station by producing a receipt the next day. Next morning, about eleven, he gave George at The Vineyard £35 for the £14 bill and they all hugged each other and then had a consolatory drink together.

On the Monday, after settling with George, he joined a couple of Monday Clubs in various parts of the Town. Things as usual got a bit out of hand, he had been all over the place and dabbled in various different illegal substances during the process. Then, whilst toasting last orders, in The Thurlow, Edward Street, Barry remembered, that he was supposed to show proof of paying the debt from yesterday's palaver.

He announced, "I shall now have one last drink. Before I have another one." After that he had made his way across the road. He had left it too late and so that was when he arrived at the Station in such a pickle and been nicked again.

*

12. Now Where Was I?

Back to the story, I did warn you that I go off at a tangent from time to time, but now you do at least have a good idea with what and who, we are dealing with here, sorry about that.

The short detour up Gloucester Road to The Basketmakers, before seeking the whereabouts of Tommy Barnes, was of no consequence to Frankie as he could certainly do with wetting the whistle with a swift half of Harvey's Best Bitter. Lo and behold as they entered, none other than the man himself was just getting a round in, so things worked out fine.

Frankie was well aware that Tommy was one of the most reliable sources of immediate cash in town. Especially once he was made aware of being given first refusal of the stuff that was soon to be available. In this particular case, the instant production of promised funds would be paramount to everything going smoothly.

He could lay his hands on a few bob for sure, but this would take time, which he did not have at his disposal. A quiet word in the bay window seats, with a couple of cigarettes and another swift Light Ale. Tommy was put in the picture and more than happy to comply with Frankie's request. Two grand would be ready and at his disposal by 9:30 am.

Then by some will of the Gods, the other important factor to his plans for the following day also walked through the doors. Coco Collins was a well-respected member of the Brighton Knocker Boy fraternity and Frankie was well aware that things had been going well for him recently.

His brother Bertie had recently mentioned that they had had a nice touch up in Coventry, which kept them all flush for the time being. Coco had purchased a practically brand new beautiful burgundy Jaguar 420 Saloon with all the spoils. With it's 4.2-litre engine it only did 16 miles to the gallon but cruised like a limo on heat. Coco was not a keen driver and Bert was on the insurance so Frankie's intentions were to borrow the car. At an exorbitant rate for sure, but it would be the icing on the cake.

They were well known to be keen on the up and coming boys in the game and The Buzz was related in some way or another, he was

A Lovely Pair of Knockers

sure. He put his proposal to Coco and it was no big deal as they were planning a day off anyway. A challenge game of Snooker at Chick's at the bottom of Middle Street was on the cards, with some travellers from down Pompey way.

There had been a territorial dispute when both firms were working Torquay, so things were to be sorted out in a Gentlemanly fashion, and Coco was having a nice few quid on brother Bert. Bert was well pucker on the green baize, but kept it well under his hat till the readies came across. All fine and dandy.

Things were going great, so when Barry re-appeared from visiting Eileen upstairs, hair in a mess, with flies undone, shirt hanging out and no tie, Frankie could do nothing other than laugh out loud and raise a glass to his new accomplice.

Frankie steered Barry away from the Bar and back into the bay window seats, out of earshot of the few others in the Pub. No need to broadcast to all and sundry of their good fortune. It was deemed unlucky to count your chickens in this game but Frankie felt extremely confident of things going their way from here on in. The fact that their first stop had saved potentially a whole evening searching for Tommy, and tomorrows transport in luxury in the bag, was a clear indication of this.

"Now Buzz," asked Frankie, "Would I be right in thinking that your Mum still does the cleaning at Ragsby's, that slippery little git of a Solicitor in Marlborough Place, next to The King and Queen."

"Yeah she does, how did you know that?"

"Well I seem to recall a few months back that she asked my Mum to fill in one morning, coz she had to go up to London early that day for a funeral or something."

"Yeah that's right," replied Barry, "Her brother, my Uncle Alf, finally karked it, after fighting the 'Big C' for a couple of years. D'you know what? I remember now, my old dear even remarked how your Mum still left her wages in the jar, after doing her the favour. They don't have the same principles, the youngsters of today, not like them or us. Cheers mate. Now what is it that you want? I know something's coming. But don't worry, if it's nothing too much and on the up and up, it won't be a problem I'm sure. If there's anything that my Mum or I can do."

"Alright. Alright." Interrupted Frankie, "Don't go all soppy bollocks Laurence Olivier on me. It's nothing much. Just get her to leave a message on his desk for when he comes in. One that he can't possibly miss. Telling him to be expecting a very important client first thing in the morning nine o'clock prompt."

"No sweat," replied Barry, "Now what else have we got to do this evening that is so important?"

Frankie was relieved to inform him that there was not much more to do as good fortune had smiled down on them this evening. Barry immediately swung into action and shouted over to the Bar, "Come on Eileen, we can still make that film if you get your skates on. Come on, come on Eileen."

He then jumped up and ordered more drinks, then waltzed light footedly up to the Bar with a broad grin on his boat. Any body would think he was writing a song or something, a couple of the lads joined in with the request and within five minutes they all had her at it.

All these years later, Come on Eileen, by Dexy's Midnight Runners still gets the locals going when played on the juke box.

I think the lead singer Kevin Rowlands still lives in Brighton.

Barry was under strict instructions to keep schtum about everything, but in all fairness he was not really aware of much anyway at this stage. It would all change the next day though that was for sure. He was now aware that their new form of transport had been confirmed.

Frankie advised that they would meet at 10:00 am at The Market Cafe next morning. To be sure he had already scoffed his breakfast by this time and made sure the motor was filled up with fuel. He wanted to be away sharpish with no poncing or flaffing about. Everything would be explained on the way to Forest Row he assured him. This was all okay with The Buzz and so they bid one another farewell.

*

13. Getting It Together.

Frankie was up at 7:00 am the next day, as he couldn't get back to sleep after visiting the Bathroom. Still there was not much he could do about it so after a shower and selecting his attire for the day he went for a walk. It was a bright breezy day and the forecast was good for the time of year, but the weather was the last thing on his mind. A blizzard could not prevent him going about his ways this day.

Purely by chance, or was it? He passed by the Solicitor's Office and said hello to Mrs Bubball as she let herself in the main door.

"Well this is a coincidence," she said "We was only talking about you last night and my Barry asked that I leave a message for Mr Ragsby on your behalf. Not in any trouble with my boy are you Frankie?"

"Nah, nah. Nothing like that Mrs B. Just a bit of official paperwork for a potential client, that's all. Don't forget now, will you."

"Consider it done Frankie, my pleasure. He owes us a few favours, he does, so don't you worry you're pretty little head about a thing. Leave it to me." And in she went.

He may as well get breakfast over with he thought, but upon entering the market cafe any appetite disappeared immediately. There were far too many faces in this gaff for him, and they were all seemingly staring and glaring at him in a new, never before witnessed, menacing light. They all knew what he was up to and wanted a piece of the action. Even Vince Nearly, and his brother Harry seemed to be scowling at him and why did the Bowles Boys seem so friendly, today of all days.

Which ones would follow him and Barney once they set off a bit later? Who would be lurking at the Black Lion Hotel in Patcham, or waiting outside The Robin Hood Garage at the beginning of the A23 when they made their move?

They would take the A27 Lewes Road route today, and foil any plans for ambush, that might be afoot. No flies on us, thought Frankie.

He somehow imagined himself as a wounded wilder beast in the desert, with vultures circling above him, ready to make their move. He was the easy innocent and vulnerable target for these evil birds of prey. Poor little Frankie.

He had broken into a cold sweat and his hands were trembling around his mug of tea when Micky McCracken plonked himself down opposite, and quite innocently enquired,

"Where are you off to so bright and early then Frankie?" he enquired in his usual jovial manner. Frankie snarled back through gritted teeth, "Why? What's it got to do wiv you? Who's been saying anything?"

"Whoa. Whoa. Easy tiger. Whassamatter? What's going on?" Frankie calmed down a bit, "Sorry Micky. I'm a bit on edge. Lot's of shit to sort out today. Sorry about that, I'll see you later." Got up, left his tea, and swiftly departed.

It was all in his imagination of course. But the sheer enormity of the task ahead and the potentially life changing benefits were beyond comprehension. At this stage Frankie had all the weight of the world on his shoulders, all alone. Still, just a few more hours to go and God willing the world would be a different place.

These thoughts had to be confined to his mind alone for the time being. Just stay cool. Keep your cards close to your chest and play it like the best poker player in Vegas that you are. In these situations he always took himself out of the situation and imagined he was elsewhere, in some form of competitive great sports arena, in the Grand Final of course.

He popped round to Tommy Barnes yard but there was nobody about. He did some window-shopping. Then had a stroll along the seafront, popping into one of the Cafe's under the Arches and managed a bacon sandwich with too much brown sauce, that spilled onto his tie, with his cup of four sugars with tea.

By the time he had got home and changed his tie it was ready to get the show on the road and put all his plans into action.

He killed another twenty minutes by getting a quick trim in Derek's Barber Shop.

First open for business in 1957, Derek's at 169 Edward Street, has probably groomed more of Brighton's Knockers than any other establishment in town. For sure he has witnessed the rise and fall of more Brighton Knocker Boys than anyone else in History. The stories

A Lovely Pair of Knockers

he has heard over the years could fill another book easily, he was of course beneficiary of generous tips his whole career. How can someone tell the whole shop on a Saturday morning that they have earnt fortunes and not tip generously. The 2/6 was usually doubled and then 'something for the weekend' was also tucked into their top pocket.

Still working to this day with son Lance by his side, Derek enjoys talking about another subject close to his and wife Betty's heart, his Grandson Joe, Lance's boy. He continues the family tradition, but works in a swanky Chelsea Salon run by Richard Ward, and is a stylist to the stars. The Sloane Square venue with the SW3 4LY postcode says it all; even I have to cheque my bank balance and think twice before booking an appointment.

Derek of course invented the very first 'Air-Cut'. Similar to an 'Air-Shot' in Golf terminology. Whereas the client has very little hair but still receives the full treatment and the whole operation still takes fifteen minutes, justifying the fee charged for the service. Nothing ventured nothing gained, but as long as the punter is happy, what's the problem? Went into one again there didn't I?

Back to Frankie.

He was at the office just before nine but convinced the secretary at the door to let him in, as it looked like the heavens were about to open. Who could resist that cheeky grin when accompanied by that doleful look in his eyes?

She was 6ft 2in, in her patent leather high heels, with a slightly anorexic look. Black pencil skirt, fishnet stockings, held up blatantly with suspenders, and a cheap beige silk blouse with black contrasting cowboy bow-tie. Her hair was tied in an untidy bun, false eyelashes, heavy make-up and the most dastardly dark ruby red lipstick. Some of which had managed to get on to her two protruding front teeth.

Still she had a very alluring and under-the-counter type of sexiness that always had customers wondering what she got up to in her private time, and whether or not they might be able to get more acquainted.

When ushered into Mr Ragsby, Frankie's opening gambit was to apologise for the unorthodox manner of his appointment, or lack of it. The Solicitor was not in the most hospitable of moods and the frown, which greeted Frankie, did not hide such emotions.

He placed his glass of wine onto a filing cabinet, as if it had been left over from the day before. Frankie knew full well that it was simply just the first of the day, as it was common knowledge that Raggers saw no one until he had had his first glass of Piersporter.

The man was quite rigid, balding from an early age, he had mastered the Walnut-Whip hairstyle for quite a few years now. He had quite a large beak of a nose, the nasal hairs had a mind of their own, curling out, as if to entice you amongst the bogies that waited within. Spooky.

Sallow skin and jutting chin, which had an ugly little tuft of bristle from his lack of attention whilst shaving. His eyes were sunken and were burdened heavily with very thick spiky eyebrows. The slight hump in his back required made to measure suits, but he had given up on them years ago, so the back of his jacket jutted out by a good seven inches at the back.

The trousers were shiny from wear and tear, held in tightly at the waist by a raggedy leather belt. They were now four inches too big due to weight loss, he was wasting away really, down to the drinking rather than lack of eating. This of course created the domino effect of his strides being three inches too short. Revealing his ankles in fact, and the raggedy grey socks that hung on the shoulder of his shoes. To all intents and purposes, he was simply a scruffy git.

His personal hygiene these days also left a bit to be desired, but he did at least try and smother it up with a good old splash of Old Spice or a large dose of Henry Cooper's best.

He was also, one of the few seen around the Pubs and Clubs who did not keep up with the shiny shoes syndrome either. He settled for the tried and tested comfort of his hush puppies, and didn't bat an eyelid at any comments aimed his way on the matter. Still, at times like these, he was considered an important cog in the wheel, so would be treated with respect and paid accordingly.

He did, however, make a concerted effort for Court appearances, but these days his services were more restricted to paperwork. Such as Frankie was in dire need of today.

Ragsby discarded any attempts of sympathy for Frankie's yet to be announced predicament. With an exaggerated waving of the arms up in the air, he just demanded to know what the problem was. So as to ascertain the necessary actions needed to resolve the issues at hand in the quickest and most efficient manner. Without, of course, generating high expenses that may be generated. (Even the Lawyers seem to repeat themselves twice in the same sentence in Brighton) Frankie realised immediately that the Brief had the wrong end of the stick.

This would have been an ideal introduction under normal circumstances. Where the client (Frankie in this case) was being accused of some outrageous diabolical liberty or indisputable behaviour that required Police attention and subsequent legal proceedings. The Raggers, as he was known, was well used to defending plenty of Brighton's now notorious Knocker Boy's, who were regularly fitted up by the plod for just trying to earn an honest living, knocking doors.

Frankie jumped in and managed to explain himself, before he could be dismissed and asked to make a proper appointment later in the week, within the next thirty seconds, remarkable.

He desperately needed an official document, or declaration of intent, to purchase the property in question and all it's contents. Not the entirety of the contents, but this matter was not under contention and would not, at this time or any other cause any need for conflict. Trust me Mr Ragsby that is not the issue. Trust me, all of a sudden made the Lawyer feel slightly uneasy, due to previous dealings with similar characters, but he need not have worried.

Frankie swore on his Mother's life that the £2,000 promised in the contract was already set in place. Therefore the contract to be produced would confirm this and the agreed final price would be paid in cash upon exchange of contracts.

Edward had provided, in his own writing, all the relevant details that were required for the draft of this contract. Frankie was not illiterate, but it just made sense for Edward to do it, and it certainly looked tidier than if he had done it. Edwina had countersigned at Frankie's request. You know, just in case.

Everything was in fact, in order, and there was no reason that the requested paperwork could not be taken care of, advised Raggers.

Sensing the anxiety or even impatience regarding this matter, when Frankie took his turn to throw his arms up in the air, Ragsby advised he would take care of things A.S.A.P.

Change of heart, then added in a reassuring tone of voice, "Okay, Okay, Mr Slimtone, I'll get something drafted, have it all prepared accordingly and have it ready for you by Thursday, how's that sound to you."

"Thank-you, thank-you so much, Mr Ragsby. Now. How much might I expect to pay for these more than adequate services, Sir?"

"Well, I don't know offhand. Family, friends, employee discounts and all that. Let's say fifteen pounds."

"Fine," agreed Frankie, "Howsabout fifty pounds now, in cash, in advance. Then I'll pop back at ten o'clock later this morning, on the dot, and pick it up personally, whaddayasay?" Irresistible.

"My, my. You are in a hurry, aren't you young man. Alright, come back at ten and it will all be ready for you." Clicking on his intercom, whilst greedily shoving the ten crisp five pound notes into his inside pocket.

He announced like a seasoned Airport operative declaring all flights cancelled,

"Miss James. Miss James do you hear me? Would you please come through immediately and take a memo please. Thank-you Miss James."

Indicating towards the door with a complete tone of disregard and contemptuous air of authority, he commanded Frankie, "Go on then, off with you. See you in one hour, our business is done here for the time being. It has been a pleasure. May I add, it would be nice to start every day in a similar way. Oh would you believe it, I'm a poet and didn't know it."

"Heard it all before Sir, thank-you, see you soon, but I do not think this afternoon." Then added, "We all do it you know."

Miss James entered and requested what Reggie needed doing in such a rush. Frankie hesitated and overheard, as Ragsby replied, "I need you to take something down."

"What's that Sir?"

A Lovely Pair of Knockers

"I can think of a couple of things, but it's a bit early for that," he said under his breath, then continued, "Tell you what I want, what I really want. Quote, to whom it may concern......" Upon ear wigging this, Frankie then left the building.

Smiling as he walked out, Frankie knew the tide was turning, and it was all going his way at the moment. Let's just hope it stays that way.

This had barely taken twenty minutes so Frankie high-tailed it sharpish round to Tommy Barnes yard in Ship Street Gardens.

As arranged the previous evening Tommy had the cash waiting as promised. He had time for a quick cup of coffee whilst signing for the readies and confirming that later on today, Frankie and his new partner in crime Barry Bubball, would return with a couple of tasty bits of furniture to cheer Tommy up no end.

Tommy merely shrugged his shoulders and wished him all the best. Well aware that he would make a nice few bob on his investment. After all, if someone should welsh on Tommy, once that got about, the said offender would find it hard to get credit anywhere else in town. It just wasn't worth it. Nevertheless of course, plenty of plonkers did it all the same.

Frankie was well educated and fully aware that the few particular pieces he would unburden the two Eds of today, would more than make up for the meagre expenses he had so far incurred.

The relevant paperwork was ready and waiting for him at ten on the dot. He did not even check it. The authoritative manner in which Miss James handed him the manila envelope, expressed an air of confidence that need not be questioned.

He was well relieved when he turned into Circus Street and saw 'The Buzz' was already outside the Cafe having a smoke. No need to go back in the Cafe now he thought to himself, and the Jag borrowed from Coco Collins looked the absolute dog's bollocks. Good for the business at hand.

As he approached, Barry got up and began to say something but Frankie discarded any futile explanations, just ushered him towards the car and told him to get going. Barry then protested that he had promised to give Bertie Collins a lift back home, as he had delivered the motor.

Frankie simply instructed him to wait a minute. Got out and went into the Cafe where he saw Bertie conversing with Billy Green at a corner table. With a forgiving smile he approached them and reached in his pocket for a fiver, two came out together by mistake. He was quite proud of himself the way he handled the situation.

"Bertie, thanks ever so much for dropping the motor off. I'm really sorry we can't give you a lift, but we do have a most pressing engagement out in the country. It's imperative we are not late for this appointment. I know you understand how these things work out, so please accept this little token in appreciation of your understanding. How does a cockle suit you?" Bertie was no mug and had already charged brother Coco for delivering the car anyway so was well chuffed.

"You are most welcome Frankie me old son," he replied with a genuine smile,

"Anytime, any place, anywhere. Bertie Collins will always be fair. Maybe we can have a little Martini later matey. Whaddayasay?"

"That sounds like a date Bert. Maybe a little game of pool Friday evening in The Kensington."

"I'll be there," Said Bert. Then burst into song "I'll be there. I'll be ther'ere. Just call my name, and I'll be there."

A few of the boys started joining in and it looked like things were going to get a bit involved, but no worries, it fizzled out as quick as it started. Frankie turned on his heels, smiled to himself and joined The Buzz in the car.

"Let's go Barry Boy. We have work to do. Don't spare the horses." And off they went.

There was a lot of traffic about for some reason, but they were soon on the A27. Barry was obviously quite curious as to all the cloak and dagger stuff of the morning and night before, but waited patiently for Frankie to shed some light on the situation.

He was still very satisfied with himself anyway, as things had gone a lot better with Eileen than he had expected. He started to rant on how Butch and Sundance would have been right good on the door. If they couldn't get in a drum they would have just blown the bloody door down. The film was very good anyway, and they had managed to get 'The Finger Stalls' as they were referred to in the Astoria. Which meant if the film wasn't up to scratch, the immediate company could still ensure a stimulating evening. Less said about that the better on that one.

*

14. Sealing The Deal.

    As they passed the Newmarket Pub, Frankie began to unravel the details.
    "First and foremost Barry," he began. "Not under any circumstances whatsoever, over the next few weeks, do you tell anyone, not one poor lost single soul. I don't care if you can talk to your Great Uncle Albert who died in the Crimean war via some poxy back street canuyvin' money grabbin' medium. Gypsy Rose Lee must not know about any of this business."
    "Or even if you go to confession at church on the most glorious of Sunday mornings, do you mention any minute detail of the transactions that you and I are about to be taking part in over the next few weeks. Do I make myself clear? It is of the most supreme importance that not one single person is aware of what we are up to. I cannot state categorically enough, how important that is. Do I make myself clear?"
    "Okay, okay Frankie," Trembled The Buzz. "You have made your point. But, before we go much further, I do need to ask. How bad are we gonna be? And how much bird are we looking at if we get caught? It's only fair to let me know what the hell I am letting myself in for. Seeing as how you are laying down the law and all the rules and bleedin' regulations my old son. I wanna know what the 'Bubball' this is all about. And for another thing, how much is it gonna be worth and why am I the only silly little prat involved in all this bollocks? What's Tommy Barnes got to do wiv it? What's the Collins boys end? And, well, and I'm not quite sure what else at this particular moment, but come on, spill the beans. Oh and by the way, not so much of the Boy stuff."
    "Well, I find that quite reassuring, at this stage," answered Frankie. Then as he lit up a cigarette, he glanced distantly out of the window, adding, in a contemplating manner, befitting one of the world's great thinkers, "That is exactly the correct kind of question to ask. Elementary my son, very well done Barry Boy."
    The Buzz just grimaced. The following silence for the next two minutes simply drove Barry absolutely cranky. To the verge of pulling off the road right by the Kingston turn off,

"Well don't go all willocky chops and Sherlock Holmes on me now Frankie, let's have it, or I'm turning right round, right now."

Frankie held up his hands in mock surrender and told him to keep driving and all would be revealed.

"Now keep schtum for ten minutes Baz and I'll let you know what the apple is. Reassure you that everything is kosher and how this little clue is gonna change both our lives forever. This my son is gonna be one of the best deals that you or me is ever gonna get. Old Johnny Widdy has a great saying, 'Your speaking, when you should be listening'. Now, is one of those moments, believe me." Frankie was now becoming quite animated and The Buzz recognised that now was one of those precise times to listen and not interrupt. He was not wrong either.

Frankie continued to explain about his discovery. Filling in about how he had overheard of the slim chance that this particular abode may have some hidden treasures. Barry interrupted at this stage and confirmed that he too had heard the rumour.

"Don't start interrupting me Barry." Said Frankie in an agitated manner. "This shit is far too important than to waste time wondering who said what, where and when. This is our danny, and our one and only Danny, only. Did I say that right? And anyway, if you think I am gonna let anyone else have any slices of this bubballiscious pie you want locking up. This is gonna be huge."

"Alright, alright. Calm down, calm down."

"Don't you worry about me calming down? Just be wary, that some proper faces are going to be none too pleased, when eventually it turns out that us two herberts have had the deal of the century."

He did calm down however. The situation was far too serious to start having fallouts with each other. He continued to explain how there were certainly some fantastic pieces, worth God knows how much, to get from the gaff. Then, how he had already convinced the brother and sister what great opportunities he and his mate Barry could offer them.

Barry was not too impressed at first and went back to his first instinct that Frankie was just after a piece of skirt. This really pissed off his partner, and so he became more aware of the sheer magnitude of what might lay ahead and paid a bit more serious attention as Frankie continued.

Once Barry realised how enormous this job could be he adopted a much more sombre attitude. The fact was, assured Frankie, that if everything in the kennel was as he suspected, this really had to be kept under wraps for quite some time or all and sundry would be wanting a piece of the action. Even though they had 'Got In', so to speak. The likes of the Nearly brothers, the Missin's and even the Bowels mob would all consider themselves privy to a share of the booty.

"Them Widdy's are sure to wanna know what happened if any of this gets out. The thing is everyone in this game is getting so green eyed these days that no-one reckons anyone else should get more than them. And that goes for every one of the greedy bastards." Finished Frankie.

Now, understanding the sheer undulating severity of the situation, he congratulated Frankie on achieving so much so soon, albeit without confiding the gory details. Barry could not disagree with the summary of the potential pitfalls and likelihood of insistent overbearing 'new partners'.

So, there and then, both agreed, to adhere to all Frankie's proposals for dispensing with all the gear coming their way. A 'Blood Brother' bond was initiated and they swore allegiance to one another forever, in the car right at that moment, 'Come Hell or High Water', 'Till Death Do Us Part'. Trying not to sound too poufish, of course.

Frankie was now content that he had found the right partner to go on this journey with, but still secretly kept his fingers crossed. Barry on the other hand, crossed his fingers as well. Thanking his lucky stars to fall on his feet with this cheeky little bastard who seemed to have pulled off the call of the century. Not realising of course, he was not wrong on that assumption either.

It started to drizzle with light rain as they approached their destination. The Buzz, had still managed to have a quick joint after breakfast, so was a little high. He started to hum, then broke into song, "Raindrops keep fallin' on me head. Da da dadadada dum. Just like the way you keep' a playing with my cock. Da da dada dada da."

A Lovely Pair of Knockers

"What the hell is all that about?" queried Frankie. "Oh it's that bloody film innit. I just cannot get that catchy tune out of my head can I. Sorry mate." Then the Forest Row 3 miles signpost was sighted.

They were both a bit nervous as they drove up towards the house, with Frankie inwardly panicking that he had imagined it all and it was a nasty trick or crazy dream. They need not have worried, Edwina waved at them from the window as they parked up.

Bang on eleven, as promised!

As they approached, "Last instructions" said Frankie, "Do not under any circumstances make any silly remarks. Like 'This is fantastic' or 'I've never seen one like this before'. Because my son, you are about to witness some things you would never have dreamed possible. Keep it easy and play it cool. Remember some of the stuff I showed you on the itinerary? Well none of the stuff in the loft, office or Garage is on that list. So, let's go and get our fortune Buzz. Don't go all quiet on me though. I've already told them you know plenty of people back in Brighton who can help them with their plans. We are not after everything today, just to seal the deal. Take a few bits and pieces and then put the major plan into operation. Breathe in nice and deep, you are going to enjoy this."

The door opened as if by magic as they approached. Frankie said under his breath, "Open sesame."

They were greeted by the two Eds, who were smartly dressed and just as excited as Frankie and Barry.

Sounds like a Restaurant that doesn't it.

"Please come in gentlemen," said Edward.

"This is Barry," introduced Frankie as they entered, "I think you met briefly yesterday."

"Of course, of course. Pleased to meet you I'm sure. Please come through, my sister is just about to make some tea. Would you care to join us in the lounge, or the dining room? What do you think Frankie?"

"Oh I think the dining room Edward," answered the main man of the moment, "It will be easier to lay out the paperwork, for all to see perfectly clear. Nice and comfortable, and then my associate can get to know you both in a comfortable setting." "Perfect." Was the reply.

"We'll take tea in the dining room please Edwina."

"No problems Brother dear," was the shrill reply from a distance.

Barry tugged at Frankie's cuff as they passed the side table that had at first caught Frankie's eye when he came this way yesterday, in the hallway. (Sorry about all the rhyming words, but I can't help myself sometimes) This of course, brought an agitated grimace from his pal. Keep yourself in check thought Barry, this lucky little sod was onto something and certainly not joking about this drum. Absolutely amazing, and we're only in the poxy hallway.

Edwina was glowing as she arrived in the dining room. With a silver tray laden with home-made fruitcake and plain chocolate digestives. She had remembered Frankie mentioning yesterday that they were his favourites. The short walk into the village first thing this morning, to purchase them, was just one of the things on her hit list today. Her glow did not go unnoticed by anyone in the room.

"You look decidedly radiant today Edwina," was Frankie's opening comment. Blushing instantly, she simply cooed in a girlie way, that only smitten girls could.

"Oh don't be shy Edwina," he continued. Not wishing Edward to become wary of any awkward moments or inappropriate advances towards his sister.

"Let's all just have a quick recap on yesterday's events. So that we all feel comfortable with the business at hand and the arrangements proposed by myself. Also, of course, with both of your consent."

Taking total control, he proceeded. Including the knowing nod, indicating for Barry to keep his mouth firmly shut. A knowing nod came back in return, that this was firmly understood.

Placing a folder that he had received from Ragsby, containing all the relevant documents, Frankie began.

"Right then. Here we go. Despite the outrageously low offer of some despicable local Estate Agents valuation of their property." Index finger pointing accusingly at Barry, as if he were the accused himself.

"I have taken it upon myself to try and do what any like minded honest citizen would and should do under such unusual circumstances."

Still focused on Barry he continued in the same manner. Mimicking the actions of a solicitor, defending an innocent man, summing up in a murder case in front of a jury.

"As promised, I have here today," slowly taking the papers out of the folder as he spoke, in a most dramatic way. As if this was the last prize in a pass the parcel contest.

"Official documentation of myself and much trusted friend and business partner Barry, (more pointing, but more decisive, as if shooting him straight through the heart) letters of intent to, purchase this lovely but unloved or necessary property. Known as The Green Gables, Discovery Lane, (quite ironically) Forest Row, East Sussex. The documents also describe that the present and rightful owners, Mr Edward and Ms Edwina O'Malley, have no responsibility for the contents of said property or attached buildings. The silly bit of land opposite is also included but this will save any pathetic complications at a later date, you know it makes sense."

His tone now became much more relaxed as he added,

"It's all quite run of the mill really, bog standard stuff. My own personal attorney arranged all this in the last 24 hours, at my request."

He'd been watching an episode of Hawaii Five 'o' on the telly last night. Frankie felt for some reason, that a bit of Steve Magarrat, giving it the large with the attorney bit, might be impressive to the pair of em'. It was wasted of course, right over their heads, as neither had ever watched the top rated show, and didn't have the foggiest idea what the hell he was going on about!

"To express how simple such an important arrangement can be certified when all parties concerned are in full agreement and give their full consent. You know, all singing from the same hymn sheet, so to speak." Before anyone had a chance to catch a breath or say a word, he carried on with the clincher.

"As I promised yesterday. (Long pause, as the two Eds waited with baited breath. A fact he was well aware of. Even Barry was captured for one mesmerising moment) I have of course brought with me today. (The classic production of the two magical envelopes from his inside pocket) The sum of, (short pause) two thousand, yes that's right, two thousand pounds. Two whole thousand pounds. As a secure deposit for all the proposed transactions between ourselves."

"Here it is. One thousand pounds apiece. One with F.A.O. Mr. Edward O'Malley on it, the other addressed F.A.O. Ms Edwina O'Malley." They both took deep breaths.

"Just to tied you over until all the details have been finalised, rectified and set in stone. Then, and only then, (pointy finger back in action) will you both receive a further sum, which will amount to another twenty-nine thousand pounds apiece. I have also taken it upon myself, I hope you don't mind, to arrange for my solicitor to take care of all the property deeds on both our behalves. You know it makes sense, eggs in one basket an' all that. Whaddayassay?"

The sheer look of disbelief on their faces, momentarily put Barry ill at ease. He thought for a moment they were going to start laughing and tell the pair of them to 'Piss Off', but none of it.

There was in fact a momentary silence that came over the room as all parties looked at one another. Like some kind of spaghetti western face-off or something.

Edwina kicked things off. Raising her hand to indicate she was not to be interrupted.

"Well Frankie. I must confess, and can safely say. My dear Brother did show some concern last night when you departed and for some time had me in the same train of thought, that we would never see you again. After such a fortuitous chance meeting yesterday. I did voice my concern that you may have got slightly carried away with such a generous offer."

"Maybe you would return, but with an offer far less than first discussed. For this I must apologise, the slight doubtfulness on my part that is. You have shown an extremely honourable and professional courtesy to both my brother and I. For which I now thank you most gratefully."

A Lovely Pair of Knockers

"Well Edwina. I can't say as I blame you for one minute. Who the heck knows what type of scoundrel or ne'er do well could knock on yer door at any given time of day or night. Let's just say, the timing was right. For all and sundry." He was outwardly beaming.

"Everything is just pucker then," added Frankie.

"Most certainly," came in Edward, "Where do we sign?"

They then proceeded to sign precisely where Frankie indicated. Frankie countersigned accordingly. *The deal was done!*

Barry Bubball, at this time, was, as you can understand, in a slight state of shock. Therefore he was rendered utterly and completely speechless, as to what he had just witnessed. Anyone else would have had their eyes popping out of their head and mouth agape. He was, however, now getting used to taking his new partner at his word. A very sensible and wise move at the time.

"Right then," asserted Frankie, "We can all safely say. That everything is now in order. We can proceed with all things as intended."

"Excuse me please for one moment Frankie." Interjected Edwina, "Can I just propose a slight celebration that I had in mind?"

"Of course, of course you can. You can do whatever you wish. I already told you both, that all these decisions are yours and yours alone didn't I?"

"Oh yes, of course you did Frankie, but I just wondered if we might pop down to the Pub for a celebration lunch. You know, just to, just to, make it all official, and all that."

"Don't you worry you're pretty little head about any of that old cobblers my little darlin' Edwina. Everything is now well and truly set in stone. So set in stone in fact that, King Arthur himself could not remove the sword from it. Not even with the help of that silly old prat Merlin. You stand on me girl. Nothing, absolutely nothing, on this Gods earth, is about to stop, what we have put in motion today. Let's not bother with any other members of the village for the time being. Do you recall me mentioning yesterday that such dealings may cause a few green eyed monsters to surface from out of nowhere? We don't want to rock the boat before we have even set sail now do we?"

Then raising his voice a tad, whilst revealing the palms of both hands for maximum effect, but not to seem threatened in any way.

"It's got sod all to do with them anyway. We have plenty of things to sort out for the time being. Why don't we just have a nice simple soup and a sandwich for lunch? American style, and take things nice and slowly? Whaddayassay?"

"That sounds quite amicable to me," she replied. "What do you think Edward?" "Sounds good to me." Said Ed.

Hee, hee, hee!

Everything was Hunky Dory.

*

15. Revealing The Prize.

Just before lunch was to be served, Frankie thought it was time to reveal all to his partner. The Buzz had behaved impeccably so far. He had attempted to intervene slightly when it became apparent that he was not actually required to sign on any of the documents in question.

He was not impressed with Frankie's contemptuous wave of dismissal, and apparent disregard of him, his alleged partner, but accepted it with dignity. With what he had already seen though, he was not gonna go short this week whatever happened. So quickly chose to keep schtum and not upset the apple-cart.

"Right then Buzz, this is it." Whispered Frankie, "Now of all times in your life, is the time to follow my lead. What I am about to show you is strictly between you and me. Let's go." Then beckoned Buzz, to follow.

"Just popping upstairs for a few minutes Edward. Just to show Barry some of the things we must sort out for you both as part of our deal. He may have a couple of people in mind to offload some of the bigger pieces, you know, when we eventually have to get rid of it all, so to speak."

"Don't mind me Frankie. You two both carry on. As far as I'm concerned the place is practically all yours now anyway. Do what you like."

Edward was still a bit glazy as to what he had just witnessed with his sister. They both had thirty thousand bloody pounds apiece. What were they to do? He and she were both quite eager for these two heroes to get the hell back to Brighton and sort out the money, and finalise all the details. From the way Frankie had explained it, things were all settled and all that remained was for him to raise the cash. He had promised this would not be a problem, so what could go wrong. It was time to start making plans. Big plans. For the pair of them, and each other. Our parents would be so proud, he thought to himself.

As they crept up the stairs, Frankie couldn't help himself when he turned round to Buzz, put his fingers over his lips and whispered shush, in a creepy pantomime way, as if they might disturb a sleeping giant. Barry looked up at him quizzically, and shoved him in the thigh. Not for one moment buying any of this silly old bollocks about ghosts, or mysterious goings on.

"Come on then, show us what all the fuss is about. I've been patient enough Slimtone. Let me see something worthwhile, all this cloak and dagger shit is getting on my tits." Now he was coming across a tad impatient.

They got to the top of the stairs and approached the door. Frankie, realising that it was now crunch time, and in fact the crucial moment to reveal what the whole thing was about to his partner. Suddenly he became slightly nervous. Retrieving the key from his waistcoat pocket in a most dramatic fashion that irritated Barry even further. Then he just opened the door in a totally matter of fact way and ushered his pal through the door, closing and locking it behind them in one swift silent manoeuvre.

The first thing to hit the Buzz was of course the desk with the pair of Regency bergeres either side. The cabinet just behind was equally impressive. He then marvelled at the tapestries and fantastic mirrors adorning the walls, and was then equally astounded at the rug.

Without uttering a word, Frankie pointed towards the loft, as he lowered the steps leading up towards it. The Buzz was of course speechless, and was mesmerisingly guided up the steps. Frankie remained in the Office and waited for a good three minutes before joining Barry in the attic.

He looked a broken man. Resembling someone who had just lost his wife and child in labour. He was sitting on a George III mahogany chair with one hand on his knee and his face covered with the other. He looked up ashen faced as Frankie approached.

Then, grabbing a hankie from his top pocket to mop the cold sweat from his brow, he stuttered, "Wh-Wh-What the, What the fucking hell is this all about?" Then he slipped momentarily, and dropped, in slow motion to his knees, as if in surrender. Frankie quickly jumped to his aid and helped him back into the chair. He was in a right terrible state.

"Calm down mate, don't get all soppy on me. Cor' I thought for a moment you had damaged this wonderful chair you're sitting on.

Don't start ruining any of this wonderful stock that we have only just purchased. Whasssup?"

Barry gradually came to, and soon had his wits about him, "Well my son. You certainly seem to have come across one here. Sorry for the temporary show of uncertainty, but where on earth has all this shit come from and who does it belong to? What the hell are we gonna do with it? How can we deal with so much of all this cream gear?"

"Well Buzz, that's what I have been working out. Number one, we own everything. I don't give a toss where it came from, and once we have managed to sell off sixty grand's worth of this gear, the rest of it is ours. To do with as and when we please."

"Then, we still own the gaff an' all. Plus, you haven't seen what's in the Garage yet, none too shabby I can assure you. Then there is also a nice little plot of land across the road, which we also own. If we play our cards right this little drum could set us up for life. I've put you in half of everything."

The next words issued by Barry would haunt him for many years to come, "Half in it. You have got to be joking Frankie. All I want from this call, is my share of the Furniture, Paintings and all the other normal stuff. It's your call, so it's your deal, as far as I am concerned. You keep all the property and all the aggro that comes with it."

"Look 'ere, I know I am not named on all the stuff you got from the Raggers, so I just wanna be half in all the gear. I will help you with everything, for as long as it takes mind you. I just don't wish to be involved in any of the legal implications. Is that clear?"

Now, this may seem ridiculously flippant or generous to you my dear reader, but Barry Bubball had heard of such deals coming unstuck before. He did not want to get involved in any legally binding deals and end up losing out on the pickings. A bird in the hand worth two in a bush, and all that, his choice of course, and who was Frankie to argue, at this crucial stage of the game.

He was slightly taken aback of course, but in that moment of clarity, realised that this was surely his destiny and he alone would benefit substantially, in a life changing way. Maybe Barry just wasn't ready for the 'Big One'.

"Right then," began Frankie, offering his hand, "I'm not gonna start arguing, or any silly bickering about anything at this stage. If that's how you want it, that's how it's going to be. Put your hand there and we need say no more on the matter."

Barry agreed with a nod of the head, shook his hand and that was it. Done deal, never to be re-negotiated.

They then began to converse on which items would be the most beneficial to get rid of first, and so reap the largest sums to clear up the purchase price A.S.A.P.

Then, by chance Barry opened one of the drawers in the Regency ormolu-mounted cabinet, which matched the desk. Unbelievably, upon closer inspection, all the files contained within, referred to what seemed to be all the items in the office, attic, garage and the rest of the house.

Then they realise, that everything had been meticulously categorised under dates of delivery, date and place of origin, approximate value, and estimated value at auction on future dates. These were also categorised with an elapsed time of receipt to sale. The elation and relief was overwhelming. They no longer had much more to worry about, surely. As they dug deeper, and became more familiar with the system, they noticed how certain periods, in historical times, of furniture were favoured.

Then of course this source was revealing that a number of items originated from prestigious properties. Some had large question marks, then footnotes that there had been reports of thefts from those locations. The question mark representing suspicion of original location.

Later to be assumed as Windsor Castle, Brighton Pavilion, Preston Manor and all other Manors across the South of England, West Country and anywhere bloody else for that matter.

They then discovered some of Ted's contacts in another file. These included private numbers for Auction Rooms. Sotheby's and Christie's were dominant, London, Boston and New York area code numbers all underlined with different names indicating different categories; Furniture, Art, Watches, Glassware, Pottery etc etc. There was even a Boston number with 'The Kennedy's' next to it.

After all this, yet another discovery, a plain looking George III mahogany bome commode, in pristine condition, the contents lit up The Buzz like a long line of coke. Ted had not been a heavy drinker, but over the years his Christmas tipple, presents from his many satisfied clients, customers and fellow villagers, had been logged and labelled in the same meticulous fashion.

There were untold delights in each drawer, laid down and carefully wrapped, some still in their original Christmas wrapping paper. This revealed that a number of bottles in particular, ten and twelve year old malts, were actually seventeen and nineteen years old, by the dates on them. Not that either of them knew what difference that would make, to either quality or value.

There were a few cases of fine wine also, and The Buzz attempted to claim this part of the haul. Frankie knew how to press his buttons and agreed Barry could have the contents, he would take the Commode. They shook hands and never thought about it again.

Not until, a year or so later, when Frankie was invited to Barry's flat warming party, and invited to officially open 'The Buzz Bar', as it was to be known. He then saw how glorious these vintage bottles looked when professionally displayed. Magical.

Not for a moment though, did he regret the bargain he had made. The commode would later fetch £35,000. He had of course already pocketed a pocket watch and a nice looking wristwatch that was in one of the drawers of the desk. No need to share everything he convinced himself.

They had been studying their find for twenty minutes when there was a call from the bottom of the stairs that lunch was ready. They were now aware, due to the files, that everything downstairs could safely be sold without suspicion, to a dealer, auction room or private punter.

Frankie reminded The Buzz that neither of the Eds knew anything of the contents upstairs.

But they both feared the worst, due to Mother's dour warning, "Let's not make too much of it," advised Frankie, "We don't want them to suddenly get curious. I don't think it would matter much at this stage. But think about it. You just wait till the day one of them visits The Pavilion, and remarks to someone in the queue that the desk over there is just like the one Father had in his office. Then they add that at least Daddy had a matching filing cabinet."

They both got the giggles then, but Barry managed to indicate with a whimper that they would be right down.

They came down the stairs for a quiet lunch with not much said. Edward and Edwina both felt it polite not to enquire how the experience of entering 'That Room' had been for Barry. He too had seemed to have been affected by the visit upstairs.

After agreeing what a lovely lunch they had enjoyed, Frankie informed Edward that he would just show Barry the garage quickly. Then they would take a few items with them today, with appropriate receipts of course, then pop back on Thursday to arrange for more items to be collected. He assured them both that by the end of the week they would hardly recognise the place. They would, however, be so much closer to making those plans for the rest of their lives.

Ten minutes of pure bliss in the garage saw the pair of them back in the Dining room for a cup of tea. Some small talk was now engaged upon and Frankie thought it might be a good idea if the pair of them made plans to come into Brighton at the end of the week. They could then explore a little and have a serious look at what their futures may have in store. He couldn't guarantee that he and Barry would be available all the time, but they would be well looked after.

This seemed to be amicable for all concerned, so Frankie confirmed that they would all have a nice dinner Friday night at The Grand Hotel and Edward accompanied by his sister would be their guests for the weekend. Sorted.

"Well," began Frankie, "Everybody is happy, fine and dandy, if I had a nice bird I might get randy. Nah, sorry about that inadequate comment Edwina, please forgive me. It's just that I am so excited for you and your brother. Barry and I are both very pleased to have come into your lives at such an important and convenient time. However, on a more serious note, are you sure there is no particular piece of furniture or set of china that either of you have had second thoughts about?"

A very risky question to ask, at such an important stage of the game. Barry went as stiff as a board, this was tantamount to breaking an unspoken rule of the Knocker game. What was he thinking? But

Frankie was confident that now was the best time to go with it. If tomorrow, one or the other wanted to keep something, he did not want to have to confront them with the signed documents he had tucked in his little folder. The risk was worth the ruck, as far as he was concerned, so let's get on with it.

Both Edward and Edwina looked stunned for a moment. Then Edwina simply replied, "But Frankie, we have both signed all the relevant paperwork. Surely, you don't expect either of us to go back on our word. Do you? Are you insinuating that either of us would try and swindle you and Barry out of anything that you might gain from this honest and genuine transaction? Oh, anyway, Edward, is there any single item not in your room, that you have decided may not be appropriate to be included?"

He hesitated slightly. "Come on man, speak up now if there is in fact something that you feel you need to hold onto. No, of course there isn't. Frankie I can assure you that we were both fully aware that some of the china, and maybe the silver tea and coffee sets are of some value. But we are not stupid. We do of course, understand that you need to earn a bit of money for yourself out of this deal."

She had never before spoken to her brother in such an abrupt manner, but it did give her a glowing feeling of righteousness.

"If, at some stage, I suddenly realise I have some form of sentimental attachment to any particular item, once it has gone. That I never previously recognised. I am confident and sure you would do everything in your power to regain it. At this stage, however, that is not the case. Please let's get things underway. No more of all this sentimental nonsense. I do appreciate your concern for our well being, but for now let us all just enjoy the moment."

Then with the most mischievous look she had ever made in her whole life, she exclaimed, "Whaddayassay?"

"Well," shot back Frankie, in an instant, "I think that pretty much sums it all up. Come on Mr Bubball, let's get that ugly little side table, with the shitty little clock on it, onto the motor. Then we will just take a couple of items from, 'That Room Upstairs', pointing menacingly to the ceiling, get rid of a couple of bits of shit out of the bloody garage and we can be on our way, whaddayasay?"   "Sure thing boss, I'm with you." Came the reply.

16. Let The Games Commence.

The rest is history really, but of course you do need to be informed of what actually happened, and the events ensuing over the following months. It's only fair.

They cleared a few bits and pieces and ventured back to Brighton.

All the while, The Buzz could not stop talking about the amazing amount of gear in 'The Gables'. "How much do you really think we are going to cop for this lot then Frankie?" Had been mentioned about twenty times before they eventually arrived back at Tommy Barnes yard, at about two-thirty in the afternoon.

"Listen to me now Buzz, pay attention now," warned Frankie as they parked up, "Now this Tommy Barnes, is as fair as they come. He pays good money. But not everything is his cup of tea. So, on some stuff, it's not as good as it gets, but don't worry if it don't seem we are getting the right colour of money. For the time being we are gonna let him earn a nice few quid, but he does not have to have every bit of gear we have got coming. On top of that, we do not want certain people, you know who I mean, to be aware of what we actually have laid our hands on."

"That's why we made our promise to each other. Loyalty is going to be our one redemption mate. We have hit the big time. But we are not about to announce it to the press. Now are we?"

"Of course not Frankie. I'm not one of the Three Stooges y'know. I know the score by now mate. I am more than just happy to be an observer, you have looked after me so far, so why would I put the pickle in? Whassamatter wiv ya?"

"Fine, fine. It's all kosher. It's just all a bit too much to take in at the moment, but I'm sure we'll get used to it. Just stay cool, and everything will work out okay. But I know that there are a couple of other dealers that will be drooling with their tongues on their chins once some of this gear starts appearing on the scene. I don't wanna upset Tommy, but also, why should he make more dollar than us. I'm not being greedy, just looking out for our best interests."

"You just crack on mate, don't worry about me," affirmed The Buzz.

A Lovely Pair of Knockers

In they went.

"Well then boys, what glorious goodies have you brought to cheer me up today?" said Tommy when he saw them stroll in. "I don't suppose you have any Nelson's for me Frankie?" he asked.

"Far from it Tom. Far from it. But, I do have a couple of items to run past you, if you have a moment."

Indicating that his services were no longer required for the day, Tommy gestured to his driver Steve, to go over to The Cricketer's and wait for further instructions. This form of communication needed no interpretation and he disappeared like a magician's assistant.

"Lovely Frankie. I trust everything went to plan then. Well then boys, let's have a gander." Then glancing in Barry's direction, "You've fallen into one then Buzz, how does it feel?"

"For the time being Mr Barnes, I would prefer not to comment."

"This ain't a slippery snidey police interview Barry, relax, we are all friends here. From what Frankie has already told me, we are all about to become very acquainted with each other over the next few weeks. Don't start getting all coy with me. I have plenty of contacts in this game and I am sure we are all going to be well and truly flush after all is said and done."

Barry knew of Tommy Barnes by reputation only and had not had the pleasure or privilege yet to deal directly with 'The Boss'. Oh how life was going to change for him, in a good way that is.

Tom continued, "Now, I have it on good authority that there is more to come, but I am not greedy, if it's not for me, I will steer you in the right direction to the proper place. Let's be fair boys, you know me, I will always do the right thing. I don't have to rip you off like some of the other toe-rags that think they can con a Conner just coz they've got a shop."

"We don't have to worry about any of that bollocks Tom," said Frankie, then opening the boot of the Jag he asked, "Whaddayafink of that my son?"

Tommy was well known to never show any emotion, and was the last person on the planet to have any sentimentality towards the things he bought and sold on a daily basis.

A Lovely Pair of Knockers

Standing back, as if struck by a lightning bolt, they both thought that he had had a heart attack. Clutching his chest, Tommy, out of breath, advised them to both join him in the office immediately.

"And shut that fuckin' boot sharpish, for cryin' out loud." He ordered them.

Once settled, and each of them with a nice stiff drink of differing spirits in front of them, Tommy began.

"Frankie my son, that there side table bares a remarkable and worryingly strong resemblance to one that mysteriously disappeared from a very well known location a few years ago. There was a right scream-up at the time when it went on the missing list. I remember it well, because the filth were sniffing around all of Brighton's big players at the time, and I distinctly recall being shown a picture of that very same table. I am absolutely positive. Where did it come from?"

"Well, that is none of your fucking business at this stage Tommy. Do you wanna take it off our hands or not, is the question. Because I can assure you, I am in no shadow of a doubt that I can find someone who will. I know you have been very accommodating so far, but if this is too big for you, and you don't wanna be involved, I totally understand. I can go and get your two poxy grand this afternoon, if you so wish."

"At this stage, however, I can assure you, that everything is all above board. If you need to see any documentation and authorisation of sale I have it all here in my folder."

As he reached inside his jacket, Tommy just waved his hand in the air and indicated that there was no need.

"Don't you worry about any of that matey, I couldn't give a monkeys. I should apologise for even asking in the first place. I just wasn't expecting that particular piece. What else have we got then?"

As he walked back out to the car in the yard, he asked,

"Ain't this Coco Collins motor?"

"Yeah, we just borrowed it for a bit of PR, didn't we." Piped in The Buzz.

"Thought so. Still, this deal hasn't got anything to do with him and his little mob has it?"

A Lovely Pair of Knockers

"Nah, nah," said Frankie; "We just borrowed it as a one off. He will get his just rewards as the deal goes on, but no interested party as to the bigger picture, so to speak."

"Good, good, glad to hear it" said Tom, "Now, open her up, and let's get the party started." He then did the proverbial double one armed bandit, with the gyrating hips, and it really did look like he had dollar signs in his eyes.

The side table was a given. They all knew it was very rare, but someone still had to find an extremely wealthy buyer. As far away as possible. Tommy uncharacteristically, told them both, he had a Norman in Texas that would gladly pay top dollar. They happily consented to fifteen thousand pounds and forget about the two grand he had given them this morning.

That cash was counted out there and then. Tommy had anticipated the arrival of some extremely beneficial goods. After speaking with Frankie yesterday. He didn't lend two bags without expecting a quick profitable return. This would be one of his best investments ever, and eventually be the reason for paying off the mortgage on his Shirley Drive home. Vince Nearly had introduced Frankie some time ago, and he had a good nose himself anyway. He liked the kid.

The clock was in fine condition, and he might even keep it himself, just to remind himself of the day. Bit of bullshit on Tommy's part, but he said three grand would be coming their way, but not today.

The tapestries were a revelation. Frankie knew full well that there first port of call when they got back to Brighton, Tommy Barnes, had a soft spot for these. Not because he liked them, but because he happened to have a private collector somewhere in The Channel Islands, who was absolutely polluted.

The Buzz had thought Frankie was taking the piss when he claimed that the tapestries were worth good money. Barry himself had bought some very similar ones when working with one of the Widdy brothers. They had convinced him, at the time, the Taps were two- bob apiece and agreed to be bought out of the deal. His share had come to thirty five quid and there must have been four or five of them.

So when Frankie had suggested they could be worth up to eight hundred quid each, he had a bit of a hissy-fit, and declared Frankie was mugging him off.

"If I was going to mug you off, you silly little soppy twat, why the Bloody Bubball would I tell you they are worth money, you greedy little shit."

See what I mean, here we go again with the same word, little, twice in the same sentence.

Anyway. They had collected thirty two in all. Some from upstairs and a few from the garage, rolled them up and thought they would take a punt. The tapestries after all did not take much loading once rolled up, and caused no particular concern to the two Eds. They all got slung in the back, some on the floor but most piled up on the back seat, which caused Frankie slight discomfort due to the lack of vision in the rear view mirror. Such hardship for what they would return.

There were eight Flemish verdure's in various colours, two Spanish armorials, half a dozen Aubusson panels in rose pink and green. One wall hanging depicting the departure for the hunt. This had the arms of Philippe de Bourbon-Parme, and was related to Audran at the Gobelins. It's a bit boring going through all the details of each and every one of them, so we won't bother with the intricate details.

BUT, when Tommy Barnes said that the most he could give for them was fifteen hundred quid each, each one that is, it's no surprise that The Buzz had his second near heart failure of the day.

This of course came to an unexpected yet staggering £48,000. Even Frankie had not envisaged such a large sum. Not wishing to let the moment pass, he taunted The Buzz, knowing Tommy was well aware of the joke.

"See you fat prat, I told you not to throw them in the bin you din." Never, ever, after that moment, did The Buzz, doubt a single word Frankie Slimtone ever said.

Even if he suspected it.

With this sort of money coming their way from just the first day, the pair knew that their ship had come in. It seemed only fair to invite Tommy to join them in The Cricketers for a drink. They each had another couple of stiff drinks before joining Steve the driver at the

Bar. He was given the keys to the Jaguar and Bertie Collins address at which to deliver it. The cockle for the sherbet back was more than generous.

It was to be the first of many generous gestures coming his way over the next few weeks, but he would be worth it. He had a couple of young kids, a nice wife and a mortgage. He knew how to keep his mouth shut. Could be trusted, and was not greedy. Perfect. For all concerned.

Whilst the car was being dealt with they made plans for the exodus of Furniture. When they explained about the filing system, Tommy once again got quite animated, and ordered Champagne immediately.

Steve the driver would be available all day Thursday, with the Luton Van. Tommy assured them that he was an expert loader of gear and would bring someone else to help him. All they had to do was log it as it was loaded then follow him home and confirm prices with Tommy accordingly. He advised that it would be best to leave Friday out, so there would be no prying eyes. His yard was pretty secluded, but come Fridays, all sorts of different characters were sure to pay him a visit at some time or other.

"Well, we don't want to wear ourselves out. Slogging away every bleedin' day do we," commented Barry.

"You, my son," instructed Frankie, "Are going to be grafting like you have never grafted before in your life, the next couple of weeks. You will earn a couple of years' money for it, of course. But don't think you are gonna go on the missing list for a couple of days larging it and still reap the rewards, me old cocker. Because that would be a major disappointment to your Bank Manager. Don't you agree Tommy?"

"Absolutely Frankie, you make sure you do your bit Buzzzy Boy, or you'll live to regret it. This seems to be shaping up pretty well, a right little belter, and I haven't even seen the kettle."

"Okay, okay, don't go all Mr Metcalfe on me, you two. I have no intention of letting the side down. It's just that I don't wanna miss Church on Sunday do I."

They all laughed at the irony of the comment. They only visited the place on Weddings, Christenings and Funerals, and they all knew it.

Thursday was confirmed for a 9:00 am start when Steve came back with the car. Tommy would loan them his brother Tony's Merc for the day, to show him where to go, then get back to the yard. Once the job was done.

They would then probably buy a motor of their own from the spoils. So as not to involve any other parties. It made sense. The Bedford Van could still be used to shift some stuff over a longer period. First of all though, get all the good gear sorted and then once the gaff had been bought and paid for they could take it a bit easier and relax.

*

17. The Carve Up.

When Tommy left, they decided to take a stroll round to The Waggon and Horses, in Church Street. Whilst walking, just outside the Colonnades next door to the Theatre Royal, The Buzz enquired as to his cut of the booty so far. Pondering for a short while, Frankie, who thought quickly on his feet as a rule, hesitated before replying. This predicament needed to be treated with care and trepidation. He didn't want to nause it for himself. The Buzz had slipped up when saying he wanted no part of the property deal, but now was surely not the time to remind him.

He began, "Well of course, we have made a really good start Barry. But let's take a look at the bigger picture. You have already stated that you do not wish to be involved with all the property shenanigans, and I have to respect that. This must not turn out, into one of those mine and yours, yours and mine situations, or we could end up shafting each other and ruining everything."

"My first priority, (long pause) must be, (short pause) to secure the property. If we don't keep the two Eds in check, we could put the pickle in on the whole deal ourselves. You do understand that don't'cha?"

Barry did not reply until they got inside the Pub. He walked straight to the Bar and ordered two pints of Harvey's and two large whisky chasers. Then gestured towards Frankie, announcing, "Don't look at me luv, he's in charge of the money."

Then whispered into Frankie's ear,

"Don't you worry about the readies for now Frankie. I trust you, but try your best not to leave me short mate, or I may not be so accommodating as time goes by. If I don't think I'm getting my fair crack of the whip, I can stick up for myself you know. You do have a good name and reputation, let's not nause that up, eh?"

Straight back on his feet, Frankie paid for the drinks, then steered The Buzz over to a corner, went to sit down, but slipped into the Gents instead.

"Back in a minute Buzz," he said over his shoulder.

Upon his return, Frankie passed Barry an envelope.

"How does that suit you? For starters, that is? There is five grand in there. I cannot be your keeper, and I'm no baby sitter. If you want, we can go see old Raggers tomorrow and draw up some kind of official agreement, like a contract, if you want that is. It's entirely up to you. Whaddayasay?"

Barry was well chuffed, and indicated that no documentation was needed.

"Right then," began Frankie, "What we will do tomorrow is call Edward and Edwina, to tell them we will be arriving Thursday to pick up some of the furniture. We will have some money for them of course, Tommy will have the three grand for the clock."

"Maybe we can take them for lunch somewhere. While the boys are bringing the first load back to Town, that is. It's not worth even considering for one single minute that Tommy will try and shaft us, it's not his style and just not worth his while. We will have logged all the gear from The Forest end anyway, leave it to me. We won't go to the local boozer of course."

"I reckon if we can get there nice and early, and that Steve geezer and his mate are as good as Barnes'y says, we might even get two loads done."

"That would be fantastic mate. I'd never have thought of that. Do you reckon Tommy will stand for it?" agreed Barry.

"Of course he will. As long as we sort out the driver. He only has to unload once and load twice when you think about it. The second load can be left on the motor in the yard can't it?"

"Well I must say you certainly have got things running tickety-boo me old mucker. But as you seem to have had everything sorted, so far. Where is it that you can foresee any problems? You must have thought about it?" enquired The Buzz.

"Well, it's like this," began Frankie, "As long as we can keep as few people involved as possible, the much greater chance of no other greedy gits trying to get in on our action. That's why it is so important, not to start getting all lairy about it. With a bit of luck, we could both end up with a gaff of our own after all this. Let alone a jam jar. Here's to you mate, now get us another drink, you tight-arsed little bastard," smiling of course.

"As it happens why don't we pop round the corner and have one in The Basket. Hopefully The Collins clan will be in there and we can thank them properly. Make sure they are happy and all that."

The Buzz was more than happy with this suggestion,

"Good idea. Then I can also arrange for Eileen to meet Edwina on Saturday and show her around town a bit. Are they still going to come, do you reckon?"

Frankie's answer was confidently expressed with a big grin,

"Of course they will. They have got as many plans to make as we have. Let's just help them on their merry way and make sure we get our end of things in place. The fact of the matter is, after Thursday their home will not be so very homely. Not if I have my way. And I certainly mean to have my way, I can assure you."

*

Coco thanked them for the prompt return of the motor, adding that he hoped everything had gone in their favour.

"Sweet as a nut Coco, sweet as a nut. How did the snooker go down chicks?" asked Frankie.

Bert chirped in, "The saucy sods only accused me of being a ringer. For God's sake, I was there in Torquay when it all kicked off in the first place. They welshed on the biggest bets and caused another row. Still, they didn't look too clever once Micky Douglas had something to say. One of them knew Mick from Borstal and he proceeded to advise that they pay up a bit lively. He was a force to be reckoned with in the ring, he was crowned Borstal Boxing Champion two years running y'know. But he was a much nastier proposition when the Queensberry Rules were not involved. Of course, then we had to put him in on the winnings, but let's just say that the honour of Brighton's Knocker's was served well on the old green baize today. What can I get you two lads to drink?"

"That's fine Bert, we actually came round to get you two a drink," said The Buzz.

"Oh piss off will yah, don't start all that nonsense. I asked you what you wanted to drink, so what are you having?" insisted Bert.

A Lovely Pair of Knockers

Needless to say they were all still at the bar at eleven o'clock and beginning to discuss where to go next. Frankie gave Barry a knowing nod, which did not go unnoticed, then announced he had an early start tomorrow and would bid them good night, Barry did the same. They shook hands outside and agreed to meet at nine the next day in the cafe.

*

After breakfast the next day it was over to Tommy Barnes. He had said there would be another fifteen grand waiting for them, and they would discuss which items would be best to get delivered for Thursday. As good as his word Tommy had already been to the bank and gave Frankie the amount as arranged.

It was strange how one week you could be skint and get by okay and the next, such as this one, Frankie had already laid his hands on 'Thirty Large'. With thirty-six still outstanding.

He must however remember to keep a strict log on money-in and money-out, more wise words from his mentor Vince Nearly.

Vince had recalled a deal where he had received thousands, and yet could not tally the books two months later when someone mentioned they had not been paid for services rendered.

This amount though, and the small fortune still awaiting to be redeemed, was not going to catch Frankie with his trousers down. He had now responsibly purchased a Red Diary to keep tabs on every transaction.

Mind you the way things were going, he was beginning to feel a bit petty, listing even the £50 to Ragsby, tenner here and a score there. See how things pan out he thought to himself, there may not be any need for all this tittle-tattle. Especially the way The Buzz had reacted when he mentioned the big picture, he certainly was not going to cause any upset, was he?

Frankie checked with Barry that he was okay for readies for the time being, assuring him that there would be another nice little windfall by the end of the week.

"Everything is fine by me," stated The Buzz.

They made their way to The Grand Hotel for morning coffee. It was a bit out of their comfort zone, but they didn't wish to bump into any familiar faces. The important business at hand was to go through the books which Frankie had with him. The famous lost book, as it would later be referred to.

They had sorted it all out within twenty minutes and were feeling anti-climatic. The Buzz revealed how easy this had been, "Well that was a piece of piss, Frankie. Do you wanna give Edwina or her Brother a call and confirm for tomorrow?"

"I'm on it," said Frankie, and made his way to the Telephone booths. Returning within two minutes. He had a distressed look about him, which raised alarm bells instantly. Then with that infectious grin he announced that all was quiet on the Western Front, and they were expected at approx 9:00 am tomorrow. Breakfast would be waiting, with fresh tea and coffee.

The rest of the day was now free, but Frankie was still a bit edgy about The Buzz's behaviour. So he proposed they spend it in a simple fashion and just enjoy a day off together. A spot of light lunch somewhere, a matinee showing at the pictures, early evening Bingo then a few frames of snooker. Barry was not exactly thrilled by the prospect and although none too keen, agreed that it was probably the best plan.

They were bored to tears with each other by the time they were scheduled for Bingo, so both cleared off in opposite directions, agreeing to meet at The Market Cafe at eight the next morning.

Next day, after a cup of tea they went round to Tommy's Yard. Everything was ready to go, but Tommy needed a word in the office before they left.

"I'm really sorry boys, but I have some bad news about The Tapestries."

Here we go thought The Buzz raising his eyebrows. Noting his partner's reaction, Frankie immediately intervened by saying,

"Okay, okay let's not get excited. Let Tommy explain before we start getting too anxious. What's the story Tom?"

"The thing is this," began Tommy, "I have no qualms about them, but my mate in The Channel Islands, well we haven't seen each other for ages, so he has invited me over to Jersey to finalise the deal.

This does of course mean that I will not be about to sort the readies for all the gear coming in this week."

Giving neither of them a second to interrupt, he continued, "Because my chartered flight is leaving Shoreham Airport at three o'clock this afternoon. Can you boys trust me? I will be back Sunday afternoon, and we can do a right proper stock take all day Monday. I will be returning with my pal, and he may well be in the frame for taking a nice few bits and pieces whilst he is here, top dollar of course. I'll even shut the shop till Tuesday, so as long as it all goes well, I don't see a problem, do you?"

Frankie kept cool, and indicated that he and Barry needed to consider this new development, Tommy shrugged and nodded towards the rear of the office for them to have a quick boardroom discussion.

They had their Dragon's Den moment, right there and then. Both agreeing that, with so many things already in place, it would be folly to try and find a new buyer at this stage. At least Tommy had the decency to explain the situation. They would still have plenty of cash to get by, and Frankie reckoned that now, they could practically clear the whole house, by the time Tommy got back from his trip.

"Just one issue Tom," said Frankie, "If this is acceptable, which it is. Where can we unload all the stuff? There is not enough room in this yard if we get right to work and shift it all."

"Listen to this next call lads, and then I am sure you will feel you are getting treated fairly, squarely and respectfully." Picking up the phone, he did not need to check for the number, just dialled from memory.

"Is that Adrian? Hello mate. Right, you know what we were discussing last night?" (Pause) "Yeah, that's right. They have been informed and have agreed the terms, so you can send both containers round this morning and clear everything. Every single thing, that's right. Cheers buddy, see you at ten."

"How does that grab you lads? My mate will be sending two containers round this morning and the place will be empty by the time you get back. I did have a feeling you would like to go with two trips today and that is fine by me. Consider Steve the driver and his pal, as your temporary personal members of staff. Now I am sure you won't let me down and take the micky with their wages, now will you?"

"Of course not Tom. Of course not," said The Buzz.

"Right then," began Frankie, "Let me get this straight. Your yard is going to be completely barren by the time the first load arrives, in a few hours time." Tom nodded. "So we, to all intents and purposes, can use it, as our own for a couple of days."

"That's right boys. Help yourselves, but be careful, and don't let too many people know about this special arrangement. Obviously now, you can also have Friday, but I strongly recommend, you find a very trusted person to stay on the premises between trips. With all the gear that will be arriving, a little bit of security will not go astray and you will at least have peace of mind. Get whoever you like, but I do have someone in mind, if you are struggling with that one."

"Well, we did plan to have a nice lunch with our clients today. What time are you leaving Tom?" asked Frankie.

"I have to be away from the yard by two o'clock."

"Right then, what the hell are we waiting for Barry? Come on look lively and get yer skates on. We have work to do."

Gesturing to the Luton Van in earnest, Frankie continued, "Follow us Steve, we are on a mission mate. Don't spare the horses. Tally Ho and away we go."

On their way, Frankie devised his plans for the day. It was still imperative to keep the two Eds happy. Once the Luton was loaded with the first batch of furniture, they would all leave at the same time. The Buzz, Frankie, Edward and Edwina would follow the Luton back towards Brighton, but stop off at Stroods Motel for lunch.

Let the lads unload, then they would meet back at Stroods and make a little convoy back to Forest Row. They would make all the weekend arrangements over lunch, and be able to explain how the money situation was going. The Buzz agreed that they were sure to be impressed with the ten grand each that Frankie was to present them with over lunch.

Frankie mentioned of course, that he too, had binned five large himself. What with all the expenses they were incurring he obviously needed a steady cash flow.

Then tapping his little book like a true accountant, he added,

"Don't worry Buzz, it's all logged in the book, it's all logged in the book mate. Anytime you wanna check the books, you just ask."

*

Things went exactly as planned. Tommy's two lads were masters, and displayed never before witnessed, the expertise of loading a Luton. It was of no surprise of course as they left for lunch, that the two Eds looked a bit shocked, at the now desolate looking ground floor.

They had helped tremendously by packing up some of the china and silverware in the three tea-chests found in the garage earlier in the week. But once they saw how quickly and with such ease, that these two experts filled another five tea-chests, in a quarter of the time it had taken them, they all agreed, it would be easier to let the experts take care of all the packing from now on.

Whilst browsing the menus, Frankie had broached the subject of money. Edward, like the gentleman he was, said that everything seemed rosy in the garden as far as he and Edwina were concerned.

"That may be so," countered Frankie, "But we did say that all transactions should be recorded, I have my little red book now," tapping fondly, the spine of his new best friend.

"So, just so that we are all in the same boat. I wish to make another little financial contribution at this time, and pardon me for asking, will require both your signatures. Witnessing the fact that I have begun to pay for the outstanding balance on our agreement. How does ten thousand pounds each, sound to you?"

Plonking two crisp sealed envelopes on the table.

Edwina let out a nervous gasp, that momentarily startled all those seated at the dinner table, then replied to the proposal with,

"Frankie, you cannot be serious. We could not possibly accept such a large sum of money from you at this stage."

Edward winced at this declaration, but Frankie simply explained that this was more of the deposit. If they felt they could not handle such a large sum, then they could simply deposit the funds with the Bank, or his Solicitor, Mr Ragsby, for safekeeping.

A Lovely Pair of Knockers

He explained that in his experience it usually became problematic with Lawyers, when it came time to exchanging contracts, they always wanted to hold onto the money too long. Keeping it in their high interest account for as long as possible, but there were no contracts to exchange. Once they had received all the funds they would just sign one last time to hand the property over to Frankie. If they wished, he and The Buzz would accompany them both to the Bank, speak with the manager on their behalf, and vouch for the origin of the funds. It was entirely up to them, they could do whatever they wished.

It was now clearly dawning on both Frankie and The Buzz, that the two Eds had not really taken all this as seriously as they thought. Still, everything would become clearer at the weekend.

*

How much all their lives were about to change, in such a short time.

Not to cut a long story short, but things all worked out fine.

The guy watching the yard was Peter Wright, or 'Big Sam', as he was known. He was also referred to as the oldest teenager in town, due to his reluctance to cut off his long white ponytail. His wages were taken care of by Tommy, as they had an ongoing relationship. He also blended in and raised no awareness from any of the other dealers, when he simply informed them Tommy was away and he was just watching the shop.

The clearance went as smooth as silk. Tommy got back as promised, and his pal from Jersey was to become a strong benefactor.

The whole of the ground floor was cleared by Saturday, and all price tagged up in the yard. Frankie and The Buzz, had been what they thought was generous. They had an ace up their sleeve of course, they were in possession of Ted's ledger that had all the relevant information. There would for sure be a little bit of bartering, but nothing they thought would cause any upset.

The weekend itself had been quite hectic. Edward and Edwina were more than comfortable at The Grand, but had not been in the slightest bit demanding for attention. This in one way was relieving, but also left unanswered questions as to their intentions.

Eileen had in fact met Edwina and they had simply wandered about The Lanes and chit chatted in a girlie fashion. Whilst Edward had kept himself amused on The Palace Pier, the Seafront and enjoyed The Crystal Rooms at the bottom of West Street on the multitude of pinball machines. The time flew by for the pair of them.

They had both decided, that Brighton was to be their home and told Frankie and Buzz of their intentions. They would take temporary lodgings, whilst looking for their new homes and were over the moon with everything. Sweet.

Tommy Barnes was also over the moon when he entered his yard on the Monday morning. Not only was it brimming with neatly stacked, classy furniture, he had each and every item individually tagged with it's expected price.

It was like ambling through an auction room, where you had already purchased every lot. He casually inspected each row slowly but surely, as if inspecting troops on parade. A little rub here, a little scratch there and then on occasion a loving smooth caress. Which was accompanied by a wry smile.

Frankie and The Buzz arrived at ten o'clock. Excited and expectant.

Tommy began to rub his chin, and totally as expected asked them, "Well, what do you two little rascals reckon we are looking at then, altogether?"

"Well, that can't possibly be worked out at the moment Tom. But if we can come to some reasonable strategy, to sell to you, a few selected others, and then sort out some of the higher end stuff for the auctions. With your advice of course, for which you will be handsomely rewarded. I would at least hope to secure by the end of the week, the balance owed to the clients, plus a decent week's wages for myself, and my partner of course. Does that sound unreasonable to you Tommy?"

Frankie had the floor at this stage, so finished nicely on,

"Oh, and by the way, we happened to come across another five of those tapestries in a nice little coffer, stashed it over there in the far right corner. Thought your mate might be interested."

A Lovely Pair of Knockers

Tommy was well aware of said coffer, Steve the driver had already brought it to his attention.

"Yeah, Steve mentioned that to me. By the way I will compliment you both on the way he was treated by the pair of you. Him and his mate enjoyed the meals taken with you and were very happy with the greengages. Smart move on your part, but still, no-one thought you woz mugs in the first place did they?"

All the while still circling, and stroking his chin very slowly,

"So, from my reckoning. This is what I can sort out this week. The Dining Cain and Able, most certainly George III mahogany early 19th century. Trouble is the two extra leaves have been rarely used in recent years so don't match too well. Although there is no dispute they are original, it's just a casualty of war sort of thing. The fifteen grand tag on it should only be ten. That said, the ten matching Lord Mayor's, are all in impeccable condition. I do happen to have an interested client and the forty grand you estimate is a bit low. So I reckon fifty for the set is a goer."

Raising his hands in anticipation of either of their comments, he continued,

"The commode, next to it, now you have got that all wrong. That my boys is a piece for the auction rooms, as long as you have no problem with that. The other serpentine commode, matching the dining table. Nice piece of cross banding on the moulded top, well that could be a nice bonus for my buyer, and the four grand price tag can be improved upon."

"Now I know time is of the essence, but that little deal will take a few days, so you will have to be patient there. But don't worry, that will not prevent you getting what you need this week, believe me."

Frankie could hold himself no more, so opened up with,

"Right then Tom, let's get down to business. What bits can we unload as soon as possible and get the nelsons, A.S.A.P."

"Come on Frankie, you know I love this part of the job. Making you squirm, just a little, before revealing the prize. Which in this case, happens to be this little beauty."

Tapping his fingers on the piece right next to him, (Of all things, it was Mother Emily's writing desk. For her WI work. A Queen Anne burr-walnut kneehole desk, with mirror-backed baize-lined writing surface and veneered back, 37in) You have it down for the right description, but I reckon it a lot more than twenty, so am prepared to give you thirty today, if that's okay, and see how I make out. Is that to your liking chaps?"

They both knew that he would obviously be making a nice profit, but they could hardly expect him to go to such lengths on their behalf and not make a tidy sum also. The pair of them nodded, indicating that this was agreeable; they then both also indicated in unison, without saying a word, what the next move was.

"Well," said Tom, "That's all sorted then, for the time being anyway. With the £36,000 I still owe for the Tapestries, I shall get you £66,000 a little bit later today. We still have a fair bit of work to crack on with though, so let's not get sloppy. My mate Les, the fellah from Jersey, is gonna meet us here at 12:30. We will then adjourn to The Cricketers, have a quick beverage, then all have a nice lunch in English's, whaddayasay?"

No need to answer. They all agreed that the tea-chests could be left for the time being. Frankie had already paid twenty thousand deposit, so the remaining forty of the balance on the property deal was now taken care of. This left thirteen thousand quid each for him and The Buzz. He mentioned to Barry that he'd get a nice few quid later, but he seemed to be a bit vague.

They soon got to work. Really they just followed Tommy's lead. He informed them of a whole Luton load bound for Mike Deasy, another big player, who would be shipping it all to the U.SA. This consisted of a lot of the 'Brown' furniture as it was known. At this present time though, the yanks were buying anything British. They would receive half of the agreed £8,000 later in the week.

There were a few things that were just a bit too high in price, even for Tommy to take a chance on. A pair of Regency parcel gilt and simulated green patinated bronze torcheres, 17in were worth £40-50,000.

There was also a Chippendale carved mahogany block front desk and bookcase. Signed by John Chipman, Salem, Mass, 1770-1785, 45in, this was £200,000+. He then brought to their attention two strange looking things, pointing disgustingly at a pair of Regency mahogany hall benches. They had been stacked on top of one another in the garage. Well, my gut tells me go with them, but my experience says 'Auction room'. They would go on to make £55,000, cheers Tommy.

He wanted to keep the George III mahogany, satinwood, tulipwood and marquetry Bonheur du jour, 28in. But he had had one before and some prat had damaged it. (There we go again, had three times, and never had a choice.) It was a delicate piece of furniture and at £30,000 he was not taking any chances.

He reminded them, "Always remember boys, learn from your mistakes, and never go back to the scene of a crime. Make a Golden Rule and never ever break it. It will for sure come back and bite you in the arse and be your downfall. Mark my words."

They both nodded in agreement, but never adhered to it.

This rule also applied to mirrors. So even though it didn't seem as though there were a lot, due to the size of the house, the ten various mirrors, in all shapes and sizes, were all still in their appropriate wrappings awaiting further instructions. 'The Rooms', came the answer.

The four poster, from Ted and Emily's room was George III, and although could be a good earner, simply took up too much space.

It was agreed by all, that the Card Table, it seemed so long ago, when he first clapped eyes on it, was also another star of the show. They all agreed it was of the finest quality, and had never seen better. It therefore, as far as Tommy was concerned, would only court trouble. Too many enquiries as to it's source, everyone trying to outbid one another, then asking what else might be available from the same seller. They put an optimistic reserve of £25,000 on it, anyway.

All the while, both Frankie and Barry were repeatedly saying to themselves, "Is it really worth that much?"

Bearing in mind they hadn't yet touched upstairs back at The Forest, Frankie was beginning to feel a little light headed. The Buzz looked a bit queasy too, maybe it was something they had eaten. It was a relief when Tom's pal arrived and they were introduced to Les. They went over to the Pub and had a nice refreshing drink.

18. Meet My Mate.

Les was a self-made millionaire, who specialised in care homes. Quite simply his parents died in a car accident when he was young, and rather than sell the family home, he had a few friends round one evening for a party and decided to set up a commune. The house was huge, but the idea was short lived, and did not last even for a fortnight. The commune idea appealed to the free loaders only, and Les was no prat.

He then proceeded to interview his mates and girlfriends on a more serious note. Offering them free board and lodging, with a small wage if they wanted to help the aged in the local area. By providing an impossibly competitive price bracket for nursing home facilities.

When he started in the early fifties, there were not the restrictions in place like today. The need for 24 hour care was still highly in demand for the many war veterans who were not capable of looking after themselves. He just took the industry by storm, and within ten years had monopolised the business. He had also revolutionised the industry to his way of thinking. Due care for due cost. Plough back in what you get out and keep standards high and mighty.

This had also given him an idea for the retail industry, High and Mighty clothing, as he could never buy anything off the rack. They just don't cater for a bloke with a 58in chest, 36in waist and six-feet five tall he declared.

All feeling familiar, they went round to English's and enjoyed a lovely Fish lunch. The Buzz though, had gone for a Fillet Steak, which was also cooked to the finest degree. Champagne helped the time fly by, but things got a bit tetchy when the bill arrived. Everyone insisting that they would take care of it. Les finally managed to convince the other three, that there would be plenty of other times to pay for each other, but he, as the guest, only had the one opportunity.

Over coffee, Les had already confirmed that he would give the boys £10,000 for the tapestries including the nice coffer they were in. Tommy had already confirmed this was a good deal, and that was good enough for all concerned. No arguing over that one then.

A Lovely Pair of Knockers

They agreed to meet later to settle all the financial matters, so Tommy and Les could get to the Bank in a bit of privacy.

For the time being Frankie and The Buzz would pop into The Oasis Club, in Queens Square, and have a few beers. It was only for an hour or so anyway. All agreeing the yard was the safest and most convenient place to meet.

Whilst in the Oasis Frankie asked The Buzz if he was okay, as he didn't seem himself today. Sheepishly he had to admit that yesterday he had gone off the rails a bit. A new 'acquaintance', had given him some snide Charlie, he had got the right hump about it, and gone looking for him. The search took him over to Hangleton and then he'd ended up in some shitty council house that must have been being used as some kind of low-grade brothel.

"Frankie, you should have seen this place. It was like a chamber of horrors. All the birds looked like they had some kind of disability. If they didn't have a hump on their back, a very bad limp or some other kind of disfigurement they must have been mentally retarded."

"It was all very disturbing. Needless to say, once I was out of me comfort zone, it got a bit nasty. Now you know me I don't go looking for trouble as a rule, it just finds me. But as soon as I realised things were none too clever I tried to get out as quick as you like. But the ringleader of this bunch of reprobates was on to me. Three of the bastards had me cornered out in the back garden and they wasn't joking when they threatened to bury me. I had to part with some readies just to get out. Then I ran all the way to The Grenadier to make last orders and get a cab home."

"It's like going out into the wetlands out there. You can jolly well keep Hangleton for all I care, and burn every lousy prick in it. As Tommy says never make the same mistake twice, and don't go back to the scene of a crime. Both apply to that neck of the woods as far as I'm concerned from now on. So let's say no more on the matter, is that alright with you?"

"Sure, sure," agreed Frankie, "Still, let's look ahead not behind, "I make it that we will be copping for seventy six grand in a little while. That would normally be thirty eight each. Would it be alright if

I let you have thirty for the time being and I owe you eight, till the end of the week?"

"Of course you can, I already told you that the ball is in your court with all this business. I'm not going to renege on any thing I've said. You just crack on as best you can. Anyway it's all in the book innit?"

"Of course it is mate. Course it is," confirmed Frankie.

The Buzz dare not reveal the whole truth. That he had also been relieved of the four grand he had on him at the time, and warned in no uncertain terms, to keep off of that manor.

When they got to the yard, Tommy once again revealed he could not give the amount as promised. He enjoyed a little taunt did Tom. So when he revealed it was because Mike Deasy had already paid for the container load and so he could give them eighty instead of seventy-six thousand pounds, they all had another little laugh. Les handed over his ten bags as promised so everyone was happy.

Tommy confirmed that all the pieces discussed, would be en-route to the auction rooms in London the following day. As soon as he had notification of the appropriate dates of sale he would let them know. He also assured them that his contacts at both Christie's and Sotheby's would have the items well featured in their catalogues.

*

19. Dotting The Eyes and Crossing The Teas.

So, to the final part, for the time being, of the Forest Row deal. To make final payment to Edward and Edwina. Frankie told Barry that it was probably best he went on his own, The Buzz had no problem with this and declared that maybe he would take Eileen on a day trip to London.

Frankie called Edward and Edwina, just after five, advising that he would be visiting them Tuesday, the next day, at approx twelve mid-day. To make final payment on their arrangement. Edward had taken the call. When his sister asked who had called, he simply burst out laughing and whooped with joy. Hugging Edwina like never before, he informed her that Frankie would be taking lunch with them tomorrow and settling the bill of sale for the house.

"I hope he doesn't want to evict us Edward." Was all she could think of to say.

"After all, it will be his premises once he has given us all that money. To think, we contemplated what that wretched Estate Agent had offered us, only a few weeks earlier. God has smiled upon us Brother dear."

"Indeed he has my darling Sister, indeed he has. In fact, if my memory serves me well, my very first words, when we first met Frankie, was that the The Lord had answered our prayers."

"I do believe they were, I do believe they were. Let's both go down to The Swan, this evening and have a couple of drinks with some of the villagers. We may not have the opportunity for very much longer."

"Good idea," he replied, "I'll just go freshen up, while you get yourself ready."

Frankie had decided to get the train for this memorable day. It may have been a bit risky carrying such a large sum, on the train on his own. But who could have guessed that the smart young fellow issued with a First Class ticket, actually had over forty thousand pounds in his neat recently acquired Burberry leather briefcase.

Another small purchase in the great scheme of things, but still logged as a genuine expense in his little red book. It also seemed a bit rich at £42, but he had also bought a nice Burberry raincoat in Hanningtons for £135, at the same time, and they matched perfectly. The salesgirl had clocked the huge wad when he paid for the coat and jumped right in with the briefcase idea, good girl.

He enjoyed the walk from the Station to his destination. He was a few minutes after twelve, but his hosts were well aware that the Brighton train did not drop off till two minutes past anyway. So they were both at the door as he marched up the driveway. Now inspecting his own territory and property, glancing over at the adjacent plot that he had no idea what he was going to do with.

The door opened as he approached, and Edwina had taken his coat before Edward had even closed the front door.

"Come through, come through Frankie. I am afraid we are not able to offer you lunch today, as all the appropriate furniture, to allow such entertaining is no longer at our disposal."

Frankie felt tense and uneasy, but this quickly dispelled, when Edward continued in a mocking tone, and continuing to walk towards the rear of the house,

"Still, we could all reside upstairs in one of our bedrooms and take tea. But I am afraid we still do not permit anyone to enter 'That Room'. So, for the time being, if you are happy to conduct the business at hand here in the parlour, and then join us both down at the local Pub to celebrate. We can all be quite satisfied, whaddayasay?"

This particular little saying had become quite infectious. It felt like you had suddenly joined an elite club, that others had no idea how to join.

"Well, Edward, as far as I am concerned, just a nice cup of tea will suit me fine. This really won't take too long. Can I just take a quick shifty upstairs?"

"Help yourself."

"Thanks, I'll just be a couple of minutes."

He climbed the stairs with a tinge of trepidation. Had he actually been dreaming this all the time? The key was where it should be, the spare one that is. The door opened and there it was, that beautiful desk, the two chairs, the rugs, the paintings, the mirrors, that, that, that and that. As he lowered the steps to the attic, it all came back like the rush from a class-A drug. There was that other desk, the watercolours, those prized candlesticks, that glassware, that's enough, get back down there, and seal the deal, seal that knocking deal. Now, lively.

He was, momentarily, transported back into the arena, with just one last round to go, then all the spoils would be his, with the champion's belt, crown, cup, or medal coming his way. Back to life, back to reality.

He joined the two Eds in the parlour and sat at the small kitchen table that was now their home for breakfast, lunch and dinner. He pulled out the relevant paperwork, and gently removed, in a surgical fashion, the two packed envelopes from the same briefcase. This was all done as if Cold War secrets were being revealed. To all intents and purpose, the next few moments were of more importance to them, on a personal note anyway.

He signed, handed over, they signed and handed back over.

He examined the signed document, by both parties, and sighed.

They checked the contents of both their envelopes, and also sighed.

THE DEAL WAS DONE!

No turning back now, but nobody wanted to anyway, so there was nothing left to do but celebrate. They were all overjoyed, so what could possibly go wrong?

As they made there way to the Pub, Frankie assured them both that there was no immediate rush to evacuate the Green Gables. As far as he was concerned, he would not consider it his, until they were comfortably settled in Brighton. As this was their decision, it would also be up to them, when and where they decided to settle. He and Barry were still at their service to help with their quest for the right home, no worries there. He would, of course, require a set of keys for the time being. Just in case he needed access to the house without their prior knowledge.

This raised no objections, so Frankie happily sauntered up to the Bar as they entered the Pub. The surly landlord grunted towards him, so Frankie looked over his shoulder, and remarked,

"Sorry mate, thought there was a stray werewolf behind me or something for a moment. But, oh no, it's Edward and Edwina, from The Green Gables of Forest Row, whaddayaknow?"

His sarcasm did not miss a soul.

The landlord muttered to himself, then requested of Frankie, "So, what is it that you require sir. Other than everything that these two poor innocent souls have to their name."

The penny dropped immediately. The village was now aware of what was going to transpire. But what they did not know, was that it had already transpired, and there was sod all anyone could say or do to stop it. Still, there was no need to upset the locals so soon and aggravate the situation any further than necessary.

"Well, my name is Frankie. I am indeed the sole benefactor of Edward and Edwina here, but just so you know, there has been no wrong doing here and we are all happy. Do you happen to know, whatsisname? The local Estate Agent, you must know him, surely?"

As the Landlord scratched his head, Frankie raised his voice purposely, for all to hear, "You know, that contemptuous greedy little bastard from that sham of a shop right round the corner. Well, my good man, while we are all being polite". Frankie knew he had the full attention of every single person in the Pub, so he may as well make the most of his first impression.

Wise words spoken by Perry Bowels, 'You only ever get the one chance to make a first impression. So make it count'.

He continued in an even more commanding tone,

" Well, he offered this innocent little pair, as you just referred to them, the potential to possibly receive after some time on the market, half the amount of money that I have already paid them in full. So don't start trying to stick your nose in where it ain't bloody well needed. If I am not welcome in this pretty little village, then so be it, but don't make out I have done anything wrong. And certainly don't infer that Edward and his sister here have been sold short by a

A Lovely Pair of Knockers

single solitary shilling. Or of being able to look after their own affairs in a creditable manner."

Then in a much calmer and even apologetic tone,

"Now do you have a table available for a nice light lunch, please? I hope to become a regular customer here at The Swan. My name is Frankie by the way, Frankie Slimtone, pleased to make your acquaintance. What's your name matey?"

His opening barrage, had taken them all by surprise. Both Edward and Edwina of course had now witnessed a completely different side to the Frankie they knew. Edward was puzzled, but Edwina was even more smitten with her knight in shining armour than she ever thought possible. When, oh when would she get the opportunity to be alone with him and declare her feelings? This was beginning to resemble some kind of Jane Eyre or Emily Bronte novel.

The Landlord, made an instantaneous decision. This young little smart-arse might be a bit gobby, but if he has bought that bloody big house for cash. And for the right money too, or he wouldn't be so cocky about it, he must be well and truly loaded. Then, for sure, he wanted his fair share of the money coming into the Village. He would no doubt be introducing new people to the area. To act in a hostile fashion, just didn't make business sense. If it worked out nobody liked him, and he didn't fit in, then he would make a stand, but give the lad a chance.

Lifting the Bar hatch and holding out his hand as he approached Frankie, like a long lost relative, meeting for the first time at an Airport,

"I'm Keith Frankie, sorry for any misinterpretation, my missus keeps trying to explain to me about my body language. So sorry, I might get the message one day, but why don't we get you settled at my favourite table in this lovely little alcove over here."

With his back to Frankie he led the way, pulled out the chairs, and placed some beer mats in front of them. Then proudly announced, in a conspiratorial whisper,

"We have a special lamb stew and dumplings today, with home-made crusty bread, home-made in the Village bakery that is. We all have our part to play in the Village, so why would we have our own home- made when we can get it next door. What can I get you to drink? There is not normally table service at this establishment, but today is special, so take your time, and I'll see you in a jiffy."

He was quite pleased with himself as he made his way back to his station behind the Bar.

"You overdid it a bit there Keith. Still, you certainly brown-nosed your way to the head of the class in his eyes, in one foul swoop," advised one of the locals.

"Well, let's give the kid a chance. It's not like I'm losing money on old custom. Them two have never been in here two days running since I've had this Pub, what's that? Yeah it must be seven years now." Keith would be well pleased with his decision.

There were about eight people in the Pub when Frankie approached the Bar.

"Keith my good man," he said, "Thanks for the lunch advice, we will have three Lamb Stews and what Red Wine do you have in the cellar?"

Not requiring Wine lists in those days Keith informed him they had a Cabernet Sauvignon or a Merlot available.

"I'll take a bottle of each please, and would you please give everyone else a welcoming drink from me, oh, and have one yourself. Your missus in the kitchen should join us also if that's alright with you. Will that cover it?" As he placed two five pound notes on the Bar, he knew he had played it right.

'Not too weak not too lairy, this will always keep, your opponent wary'. Another legendary little anecdote from the Brighton's Knocker Boy phrasebook. This one belonged to Phil Decanter. His version though was more like. "Never too weak, and not too lairy, but make sure the runt, is always fucking wary". Poetic stuff. And that was the toned down version.

The round of drinks went down well with all concerned. Then a skinny ginger haired man with horn-rimmed glasses around thirty, wearing a shabby suit walked in, and it suddenly went eerily silent. Frankie sensed it immediately and in one glance sussed who it was. He rose from his chair and went round to the Public Bar to greet him,

"Hello. You don't know me, but I am new to the area. I have just purchased a property up the road. You must be Petty Pete the Estate Agent?"

"Well I don't know about the Petty bit, but um."

"Don't worry about that Pistol. I'm just having a laugh. I'm Frankie, new owner of The Green Gables. I'm sure you are familiar with it. I'm sorry not to have used your services, but that's how it goes. I just got a round in, so please let me get you a drink. I am sure to be requiring your services in the near future, and may well have a few potential clients for you, now that I am based in this vicinity."

"That's very kind of you Frankie. Mr Slimtone, isn't it? Well I do appreciate the gesture, but I was merely dropping off some paperwork for some clients. Oh I see, you are dining with Edward and Edwina. Perhaps you could give them my compliments and hand them these details that they requested from me last night. Thank-you, so very much."

With that he handed Frankie a brown Manila envelope, turned on his heel like a well drilled soldier, and marched straight out the door.

Frankie shrugged his shoulders and looked at the rest of the customers, they shrugged their shoulders also, then all held up their glasses and said, "Cheers Frankie."

He smiled back, and then rejoined his table. Keith bought the Wine over and poured, whilst Edwina sampled, he remarked:

"Well that went better than expected. He was fuming last night. You've got a lovely way about you Frankie, a lovely way."

Edwina slightly spluttered on her wine, at this point. Keith disappeared on cue. They were both obviously extremely embarrassed.

"Don't worry about it, either of you. It couldn't be kept a secret forever now could it? What with the Luton paying all those visits and everything," assured Frankie. "I take it he was not impressed with your new found sense of freedom and freewill, or something."

Edward began to explain how usually in the Village, local matters were dealt with by the local business to which it applied. It was deemed disloyal if you did not use a local plumber or electrician for instance. So, by not using the services of Peter they had caused slight unrest.

When they announced last night about the sale, he had been offended. But after they explained about the chain of events that had occurred, and how this Frankie fellah, who knew so much and so many people, had taken care of absolutely everything, at no cost to themselves, he could hardly criticise.

He had in fact congratulated them on the price achieved for their home, and how no extra costs had been incurred. He could not however, fathom out how this Frankie geezer from Brighton had been able to give them such a good price, take care of Solicitor's fees, and all the land search and survey charges. He had eventually declared that it was a fantastic deal, and wished them both well.

Basically he was also a bit jealous, admitted as much and so he had offered to help them find a property in Brighton. The arrangement was to drop off some information before they came for lunch, but as things had been so quick and easy to sort out they had arrived much sooner than expected. They should have known it wouldn't take the time that Pete had mentioned.

With the air cleared on that one, lunch arrived and was enjoyed by all. The lunch was excellent, when finished the wine was also gone, so they decided to venture to the Bar.

Frankie ordered a large Brandy for himself, then the same for everybody else that wanted one, not one person disappointed him, including the landlord. At that moment Pistol Pete, a name he would never shake off, to his annoyance, came back in the Pub, and was drafted into the company with a pint and large Courvoisier like everyone else.

Frankie advised that as the property may be empty from time to time in the not too distant future, would it be possible for Pete to arrange for a decent security system to be installed.

"See, money earning work, for you already, Pistol," congratulated Frankie. He would arrange for a set of keys to be left with the agent when the time was right, everything was settled and everyone was content.

They had a few more drinks needless to say. The Pub somehow forgot the appropriate licensing hours that day. Keith thought he had ruined the day when he mentioned it was like the good old days with 'The Carrot Top Cop', in charge. But no worry there, Edward and Edwina were three sheets to the wind and began questioning as to why they didn't come down the Pub more often. Then Marjorie, Keith's wife joined them for a couple and reminisced about their Father Ted for a little while. Despite being invited back to The Gables, Frankie wandered off towards the Station and got the next train home.

*

As he came into Brighton, Frankie suddenly felt quite elated. The train departed from Preston Park, so it was just three minutes till he would be at the station. He was in fact, now a man of property. Not just a huge four bed roomed house with large attic and a detached garage. Also an adjacent piece of land which he had been assured was more than ample to build a three bedroom detached property, with the latest modern designs which could even include an integral garage.
One thing had woken him up during the lunch though, which must be dealt with as soon as possible. The land survey and search details that Petty Pete had mentioned. There would surely not be any problems there, but Frankie had not actually got around to it. There was no great issue as far as he could think.
Edward had mentioned that the property originally belonged to the Police force, and that it was part of the deal to sign up for ten years to get the discounted purchase price. The same applied to the garage space, but the adjacent plot was something entirely different.
Panic came over Frankie. Could there be some ironic twist of fate that meant the Gables was not legally theirs to sell, and it reverted back to the next Village bobby. He scanned the signed documents and could find no trace of Land and Survey searches, after all he had not instructed his Lawyer to do so, had he? The cold sweat beads began to trickle down his temples as the train pulled into the Station.
Frankie deployed from the First Class carriage before it had come to a halt. A platform station master whistled at Frankie to stop

running, but he just turned momentarily to stick two fingers up at him, shoved the tickets at the youngster on the gate and hailed a Taxi as he neared the rank. At least First Class meant first off he thought to himself as the cab pulled away.

"I know it's not far mate, but I really need to get down to Marlborough Place as quick as poss."

"If you wanted to get their A.S.A.P. it really would be quicker to walk mate," said the driver, "But you're in the car now, so I may as well take a small fare rather than go to the back of the rank again for sod all. Now that I've had to pull away from my bay."

Frankie was affronted by such an abrupt attitude,

"Having a bad day as well then mate, or what?" The face in the rear view mirror just smiled, it was an old pal from school, Gerry Powell who was driving. They had a quick catch up and Frankie was at Ragsby's at five to five. He bunged Gerry two notes, a pound and a ten shillings, then went straight in.

Miss James tried the usual diversion tactics but Frankie was still in a manic panic, so it was futile and wasted. Raggers was not too surprised to see Frankie, he in fact had been expecting the visit any day now. He let his client blurt out all his concerns, smirking inwardly at the way he couldn't catch his breath. Anyone else would have told him to calm down and take his time, relax a bit and then explain.

Raggers preferred to witness the self-inflicted pain and suffering Frankie was experiencing. This was the sadistic side of Ragsby, the element of power that he sometimes held over a client that excited himself and Miss James, in such circumstances.

Ragsby went straight to work, allowing Frankie to explain the seriousness of the situation, as he felt this was of paramount importance. He assured Frankie that he would deal with all the devastating consequences, when they arose. But for the time being he would do all the necessary paperwork to complete the deal as laid out in the documents provided.

Holding out his hand, for the signed documents, he slyly asked, "I don't suppose you thought all the surveys and land searches did themselves did you?"

"Well, no of course not Mr Ragsby. It's been a bit hectic though, getting all the money an' all that. I should have asked you to do it all in the first place, of course I realise that now. What the devil happens if there is something wrong wiv the gaff? Or I can't legally buy it? Or they can't legally sell it?"

"Well, Frankie we will cross that bridge when we come to it. For now though, young man, there is nothing anyone can do. All the relevant officers of the court and relevant departments are closed, so there is nothing I can do for you right now. Please be off, on your way, and I will take a look at this mess by the end of the week."

"End of the week, end of the fucking week!" Screamed Frankie, "What do you mean, by the end of the bloody week? This could absolutely ruin me if this deal goes tits up."

The Raggers had played it perfectly.

"Oh alright Frankie calm down. Now I do have a court appearance scheduled for tomorrow, but I'll see what I can do." Then pressing his intercom in the most casual manner,

"Miss James, would you please bring through two special coffees please."

"Nah nah, I don't want any coffee thanks Mr Ragsby."

"Don't go all formal on me Frankie," as he opened his top drawer, removing a half bottle of Courvoisier, Ragsby continued, "You will appreciate a Ragsby special coffee today young man. Your recent activities have not gone unnoticed in certain circles. So, calm down for a little while and fill me in on some of the finer details. I don't need to know the intricate details, but if you trust me with some of the finer details I may well be able to help you invest some of the good fortune coming your way. If you know what I mean. Of course it's entirely up to you."

Heard that one somewhere before, haven't you?

"If I were to have a little more insight into the grand scheme of things, so to speak, I may be of more use to you than you realise, or understand."

"Well, maybe I should give you a bit more credit Mr Ragsby," said the now alerted Frankie,

"But in what respect do you mean, exactly?"

"Well, in my experience," the door opened, Miss James in, tray on the desk, Brandy poured in coffee, sugars added, stirred slowly, Miss James out, door closed.

"In my experience, in situations such as this. Where large sums of money have already been transferred, albeit all above board, ship shape and Bristol fashion, with no apparent....."

"Alright Raggers, alright, you have made your point quite clear enough. Now, what are you actually saying for Christ's sake? Come on you slippery old bastard, out with it."

"No need to get personal with me sonny boy. Or you can take your documentation elsewhere and see where it gets you. I am just trying to educate you. Do you know how many of you lot I have had to get out of serious trouble, over the last few years. You ignorant little brat. And all because you never took take care of the proper paperwork in the first place, at the all important early stages."

Then raising his voice and standing up with a treacherous shaking of his fist, that would have made Oliver Cromwell look sheepish, He belted out in single syllables, for added accentuation and fervour,

"Like you bloody well should have done."

Then he carried on like life itself depended upon it, with shaking finger and red-faced tenacity and frustration,

"You just listen to me for a minute, you scrawny faced little toe-rag. I may not have a Saville Row suit on today, but don't you think, for one shitty little minute, that I don't know how to secure a few quid, and still manage to keep it safe when it matters most. To me, myself and I, and those important people that I keep close by. Poet, know-it. Yes or no? What is it to be?"

Frankie reflected, he didn't know the old git had it in him, "Yes."

Miss James, smiled to herself outside, having heard every single word.

"That's all I needed to hear," intercom, "Miss James, I will be needing you to stay a little late this evening, some important business has just come to light. Must be dealt with in earnest, would that be okay?"

"No problem Sir," came the reply.

A Lovely Pair of Knockers

Pointy finger by Ragsby, this time straight into Frankie's face, "You make sure the people you trust are trustworthy, is my first comment of this meeting, Frankie boy. She is one of those, and I hope that Buzz or whatever he is called, is also equal to the task."

"He's been as good as gold so far, Sir." A defining sense of respect had now been established between these two.

It only took Frankie a few more minutes to explain that everything was in full swing. The house from the signed documents he had presented, was now paid for in full. It was just this matter of the survey and searches that had him worried. He gave a bit too much information of what was still to come, admittedly, but once he got going and they had another couple of special coffees arrive, it didn't seem to be an issue.

Mr Ragsby was now informed. He was now in the loop so to speak. He had revealed the nature of his enquiry, and it was now obvious why he felt the need to be in possession of the details and seriousness of the rapid, un-interfered completion of the ownership deeds.

"Now," Raggers began, "At least if I should come across any potential hindrance, which may prevent this transaction completing smoothly and with no interference. Or, subsequent questionable methods, I will be able to confidently persuade any concerned persons that their concerns are unfounded."

Then with a knowing smile, "In other words, between you me and the gatepost, if some jobs worth starts creating a stir, I can at least bung him a tenner and tell him to get knotted. Grease a few palms so to speak. If someone starts fussing I can use my initiative, with the full knowledge that you will support my better judgement. Not question my methods and reimburse me for any unusual expenses incurred without question. Whaddayassay Frankie?"

"Spot on Mr Ragsby, spot on."

"Right then, you leave it to me. Miss James. Thank-you Miss James, one more quick coffee, and could you please bring me one of those medically excused notes for court please. Try that Mr Nearly on the phone for me as well please, we need to tell him that tomorrow's court date has been cancelled due to illness."

Then continues matter of factly, but with a sinister smile,

"Frankie, leave it with me, I will be on the case first thing tomorrow, I shall expect to see you at around twelve thirty. You will, hopefully, receive all the relevant paperwork that is legally required for your future prospects. Then we can both enjoy a pleasant lunch, at your expense of course, to celebrate the satisfying conclusion to our business on this project. How does that sound to you?"

"Fantastic Mr Ragsby, fan-flaming-tastic."

"Good, good evening then sir."

With his client departed, Raggers pressed the intercom, said nothing, and in return, got no reply.

After an almost unbearable and yet tantalising wait of nigh on three and a half minutes, in she comes. More than fully aware of the height of impending anticipation her master has already suffered. He is at the end of his tether.

Dressed as normal, she raises her diagonally but loudly coloured decorated Nylon skirt. Revealing stockings and suspenders, bought in Paris, and revealed the most desirable legs and thighs in Brighton.

His mouth was, by this time, wide open, in amazement.

She approaches the desk, with a file in her hand, it was marked Frankie Slimtone, For Our Eyes Only.

Browsing through the file, Raggers announces that everything is in order. He had of course, already done all the relevant and required surveys and land searches. At his own expense of course.

Licking her luscious lips, she leaves without uttering a single solitary word.

Everyone a winner baby, that's no lie. He had heard a whisper that Frankie had found one. Whoever got the work to take care of the legalities on this little bar-tab, would for sure get a nice drink. On this occasion, Raggers made sure he was tending bar. He didn't need to go too far, but why not get in at an early stage, you never know what might appertain at a later date.

He had given Miss James her instructions for the bill. The miscellaneous part of the bill came to an unusual two hundred pounds, this would later be explained as a bribe to a local councillor. Preferential treatment was also slightly above average at eighty quid, but he had already hoodwinked him on a Nearly case, cancellation blag. Ordinary expenses for the actual work, were doubled to one hundred and twenty five pounds and ten shillings. Then he had the bright yet brilliant idea of adding, sixty three pounds seventeen and six for expertise and industrial knowledge.

The total came to four hundred and sixty nine pounds, seven and six, precisely. £469.7/6. Raggers was quite happy with the evening's work, so requested Miss James to book a room at The Grand Hotel. They would have dinner at nine, retire and then require room service for drinks, a bit later perhaps. Breakfast was to be included but they expected to be gone by eleven. She concurred obviously, and the deal was done. This would give them ample time to get home and change for the all important appointment with Mr Slimtone at 12:30.

*

19. Let's Do Lunch.

The next day, 12:30 dead on the dot, Frankie knocked on the door.

As he was ushered into the office, he sensed something lingering in the air. A similar fragrance he had for sure, experienced before. But, for the time being, he could not quite grasp where it was stored in his memory banks, maybe it would come to him later.

Anyway, when Mr Ragsby, assured him that any and every single discrepancy that would, could or should be logged to contravene this transaction had been anticipated and counteracted. He was more than satisfied he had done the right thing. Well, it would never see the light of day as long as Greenwich Meantime was still in progress, he was assured the property was his, from this day forth.

"As you can see," pointing to the bill in his hand, Raggers explained, "There are a couple of exaggerated costs involved, but due to the seriousness of this deal, I deemed it advantageous to all concerned, to just crack on and get it finalised. Is everything to your satisfaction Sir?"

Continuing in a devious conniving manner, as if having something to hide, "Just get the O'Malley's to confirm and vindicate that they are of sound mind and absolution, and we are all in serious business."

"You twat, Reggie. I don't need anything from them any more. All I need is the fact that no person of sound mind and body can trespass on my property. Or, I am not stopping any other prick or prat from legally obtaining water or electric by forbidding them access to my land. Do you actually have any idea what the heck you are supposed to do?"

"Now, I do understand that you have grafted all morning, at considerable cost and inconvenience to yourself and registered clients, but did you really think I was bothered about anything other than the council shit. The rest of 'em can go fuck 'em selves. The two Eds are in the bag. They are no problem whatsoever my son. Now let's go and have a nice bit of lunch. Can you join us too Miss James? The Buzz, and his missus are waiting."

A Lovely Pair of Knockers

She, "Oh well, I suppose if there is no other pressing business, I could consider it. What do you think Mr Ragsby?"

He, "Suit yourself Miss James, I am your employer, not your Brother."

Enough said on that matter.

Frankie, just clicked his fingers and announced,

"Right then, let's get jolly well get going. I fancy a nice bit of fish today. You okay with that Raggers? How does Wheeler's sound to you? Don't wanna stray too far from the office do we?"

"Jolly good idea Mr Slimtone, sounds good to me. Shall I get Miss James to call and book a table?"

"No need for that my good man, the wad of money in my sky, is all we need to reserve the best place in the house. We shall take an upstairs table today methinks, and look down upon the poor people in the square, and they won't have a danny. How does that sound to you, and you Miss James?"

"Oh, positively serene sir, positively serene."

Just as they entered the Restaurant, Frankie slipped Stewart the Steward a ching, then handed Mr Ragsby an envelope containing four hundred and eighty pounds. Asking,

"Do you have that bill on you Reggie?" As he handed it over, Ragsby smiled, "Of course Frankie, there you go".

State secrets could have been no craftier.

The lunch was a rip-roaring success.

Eileen had been thrilled to be invited. The Buzz, equally thankful that Frankie had shown acknowledgement of his recent well disciplined behaviour.

Frankie had a whale of a time. He ordered Moet & Chandon Champagne immediately, winking to the waiter Stewart. Indicating that he need only take care of this particular table today to ensure a generous tip.

Ragsby was in his element, confident that he was not expected to contribute towards the bill, he went to town. Dressed Crab, L'escargots En Croute, two sharing platters of Fruits de la Mer, served like afternoon tea on three tiered stands, Dover Sole with seasonal Veg and a delightful Crème Brulee to finish off. He really was the cat that got the cream. Frankie had gladly allowed him to order for the table, aware Reggie Ragsby knew his way round a quality Menu.

Frankie of course was the cat that got the real cream. Knowing full well what a single minded greedy little git 'The Raggers' was, he knew he would take his eye off the ball. Frankie had given Miss James the nod at the appropriate moment. Between courses, their hasty rendezvous in the Gents, resulted in a sordid quick bunk-up against the wall with her legs wrapped around him like a boa-constrictor, until she had sucked all the goodness out of him. Nearly his breath an' all for that matter.

His back now resembled that of a sailor's after receiving a few lashes at the expense of the cat-o-nine-tails, as a result of her fingernails having finished clawing into his back. How nobody noticed the ruby red raw marks on his neck from her vampire like kisses, was nobody's business.

She was, after all, a nymphomaniac.

But we don't have to tell everybody? Do we? Especially not Ragsby!

Frankie paid the bill when it finally arrived, about two-thirty. He added a nice little tip for Stewart, who had made sure the 'Out of Order' sign was positioned outside the Gents, at the appropriate moment of course, so everyone was happy.

In the region of £185, Frankie considered it, worth every single penny.

Was it really worth that much?
You bet your life it was!

*

20. Time On Your Hands.

So now it was a Wednesday afternoon, Raggers wandered off with Miss James, who looked back over her shoulder, still smouldering. But, the nylon slip under her skirt was certainly not where it should be, and her stockings not strictly straight, as was usual with her appearance. The trained eye would surely pick up on this dress code malfunction.

The Buzz was going off with Eileen for an afternoon at the Bingo, and although invited, Frankie declined. As she pecked him on the cheek, The Buzz got impatient and the all too familiar, "Come on, come on Eileen," was heard in the background.

He strolled around to Tommy Barnes yard, more out of boredom than anything else. On the way he saw Perry and Simon Bowels who said they were off to The Linden Club and maybe see him there later. Tommy was over at the Cricketer's according to Steve the driver. So after a little small talk, arranging a day for next week to pick up some more gear from Forest Row, Frankie waited for him.

Even Tommy could not change Pub opening times in the Town centre. Back street boozers had a bit of leeway, but too many strangers in the Town centre locations, made it too dodgy for Publicans to stray from licensing laws. Anyway, there were plenty of other locations to cater for the more serious drinkers of the time, and there was no shortage of either.

Great news from Tom, his client liked the Dining Table and Chairs, wanted the matching Commode also, so if Frankie could manage to get back in the yard Friday, similar time to this, then a sixty grand cheque could be made payable to Frankie Slimtone Esq.

The day was just getting better and better.

They discussed briefly which dates some of the Auction stuff would be coming up, and clarified the costs and expenses incurred.

Tommy had been very generous up and till now, but still mentioned, that Frankie still had to cover the days 'His Driver' used 'His Motor.' These must still be covered by Frankie. This was simply because, Tommy had experienced this type of deal before, and usually people got greedy and started to expect things for nothing once they had got a few bob coming in. He didn't want Frankie to make the same mistake. He certainly didn't trust The Buzz, but he was a different kettle of fish entirely.

Frankie had taken Tommy's advice of opening a business account, Slimtone Enterprises Ltd, had been operating for a whole week now. This next deposit would get the ball really rolling.

It would, of course, also enable him to access and release large sums of cash at the drop of a hat, no questions asked. Immediate cash availability could earn you a decent week's money in this game. Some of the Knocker Boys would rather take two grand in ten minutes, than be forced to hang around half-an-hour for twice as much.

'It's just the nature of the game', was one of The Dealer's favourite sayings, not just Tommy, but Mike Deasy, Bubbles, Tony Spaghetti, Micky and Basher Drawers, they all swore by it. Perry and brother Jimmy Bowels, Coco and Bertie Collins were all well aware of the power of the pound in the pocket and they all used it to their advantage over the many years to come, in their chosen trade.

Frankie met up with the Bowels brothers that afternoon, had a few drinks, then got to The Waggon and Horses for opening time, 6:00pm. Then to The Basketmakers then The Cobden, Cobden Road where he bumped into The Buzz and Eileen. Then had a few in The Horse & Groom, Islingword Street, and was severely pissed, by the time he made last orders in The Albion, Albion Hill. Before finally making it home after a Gut Buster Breakfast in the All night cafe, and was nursing a terrible hangover all day the next day.

A Thursday you can lose, and he certainly lost that particular Thursday. Monday's and Friday's, though, are precious, and should never be wasted, in any shape or form. Them's the rules.

So, come Friday, everything was full steam ahead. He had already made arrangements to meet with Barry for lunch. A simple Huss and Chips with gherkin and pickled onion take away from 'the other' branch of Bardsley's, in Upper North Street. Right next door to the Dole and Tax Office. The Buzz had the same but had to top it up with a large sausage in batter as well.

After all, he only had time for two bacon and egg sarnies for breakfast this morning. Then they had a quick pint of John Courage in The Bosun, in West Street. The main meeting place, in the old days, for rivalling football fans and local street gangs, to have a tear-up.

A Lovely Pair of Knockers

Feeling full and content they meandered down to Tommy's yard. Frankie had pre-empted The Buzz, that he would be collecting a nice wad very shortly. Barry conveyed how he was more than grateful for the way Frankie had been conducting business on both their behalves over the last couple of weeks.

After all it was all logged, 'In The Book'.

Tommy indicated as they came into his yard, that he would meet round the corner in The Cricketer's. He was negotiating with Vince Nearly on some deal and it was only good manners to wait their turn, so to speak. Vince did acknowledge Frankie, but he obviously had more pressing matters on his mind.

Tommy did not seem his usual charming self when he arrived ten minutes later, but soon calmed down after a large brandy and soothing pint of cider, that was provided on request. They discussed how they required the services of Steve the driver next week, and this was no problem to Tommy as far as he was concerned.

"Just look after them," was his only comment. Money and cheques, were passed over as arranged. Then Tommy added, in a conspicuous manner, that they should be careful who they mixed with over the next few weeks. Something was not right in the game at this time, and someone was about to get a serious tug by the filth. Anyone associating with the wrong crowd in the not too distant future could well be dragged into some nasty business they would live to regret.

"Watch yer backs boys, trouble is afoot. But you never heard it from me." Was all he would say. Coming from such a staunch member of this close knit community, only a fool would ignore such a guided warning.

Frankie enquired how much Barry would need for the weekend, so The Buzz just mentioned that he would be happy with his share.

"Thirty grand will suit me fine. Thank-you very much."

"What do you want all that much for?" Frankie asked.

"Well, why wouldn't I?" Came the reply.

"Sorry mate, my mistake. Of course you can. I just wanna make sure you look after this money. It won't last forever you know, this knocking game."

"How much have you had so far? No, I'm sorry, that's got sod all to do with it. If I had to give you two bags for your share I would have already done it. Give me twenty minutes and I'll take care of it. Meet me in The Waggon & Horses in half-hour. There should be a few faces still hanging about. Then we can go and have a nice few sherberts together and enjoy ourselves. Whaddayasay?"

"Sounds good to me pal. See you soon."

Off Frankie went, he'd plonked for Barclays Bank. With no rhyme or reason for his decision other than Tommy Barnes banked there. Good for the goose, good for the gander.

When he got to the pub, The Buzz was already in fine form. Coco and Bertie Collins were there with Ronnie Burton and Phil Marshall. Morry Hughes was joking about with Charlie Hardwick. Two of the Widdy brothers were also in tow, so it looked like a decent crowd would soon be hitting the afternoon Clubs.

'The Black Prince', Johnny Warren was in deep conversation with 'Frank The Bone', and Jackie Wadman was just getting a round in as he entered.

"What are you having Frankie Boy?" Jack asked.

"I think I shall partake in a nicely chilled white wine if that's alright by you Jack."

"Piss off you little fairy. Wine's for women, restaurants and indoors only. Have a proper drink. What is it to beee, young Frankeee?"

The infectious humour was instantaneous and it seemed to trigger a knee-jerk reaction within the Pub, like the whole place was watching his every move. Suddenly they all burst into an exaggerated sing-song style, whilst at the same time everyone was pointing accusingly at him, equalling that of a synchronised swimming team,

'No wine, no wine. So what is it to beeee, young Frankeee!'

This set Charlie Hardwick immediately into full male voice choir mode, (to the tune of Danny Boy) "Oh Frankie Boy. Young Jack, young Jack is waiting. For you to choose, to choose a lovely drink. Will you, will you young Frankie please, order a drink and let us all get on with what we wish to dooo."

Rapturous applause followed, and Frankie requested,

"A large Vodka and Tonic, with ice and a slice, would be very nice, please."

A Lovely Pair of Knockers

"What a palaver. Just to get a poxy drink. What is the world coming to Barry? Anyway, cheers Jack, all the very best." Frankie then handed The Buzz two thick envelopes, containing fifteen thousand pounds in each one. Barry tucked them straight into his inside jacket pockets and raised his glass to toast his new best mate.

The Buzz, obviously had hardly done a thing to earn this tremendous windfall, but this was the nature of the game, he had hit the jackpot, by just getting out of bed a couple of weeks ago. He would also be reaping the rewards for some time to come, as long as Frankie remained true to his word. He couldn't see any problem there, unless of course, he made some serious cock-up himself. So everything was good.

Everything stayed good as well.

*

21. The Outcome Of the Forest Coup.

Edward and Edwina took lodgings at The Bowthorpe, a small guest house down Lower Rock Gardens. Run by Maxy Smith, a cousin of Ricky Opendaws and Joker Smythe. They were both intrigued how so many people came and went to this seemingly unattractive and insignificant abode.

The fact of the matter was, The Bowthorpe was more commonly known as 'The Heartbreak Hotel'. Anytime any of the Knocker Boy fraternity had a row with the missus, the first port of call, was to check in with Maxy. Whether right or wrong, there was always a clean bed available at Maxy's gaff. At mates rates the pair of them were very well looked after, and were in fact sad to leave once their major decisions had been made. They had made a few acquaintances and could quite happily have stayed the whole spring and summer. It was imperative though, to get them settled before anyone else got their claws into them. More of that later.

*

Given a free reign with the house in The Forest, it was in Frankie and Barry's interest to get the place emptied in the quickest fashion. They didn't hang about either. As everything was logged, it was easy pickings for all concerned. Tommy was a great asset, and his experience of 'questionable goods', was second to none. Working alongside Mike Deasy and Micky Drawers made things easier. Some items were loaded straight onto a container and never saw the light of day.

The money was carved up equally, and they all benefited from the lack of prying eyes when shipping across the Atlantic. Integrity was essential when these huge sums of money were being exchanged. Another extremely important factor was the exchange rate on the dollar. At two and a half dollars to the pound, they were reaping great rewards. This would come to an abrupt halt a year down the line when decimalisation was introduced, 15th February 1971.

There were just a few pieces that did not go under the hammer. Barry was not keen, but weakened against his better judgement when Frankie insisted he should keep 'The Desk, matching filing cabinet and two matching chairs'. This was to be his reward for finding the clue in the first place. The Buzz thought he was overpaying himself. Anyway Barry decided he would keep a few bits also, and in the end was more than happy.

The Queen Anne giltwood mirror, which caught his eye, with shaped divided bevelled plate, 69 by 44in, was valued at £30,000. It looked the business in 'The Buzz Bar'. He would also congratulate himself, years later, when the small Louis XVI tulipwood and parquetry mounted gueridon, by Martin Carlin, date letter X for 1775, made £100,000 at auction. Altogether neither could complain about the couple of pieces they kept from 'The House in the Forest'.

'The Smalls', as they were referred to, all gradually slipped into circulation. Either by Auction, sold to other dealers, shipped out or even sold privately to collectors. There were a few Tiffany lamps, they were good sellers and made great money. What wouldn't be great money? It was all paid for, so the odd extra £10,000-15,000 every other week was not exactly earned with blood sweat and tears.

Two though in particular, managed to raise a few eyebrows. A white wisteria leaded glass and bronze table lamp, the shade impressed 1073, the bronze tree-form base impressed Tiffany Studios New York 27770, 26in high, came in at £37,000. Then an oriental poppy leaded glass and bronze floor lamp, the shade impressed Tiffany Studios New York 1597, the base No.376, similarly impressed, 78in to the top of it's pig-tail finial, an impressive £65,000.

Needless to say, neither of our latter day heroes, were bothering to go out and knock doors in the spring of 1970, nor the summer for that matter. There were a few glass vases that Frankie liked, but neither of them made any fuss about the odd bits and pieces that either of them fancied keeping, 'for old time's sake'. Sentiment, never came into it, they simply wanted a few bits for 'rainy day money'.

It had even become a bit boring unwrapping so many of these things, one day after another, neither of them understood the vast catalogue of fine Antiques they had discovered. Tommy smiled knowingly to himself all the while. He had of course steered them in the right direction all the way, like a Fatherly figure. But at the same time, even though it was his name on the Container loads going out of the country, had of course earnt handsomely, they loved him for it.

The Auctioneers cheques though, were all made payable to Frankie Slimtone Enterprises Ltd. He knew that eventually Frankie would come unstuck with the taxman, but who was he to lecture every single Knocker Boy on how to keep their house in order, when they had a nice tickle. At least they had kept their mouths shut long enough, so as not to attract too much attention to themselves, not yet anyway.

The inventory took eventually till the middle of May to dispose of. It had at times become quite arduous, counting all that money and banking all those cheques, then getting the cash for The Buzz. Poor Frankie was tired out.

He had invested in a couple of things along the way, mind you. The Racing Green E-Type Jag, parked in the Garage of his newly acquired bungalow in Dyke Road Avenue being one of the more lavish treats. Still, it was the car of the moment, and it wasn't like he was the only person in town to have one.

The Buzz, also had invested in a property so all was not lost. In total Frankie had put £887,000 through his account. Nearly half of that had gone to Barry, quite rightly so. Then of course he still had Green Gables, sitting empty at the moment, and waiting to be refurbished in a nice modest modern fashion. A lick of paint throughout would soon freshen up the place, he might even have a go at doing it up himself. Or then he might get a local guy to do it, 'keep it in the Village' and all that old bollocks.

*

22. Life goes on, and all that.

So, what had become of the two Eds, I hear you ask.

I mentioned at the beginning that I had the all sides to this story so here is what happened. Once I had heard of this most fantastic of tales, I took it upon myself to do some journalistic investigating. The main reason for my coming to Brighton in the first place. So let's put this education to the test, I thought to myself.

It was not exactly needle in a haystack stuff. A couple of trips to the relevant Town Halls, checking Voters Registry and then Births, Deaths and Marriages records. It sounds a bit cloak and dagger but all you have to do is ask a clerk for details of certain dates and they do it all for you. As long as you have the basics, and critically, specific, or particular dates, about which you are enquiring, common sense really.

Frankie had in fact broken one of the Golden rules. He had got involved with Edwina. She had always felt drawn to him, as we know. But, once all their business was taken care of, he had distanced himself. The Buzz, by now, understood that this line had not been crossed, but still gave Frankie the occasional jibe, about not securing the main prize, on top of everything else.

Frankie had bitten, early one evening in The Golden Cannon, just along St George's Road, and paid Edwina a visit at The Bowthorpe where she and Edward were still temporarily, staying. This could hardly have been regarded as the love affair of the decade.

He invited her to Hickstead for a Show jumping event, where Harvey Smith famously gave his two-fingered salute. Champagne was enjoyed by the pair of them and then just a little up or down the road to Stroods Motel, where they had dinner. Reminiscing of the lunch they had enjoyed months earlier on what they referred to as one of the 'paydays'.

Frankie then booked a room and they consummated their brief affair.

She willingly gave herself to him, and for at least a couple of weeks had high hopes of their future together. But Frankie was still only a young bloke and had no intention of settling down.

The heartbreak that followed came as no great surprise to Edward. He could hardly blame the fellow; his sister had swooned over Frankie since the very first day they had encountered one another. He was still a bit miffed, but what could he have done about it?

By way of consolation, before making up their minds exactly where to live, Edward had persuaded Edwina to join him on a nice holiday to Thailand. He had read about it in a magazine and the food sounded sumptuous. She was only too happy to join him. To at least get away from the Frankie calamity. He offered to pay, so why not?

He owned up, during the first part of their journey, that he had actually used some of the funds from their parent's estate, to pay for a couple of 'extras', did she mind?

"Of course not Edward, but thanks for asking."

They spent the first four days in Bangkok. Which although they found a bit dirty, the sights were interesting. They could not understand why every single person wanted to strike up some kind of conversation with them, but figured they were all just being friendly. The food was indeed very enjoyable, but played up a bit on their tummies.

Then they were off to Kuala Lumpur, Edward's special surprise. The Eastern & Oriental Express was a luxury train service connecting Thailand, Malaysia and Singapore. Head office Venice-Simplon-Orient Express Ltd still has an office at London SE1 9PF. It was two days of luxurious bliss, quite distant from the seemingly poverty stricken peasants that waved at every turn. There were rumours some tried to board at the slow bends, but these were soon dispelled by their well-spoken waiter. The five-pound tip he received, was equal to three months wages.

Then they ventured to a little, yet well recommended Island, Ko-Samui, for ten glorious days. Edwina buy now, was more than happy to rest and soak up the sun's rays. A period of solitude, rest and reflection was what she needed.

She was glad to have included a typewriter with her luggage; she loved books of course, but also now had a penchant for short stories and poems. She began clacking away on it day after day, once they had settled in their independent bungalows on the beach. No

A Lovely Pair of Knockers

electricity, and simple but enjoyable communal meals at the appropriate times of the day.

She wrote a story of a brother and sister locked away in the turret of a medieval castle, and were to be saved by a handsome Prince who gave them all they thought they ever wanted. But he turned out to be a Dark Prince, all was not as it seemed, and all their hopes and dreams faded. By hook or by crook they managed to get away from their new captor, and eventually rode off into the sunset on camels.

I can't remember the actual title, but evidently it unexpectedly required two reprints to quench the appetite and demand of the public. Once this new Author had been discovered, there was no holding her. It did seem strange however, that not only the benefits of Frankie's arrival at The Gables, helped them both financially, but also influenced their whole lives in a most complete fashion.

Edward meanwhile, was getting far more attention than seemed necessary from Rose, the beautiful chambermaid, he did not complain. The day before leaving, he got an interpreter to take him to her Father, and asked for her hand in marriage.

There were some conditions, but regarded of as a trivial nature to Edward. For what he was getting anyway. She arrived in England one month later, with the whole family. Edward was no fool, so the arranged Wedding was held immediately. The timing was not bad on his part, they were all freezing cold and he arranged for the heating to be out of order, at The Bowthorpe.

Max regarded the extra ten pounds a week, for the heating to be off rather than on, as slightly ironic. Visitors all complained but he told them there was nothing that could be done. Edward correctly guessed that the Father of his beautiful bride, would prefer a nice dowry and a small monthly allowance, rather than suffer this terrible English weather.

The small reception kept things low-key, but he still felt the compelling need to invite Frankie and Barry. After all none of this would have happened without them. They both agreed to attend and were back to their perfect selves, with dignity and respect. They preferred to enclose a generous cash present in their cards, as they could hardly present him with a dinner or cutlery set from his own

A Lovely Pair of Knockers

house. And Edwina made things very comfortable when she requested a dance with Frankie who obliged in a Gentlemanly fashion.

Edward decided to buy a nice terraced town house spread over five floors, at the bottom of Burlington Street, Royal Crescent. It was a lovely part of the seafront with sea views of course. He had fallen in love with it immediately, visualising it as the perfect home to raise a family. The Estate Agent mentioned what a great investment it was and the potential to turn into flats, but this was never on the cards. It was of black bricks, with a few steps up to the front door, which meant the lower ground floor, or basement, still got plenty of light.

Edwina was not too far away in Brunswick Square. She though, settled for a penthouse apartment. Although not scarred for life, she still for the time being, wished to be alone. She was of good breeding after all, but still as vulnerable as the next girl.

The Buzz assured Frankie, that if it wasn't him it would have been someone else, so not to beat himself up about the whole business. Still, he was also feeling a little bit guilty for egging him on, in the first place. Another Golden Rule broken, and a heart to go with it.

Barry mentioned one day whilst playing snooker,

"Just think Frankie, imagine if one of them Nearly or Missin herberts had got their teeth into her. It happens to us all, at one time or another. Why should Edwina be any exception? Not only would she have been hurt in the same way, or even worse, she might have got wind of all the money we made?"

This was a weak, even pathetic attempt at consolation, but at least he tried.

When I caught up with Edward, he was in his prime, with two beautiful daughters and two handsome sons. All had had benefited from a good education locally, with his eldest son, Jai, who was now 17, preparing to go off to Oxford University, and study Law. The two girls were just one year apart at 14 and 13, were attending St Mary's Hall School in Eastern road, so just around the corner. His wife, Mrs Rosie O'Malley, as she was fondly known in the Kemp Town area, was in her element. She rarely let the girls out of her sight and insisted accompanying them to school every single day, rain or shine. The youngest boy Teddy, only 7, was much more integrated to the English

A Lovely Pair of Knockers

way of life, and had already declared he wished to be a butcher when he grew up.

Rosie blossomed in Kemp Town, I love a pun don't you. She had an account at Randall's Butchers, this was why, Teddy wanted to be a butcher. All the staff were so very friendly. She also did her shopping at The Home and Colonial supermarket, a few doors down. She visited Webb's opposite The Golden Cannon Pub, when she wanted something a bit more fancy. She collected his Dry Cleaning from Lee's on a regular basis. Edward was reflecting back to when they first settled in the area, as most of those shops are no longer around.

Fresh bread was collected every Saturday without fail from the Bakery, and this was when she treated herself to a fresh cream chocolate éclair or cream and jam doughnut. She would greedily scoff it on the way home, it was her guilty pleasure. Edward would not have batted an eyelid had she taken it indoors, but little things please little minds.

Edward had taken up a position in Hanningtons Department Store as originally proposed by Frankie, and indeed was head of his own Gentlemen's fine clothing and hire department, within six months.

He got wind of the store closing in the early nineties and had invested well in a couple of shops in the up-and-coming Duke Street vicinity. He kept his cards close to his chest and secretly collected rent on a total of seven shops. Mr Ragsby had played a good part in these proceedings and was duly rewarded. Edward knew now more than ever, that it was who you knew rather than what you knew in this lovely little town called Brighton, but now, lovingly regarded as his and his lovely family's home.

So Edward was as happy as Larry, when by chance, a mutual friend introduced us, over afternoon tea at The Grand Hotel. (Chance would be a fine thing, a carefully orchestrated manoeuvre, on my part, would be more precise) He even mentioned that he was sure I would make a nice acquaintance for his recently widowed sister Edwina. She obviously had not shared her brother's good fortune with the opposite sex. He quickly assured me though, that it was perfectly okay to broach the subject.

Her husband had been a bit of a playboy, although not in a selfish and unfaithful manner. They had been holidaying in the south of France, he had some business to attend to and Edwina had accompanied him. With some pressing documents needing his immediate attention he had hired a sports car, and whilst driving alone into Monte Carlo, had crashed on exactly the same bend as Princess Grace of Monaco. The Royal Family had attended the memorial service themselves as a point of respect. He had in fact been on his way to the Palace, to sign aforementioned papers.

Upon meeting Edwina, I was self-assured that all would be well. She had, after all, become a hugely well-acclaimed successful Author. Specialising in Children's fantasy, and of course dramatic love stories ending in disaster or glory.

She was very smartly dressed and oozed confidence. Which would have been one of the last things I expected. She also possessed a sexy husky voice, which also caught me by surprise.

She mentioned that she had an ongoing trilogy, about some of the more colourful characters of Brighton. These were to include the likes of Max Miller and Uncle Jack the children's entertainer at Peter Pan's Playground. Just below, on the esplanade, where Edward lived. No mention of the more notorious characters that I was so wrapped up and interested in.

She reminisced about the benefactor who had changed her and her brother's lives, seemingly overnight. She mentioned Frankie Slimtone by name, but, when she spoke of him, there was not the slightest bit of malice in her tone. Nor did she seem at all interested in what he was or not doing these days or what had become of him, for that matter.

She was for the time being in mourning, but had not given up hope on finding love for herself, again some day. Very refreshing, considering her limited experience on the subject. I could not of course, reveal my already extensive knowledge of her situation and past experiences.

Another comforting and reassuring belief in the human race moment, was when I enquired after the beautiful ring on her finger.

"Oh this old thing?" she said starry eyed, "This was my Mother's. Father and she picked it out together when they were first engaged, she would glow like a shining distant star when recalling how he had worked five weeks overtime to settle the instalments incurred. Someone did mention, Frankie I think, that I should have it valued many years ago, but I never did. Then a funny thing happened just recently. My insurance agent made an impromptu house call. When going over personal items of potential high value, he insisted that I did in fact get a quote for replacement purposes, should anything unexpected happen. You can imagine my surprise when a jeweller, appointed by their company, said it could not be replaced for anything less than three thousand two hundred and fifty pounds. Would you believe it?"

I would believe Abso-Brighton-lutely anything to do with this lot.

*

All in all, everyone had done very well out of The Green Gables.
Once I realised how I now knew all sides to the story, with none of the concerned parties being aware of my remarkable insight, it became quite exhilarating.
I was one of the few that knew what had happened to all of Ted's treasures. He had been the hardest done by, in my reckoning. As he had never reaped the rewards of the true value of all his ill gotten gains. But maybe this part was reward enough. As it had never officially been discovered, he had, in a creepy kind of way, 'Got Away With It'.
His good name was never tarnished. He had enjoyed being in possession of all the magnificent treasures for many uninterrupted years. If he had sold any bits off, he'd certainly hidden it well and managed to destroy any proof of there existence. His Bank account, along with his wife's, were very comfortable, but certainly not enough to raise any eyebrows let alone alarm bells.

*

Frankie and Barry had earned enough to be set up for life. Although of course they were destined not to hold on to it for as long as you might expect, they certainly got their money's worth anyway.

*

Edward and Edwina? Well they lived happily ever after!

*

But, of course, the puzzle is still not yet complete. There are more sides to this particular story yet to be revealed. Many more secrets will be unravelled, before I've finished telling the unbelievable tales of Brighton's Knockers Boys. Especially this lovely pair, Frankie Slimtone and Barry 'The Buzz' Bubball.

My own personal connection is in fact the most incredible and unbelievable part of the story, but that all comes later.

*

23. A Day At The Races.

So things were all going quite well. Nearly everything from The Forest Row coup, as it was now referred to, had been sold or safely tucked away for a later day.

The Buzz had caused quite a stir a couple of months ago. When he had announced, that due to a moment of divine inspiration, the winner of The Grand National had somehow come to him like a message from God.

After collecting a nice few quid from Johnny Poulter in Waterloo Street, he had ventured down to the Linden Club and begun to share the spoils of the day. He then changed his mind when a couple of the Missin brothers walked in.

Nothing personal, just all of a sudden, decided to join his mate Frankie at the Esquire Club in Holland Road. It was only really a five-minute walk, but he ordered a sherbet anyway.

The Black Prince, Johnny Warren, had been laying a book at The Esquire, with Siddy Berman's co-operation. Bobby, Sid's sister, was visiting relatives up in the smoke that weekend, so the coast was clear. Lee Leechin was with girlfriend Speedy and Giles Capshaw at the bar. 'Frank the Bone' and 'Phil the Till' were there, with a few others, so it was the perfect time for Barry to announce how he had decided to go for the top weight, Gay Trip, in the Big Race.

With a large Mahatma Gandhi in his right hand, and a big fat King Edward cigar in his left he revealed the source of his secret information.

"Well, boys," he began, "There I was this morning. Had a couple of liveners in The Star, off of St James's Street. Then I decided to pop round to The Buccaneer and say hello to Toby Noble. As I'm coming out, along Manchester Street, going towards The Hungry Years, there's this tranny coming towards me. He looked like he had just finished a right old night out on the tiles."

"Well just as we are about to pass, the poor sod has lost balance on the old high heels. It was one of those things you just have to witness, you know what I mean. You had to be there to appreciate it. I simply could not help myself, but with bundles of self-control. Rather than bursting out wiv laughter, I managed to keep it down to a titter. The soppy rotten twat has gone absolutely berserk at me. The tirade of foul language that was hurled at me was something to behold."

"Soppy big twit for wearing those stupid things on your feet anyway, I commented. He managed to get himself up. Then he began to lecture me. Yeah, I know. Lecture me of all people. On how the general public, or other degenerate and ignorant pricks such as myself, should not refer to the likes of himself in such a derogatory manner. Then he started to prattle on how the 'Gay Community' were still being persecuted and treated like just another minority group. That would one day be given equal rights like any other members or part of the community, and treated equally."

"I just shrugged me shoulders and walked away. He still kept shouting behind my back, but what the dickens it was still early in the morning as far as I was concerned."

Jackie Wadman couldn't help but question what the hell did any of this have to do with The Buzz knowing what would win 'The National'.

It was now common knowledge that Barry was one of a very few lucky sods to have gone for the winner, also he had had a sizeable bet. This always pricked up the ears and engaged the curiosity of fellow gamblers, as it may well lead to further valuable inside information at a later date.

"Sorry Jack, I got slightly off the point there. Well, when I get's in the Buck, they are having a sweepstake. I simply closed my eyes and picked out Gay Bloody Trip from the Lucky Bubball Bleedin' Dip. So then I reflected on the recent occurrence, and realised that this was a message from somewhere. You know the Gay guy tripping up an' all that."

"When I get's into Poulter's, a bit later, the fing is being offered at 15/1 so I had a ton, on the nose. Some clever clogs standing behind me said it was a mugs bet and why didn't I do it each way. Finking about it during the next race, I realised that Ray Comfort was probably right. So then I went and had one hundred pound each-way, an' all. Then of course, nosey bollocks Ray Comfort has told a few of the others about the 'wager of the day so far', and so he's gone and had a tenner each-way as well."

A Lovely Pair of Knockers

"I must say Johnny Poulter was not particularly impressed with my 'vision' so to speak. He did comment that maybe next time I might be a bit more discreet. Save it for the confessional or something, and not go round shouting from the pulpit. Whatcanyasay? Whatcanyadoo?"

The group at the bar were all adding up the winnings in their head. Barry recognised that he had already revealed much more than he should. So ordered drinks all round and a cab A.S.A.P.

Frankie gave a knowing nod to his pal, he was having a one to one game of spoof with Tommy Barnes so did not wish to get involved. They were also indulging in small doses of amyl nitrate, or poppers as they are referred to. Each inhalation causing them to go into fits of laughter. Some people were getting slightly paranoid about what they were finding so bloody funny, whilst others knew exactly what was going on.

Before anyone could tap him up, he added,

"Just as well I had a little tickle. I haven't paid the rent in three months so it will help get me out of a bit of trouble there. See ya later lads."

He had of course plenty of readies about him at this particular time due to the recent dealings in The Forest. He had in fact been just as crafty as Frankie, or sensible, whichever way you look at it. A ground floor flat in Sussex Square had come to his attention, number eleven.

It also had a basement that was not up to building regulations for habitation. The Estate Agent done him a real good deal and Frankie had the Raggers on the case to arrange planning permission for a Bar/TV room, shower with W.C. Sauna and even a small swimming pool to be given the go-ahead with no questions asked. In them days, a slippery nifty got things done quite smoothly. What's the harm? Everyone happy as Larry.

So, to be fair, this has been quite a long introduction to, 'A Day At The Races'. It has merely been a way of indicating how much Race horsing was an intrinsic part of The Knocker Boy's way of life. After all, many of them spent their hard earned money in the bookies. Easy money, easy spent, being the common motto of the day. This still is the way of such people.

Whether you consider them crooks or chancers, none of the characters known to me or referred to in these tales, should be regarded as criminals. That is not to say that some of the purveyors of 'Fine Antiques & Objay D'art' did not resort to darker means to gain possession of such artefacts. That subject is for others to deliberate upon. Not this girl.

*

Back to the matter at hand.

Frankie had taken it upon himself to arrange one of the many trips from Brighton, to The Epsom Derby of 1970. Pretty much all of the loose ends with The Forest Row deal had been tied up. He was now settled in his own property, all bought and paid for, with some very sumptuous furnishings to boot. Very tidy. The Buzz also, seemed to be settling down, of sorts.

He had sorted out a good deal with a luxury coach firm from Eastbourne. The last 52-seater available on the South Coast was eventually secured. The negotiations had gotten a bit tetchy at times but they had finally settled on what appeared to be a good deal for all. If they had offered him the coach free of charge there would still have been some bartering, it's just the way they were.

There was certainly a lot of competition when it came to Derby Day.

Whoever offered the best deal and 'proper' added extras was sure to gain notoriety amongst the Knocker Boy community. Which of course by now, meant that the lucky bus firm to get the best booking was sure to make a tidy sum on the day. Drivers drew lots to decide who got who. Tips would be equal to a month's wages on the biggest day of the year for this special service.

The Missin boys would be leaving in a Double Decker Bus from The White Admiral in Bevendean. Accompanied by some of the Bhargie's and the Drawers clan. The Nearly family with some of the Opendoors crew, had the same mode of transport from The Whitehawk Inn. Whilst The Bowels would be departing from The Lion & Unicorn, otherwise known as The Blue House, which had now developed into a centre point of all Brighton's Knocker Boys.

A Lovely Pair of Knockers

Frankie had gone upmarket with his coach. Rather than 'Double Decker peasant travel', as he was overheard to say one day. A comment he would live to regret at a later date. They were to depart from The King & Queen. This was due to the fact that most of the signed up contingent frequented The Basketmakers or Brighton Tavern.

Down to the fact both Pubs were situated in the unapproachable Gloucester Road, by bus or coach at least, it just didn't make sense to try and leave from either venue. He had slipped the Guvnor twenty quid to ensure the boozer was up and running by eight so everything was in place.

There were a few other groups going from St Peter's Church as well, so it made sense to try and take a few bob, considering so many would not be about later in the day. Of course in those days there was no telly in the pub, so you either stayed home or in the bookies.

Not being too far away, Epsom was considered an unofficial Bank Holiday for the working classes. The journey would always include an encounter or two with fellow Brighton families on the road. Some would wave graciously, doing the Queen bit, whilst others would stick up two fingers or shake the opened fist in an excitable fashion. It was, and still is, traditional to start early on such memorable occasions. In those days it was still held on the first Wednesday in June.

All said and done, Frankie had woken up feeling fine, with something telling him he was into something good.

As usual, there were a few people who hit the top-shelf far too early in the day, but what can you expect. Casualties of war are regarded in the same way.

The price for such an excursion was always kept at a minimum. Frankie, however had thrown caution to the wind, and was charging £15 a head. It had been shunned at first, by nearly everyone. Then the rumours had got about, that this would be the best Derby trip ever. Anyone missing out on the Frankie and Barry trail would live to regret it. Vince Nearly even asked for availability at one stage, but by this time it was a sell-out.

It was now common knowledge that Frankie Slimtone, with Barry Bubball in tow, had found one. Had come across a right clue

A Lovely Pair of Knockers

and would soon be a couple of the biggest players in town, just don't tell anyone I told you. You know the score.

Frankie had indeed made his mind up to make sure that his would be the most talked about and remembered of the 'Derby Day Outings', this year. He had a word with Frankie Leach about the Seafood. His brother practically had a monopoly on the best of the seafood available locally.

Two big buckets of jellied eels, whelks, cockles a' plenty, prawns, shrimps, smoked salmon and a few extra special dressed crabs had all been paid for at great mates rates. Kindly delivered by their ever reliable family friend, scouser 'Del Boy Mc Quade'. He had other plans for the day, unfortunately, and was unable to join in the frivolities. Frankie loved the Races himself and was only too pleased to help.

The booze was secured by the coincidental news of a local Off License, Unwins, in St George's Road being ransacked. No need to go into that much further, as the case was never solved. Needless to say, it turned out to be very profitable for the culprits that carried out the military style operation.

Frankie had got first dibs, picked out all the cream, then kindly guided them on to other interested parties. He of course was holding plenty of readies at the time, so it made sense to see him first. It was a certainty that all the other interested parties would try to squeeze every last drop at a minimum price. Or potentially not even come up with the money at all. The tea-leaves involved could hardly go to a small claims court or complain to the old bill that they hadn't been fairly paid for their black-market stock.

As they were only small time they had to take what they could, messing with Missin's or Nearly's was just added aggro, above and beyond their call of duty.

So, needless to say, Frankie's coach had enough alcohol to keep a Pub going for a weekend. They didn't care for refined wine too much in those days. He had purloined a nice case of Chateau-Neuf-Du-Pape for himself. There were also three cases of Moet & Chandon; another case had been dropped off to Frankie's Mum for safekeeping. That particular one had something to do with Don Quixote.

There were loads of Party Seven and Party Five tins, cases of Light Ales, Brown Ales and twelve cases of Double Diamond. That would work wonders later on!

They still had four cases of Blue Nun, two cases of Matteus Rose, and four cases of various Red Barolo wine.

The 'Top-Shelf', consisted of four bottles each of Smirnoff, Vat69, Gordon's, Bacardi, Johnny Walker, Martini, Rosso and Bianco, Remy Martin and Courvoisier V.S.O.P. There were also a couple of cases of Babycham and two bottles of Dubonnet, just in case.

A stray R.Whites lorry had parked in the wrong place, the old depot was later to become Mike Deasy's Yard, and was therefore relieved of six crates of Lemonade, two Cherryade, three Limeade and five small cases each of tonic, soda and bitter lemon. Having to actually buy two cases of Coca-Cola from the Pub was heartbreaking.

All the fruit to go with it had already been delivered when he arrived at 7:45 am.

Smudger, who had been given a complimentary ticket to take care of all the catering, confirmed that all the ordered meat for the barbecue was in order. Fresh bread and rolls, plus a sumptuous selection of pastries and fresh cream cakes from Zetlands were on their way.

With a mocking salute, to his pal, he announced,

"All ship shape and Bristol fashion, Sah!" He was a Navy man Smudger, fortunately out on leave that week, and his first class Navy training in the catering core would benefit all for sure that day. Timing was everything.

Frankie thought he would start the day with a flourish, and had a master plan to get everyone together from the start. So as to ensure they all knew each other and enjoy the whole day as a family group.

He had a clip board with all the paid up punters on it and was checking them all off as they arrived. The Collins clan, all eight of them, were all prompt at eight, and were enjoying a smoke (apart from the four kids of course) in the beer garden along with early Irish Coffees. The Buzz was with Eileen, from The Basketmakers, her two sisters, two brothers plus Mum and Dad.

Tommy Barnes was with wife Margaret and two young daughters. Also his kid brother Tony and his girlfriend Sally, they

A Lovely Pair of Knockers

would later marry in 1972 and have a beautiful daughter Lucy. He'd closed the shop and also included his driver Steve and his missus for the day.

Also closed for the day was Raggers, he was to be accompanied by Miss James of course. His part of the Forest Row coup was major, so the two complimentary tickets were cheap by any standards.

Georgie Balcock turned up unexpectedly; he looked a bit out of sorts, but paid up immediately after explaining he had missed the Nearly Bus from The Whitehawk. He had of course got the time wrong, as they always left earlier than most, to make sure they got a prime location on site. He had a bird in tow, with another two herberts who were also late, and got a Taxi from The Broadway, Frankie had allowed for such an occurrence, so was not put out whatsoever.

Lance King, who ran The Freshfield at the time, did not fancy all the hassle this year of doing his own bus. So had been one of the first to sign up, and was fervently followed by a few of his regulars. These Frankie was not so sure about, but he wasn't about to try and start some exclusive membership club, just to go to the Derby. He didn't want to come across as some kind of 'Jack The Lad', amongst his own.

There were a few other Knocker Boys from the Hove end signed up, all accompanied by their chosen W.A.G. Not terminology of the time, but most certainly an unspoken understanding by all concerned. It was a bit sad how some of the wives were forced to enjoy the company of a girlfriend one week and then the wife of the same fellah the next. They must have seethed at the blatancy of such behaviour, but rarely did they crack a note. Just as well, or the female in question may well have witnessed similar indiscretions, whilst their old man was away. Nobody was sweet and innocent in those days, nobody.

Bringing everyone to attention, Frankie announced his first generous act of the day.

"Ladies and Gentlemen please. Let me first of all, welcome you all and wish you all a very happy, enjoyable and prosperous day. Let's all have, a bloody good day at the races". As he raised his glass of

A Lovely Pair of Knockers

sparkling water, they all cheered back, did the same and drank to his health.

"Right then," he continued, "How does this grab you? I know you have all paid handsomely to come on this little adventure with me and me old mucker, The Buzz over there, today. But to show my appreciation, I would like you all to have a go on our exclusive Derby Sweepstake. No, no, no." Raising his hands in mock surrender,

"Don't you worry your pretty little heads about some slippery little scam to cajole some more money out of you. This is I can assure you, will be the best value sweepstake you ever have had the pleasure to enter. We have, if my calculations are correct, 44 happy people on our little excursion today. Kids included of course."

"Now there are eleven runners in the big race, and therefore there are how many jockeys, yes, that's right eleven jockeys also. Barring any late changes, we know who's who, on what and where they are going. This is my proposition. £5 a ticket and everyone gets two. But the thing is, I don't want anyone to hand in a single sixpence."

"That's right folks. I am gonna donate £10 a head into the kitty for the sweepstake, so all you have had to pay is a ching each for the day. That should cover the entry onto the Downs and give Eric here our driver for the day, a nice little drink. Now, whaddayasay?"

Although quite taken aback, everyone cheered like it was a cup final win for their favourite team.

"So," he continued, now well aware that he had everyone's full attention,

"That means we have four hundred and forty quid in the pot. We have here, holding up two champagne buckets, the two gold mines of good fortune. One contains the name of each horse, and this one has the name of a jockey. Now obviously, there are only 11 horses in the race, so it is to be divided up in the following way."

He then explained how things would proceed; each horse and jockey had been entered twice, so everyone takes two horses and two jockeys. This meant everyone had four selections. First, would get the lion's share naturally, but Second, Third and even Fourth place, would all redeem some amount, in smaller increments.

A Lovely Pair of Knockers

First horse and first jockey x 4 tickets = £60 each = Total = £240
Second horse and jockey   x 4 tickets = £25 each = Total = £100
Third horse and jockey   x 4 tickets = £15 each = Total = £60
Fourth horse and jockey   x 4 tickets = £10 each = Total = £40

    Everyone was happy with the state of play, and congratulated Frankie on such a generous and unexpected kind gesture.
    With all the sweepstake taken care of and duly recorded, it was time to make a move, Eric was given the nod and they all piled onto the coach. Frankie was in his element, up front on the coach. Then realising that all the booze was in the luggage hold, held things up for a few minutes whilst unloading four crates of DD's along with some light ales. This of course brought loud cheers of "We're only 'ere for the beer," from all aboard. Just to keep the juices flowing of course.
    The tried and tested experience of the likes of Tommy Barnes and the Collins boys were quite content to swig from their hip flasks. Whilst others already had flasks out with prepared tea and coffee. Frankie himself had the master plan of not taking a drink till about two o'clock. Wise advice from someone that had taken on a similar task the year before, and been taken advantage of because they got too, pissed too early.

*

    As they cruised up the A23 Frankie got a little tap on the shoulder, from one of the guys from The Freshfield. He at first thought it might be a complaint about the strong odour of The Buzz's illegal smoking at the back, but not to worry.
    Pat Sargeant introduced himself politely to Frankie, then began to explain that he had a couple of passes for the owners and trainers enclosure, and would it be okay if he and the missus Jean slipped off a bit later, to enjoy the experience.
    "Of course you can mate, don't you worry at all. You do whatever you like. We won't be leaving early anyway today. Off to the Fair after the races, let the queues die down for an hour or so, then probably have another bash at the grub before we make a move. I heard that those passes were like gold dust, and were strictly checked

with an evil eye by the stewards on the gates. You be careful won't you."

"Don't worry about that Frankie," replied Pat,

"Have a gander at these," showing Frankie the official laminated identification cards.

"Look, Sydney Starr the bookie gave 'em to me when he realised he had to be elsewhere today. I am today Mr Jeremy Thorpe, leader of The Liberal Party, with guest, my beautiful little wifey Jeanie. I can get in anywhere I like today."

"Nice one Pat, nice one. Still, you will be with us for the first drinks and barbecue an' all that won't you?"

"Of course, of course. Looking forward to it. Should be a lovely day. Weather's great an' all innit."

"Absolutely mate. Abso-Brighton-lutely."

*

Everyone was in high spirits and the journey was soon done in good time. Just after eleven o'clock they got a nice position on the rails, right next to the Missin Bus, loaded with Colt 45's. Beers not guns. Then lo and behold alongside them came the Nearly Bus, with plenty of Red Barrel on board. Frankie announced that they were surely like a rose between two thorns. Everyone agreed, it was certainly going to be a day to remember.

Smudger was straight on the case as they disembarked, and within twenty minutes he had the barbie on. He had already explained to Frankie that it was best to get most of the cooked food sorted out first, so that everyone lined their stomachs a little.

Anyway, once the races started, nobody would give a toss about the grub. They did of course all steam straight into the glorious array of seafood on offer and all marvelled at how beautiful it looked.

The Smudge was indeed an expert, and the whole poached salmon resting on struts, resembled a flying fish. With the delicately and ornately placed assortment of other seafood surrounding, it was totally captivating. Everyone remarked that it looked too good to eat. So it was all of fifteen minutes before the whole bloody lot was demolished. They all sat around afterwards like the cat that got the cream, or the fish for that matter, rubbing their tummies with great big satisfying grins on their boats.

The looks on their faces though, when Smudger unloaded some whole skewered chickens, then started carefully placing them on the nice glowing coals of the barbecue was something to behold, and to be one of the nicest moments of the day. He had marinated them overnight, in recipes picked up on his excursions in the West Indies, Asia, North and South America. The smell was out of this world. Although not short of a few bob, nobody in the near vicinity had yet ventured further than Blackpool or The Isle of Wight for their holidays.

Gathering around, they all enquired how the poor little things had got into such a state, and if this was some kind of Religious ritual that they were not aware of. What with all those skewers going in one end and out the other, resembling a crucified chook.

Some even started singing one of the popular songs of the time. 'Do the Funky Chicken' by Rufus Thomas.

"This my friends, is called a spatchcock chicken," announced Smudger. Now revelling in all his glory and certainly not used to such respectful attention.

"These birds have been prepared in such a way that they are all cooked evenly over the coals. They will retain all their natural juices and have many different flavours. Mexican is my personal favourite, Pollo Loco as it is known. Then we have the Caribbean, Argentinean, Italian and even Chinese Five Spice Spectacular, they will all be available for you good folk today. As you can see we have plenty of potato salad, fresh salad and bread to go with. Just be patient and when it is at it's best, we can eat the best tucker on the Downs. Courtesy of course, with our dear hosts blessing, Frankie and Buzz, over there. No expense spared."

He reckoned years later that he received one of the biggest cheers of the whole day, barring the winner of the big race of course.

At this stage the two neighbouring Bus loads began to mingle with the King & Queen crowd. Eager to get a taste of the tantalising grub, that was beginning to become the centre of attention all around. Frankie had anticipated such actions, so announced that only those

A Lovely Pair of Knockers

with King & Queen tickets were able to approach the barbie to collect food.

These were of course the Sweepstake tickets that he shared out evenly earlier in the day, with a little K&Q rubber stamped in the corner. However, once all the coach party had had their fill and were happy, there were no objections to everyone joining in with the frivolities.

Both the Nearly and Missin families were more than welcome to join in. After the chickens had been evenly distributed, of course.

Smudger then loaded up with bangers and burgers, but still got plenty of ooohs and aaahs when the irresistible smell of onions started to reach anyone within a fifty yard radius. By this time all the Brighton mob were well solid, so any strangers were quickly warded off, in no uncertain terms.

The Buzz took Frankie to one side to congratulate him on such clever and meaningful foresight.

"Blinding idea that with old Smudge. He's done a corking job. There's not one single soul can say we haven't pulled it off. Look at that, everyone is havin' a blindin' time."

"I wish I could have eaten a bit more, but me and Eileen ended up in the Taj-Mahal, Duke Street, last night. As usual she only had half of hers so I made a bit of a pig of myself. Suffering a bit wiv the old Gandhi's revenge. Still, a nice bottle of that Red wine we got in the boot and I'll soon be me old self."

"You just crack on Buzz, have a lovely day mate," Frankie reassured him.

They had some great background music to add to the atmosphere. Someone had brought one of those new big radio 'Ghetto-Blaster', contraptions, and not only could they get the radio, they had some tapes from recording the top twenty from Sunday night, a couple of weeks ago.

Daughter of Darkness by Tom Jones, Everything is Beautiful by Ray Stevens, the memorable ABC by The Jackson's got 'em all dancing, the classic Can't Help Fallin' In Love from Andy Williams. Then Elvis with Kentucky Rain and Yellow River by Christie all got their fair share of airplay.

The favourite of the day turned out to be Spirit in the Sky by Norman Greenbaum, when absolutely everyone joined in the chorus.

*

The first race was at 2:00 pm, and at this time Pat Sergeant and wife Jean bade farewell and wished everyone a great afternoon. They had other important places to go and people to meet, you understand.

It had tickled Frankie earlier on in the day, when they were all enjoying the chicken and having a bit of banter. Pat Sargeant had declared that he had had to have a word with his Guvnor on the Monday.

"Well," he starts, "I asks him if it's okay to have Wednesday off, 'cause we fancy a trip to Epsom for the Derby an all that. Now I didn't fink there would be a problem. Then all of a sudden he goes a bit cranky on me, and informs me that nobody can have Wednesday off, under any circumstances whatsoever. What a prick. Proper willocky chops jobs-worth he is. Due to some deadline or some other old tosh."

"Then he has only given me the once over and gawn, 'What the blazes are you doing' 'ere on a Monday anyway Pat? And, come to think of it, I have been meaning to ask you for greengages, why you only ever work four poxy days a week? What have you to say for yourself young man?'"

"He was getting right out of his pram and up his own arse, so I just says to him, 'Well. I can't get buy on just three days money can I?' Well to be fair, he didn't have much to say after that, shrugged his shoulders and told me to do whatever the heck I liked, coz the chances are I would anyway. He was right about that one anyway, that's for sure. Cheers everyone, and cheers to young Frankie Slimtone and his mate over there for giving us all such a lovely day. Whaddayassay?"

Everyone else joined in, with the cheers. Even the two neighbouring bus-loads, were now feeling a little envious and slightly upstaged. Of course this was by no means any accident. Frankie had of course already pre-empted The Buzz that the day would not go

A Lovely Pair of Knockers

without incident. As far as he was concerned it had only just got started.

The Nearly Brothers had decided to set up a book, (Take Bets from all-comers, that is) under the banner of John Kent, so nobody had to travel too far to place a bet. This suited everyone. As long as they didn't run out of money. They never did, so it didn't matter.

After the first race, Frankie caught the eye of another couple, from The Freshfield, Mr & Mrs Town. They would indeed, prove to be, the classiest couple of the day. They did however, have two youngsters in tow. Lee and Kevin. A couple of little scallywags, you could ever wish to meet, it would only be fair to say.

He had backed handsomely the winner of the second race, My Swallow in the 2:35, at 8-1 with Lester Piggot on his back, was probably the best bet of the day. So with their consent, decided to bung the two young whipper-snappers, some loose change. Two minutes later, Lee comes back and tells Frankie, that his bruvver has eight shillings, and all he had is seven and sixpence.

"Well pardon me," goes Frankie, "I'm really sorry about that. There must have been a mistake in the accountancy department."

Shuffling through his pockets though, there was not an immediate solution,

"Sorry, son, I do not seem to have a spare sixpence to even the tally. Would you be prepared to accept a shilling, y'know, to even things up? Oh, and by the way, you won't tell yer bruvver, will ya'?"

"Nah, that's okay Mr Frankie," with the cheekiest little grin you can imagine,

"It'll just be our little secret." (Alias Smith & Jones would, years later, use the same line). Then young Lee sprinted off to join his brother, knowing full well, that they were probably the richest little kids in the whole of the bloody Fairground. Yippee!

*

Townie would, just a few years later, get to a Junior A.B.A. final under the guidance of renowned trainer Bert Barrows. He had a very good jab. Brian Cordier would have helped with that part of his make-up, another great coach, but always took the back room approach, not wishing to accept any compliments or responsibility, for their combined successes. A true Gentleman.

This particular pair, (Bert & Brian) were responsible for a glut of Boxing talent from Brighton in the 70's. Phil Cooper, who captained a winning Queen's Park Boxing team one year, cheered on his two brothers, Alan and Victor at every opportunity, while Brian's kid Brother Malcolm did okay. Barry and Keith Price were probably the best Brighton brothers to ever get in a boxing ring. The 'Two Towns' weren't bad, Keith Funnell joined later. Pat Kerrigan and brother Dave Marchant, along with Colin Brownjohn helped develop a nice junior squad. Lance Wheeler was successful in later years, along with Steve Martin. The Clarke brother's, Wayne, Brent, Dean and Ricky, all accommodated themselves well, along with a couple of the Missin boys. All said and done, they turned out a nice few tidy fighters between them.

They should, most definitely, be subsequently proud of themselves.

Well done the pair of you.

Hove ABC was another local Club, the Danahar brothers were ok and the only Grammar School Boxer of any stock, Steve Wood, represented them also. He did well, but really and truly, he was just too nice a person to hurt anyone. But he always loved the sport and continues to this day in supporting local Boxing and Ex-Boxers Associations. A little later Mark Snipe, who's Father had been a well respected Ref, also represented Hove.

*

There was not too much more to report for the next couple of hours. As long as you choose not to mention Smudge going to the luggage hold for some more salad stuff, and to his amazement there was a couple having sex in there. Not too close to the actual food, so no harm done.

She had been propped up on a case of Double Diamond, so that must have worked wonders for her. It is not important to mention the actual culprits, but they certainly had to take a fair bit of stick for their indiscretion.

A Lovely Pair of Knockers

Puns a plenty on Derby Day.

Anyway, anyone there that day, remembers who they were, and obviously the perpetrators also, 'just anuvver day at the races', was everybody's view.

The first ever genuinely recognised Tipster even paid The Brighton Boys, a visit, Prince Honolulu. He charged half-a-crown for three selections. It was a bit of a con really, you had to pick a number out of his hat, so he wasn't responsible for you picking the wrong ticket, was he? As long as he sold out for each race, he was sure to make someone happy. Of Indian descent, he also complimented the chef, when he managed to blag a nice piece of that spatchcock chicken.

The Big Race came and went. Lester Piggott with his 5th win on what he referred to as one of the finest horses he ever had the pleasure to ride, Nijinsky. Most of the Brighton crew had managed to get up on Tattanhum Corner to watch the race, and a sense of anti-climax came over them all, once it was all finished.

At this time, always perfect timing, of course, Frankie announced the Winners of the sweepstake. Not that they needed telling of course. Ronnie Burton and Mrs Town had Lester Piggott so both received £60 each, with Frankie Leach and young Delia Barnes, Tommy's daughter, who had both plucked the winning horse Nijinsky.

The also-rans were also pleased to get a nice return, with Smudger, Georgie Balcock, Eric the Driver and Miss James receiving £25 each for Gyr with Bill Williamson riding it home, 2 ½ lengths behind.

Third was another French runner, Stintino, 3 lengths behind, ridden by G. Thuboeuf, the winners here were Bertie Collins and brother Coco who both had the same jockey and joined by Eileen and Jean Sargeant, not present at the time, but still entitled to her winnings for picking the right horse.

Fourth place went to the game Great Wall ridden by Joe Mercer, at 80-1. Raggers did not complain, neither did Melvyn Foster, Eileen again because she had the jockey along with Tommy Barnes.

Money was all dished out and they all got back into the party mood, realising most of them had benefited sufficiently to call it a free day out. This was now also the moment for Frankie to take his first drink of the day. He considered his work here done, so was going to enjoy himself from here on in. He popped the cork on two bottles of champagne and shared it out immediately. Now things were going to start occurring.

Almost on cue, The Buzz, asked Frankie where the nearest toilets were, he was pointed in the right direction. It was unfortunately to be in vain.

As he marched off he thought he was going to pass wind, but passed something much more substantial. He had on a brand new Prince of Wales suit, which would give away his predicament like a lighthouse in the dark. More bad fortune.

He had a minor explosion and it was like a downward chocolate fountain, the stain slowly appearing down his trousers. Frankie regretted it immediately, but could not help point out to everyone what was happening. The wicked stain materialising right before their very eyes, as he walked towards his destination. It was warm for The Buzz, as it trickled down his legs, but certainly not in a comforting way.

It was equally embarrassing in the queue, people began to edge away from him and he was suddenly standing alone with an ominous group of people holding their noses and pointing at him as if he were a leper in their midst. He may as well have been. When the booth in front of him opened, things just got worse. The awful stench hit him smack in the face like a lump of wood. He managed to scramble in, but it just wasn't his finest hour to be sure. The toilet was blocked with three soggy rolls of toilet paper and there was no more in sight.

Then to top it all off, a young traveller kid kicked the door in and demanded for him to,

"Horry the fock op will ya. Me mam's pregnant and needs this bog more than you, ya fat twat."

This outraged The Buzz, but as he lurched forward to reprimand the kid, he fell straight out of the cubicle and was left stranded with his damp dark strides around his ankles. He hadn't even managed to remove and get rid of his pants yet, and they were in a right soggy mess.

The gram of cocaine and four Acid tabs had also been ruined by his own excrement, so he was none too pleased about that either. A large wad of fivers were also quite sticky with a rottney smell on the outer notes, and badly stained into the bargain.

Unbeknown to Barry, that very same day, Persil washing powder, was introduced to the Great British public. But a fat load of good it was doing him at the time.

There was nothing for it, he would have to front the whole thing up, and face the music and humiliation. Hopefully there would soon be another subject to talk about and this little episode would soon be forgotten. Some chance. It's only forty-six years ago now, so you can see how that worked out for him. The light at the end of the tunnel came from Smudger.

He had a spare pair of Chef's trousers and jacket that he lent Barry. He also had to borrow some rubber non-slip sandals, once he had rinsed his feet and thrown away his socks. Even his shirt tails still gave evidence of the catastrophe, so that was also thrown away. He finished the look off with a matching chequered cap and if you didn't know him he quite looked the part.

He then proceeded to explain to everyone that it was down to the Curry and the strong red wine he was drinking today that had caused the physical embarrassment. Not mentioning the extremely strong cannabis he had been smoking. Everyone was aware that the strange Grapefruity smell, was not from a healthy tobacco substitute he was experimenting with, for a friend at Holland & Barrett, like he said.

"Don't worry Buzz," they all said with sympathy, "Just get on with the rest of the day mate. Today's news is tomorrow's fish n' chips."

"What do you fancy in the next race?" enquired Richard Nearly, "I'm not laying it though, I bet it'll shit home."

He had to laugh of course; after all he had made quite a spectacle of himself. Just felt a bit sorry for Eileen, she had to sit next to him. The Suit was disposed of and never seen again. A one-day wear, 'Throw away suits are all the rage you know?' he was later to remark.

After the last race, the last few bangers and burgers were on the go, and the sudden urge to eat was soon being satisfied. Pat Sargeant and his wife rejoined the group, having had a nice few bevies themselves. After collecting the sweepstake money, he declared it was his only draw of the day. It had all been very well to mix with the hoy-polloy, but they were much more at home now they were back with their friends.

More champagne was opened and they toasted one another again. "No more of that red wine for you though Buzz, we don't want any more accidents," came from some mystery person at the rear of the group.

Frankie was unstoppable, he had his money on Nijinsky in the Derby, so was well up. He then came across an old pal who now lived up north, but had heard about the great grub and beer over at the 'Brighton End', that was on offer. He gave Frankie a tip for the penultimate race, Tudor Harmony in the 4:10. He knew the jockey R.P. Elliott, who right fancied the ride. Two hundred pounds at 13-2, saw Frankie's tally rise to in excess of two grand for the day. More than covered all his expenses.

R.P. Elliott would later become involved in a minor scandal, as a result he went across the water and rode in the U.S.A. Upon his return he was allowed back into the fold of the racing world, but could not curtail his habit of unscrupulous behaviour.

No, I have no idea where he is now.

*

Then the first bit of concern of the day began. Young Townie came back from the Fair, sporting a fresh shiner on his left eye. His Dad enquired if he had been fighting with his brother again, but Kevin stuck up for his brother and told them that some adult had cuffed him, for fighting with his son.

"We, ain't standing for that," declared Arnie Missin, "Let's go and have a word with this bunch. It's down to the parents to discipline the kids, not some uvver jumped up little prats from God knows where. Come on boys, it's off to the Fair. Whereabouts, are they young Lee? You show us the way."

A Lovely Pair of Knockers

There was no point trying to reason with any of them. But no-one was interested in trying anyway. Timmy Missin, backed up his brother, along with Big Sam, Basher Drawers, a couple of the Bhargie's and all the Nearly Boys followed in earnest. Coco and Bert Collins with Ronnie Burton in tow, also joined the quickly assembled posse.

The Buzz couldn't help adding that there could be 'No Bridge Over Troubled Water', to solve this matter easily, another of the popular tunes being played that day. By Simon & Garfunkel, of course.

Once they confronted the offending man, it turned out to be the same little firm from Portsmouth. The ones who the Collins boys had had the turf war and ensuing Snooker match with, back in January. This was not going to be a sit down discussion situation. To achieve any kind of resolution, there was gonna be a fight. Frankie managed to come between them briefly and suggested the Boxing Booth as a solution to their problems.

This seemed acceptable to all concerned. Timmy Missin was first up, but during the traditional touching of the gloves ceremony, stuck the nut straight bang on the nose of his opponent. The crunch of cartilage was heard at the back of the tent, and the guy's nose resembled Niagara Falls. He fell to his knees, but Timmy was not deterred and continued to rain punches down on him. He must have lost a pint of blood through his hooter by the time the ref had pulled the Brighton man off his victim. The bloke was well mullered.

One nil and counting.

Next up was young Harry Nearly. He had done a bit of Boxing training at The Brighton Boys Club, and years later would actually box as a professional Heavyweight. He was still a youngster then though, but still gamely agreed to take on someone a good ten years his senior. They were both very cagey in the first round, sussing each other out.

Then Vince Nearly decided he was Angelo Dundee all of a sudden, and jumped up into his corner,

"Just shove him into the corner and smack him straight on the Vera," were his pearls of wisdom. Mind you, that was exactly what Harry managed to do, and his opponent had to be aroused with smelling salts after Harry knocked him spark out, with a sickening left hook, smack on the jaw, as instructed.

Vince took all the accolades like the proud brother he was, "What a team, we are," he declared, to anyone who would listen.

Two nil and still counting.

The third and final match saw the offending Dad, that had clouted young Townie step forward. He wasn't that much to look at, but he had been warned by his fellow travellers that he needed to step up to the mark. To save face, and, well it was all his fault in the first place.

Nobody seemed keen to step forward, and they were all sort of looking at each other for encouragement, Dutch courage or something.

Jimmy Bowels stepped forward, from the back, and declared he would defend the honour of Brighton, and finish the day off in style. He was probably the most skilled Boxer of the day, but the Bowels boys didn't mind dishing out a bit of punishment when the situation required.

He jabbed with precision and speed for a kid of his size and stature. Didn't waste a single punch and held his opponent up at least twice in the first round. They wanted to stop the fight but his brother Perry insisted the decision was up to the ref. Jimmy continued to destroy the bloke in the second with some punishing body blows. It was only the two-inch split above his right eye, from an out of nowhere, crashing windmill right-hander, that saved the Pompey boy from annihilation.

The harsh leather horsehair filled gloves could not have helped. He went flying through the ropes and was obviously concussed. Someone from his gang threw a bucket of slushy water over him, and shaking his head, he struggled to his feet. Once he realised where he was, he criss-crossed his gloves to indicate he was not getting back in the ring. He was in such a state that nobody could genuinely argue with his decision. The most and only sensible thing he'd done all day. He still needed medical attention afterwards and a hospital visit was on the cards.

Someone even mentioned, whilst laughing out loud,

"Did you see the state of that poor geezer's face, it was more of a mess than Barry Bubball's pants. Poor sod. That mate of his throwing all the spit-bile bucket over him couldn't have helped much either."

Three nil Brighton.

Game, Set and Match.

The great thing about settling scores in the ring, was that it generally ended with everyone shaking hands and making up. This was not to be the case with these two factions, and there is still rumour of bad feeling between them, till this day. But who am I to say?

The warring done with, they made there way back to the Buses and had a few more drinks before deciding to make their way home. It was definitely a day for camaraderie, just a shame it was not to last forever.

*

Back at the Coach a couple of the women complained that Ragsby, who had consumed probably more wine than anyone else. Had got a bit too fruity with Miss James and she had had to give him a slap. Shouting at the time that he was a filthy rotten, dirty old bastard, and would never work for him again. They could not work out if it was all part of the role-play or they actually had something going. He had been very sheepish since the incident, but she had still taken the seat next to him for the journey home. Oh well, it takes all sorts.

Someone also demanded impatiently, to 'turn that poxy music off'. The second set of batteries had run down and The Beach Boys, singing Cottonfields in slow motion, just didn't cut it.

As they joined the slow stream of traffic that was still departing from The Epsom Downs, Frankie recognised a couple of very attractive girls he had come across somewhere before. He asked Eric to cut across them so he could get a closer look at the other coach. This done Frankie realised it was the Brighton & Hove Albion Football Team on board the coach alongside. It was common knowledge that they always left from, and therefore obviously returned to, The Black Lion Hotel, Patcham.

He saw a few of the players, John and Kit Napier, one of them was the Captain. Alex Dawson, Eddie Spearitt, Nobby Lawton, Howard Wilkinson, Stewart Henderson, with Willie Bell the Coach, and George Patton the Trainer. Peter O'Sullivan was there too sitting next to Geoff Sidebottom the goalie, years later he would enjoy playing golf with the pair of them. Chairman, Mike Bamber was full of the joys of spring despite recent activities within the club.

It had only just come to light last week, that Manager, Freddie Goodwin, was in talks with Birmingham. So he was not on board. He would subsequently take the Coach and Trainer with him when he left the Club. He was replaced on the 17th June by 39 year old Pat Saward, formerly an assistant at Coventry.

At this point there was suddenly a terrible stench of rotten eggs on board. All eyes focused on The Buzz, who declared his innocence immediately, raising his hands in surrender and shaking his head in denial. Frankie, instructed Eric to open the doors so people could get some fresh air. He jumped out of the coach as well and approached the other one, carrying his intended prey. He knocked on the door and was let aboard.

He made a beeline for the two girls in question and was well chuffed to discover they were all on the same wave length. A few of the players had drunk far too much so were of no interest to either of them any more, not tonight anyway. So, the girls were up for it. Frankie was like a breath of fresh air. He waved to his coach as they passed them, and received a few mooners when passing the Missin Bus. The Nearly crew were all fast asleep from what he could make out.

It was later revealed that it was in fact young Lee Town, who had let off a stink bomb. He had bought them in the Fairground joke shop and just wanted to know if they worked. As if he hadn't caused enough attention to himself for one day. Mind you he and his brother were both promptly marched off the coach in shame, by their Dad. Then, due to all the ice-cream, candy floss, chips, barbecue food and pastries they had been stuffing in their faces all day, joined a few of the others as they spewed up alongside the Coach. Lovely.

Thank goodness there were still a few soft drinks available. Mrs Town and Miss James handed out Mint Imperials or Fox's Glacier Fruits to those who required them.

The biggest winner of the day though, was Melvyn Foster, a member of the Collins crew. He had recently spent a lovely weekend up in London with his wife Pat. After dropping a load of bills in Anglesey, they had found a right proper clue, and his end of the wedge came to fifteen hundred quid.

Celebrating in grand style, with his wife Pat. They went for afternoon tea at The Ritz, delightful. Followed by a matinee performance of Paint Your Wagon, with Lee Marvin and Clint Eastwood at the Leicester Square cinema. After a light supper, they attended a Shirley Bassey show at Ronnie Scott's in Greek Street.

Whilst there, Melvyn had bumped into a common acquaintance of his pal Bingo, none other than Mickey Blewitt. He mentioned that there were some very good Skin Divers on the market, at 12/6 apiece, and would he be interested.

"Lady Gaduivers are right up my street me old son," was the reply. Hence Melvyn had bet five pounds on every single eight to one or better horse with each and every one of the shy-locks on Tattanhum Corner that day. Knowing full well that his counterfeit currency would probably be passed on to other innocent punters in due course, this was the perfect set-up. His ship came in early when the winner of the 2:35 came in at 8-1 and he cleaned up proper. Then Frankie had steered him onto the 4:10 tip, which he went to town on. Clearing a final total of £1,080 after collecting all his ill-gotten gains.

He was a little bit perturbed when he was counting up, that he had been given back £90 in the very same dodgy notes. Still you can't have everything your own way or it wouldn't be a challenge, would it?

He did however have the last laugh when he sandwiched one between two genuine bills, when purchasing a 'Budgie Jacket', all the rage at the time. At a newly opened fashion store in Carnaby Street, he was also able to use two for his train fare of £5:40, so got his profit back in the change. Then he used the rest to purchase tickets for West End Shows from the ticket touts, it was only a bit of a laugh, but ended up very profitable.

Who said Melvyn was just a bill dropper? He picked up on all the tricks of the trade and therefore found his own clues. It should be pointed out, that the purple, orange and black combination of his jacket, was not pleasing to the critical eye.

This admittedly, did not equal Frankie's earnings for the day, but to be fair, they were in different leagues.

Eric had already been given a very healthy tip and instructed not to put up with too much aggro when back in Brighton. Just unload all the booze in the King and Queen lift facility, in the small car park, and everything else would be taken care of.

When Frankie's new mode of transport arrived back at The Black Lion in Patcham, he confidently ordered a double room and escorted the two bright young things upstairs. With that he requested Champagne and smoked salmon sandwiches to be delivered to his room, post haste. What a way to finish the day. The one problem with such an incredible day, Frankie was never to go to the Epsom Derby ever again. The memory of that day could never be surpassed, so why try?

It sure was one hell of 'A Day At The Races'.

*

24. Frankie's Story.

With such a fantastic day at The Derby still being talked about, The Buzz managed to convince Frankie into joining him at Brighton Races on Monday 15th June. Frankie checked the entry prices in The Argus, 25/- Tattersalls and Paddock, 12/6 Grand Stand, 7/6 Silver Ring and 5/- East Enclosure.

"You have got to be joking Buzz," declared Frankie, "These prices are ridiculous for crappy old Brighton."

"Don't you worry about that Frankie, once you've got the jist of my master plan, you'll soon be on board, and we will be in a position to make a right killing. I will have inside information on all the prices, before they come up, and we, my son, are gonna lay a book."

He proceeded to explain his plan. He had someone in the main office who would convey the odds from all the other meetings of the day, via teleprinter. Before any other shy-locks on the course had any idea. They would lay the odds before any others had a chance. An unheard of, five minutes before anyone else had the relevant information. Frankie agreed to give it a go, and they were set up bright and early.

The first race at Ripon was 1:35, and on cue, The Buzz, indicated the first show of odds. It was not a huge field, with nine runners. Nothing stood out, with the favourite number four at 9-2. Number three was 20-1.

Vince Nearly came straight up and had a cockle to win, the three horse, 'Twenty Tenners for Mr Nearly'. Frankie lowered the odds to 15-1. Perry Bowels, not known to gamble too often asked for a score on the nose. 'Fifteen Scores for Mr Bowels, number three'. Then Trevor Thomas stood alongside him and had a fiver on it. 'Fifteen Chings for Mr T.T. number three'. Frankie felt a tinge of doubt, so reduced the horse to 10-1, Jack Wadman strolled up and had thirty pounds to win, and before he could do any more Vince Nearly had another twenty quid, on the nose.

Frankie, now in a slight panic, indicated for The Buzz to join him. When he came alongside, Frankie pointed to number three and advised he had taken enough bets to clear them out already. "What's going on, I didn't know they had such huge bets on such huge odds, and all to win. What's all that about?"

The Buzz looked up at the chalkboard and gulped, like he'd just swallowed a golf ball,

"Oh shit," he said. Then with another huge gulp, this time it could have been a snooker ball though,

"Oh shit," he repeated, "Number three is the favourite. I didn't read it right, missed one of those silly zero's, should have been two's, sorry mate. Look at that, (pointing) it has just opened up at two to fucking one, would you Adam and Eve it, 2-1. I fink we are in a bit of hubble-bubble Frankie babe."

"Don't you fucking babe me, you sausage. How much money are you holding anyway? Don't worry about that, just give me everything you have on you. The whole fucking lot you fat twat."

"I don't see what is jolly, if you don't mind me saying," said The Buzz meekly.

"There is absolutely nothing comical, in any way shape or form my son. Now let's see how much we are going to need if and when this old nag comes in……. Sorry Sir we are not taking any more wagers on this particular race………. No sorry Sir, we are not taking any more bets………. I said, we are not taking any more poxy bets, now piss off will ya!"

The number three horse duly romped home by seven lengths. First up was Perry Bowels as he had an inkling they might not have enough to cover the bets, and collected his £320. Straight behind him was Jackie Wadman who was due £330. Then Trevor Thomas for his £80.

When Vince marched up with a big grin on his boat, he remarked, "It's funny innit, not everything comes out rosy all the time. I make it £430 boys, would you agree?"

"You are bang on the money Vince. Let me count it out for you," said Frankie.

"Nah, that's okay me old son, I trust you. It's funny how quickly you can do a bag o' sand at the races, don't you agree. I suggest you have an early day, before you do your absolute Brighton Beautiful Bollocks Boys."

A Lovely Pair of Knockers

"I think that is sound advice. Come on Buzz we're off," announced Frankie. Vince could not help himself and commented, "You're off, and I thought you woz only under starters orders lads."

As they packed up, there were a few sniggers, and he thought he heard someone say,

"That'll teach the flash little runt to steal the show at The Derby," Frankie could not help wondering whether they had been set-up or not.

This little escapade had cost them just over £1,100.

*

So it was the end of June, and Frankie Slimtone had arrived. He was now an accepted and revered member of the Brighton Knocker Boys fraternity. It had for some time now, been regarded as common knowledge that he had pulled off a really good clue. His pal Barry 'The Buzz' Bubball had also come up in the world.

He just wasn't interested in some of the things being offered to the pair of them. Many new business opportunities had become available to them. Doors they never new existed, were suddenly opening and they were being welcomed with open arms.

It was of course only due to the fact that it was widely rumoured, or at least substantiated by very reliable sources, that they were sitting on a small fortune. It didn't hurt either, that neither had revealed the true source of their good fortune.

They had eventually, after much deliberation, decided to rent a small shop in Prince Albert Street, in The Lanes obviously. It was, after all, right smack bang at the heart of all Brighton's Antique dealings during this period. Not only did all the Knocker Boys make it their first port of call when returning from a hard weeks graft knocking doors; it was also the best place to find an inexperienced punter, who would pay top dollar for a nice piece. Whether it be Birmingham, Torquay or London, they would come here to sell-up, before anything else. Also the general public were constantly window-shopping for that special piece to adorn their home.

The best part of this was that they could beckon to the shop-owner to come outside and view the goods, still tied tightly onto their vehicle. Some had vans, a few stuck with nice saloons. The preferred motor of the day was the trusted old Volvo Estate, with full-length roof rack. Plenty of room inside and on top, some racks even extended to the front of the bonnet. It just made sense; they would arrive in style like any other genuine businessmen, and then depart, once the deals were done, like the proverbial old 'Steptoe and Son'.

The transformation would always be appealing to those playing soccer in Preston Park, London Road, on a Friday afternoon. As the stream of motors, loaded up as high as ten foot at a time, would follow each other into Town, like some kind of rally for second-hand furniture merchants.

The more interior shops of The Lanes, the backstreets if you like, catered more for the Jewellery side of things. But the doors here, would also be constantly opening and closing for dealers to buy and sell all and everything they had got their hands on, that week. Most modern day Knocker Boys, are only interested in Jewellery or 'Old Unwanted Gold' as they refer to it. This of course, is mainly down to the fact, that their predecessors, have already bought every piece of furniture worth more than firewood before them.

No modern furniture, barring specially designed pieces by renowned designers, has been worth anything in the second-hand market for years. You can bet your last cherry picker that anything bought from Ikea, will only ever gather dust in the attic, and never get to be worth the kind of money that they could earn in the seventies with old pieces of furniture.

Some seventies bits do in fact have a collector interest factor, it could be said. However, surely nothing like the George II and III, Queen Anne or even Victorian period pieces that Frankie and The Buzz had encountered. Injected Plastic on a huge scale, versus 150 year old quality craftsmanship in mahogany or burr-walnut, I don't think so. But who knows?

*

A Lovely Pair of Knockers

Back to Frankie. He had of course suddenly become the 'Toast of The Town', whichever restaurant he entered, the best table would be readily available. He would be escorted to a front table with champagne on ice whenever he chose to visit Jenkinson's Cabaret Bar on the seafront, or Sherry's at the bottom of West Street. Usually, after cocktails in The Grand Hotel Piano Bar, to which he had grown fond of, and become accustomed to. There was no shortage of female company, needless to say, but so far Frankie was simply enjoying himself.

He was quite proud how his mate 'Barry The Buzz', had seemingly kept himself contained, even quiet perhaps, and himself to himself. He put this down to the calming influence of Eileen. It was more due to the fact he had developed an almost addictive habit of smoking Marijuana. From the moment he woke up, he was in a constant state of lethargy and was relatively stoned all day long. He only acted up a bit more these days at parties, when he would indulge in heavier drugs and get completely off his face.

This was much more the case behind closed doors of course. He could invite some mates round for drinks, and line up the Charlie without anyone casting aspersions. Who wanted to sneak into some grotty Pub khazi, like a common street junkie, when you had this perfectly suitable, mirrored coffee table to suit your needs?

Eileen had moved into the flat in Sussex Square, and enjoyed entertaining and clearing up. She certainly didn't have to pour pints in The Basketmakers any more. She never tried to get above her station though, and was a genteel hostess. In other words she left them to it, made the tea or coffee when required and joined in whenever it took her fancy.

*

Other interests now presented themselves. Frankie was well aware that Brighton's Knocker boys were always found to be generous, at charity or sporting events, and was keen to get in on the act.

This was most prevalent at Amateur Boxing Shows. Not only were they benefiting and supporting the local community, they thoroughly enjoyed themselves. They larged it and paid fair and square. Tables were sold in bulk and would be adorned with Bottles of Spirits, Wine, Champagne and Beer. The shows were held at venues such as The Grand Hotel, so the booze was not cheap, by any means. That was their favourite any way, held by The Bourne ABC, later to become The Silver Ring.

It was known as The Bourne ABC due to the fact that Arthur Bourne who owned Lewes Racecourse, allowed them to use an old barn as a gym. A noisy generator whirred all night to provide electricity. This unfortunately got flattened during one winter storm and was not rebuilt. They then trained outdoors down at Peter Pan's playground for a couple of years till someone persuaded the council more permanent premises were in demand.

Local Amateur Boxing Club, The Silver Ring, were rumoured to be keen to gain independence from the Missin boys. Timmy had held the position of President for some time, and nobody could deny he was a great money getter, when it came to the raffle. The main problem was though, he was thought by some, to be a bit of a bully. As he conducted the raffle and auction during the intermission, he would have consumed quite a bit of alcohol himself, naturally, and it went on for ages. Some people who fairly and squarely won a prize would be intimidated by him, and put the prize back in for auctioning. To then be taken home by the biggest cash offer once the auction had taken place.

In all due respect, Arnie Missin and his partner on the door at the time, Powders, representing The Silver Ring, were the first volunteers to actually achieve official A.B.A. recognition by completing a week-long course to qualify at A.B.A. Competency Standards.

These days you cannot even hand-up the spit bowl, without such status and official clarification by way of producing an official License. Back in them days, any Tom, Dick or Harry could have a go. But these two had done the course and gained appropriate certification as Coaches.

They had taken a whole week off work to do it as well, so should be duly recognised and commended for their honest, wholehearted and genuine commitment.

A Lovely Pair of Knockers

It was held at a sports complex called Nash Court, on the outskirts of Birmingham. The English National Squad were there on a training camp, Kevin Hickey was in charge at the time. Supported by the likes of Ian Irwin, from up North who would later take charge, and Alan Sanigar of Plymouth. Right Good company.

The unaware, Father to be of my two children, Steve Martin, was also there, enjoying a weeklong holiday, as one of the much needed students of the fine art of pugilism, or better referred to as the Science of Boxing. You can only learn to be a trainer, when you have kids to train. He along with his mate, Michael McCullough, also of The Silver Ring A.B.C. Brighton, stationed up at the racecourse in those days, travelled up with them both in Arnie's Mercedes. There were also some other hopeful young boxers from neighbouring Newhaven A.B.C.

Only Stevie Martin would go on to represent England on multiple occasions, having more Amateur International fights than any other Brighton born and bred Boxer. He was even England Captain on one trip to Hungary, and his pal Lance Wheeler boxed alongside him.

Steve once told me that upon their return it was the only time he had ever been met at the airport. Lance's Mum and Dad, Betty and Derek were there with family friend Ricky 'Ginger' Thomson.

Frankie had attended one of the shows at The Grand Hotel. Vince Nearly attempted to cadge the 'Best Fight of The Night', privilege. He could then choose his favourite match and award the two relevant fighters and present the trophies. He had offered £100, but Frankie topped him up and took £150 out of his pocket to take the honour.

It was common knowledge that Perry Bowels had first pledged his allegiance to the Club and offered £40 for the two extravagant trophies, commissioned from a trophy shop based in Sydenham, Kent. Pat Toope of Redhill would take over later, he was attached to the Rosehill ABC. This was an extremely generous gesture, once it was known how much he donated, it was easy to get tenners and scores from other sponsors and so the Club earned a decent profit on the trophies alone.

By the same token, not to be forgotten when you are starting up, a generous monetary benefactor such as this, should not be taken lightly. In 1972, their first show at The Grand, £40 was the equivalent of a decent Bricklayer's weekly wage at the time.

Competition Secretary and stalwart of the Club, Alan Martin refused both offers, and advised that Perry Bowels had done it from day one and would continue to do so, for as long as he wished, money was not the issue. Loyalty and respect won the day. Perry went on to honour this commitment, for all the time the Club continued to stage events. Not always did Brighton's Knocker Boys run the show.

The Silver Ring gained a good reputation by adopting this attitude, and went on to become renowned for awarding the best prizes for Club Shows, and fantastic refreshments for the Boxers and Trainers afterwards. Rather than a sandwich or burger, they got to sit down to a Grand Buffet style meal, with Grand Hotel Silverware, and all the trimmings.

The cakes and pastries never lasted long enough to be available for the last few boxers, they were just too nice. This in turn assured top Clubs and their Boxers were always willing to travel and make themselves available. The quality of Boxing was raised in standard and now on show in Brighton, and as a result, the standard of Boxing and local fighters went up with it.

*

` Frankie now also had an account with Jack Ellis a local Bookmaker. Jack had an office in Kensington Gardens, handy for those in the Pub. He was the first bookie to actually take bets over the phone and had a friendly team available, during working hours.

Of course this was many years before mobile phones.

Many of the boys would prefer to remain at home on a Saturday afternoon, in the comfort of their own sitting room. Tea and cake readily available and it kept the wives happy into the bargain. Away at work all week, and Friday night out with the boys, Saturday morning at the market, they couldn't have it all their own way. Spending all afternoon in a smoke filled Betting Shop, did not appeal to all of them. It also gained brownie points with the missus. The big losers on Saturday afternoons would be the kid watching telly with his Dad, constantly up and down changing from BBC to ITV for the different race meetings. Pre remote control days of course.

*

It took Frankie a while to work out why he was now being asked or contacted, then taken to one side at one of the drinking Clubs from time to time, and invited to go on a call. The penny finally dropped after one such occasion.

Giles Capshaw, approached him one Thursday in The Esquire Club, over a game of pool. Advising that he and Murphy McCuigan had 'found one' in a little Village up in Norfolk. They swore the place was polluted, but had no joy in getting through the door. Bubbles was asking for far too much of a cut for them to consider his services, so would he give it a go? Frankie had felt honoured. He had only heard of this course of action being resorted to, once plenty of others had tried. Vince Nearly was well known to be able to 'get in', where no-one else could, so he readily agreed.

Off they went the following Monday morning, and arrived at their chosen Hotel in Norwich, The Laughing Cavalier. They had checked in and Frankie fancied a swift half. Whilst enjoying this, he won fifty quid on the fruit machine, much to the chagrin of one of the locals, who claimed he had filled the machine up and now this southern twat had taken all his money. Frankie sneered in his direction unperturbed, and informed him that he was indeed a paying guest, so suck it up Farmer Boy.

He then proceeded to pay the Hotel Bill in coinage.

"That's the expenses sorted out lads, now let's have a look at this drum," then without so much as batting an eyelid, "Let's not worry about that dinlo carrot cruncher. Oh I must say, it's good to be back on the road again."

They drove the forty miles up to Hunstanton and they showed him the mid-terraced old fisherman's cottage right on the coast.

"What can they possibly have in that crappy little shithole?" Was his first comment. Giles informed him that the whole row of four cottages belonged to the same couple, and they were getting on a bit, and with no apparent heirs, looming in the shadows.

"Okay," announced Frankie, "Here we go then," his two associates were both astounded.

"Ain't you gonna make a plan or something then Frankie," asked Murphy, "Or at least ask us what we think is inside?"

"Well, surely it's quite obvious Murph, there's gonna be a shit load of fishing gear for starters. Do you really think I just came up here for the ride? I have it on good authority that this little bit of coastline, was rampant with smugglers years ago. See that?"

The Light Yellow Ford Granada Mk 1, they had driven up in, was facing the sea, so pointing to the bay towards their left, he gesticulated with the always reliable 'old pointy finger'.

"That there is called 'The Wash'. Now, the strong hidden undercurrent lying beneath the waves in these treacherous waters infamously drew in merchant ships, to be dashed upon the rocks. The nearest lighthouse is thirty five miles away in that direction, (pointing right) at another little village along this coast called Cromer."

"Now, that was of course many years ago. I would bet my brand new Rolls Royce, that these two, and their ancestors before them, have been Treasure Hunters, all their lives. Picked up plenty of untold riches, tax free of course, over the years, that have simply just washed up on the beach right in front of their very own little home."

They both stared at him in disbelief, how could he have possibly found out so much in such a short time. It was simple really, a quick call to a couple of other knocker boys who had worked the area, revealed that this was an old wives' tale.

Except in this case, one with substance.

The couple in question were semi-hermits, and only came out at night. They would have a few drinks in the Jolly Boatman, the Village Pub, then scour the beach with torches. They did also have a motorbike and sidecar, for the weekly trip to market. Where, not only did they do their shopping, but also attended the auctions, where they always collected money for goods, tendered the week before. They were very well known in fact, but kept themselves to themselves. Someone also mentioned, probably one of the Widdy Brothers, that they did also have an Irish Wolfhound, that was not to be taken

A Lovely Pair of Knockers

lightly. As no-one had ever gained entry, who knows what the reaction would be, or How the Hound would react? This was then followed by a mock howling, mimicking a werewolf.

"Charmed I'm sure," was Frankie's reply.

Always get as much information as you can, had been ingrained into him by another of his trusted mentors, a chap known as Bingo. Someone else with a bit of inside information had been Michael Lee, who had worked the area with Murphy before. Whilst having a drink in The Montpelier with him, somehow the subject of East Anglia came up. Michael happened to mention that they had actually decided to stake out some joint once, near 'The Wash', a group of cottages it was. The only visitor though, all day long, was an elderly fellow who tapped the door, waited thirty seconds and was then handed a few newspapers.

Michael was not a shy chap. so had investigated further. Striking up a conversation with Mitch, the chap he had witnessed knocking their door, in the Jolly Boatman, he discovered some interesting and possibly useful information.

It appertained that the 'Couple in The Cottages', as they were to become known, had no T.V. but kept up with what was happening in the world by ritually reading three newspapers apiece everyday, delivered at a very early hour. They were finished by 11:30 am, so Mitch collected them and delivered the 'fresh enough papers' and shared the spoils with the rest of the Pub. This saved the landlord a pretty penny over the course of a year, so Mitch benefited by a complimentary pint every now and again. Michael also confirmed, as far as he could tell, there was not a dustbin lid in sight.

"If you don't mind me saying Murphy. I also have it on a reasonably good authority that they are known as Mr and Mrs Crown. Some more sound information, confirmation, that you and some other slippery associates have been up here sniffing around this manor before. That means you could quite easily have given me most of this information yourself. So why didn't you? But let's not worry about that for now, eh?"

Murphy looked a bit indignant, once this was revealed, but chose wisely not to deny any of it. Instead he changed tack and remarked to Frankie,

"Since when did you have a roller anyway?"

"Not right at the moment, but after this little bit of work, my order will be placed, matey. Don't you worry yourself about that me old cocker sparrer."

With that, he then left the pair of them sitting dumbstruck in their seats and slammed the door, behind him. What followed is historically regarded as Brighton Knocker Boy legend.

Frankie, marched straight up to what was deemed as the front door, and gave a sharp rapid jingly knock. Indicating a friendly caller. The man who came to the door sounded a bit shaky and infirm. Enquiring as to the nature of the call at this untimely moment, with no appointment.

"Well if you just let me in for a moment I can explain everything. Mr Thomas Crown I presume? It's rather awkward talking through such an imposing lump of wood. Won't you please let me in? I mean no harm, and I fear you may be the only person that can help me in my hour of need. I am in dire straits, and have been warned that my plight may be in the hands of the Master or Mistress of this abode."

"If the matter cannot be resolved in the very near future, I fear my dear younger brother may well be cast off to Australia, with many other orphans and unfortunate unwanted children. Never to be seen again. Please Sir, I beg of you, at least hear of my predicament," the desperation in Frankie's tone did the trick.

The door creaked open slowly; the bearded man squinted at the bright summer sunshine outside, and put his arm over his eyes.

"Well you had best come in for a minute or so young man. But I can't imagine how I, or my wife could possibly be of any use to you."

The old man, although he was only in fact 62, turned as Frankie entered. Then beckoned with his finger for Frankie to follow, as he trudged slowly to the back parlour. There was no sign of the dog, to Frankie's relief, but he would soon meet the animal, but for the time being, it was safely chained up in the back yard.

Giles Capshaw and Murphy, staring wide eyed at each other in disbelief, were left speechless and incoherent for the second time in twenty minutes, as Frankie disappeared into the property.

He was in there for forty-five minutes. As he left, the old lady that had opened the door to let him out, paused momentarily, stood on her tiptoes and allowed him to bend down and kiss her whiskery cheek. There was a faint farewell in the background from her husband, to which Frankie waved lovingly, blowing a kiss as he walked towards the motor.

Neither of the two guys sitting in the front uttered a word, so Frankie instructed, to both of their amazement,

"Well, it's no point having the wheels of the Fucking Flying Squad at your mercy and not taking advantage. Come on Murphy, let's go and freshen up and get some dinner down us. Let's go boys". Then he mimicked the popular TV programme of the time, The Sweeney, da-daadaa, da-daadaa. Da daa, da daa, dada, dada, da, da da.

They both turned at the same time and demanded what on earth had just occurred.

"Don't you worry boys, all will soon be revealed. Tomorrow I will show you both how I go about my business. Fresh blood. That's what this knocker game needs, fresh blood. Welcome to the Frankie Slimtone Bank of Fresh Blood fellahs. You are gonna love what I have to tell you both. So, where are we having something to eat tonight? I fancy a bit of Chinese, do you know any nice Restaurants near The Hotel? We will all be Laughing Cavaliers tonight Murphy, mark my words."

They both tried to squeeze the tiniest of clues or even the unworthiest detail of the recent meeting, out of him. Frankie was not to be swayed, and remained adamant that it would all be worth waiting for.

Murphy attempted just once more to squeeze some information from him, asking desperately,

"Come on give us a clue", Frankie completely blanked him. So Murphy getting tetchy, shouted at him, in a non-appreciated aggressive tone, "Are you fucking deaf or something?"

Frankie had had enough and screamed at the top of his voice, "If I was fucking deaf my son, there would be not be any point in shouting now, would there? You saucy little bastard. Now shut the fuck up and get us back to the Cavalier, I'm Hank Marvin".

Then in a much calmer tone, added,

"Just be patient chaps, it all comes to those who wait."

They tried telling him not to count his chickens, not get too cocky, and why didn't he at least try and 'get a couple of bits and pieces out'. But he was having none of it.

He was now fully aware of the superior control he had over the situation. This was now his call. They would cop handsomely of course. But he, Frankie, would be gaining more kudos from another call, and getting the credit for cracking another tough nut, and getting through another, never before opened door.

They met in the Hotel Bar at 6:15 pm as arranged and each had a pint of the local Real Ale. Murphy advised the Chinese a mile or so up the road was always reliable, and their sizzling platter of steak with black bean sauce was the best he'd ever had. Round the corner and up the road was their destination, but if they fancied a few beers first there were a nice couple of boozers on the way. This was confirmed as the plan of attack, but first Giles and Murphy wanted a quick heads up on the capers of earlier in the day.

"Well," began Frankie, "Without going into the nitty-gritty, and needing to know the inside leg measurements of the mark, let me explain."

His two new partners were all ears.

"I did a little bit of research before we set off. Realised that this call was hardly covered under the Official Secrets Act, and managed to get some critical yet crucial information, that I set in motion on the spur of the moment. The way I work, you can't have a contingency plan that must be followed strictly to the letter of the law. If you have just the one angle, if that doesn't work out, you're cattled right from the start."

"But you only said 'Hello', you prat. How can you say that, and expect us to swallow it? I spent twenty minutes on that doorstep a couple of years ago, and a couple of times since I haven't got a word in. A few others have given it a go also, admittedly. I apologise here and now for not giving you the heads up, but I didn't wanna confuse the issue, with too much history on the joint. Giles had a good quarter of an hour last week, on that very same doorstep, obviously he had no joy. It's like Fort Knox in there." Murphy, stated in an exasperated fashion, that brought a dark crimson glow to his cheeks, almost spluttering,

"That was when we decided to give you a pop at it," he was obviously now getting quite wound up. But Giles was a smooth operator and calmed him down before anything was said that might be regretted later. Frankie merely rose to the bait, explaining how he had heard about the Newspaper scenario. He was also an avid reader of the Daily Papers, that's why he preferred to work with people who didn't mind doing all the driving.

He began to explain, in an educated tone of voice,

"There has been a lot of hoo-ha lately in the press, about young kids being separated from families and getting shipped off to Australia. The Ten Pound Poms, exodus is in full swing. Any spare kids that could tag along with newly married couples, yet to have children of their own, had been encouraged to do something that resembled 'A Mock Adoption'."

"There has been a lot of speculation, and much objection to this process, even mentioned briefly in Parliament. Still, as yet, nobody has completely committed themselves to curtail this terrible behaviour and seemingly illegal method, of not only reducing children in care, but also helping to boost the population of Australia. Nobody was prepared to take any responsibility for what appeared to be an atrocity on British soil. The bulk of these cases could be linked back to South Australia. Adelaide mostly."

"A lot of the children have, it appears, been abandoned once on the other side of the world, and been taken in by monks or church-based charities. These kids are certainly not getting the opportunity to start a brave new life, as advertised. The ones that stayed with their adoptive families, it seems, are being treated no better than cheap labourers."

"Or in the worst instances, playthings for the men who are working on the Farm or Ranch. It is generally accepted that the Men of Australia have little time for romance. 'Any Sheila Will Do', was hardly a term designed to cause a flutter in the heart of any young girl just arrived off the boat. And that's it in a nutshell really." He finished it off with a smirky grin that made Murphy's blood boil.

"What the fuck? Has any of that old bollocks, got to do wiv trying to get two silly old gits on the Norfolk Coast of England, to open their front bloody door, to some silly little prat from Brighton?" Demanded Murphy, who was now nearing the end of his tether.

"Well if you just calm down and let me explain, all will be revealed. It's your round Murphy innit?"

"I'll bleedin' well swing for you in a minute if you don't stop playing silly buggers Frankie boy. I don't know what the world's coming to. Anyway, what'll you have? It's thirsty work listening to you and your ridiculous tales of poor Australian bloody orphans."

"They're English. Not Australians yet, they haven't had the operation. Have they?"

"What operation?" He could not help himself asking.

"The one where they have to have a piece of their brain removed, of course."

Saying to himself, 'Now I've got it'. Murphy had finally seen the light, and come to the conclusion that Frankie was playing him and Giles at his own funny, self-amusing little game, seeing the comical side of it.

This young Frankie was at it 24/7. Trying to get everyone under his spell, and leading them on. At this point, however, he was more than willing to listen and ready to learn whatever this kid was about to teach them. This game was not restricted for just one person to know it all. So learn whatever, whenever you got the opportunity. You would never know when similar tactics would apply to another clue. Then he would not have to request the services of such characters as Vince Nearly and young Frankie here.

Returning with the drinks, Murphy smiled and said,

"Well then, let's be having you Frankie, how on God's green earth did you manage to get in so easily? Please, please, put me out of my misery so we can go and enjoy a nice bit of scran. Whaddayasay?"

Frankie began to explain in earnest, so they listened, intending not to interfere. He had decided on the spur of the moment to tweak at their curiosity. Armed with the knowledge that they had most definitely, 100%, heard of the 'Mock Adopters' scandal. How would the intrigue of his dire consequences, or their curiosity react, to the fact that, unbeknown to themselves till this very moment, they may have some distant relative involved in it all?

See for yourself as an outside neutral observer, what happens next.

His opening gambit had been about how he had been searching for months for a man, believed to be his father. Who originated from the Hunstanton area, but had disgraced the family and been banished. The unfortunate mother had died in childbirth with the second child they had conceived.

There was a considerable period of time between the two boys, and this was presumed to be because of the man going away to sea. He, Dominic, as he referred to himself, once reaching a certain age had been given papers by the orphanage upon his departure. These indicated his younger brother was also given up for adoption, but at a different similar charitable trust.

He had at first, been under the impression this all hailed from Hucknall, on the outskirts of Nottingham. Then, as he had spent years in the West Country, he had searched fruitlessly in Wincanton. Not having any joy in either area he had scanned the maps of Britain for some clue as to where he had actually come from. In his last final hope of finding some answer to his prayers, he had come to the conclusion it must be Hunstanton.

A lot of the documents in his possession, he had in fact taken without permission, but felt no guilt for this. Growing up as he had, there were times when you made choices, that under different circumstances, you may not have made. A lot of the paperwork had also suffered water damage and addresses were not legible, hence the uncertainty of it's origin.
Some began with Hun....... and others ending ....anton.

He added that a lot of his research had been done at Somerset House in London, but it all lead back to Hunstanton. From what he could ascertain, this very row of cottages, known locally as 'The Last Wash Cottages'.

Various teachers and administrators had vague and distant memories of his arrival. Yet, they all agreed, after persistent questioning, that the chubby little fellow arriving eight years later was from the same unfortunate source and circumstance. He had pieced together all the relevant discoveries and purely by chance, traced his brother recently to an orphanage in Southampton.

The very same port that all those poor orphans were being cast off from, to who knows where and to what disgraceful fate? His brother had somehow received, against all the odds, some of his attempts at communication, by letter, telegrams and even a lucky phone call one day. This had been a bit extrovert on his part admittedly, but if you are taking a liberty it may as well be a blindin' one.

He had somehow attained information that the man responsible for him and his lost brother, was highly likely to originate from Hunstanton. Cast away in shame, many years ago, from all of his family for all eternity.

All very dramatic stuff. Especially in the way it was being conveyed, by such a poor young innocent chap.

Did they, or could they have any recollection, of a cousin, brother or uncle that had suffered such treatment from his own flesh and blood?

Of course he explained, and promised on his oath, that he would never tell a single soul of the scandal. As long as they could or would find it in their heart to help him save his only living relative.

Then of course it dawned on all of them, in a moment of clarity. If his information was correct, that they too were all related. Once all this gathered information could be confirmed by the local authorities, a whole new family could rightfully be reborn, and brought back together.

All these unexpected revelations had taken the pair completely in. He then allowed the Crown's to reveal their take on the situation. They both had vague recollections of such an Uncle being told to leave the family home. At the time all four cottages were lived in. The oldest inhabitant was Granddad Alf but when he passed away thirteen years ago, the family fell apart. As with most families there is usually one steadfast member that keeps them all together. Once he went, that was it.

The photo albums came out, and there was definitely a strong resemblance between Dominic and great Uncle Albert. He had been a Fishing Boat Captain, but alas lost at sea. Then turned up ten years

A Lovely Pair of Knockers

later claiming that his boat had been boarded by Pirates and the whole crew had been slain, right before his very own eyes.

"Marched straight off to the fonny faarm, he woz," informed Thomas, then "More tea, young Dominic?"

"Oh thank-you sir, you are so kind," in a meek and humble fashion.

"Fetch the poor lad some more tea then please Hilary, and let's have some of those Garibaldi's too, if you loik moy lov?"

She replied in a loving manner,

"We certainly are pushing the boat out today. Our first guest in ten years and the Great Garibaldi's out in the same day, what am I to say?"

"Ooh, hark at her," said Dom, "She's a poet and don't even know it."

"Oy tink oy moyt even 'av a smook on me poyp," announced Thomas.

"Nice accent there Mr T, nice accent," complimented his guest.

They then passed on the grave news that the man he thought may be his Father, Uncle Albert, had been certified insane. To add insult to injury, the medication prescribed him at the Asylum had initiated terrible side effects. He had therefore suffered a major and sub sequentially fatal heart attack and it was in fact four years ago that he had died. They had not even been able to attend the funeral, as he was cremated by the authorities, and were only informed of what had transpired, two months after the event. What could they do?

Any hopes of Dominic being able to save his brother seemed to be dwindling rapidly. He was devastated at this news, and broke down like a lost soul in uncontrollable tears, right before their very eyes.

"We are so sorry Dominic," said Hilary, "But alas there is nothing to be done." They both tried to console this poor wretch, who had come to them under such desperate, yet hopeful circumstances. Thomas suggested that he introduce Dom to, Horatio, their dog who resided outside in the yard. He felt it might bring some comfort, and he needed a brief moment to discuss something with his wife.

With a slight hint of trepidation, Dominic was introduced to Horatio, who was as friendly as you like. Frankie accepted the good natured intentions with gratitude, in a most sombre and surrendering mood. Worthy of an Oscar nomination, the whole pitiful scenario.

Then, when they asked him to come back inside, there was a more positive aura about the pair. They enquired as to the requirements of someone who wished to take responsibility for a child destined for this terrible fate. What they regarded as tantamount to modern day deportation to the New World.

He advised that his understanding was that he would at the very least be required to provide a safe and reliable home of a secure nature. With no outstanding debts or monetary responsibilities. He would also need to prove a regular income or substantial financial stability with which to support both himself and younger Brother. This at the present time was impossible, and hence the reason for his search of some living relative prepared to take this responsibility on, or at least help in some way.

They beckoned Dominic to follow them to another room. The spectacular sight of items stored here were absolutely breathtaking. Thomas indicated towards a large chest, sitting next to a wardrobe against the wall. Dominic ventured nearer and as he did so Hilary lifted the lid to reveal what could only be regarded as incredible. It was filled with what looked like precious gemstones, set in gold bracelets, necklaces and earrings.

They had a certain dull glow, which meant they could maybe do with a decent clean. It was also a sure sign that it was all genuinely of a high quality. Imitation gems were always sparkly and glassy, to the trained eye all this looked pukkah, but young Dominic simply looked questioningly at the pair. Asking:

"But what has any of this to do with my predicament?"

Hilary explained, "We would like you to take some of these rare gem stones, with our blessing, and go get your brother. We think that some of the larger stones could be worth quite a lot of money, and hope that in some way we can be of help to you both." "I don't know what to say. How could I possibly accept such a gift? It is not possible, sorry, I cannot do it. You don't even know me, how could you make such a ridiculous gesture?" replied the astonished Dominic.

"Well we have discussed the matter, and decided that as there are no other family members known to us. They have all deserted

A Lovely Pair of Knockers

what we regard as the family home, so why not make use of the possessions left under our care."

"We will not live forever, and we will gain comfort by helping you, in your hour of need. There are a couple of young lads that store some stuff here in the Cottages but we haven't seen them for years now. They may never return. We realise you cannot take all this with you today, but if you can return tomorrow, at just after 11:30, when our friend and regular visitor Mitch has come and gone. Would it be possible for you to arrange the means of transportation? We are confident you will find a way. We will have sorted out for you what we would like to think, enough goodies to sort out all your problems. We would have only one request."

"Anything, absolutely anything whatsoever. What might I ask is your request?"

"That should you be successful in your quest, you come back and visit us. The pair of you, when you are re-united."

"You have my word of honour, I promise," he assured them. "I shall return exactly as you request. Of that you can be sure."

With that he bade them farewell and looked forward to visiting them next day. When he had finished revealing all this to his two pals, Murphy just looked at him with utter disgust.

"Do you think that they are really going to stand for that crock of old shit, you must be absolutely crazy or just simply off your rocker, Jesus H fucking Christ?"

"Stand for it Murph, they already have my son. They already jolly well have. They have swallowed it whole, so now let's go and swallow something ourselves. So can we please go and sample some of that Chinese food you have been raving on about all week."

Murphy continued expressing his utter disbelief,

"Incredible, un-remarka-fubball. I have never heard of such a load of old crap in all my born days. What do you make of all this Giles? Come on be honest, do you believe a single solitary word or what?"

"Well," answered Giles, "If Frankie thinks he can pull it off, I reckon we should go along with it. What have we got to lose?"

"Unbelievable. Fucking unbelievable," was all Murphy could bring himself to say, shaking his head in pure disgust.

They arrived at the New Lotus and proceeded to enjoy a lovely dinner. Frankie had gone for the King Prawns Sizzler Plate in Black Bean Sauce and complimented Murphy on his recommendation. Giles had Sweet and Sour Pork Balls and Murphy stuck with the Steak Sizzler. They enjoyed a few Singha beers with the meal and were all totally satisfied. Banana Fritters and ice-cream were accompanied by Irish Coffees.

The walk back saw Murphy in a slightly more optimistic mood, and he even congratulated Frankie on his pure genius. He was still a bit dubious, but then he was a man of constant doubt on most subjects. His glass was always regarded as half-empty, whilst Frankie regarded his as half-full. It was just the way they were.

Still, all would be resolved in the morning. A couple of nightcaps in The Hotel Bar, ensured they all had a comfortable nights sleep.

They had a pleasant English Breakfast together at 8:30, and decided to check out, so they could drive straight home after the morning's appointment. Murphy was now back to his old self and in a pessimistic mood once again. Giles told Frankie to pay no heed, he at least had confidence that Frankie was on a winner. They arrived in plenty of time.

After observing Mitch stop to pick up the papers, Frankie told the pair to wish him luck, and approached the Cottages. Murphy could not help himself, sighing heavily and tut-tutting, then remarking sarcastically, "Absolute waste of time all this. No sodding chance whatsoever. Them two are going to completely forget what happened yesterday. I'll be surprised if they even let him in."

"For God's sake," said Giles, "Anyone would think, you didn't want him to get in, the way you're carrying on. Whassamatter wiv ya? Cheer up for Pete's sake."

"Sorry," said Murphy glumly.

The reception he received when knocking on the door, astounded even Frankie. Thomas and Hilary had been up late, washing the jewellery in soapy water, and they had done an excellent job. He guessed that his first assumption of the gems being of high quality was correct. He felt a compelling need to get in and get out, as quick as possible. But knew full well that this was not the best ploy. Play it cool he coached himself.

To all intents and purposes, they did not have very much to say either. They had the obligatory cup of tea of course, with Dominic declining toast. Then Thomas mentioned that there was another article in The Daily Mail, on the 'Aussie Orphans Going Down Under'. It was more about some young female politician, really, than the actual subject at hand. Margaret Thatcher, of the Conservative Party, brought it to the attention of the House that she would soon be championing the issue.

"And, anyone that standing in her way, should be wary. This woman is not for turning, or something."

He confirmed that he would get in touch with them as soon as he had any news. They reiterated that he had both their blessings, and looked forward to his glorious return. No receipts were requested or offered. They all studied the chest of jewellery, so then Henry simply asked how much he would actually require.

"Well, I may as well take the lot really. I can always return any jewels that are not required, can't I?" Was the obvious reply to such an open request.

Hilary offered the use of an old suitcase, along with a small vanity case, to transfer the extra pieces of jewellery into for ease of transportation.

"Before you go Dominic moy boy," said Thomas.

Here we go thought Frankie.

"Oy wood jost loik to show you moy little collection of bosts, wot do you think of these?"

Opening another connecting door he revealed a small room, decked out floor to ceiling, with shelves adorned with many busts of what appeared at first glance to be Navy personnel.

"Very nice, very nice indeed," said Frankie, "What a nice collection, I bet you are very proud of that lot, Mr Crown."

"Oy am for sure, young Dominic, but if you found yourself short, please remember these, as they may have some value if requoired. Just in case, just in case."

"Very well, I shall bear it in mind." Immediately thinking of Abdul at Alexander Antiques, who had a shop in Hanover Place at the bottom of Elm Grove. Always had a good eye for such things.

Frankie added that he had a friend who collected busts and may well be interested in offering decent money for such a nice collection.

"Foin, foin, you jost be getting along and we sholl see you soon, take care moy lovly."

With that Frankie said cheerio to the pair of them and departed with smiles all round, telling them that he had a local driver waiting around the corner.

When he walked around the corner with the brown leather suitcase and small pink leather vanity case, he was actually impressed by the reception he received. He had anticipated snorts and derision, but there was a serene expectancy. Respect, even.

Giles obviously mentioned that he never doubted it for a minute and Murphy held his hands up in total surrender. He even resorted to waving his white hankie in Frankie's direction.

When he mentioned that it was all probably just costume jewellery anyway, the pair of them gave him such a menacing glare that he literally shrunk visibly into his seat.

Once safely deposited into the boot, off they went. It had been a bit panicky for Murphy, what with the sudden arrival of the successful outcome of the visit, he still managed to get a negative quip in:

"Cor blimey, I didn't think you would be so quick. I was going to pop in the Pub and have a drink wiv Mitch."

"You are without a shadow of doubt welcome to my son," replied Frankie, "Drop him off right now Giles, and we'll see you next Tuesday, you melt." They all laughed together, at this appropriate gesture.

It was a good few minutes before anyone spoke, but Giles could contain himself no longer, and eventually broke the ice with:

"Do you seriously think? No, really Frankie, I'm being honest with you now. That all of that gear is really actually on the money? Come on now, be honest? It can't surely, all be top jolly. Can it?"

"Course it can Alice."

"Who the fuck is Alice?" chimed in Murphy.

*

They made their way back towards Norwich.

"Tell you what," advised Frankie, "Let's go back through King's Lynn, I have a pal in Wisbech. We can stop there for a bit of lunch and then have a good gander at this gear. Then through The Fens, and down to Cambridge. I know a decent bloke there who would be seriously interested in having a go at this little lot."

"Don't you worry about that Frankie Boy," came in Giles, "Whilst Murphy may not have been as confident as myself. Nevertheless, we both reckon that a mutual friend who has a Shop in Camden Passage, Islington, is definitely the right buyer of the stuff we have on board. Then no-one has to know exactly how much we have copped for. When we get back home. Whaddayareckon?"

"That sounds okay to me. Let's go," agreed Frankie.

They had a very quiet lunch in Wisbech. Due to the fact they had already scanned over the haul. Giles and Murphy had never experienced such a vast amount of high end, and obviously quite ancient and unbelievably oversized range of precious gemstones.

They were both basically in a state of shock. Frankie's pal, Mr Lee, in Wisbech, well he just let them use his little bit of private land to go over the gear without any prying eyes. His reward would come years later when Frankie would help to sponsor his son Simon, with his Amateur Boxing career.

Murphy in his defence would eventually declare that he was completely flabbergasted. He also felt that this haul should in fact be split up. Some of the gems would need to be separated from their present home.

"Split the lot up. Carve it right up the middle I reckon. Let's at least get a nice few quid, and not be greedy," was his rationale.

This of course sent Frankie down a completely different track of thought,

"That is most certainly not the road we are going down on this job mate," came back Frankie. "Now I know I may not be as experienced as you couple of 'old timers', but you are not going to persuade me to accept anything other than what this little lot is truly worth. If you two wanna take a quarter share, then that's fine by me, but I want exactly what I think I've got coming. I am not saying I want more than you, and I don't wanna get into an argument. But some of that stuff could be worth an absolute   fortune, and I am not about to start giving it all away."

Another little song title slipped in under the carpet, but by Who?

Under protest, Murphy succumbed. The fellah in Camden Passage, was straight-up about the goods concerned, which gave Frankie even more confidence. He could only take on the smaller pieces. He did, however, have a pal up in Hatton Garden who had an Uncle, who had a cousin, who's Father could well come up with the sort of readies that some of the bigger bits should command.

We are talking about ten and twenty carat sapphires here. Individual stones that is. Very few pieces were without diamonds. These though were only one and two carats each, in between the dark blue beautiful gems, it was truly a spectacle to behold.

There were also four identical bracelets, each adorned with five three carat Emeralds, with alternate two half carat Sapphires, Rubies and Diamonds. Even Murphy admitted it would be nothing short of high treason to break these pieces up.

Some of the necklaces had up to sixty gemstones incorporated in them, the eighteen and twenty four carat gold, connecting them altogether, would surely come to a nice few quid. But they must be sure to keep their cool.

It would in fact take nearly three weeks before they carved up the money satisfactorily between them. The final tally has never actually been confirmed by all the concerned parties.

Frankie did indeed though, make a one-off payment, to a company named Rolls-Royce. Using around about one-third of his share from the Thomas Crown affair. Ordering one of the very first Two Door Corniche models that he had been enquiring about recently. He'd gone for a delicate light shade of Blue, with Navy hood, that came to £24,650 with all the extras.

The Navy leather seats with pale blue piping and burr-walnut dashboard, that you could see your face in, was very impressive. He took delivery in July 1971, and was proudly driven to the Glorious Goodwood meeting in it by his old pal Gerry Powell. The Taxi Driver was more than happy to drive the Roller from time to time, instead of the Cab, and earn the same money but without any of the aggro. Giles Capshaw and Murphy McCuigan accompanied him on the first day, and they all enjoyed Silver Service Dining in The Member's Enclosure.

Did they back any winners? They could not recall, when asked.

*

Frankie had decided at this time to look after his parents, at least that was his intention anyway. Without their knowledge. He bought a nice little bungalow in Patcham, for their impending retirement. He picked them up in a Taxi, and advised that he had lunch booked to celebrate their Wedding Anniversary. A table was reserved at The Black Lion Hotel. He devised a little scenario, that he had to pick up a friend, and invited them up a quaint pathway.

This was Ladies Mile Road. As he led the way he chucked a set of keys to his Dad saying:

"All yours Dad, you won't be needing that allotment of yours any more."

It did not have the desired effect. His Mum turned a delicate shade of purple and went as silent as a church mouse. His Dad just threw them back at him, practically barking,

"What the bloody hell do we wanna live all the way out here in the sticks for? Sandwiched between next to God knows who? And right next door to a poxy all Girls school. Margaret and Hard Ups, they call that place. Your Mother will go out of her tiny mind, and it'll take me ages to get to the Pub on a Sunday lunchtime."

Frankie in the moment was devastated; the anti-climax was hard to accept. He had bought it for cash at auction, for five grand, so there was no turning back on the deal.

They still went for the meal but his attempts to convince them they could be happy out here in the developing area of Patcham, were in vain. His reasoning fell on deaf ears, they were just not interested and having none of it.

The subject never came up again, except at other family gatherings when his Dad would point out sarcastically that he hoped his one and only would not be making any more over the top and unnecessary grand gestures, and embarrass his poor mother.

He proceeded to furnish the bungalow in a reasonably modern fashion, and left it with an Estate Agent to rent out. A separate Building Society account was duly opened, for rent deposits to be made by the Agent or tenant, and he shrugged his shoulders and forgot about it. Years later after being advised that the place needed refurbishing to achieve a better yield. He invested a few quid in it and had a sudden fondness for the place. From time to time Frankie shacked up there himself, but the property had no great sentimental ties.

*

So there he was, all set and sitting quite flush. He and 'The Buzz' had equally lost interest in the Lanes situation. Neither of them qualified when it came to the desired responsibility of opening and closing a premises every single day. The deciding factor of course being, that neither had the desire to work, every single day. They certainly didn't entertain the idea of going on the road and knocking doors again in the near future.

Frankie felt, in his heart of hearts, that his new found wealth entitled him to broaden his horizons. He was now qualified to branch out into other fields and secure his future. After all, the Knocker Game couldn't last forever.

He had been introduced to a few faces from London by now, some sweet, some savoury. The more unsavoury types were now settling in Spain these days, not for the weather, but to avoid another type of heat. He had joined a couple of Gentlemen's Clubs, and frequented some of London's better Restaurants. He though, for the life of him, could still not fathom how sniffing a bottle of French Wine, indicating with a smirk, that it was favourable, could suddenly demand the price tag of a decent Greyhound.

He had been introduced to a Tailor in Saville Row, during a lunch in a little back street behind Regent Street. The ensuing appointments for measuring, fitting and final fittings, drove him to despair. He paid without protesting the ridiculous fee involved, but felt that he had been mugged right off. Swearing not to bother with all the pomp and false pretence ever again. When he mentioned this unfortunate experience, whilst visiting Mum and Dad a couple of months later, his Father laughed out loud and beamed,

"Well, now you know how we felt when you pulled that stupid stunt out in the bleedin' countryside. You silly little prat."

He was having a drink one lunchtime in The Prince of Wales Pub, right by the Angel in North London. The Angel Tube Station has the longest escalator in the whole of the London Underground System. Needed to know that, didn't you? It was also quite close to Camden Passage, where the contact for the Jewellery from Norfolk, still had a shop. He happened to pop in for a quick drink and introduced Frankie to someone he felt, may be of interest. They enjoyed each other's company straight away, they were both of a similar upbringing. Geography only separated their origin and appetite for success aspect.

This guy, Adam Damario, was a Cockney from The East End, and was already doing reasonably well for himself by all accounts. Into Hi- Fi systems for the home or something. There was one major thing differing in their outlook on life at this present time. Adam had never quite got out of the habit of hard graft, so had not slipped into any bad habits.

He was rabbitting on about going into Music systems, which could be manufactured at incredibly low costs in Asia. They looked the absolute dog's bollocks and he could get them shipped to England at remarkable rates. The mark-up would be exorbitant and could change the face of Home Entertainment, if he managed to get them into the right High Street retailers.

He had found a way to cut out the middleman,

"And that my son is the answer to all our prayers," he finished off. Frankie saw it all coming as a bit of a sales pitch, but agreed to meet the guy a week later at The Telegraph Pub, on Streatham High Road.

This Adam geezer was looking for like-minded, ambitious, new-wave entrepreneurs. Respectable investors only of course, but if he wanted to get his foot in the door at these early stages, he was welcome. Assuring Frankie, that a positive attitude could result in returning a proper lump of money, and get respect to go with it. He gave him his business card and the invitation was left open.

A Lovely Pair of Knockers

They did in fact meet the following week, but Frankie shied away from the deal on the table. The music was very loud in The Telegraph, and it had been difficult to hear all that was being said. They shook hands after Adam Damario paid the bill, with The Rolling Stones belting out 'Brown Sugar', on the jukebox. Frankie joked in the Car Park, as they got into Adam's Chauffeur driven Daimler, that he would always remember his new acquaintance as 'Demarrera' from now on.

He gave the Brighton boy a lift to East Croydon Station, declaring,

"I like you, you have got potential Frankie." During the journey they stopped off at a recently opened fast food outlet. Demarrera predicted this place would soon be all over the country, and proceeded to recommend three pieces with chips and a small coleslaw. He had bought shares in the company, and reckoned it was a risk worth taking. Kentucky Fried Chicken went on to do okay.

They had got a bit pissed, naturally, but on the short journey, Frankie assured him he would give the proposition serious consideration.

"Don't you worry matey, if this isn't for you maybe the next one will be." Then pointing his finger at him, as Frankie departed from the vehicle, he repeated in a slightly slurry manner,

"I like you Frankie, come and join me on the journey, if you do decide to say yes next time. Then I will tell you, you're hired."

On the rattler back to Brighton, Frankie browsed through the Evening News. There it was, a full page advertisement for Amstill Sound Stack Music Systems, available now at incredible prices, Woolworth's, Dixon's, Curry's and all good Home Entertainment retailers.

He contacted and then subsequently visited Adam a couple of days later. Mr Demarerra, took the meeting under duress. Things had happened so quickly, some very big players had got involved as promised and things had gotten out of control. The previous offer of just a few days ago, was no longer on the table. He would speak with some major investors and see what could be made available. The proverbial:

A Lovely Pair of Knockers

"Trust me Frankie. Just be patient. Now my old man's a dustman, but true to form, as with him and me, the right deal will soon come along, and I will be with you all the way. Keep in touch. Maybe I can pop down to the coast soon and visit. Whaddayassay?"

"Sure, Adam, sure. Keep me in the loop. I have the dosh to make a difference, just let me know."

Frankie had confidence in his new associate, but could not get any decent response from any of his Brighton pals. The Buzz insisted that you should stick to what you know, 'All that high finance shit will only get you in the shit,' was his simple but shitty conclusion.

Tommy Barnes also showed little enthusiasm. To dealing in the world of manufacturing without having the training and experience of what you were dealing with sounded a bit risky. Being aware of all the new technology and the latest methods of production was surely tantamount to getting the best out of the industry, or your fingers burnt.

"Surely Frankie you have to be properly educated to deal with this stuff, and the herberts that run the show as well. It just doesn't make sense that by simply throwing a load of money at something, it earns shit loads more without any risk. I might have been interested with more information, but as you know, I am making plans to sell-up and move to Majorca. I strongly recommend, however, that you tread carefully, but all the best anyway, mate."

All this negativity just spurred Frankie on. It made him all the more determined to get in on this golden opportunity, he had created for himself. He would show 'em all.

His big break came sooner than he had expected. Adam contacted him and requested he attend his offices in Spitalfields, E1. It was just a short walk from Liverpool Street.

Once they were alone in his office Adam had a quick trip down memory lane. Pointing in one direction to Petticoat Lane where he first embarked in sales as a market trader. Then with the pointy figure, in another direction towards Brick Lane, where he first rented out to other traders, selling his goods at what he felt were reasonable and fair rates.

"Trouble is there are too many foreigners getting their teeth into that game these days. Still, as we all know, nothing lasts forever.

You have to move with the times. That's something I respect about you Frankie, you have vision. Now let's get down to some serious business."

The upshot was, he was no mug, and had not got where he was today by pussy footing around. He did not suffer fools gladly, and certainly wasn't about to let just anybody share the spoils if they didn't pull their weight.

They needed to show true commitment. As well as being in a position to invest some serious money they also had to be prepared to invest their time, no free rides were available. There was indeed, however, an opening with a soon to be newly formed company, that he felt would be of interest.

Frankie signed up. He didn't actually sign his name to anything but you get the drift.

Commuting was a pain in the arse. He had at first driven up, which was okay, but invariably, every meeting he attended finished up in some Hotel Bar or Private Members Club. Spending the night in a random Hotel and then trying to figure out where he'd left the car, the night before. This became a job in it's own right.

The meetings he went to all seemed the same. A rough draft was presented, everyone agreed things looked promising, then they went for a late lunch or early dinner. Nothing seemed to get actually achieved by all this though. They all spent copious amounts of cash on food and drink, business expenses evidently. Congratulating each other on another great accomplishment. This actually became boring.

He paid his fair share, but sometimes felt that his turn came round much sooner than expected. He also never seemed to get reimbursed for his share of the bills, without having to provide specific receipts. Which were not always available, due to the slackness caused by the excessive alcohol consumption. This had started to grate on his nerves a bit. Then out of the blue, he was informed that Adam was expecting him at a presentation at The London Sporting Club, otherwise referred to as The Cafe Royale, in one of the conference rooms.

He was advised in a memo, that he was required to attend early as there was a matter of the utmost importance for his consideration.

A Lovely Pair of Knockers

Upon arriving he was ushered into a private suite. Adam conveyed that they had developed a brand new product altogether that would take the country by storm.

He was very excited and animated,

"The best thing about the project is this though Frankie. When I reveal tonight this revolutionary instrument I want you to be named as the Chief Executive of the newly formed company. Have a gander at the contract I have had prepared, it's all standard stuff, and if you like what you see, sign it later before you leave."

Adam Damarrera did the presentation himself. Before what could only be described as all the leaders and buyers, of all Britain's High Street Retailers.

It was called a 'Slimtone'. At this point his business partner gave a knowing wink to Frankie. It was of course a state of the art, handheld, battery operated Xylophone keyboard. This was a proto-type.

Not only was this new concept designed and produced to the highest of standards, in Tawaiin, it would be the best thing since sliced bread and every home should have one.

It bore Frankie's name, so now, not only did he feel honoured, but also secure that his input was being truly valued by the company.

Frankie proudly signed up to be C.E.O. at the reception afterwards and received the customary slaps on the back. For yet another decisive step towards global domination and success.

It was unfortunately a smokescreen by the conniving little git Demarrera. Frankie was to be the figurehead of a new company set up for this one product. He was now able to persuade Frankie to fully commit himself, and purely on an egotistical falsehood Frankie agreed to everything. Financially committed and devoting all his time, although he still didn't quite recognize his role as per say, apart from the title bit. It was September, and the 'Slimtone', would be on the shelves all across the country by November, and become a Christmas bestseller.

The 'Slimtone' phenomenon, of course, was short-lived, to say the least. The proto-type that Frankie and market leaders had marvelled at, was not re-produced to the same standard. Half of them never even worked from the start. So all the huge orders placed with the main retailers were never fulfilled as they were returned prior to completed delivery dates. Why couldn't people just have a bit of patience and wait till bloody Christmas? Thought Frankie when they realised the shit had hit the fan.

At first customers were given replacements, by order of Management. But then, when half came back again, with all the customers now demanding their money back. On top of that the complaints of how Christmas had been ruined for the kids because of it, the customer relations team were kept very busy. Not even Woolworth's kept it for more than two months.

When the stores had thousands more returned in January, they obviously sent them back, and asked for a refund of the deposits they had paid in good faith. Unfortunately there was no good faith or money available. The holding company, of which Frankie had been made C.E.O. and President, went into liquidation.

The 'Slimtone' was destined for Sunday Morning Markets, cheap discount stores and fly-by-night traders. Exactly where Mr Demarrera had started, but not where he was destined to end.

Frankie, naturally, was despondent at the astronomic demise of this failed project. Also extremely annoyed, but the worst was yet to come. Yom Kippur, that year, was surely the longest Jewish Holiday in history. It was weeks before he could get a meeting with Demarrera, in the boardroom, who had been avoiding him like an antelope in a Lion's Den.

"It's a diabolical fucking liberty," he screamed at the man in the big chair. This little Jewish market-trader had come up in the world a bit more by now. So wasn't about to be upstaged by some smart-arsed little toe-rag from Brighton, who'd just got all his money on one lucky day.

He raised his arse slightly off of his heightened leather Chesterfield, for maximum effect. Pointed his finger menacingly at Frankie and glared,

"I used to be just like you Frankie. But you my son have served your purpose. Your journey here is over. So now, why don't you just fuck right off?"

Frankie realised there and then, he had met his match.

The next year or two became a bit of a blur for Frankie. After wrangling with Solicitors, being bogged down with paperwork, and one summons after another for two years, he eventually got some of his money back. But his reputation was shot to bits. The Lawyers took most of what was left though. He was absolutely exhausted and totally drained by it all.

'Businessmen have no loyalty or moral conscience when it came to business', was all he could gain from the experience. Small, if any, compensation.

Old Demarrera, well he went on to bigger and better things, and never got in touch again. He certainly never made the promised visit to the coast. To say he never gave Frankie another thought would be harsh. When once questioned about the Brighton boy involved in the 'Slimtone Fiasco', he laughed out loud, and was quoted as saying:

"Oh you mean 'Frankie The Fall guy', sure I think of him from time to time, then I just get myself back to work. Whatkanyasay? Whatkanyadoo?"

I hear he is a bit more polite in the Boardroom these days, but still a hard nut to crack. Rumour has it, that a knighthood may even be on the cards, as long as he can continue to keep ahead of the competition.

*

Frankie slung his complimentary stack stereo system in the bin, when he got home one day, after another dogged day in court. The next day he bought an old Radio Gram from a second-hand market in Kensington Gardens. £15 plus £2 delivery. He then ventured into The Kensington for a couple of pints, met The Buzz and a couple of other Knocker Boys. Then had a couple in The Brighton Tavern, where they decided to work together again. Then a few more in The Great Eastern, where they decided to find another 'real nice clue'. They had a quick one in The Big Northern, along with a quick line of Charlie, as it was now deemed a special occasion.

The Buzz had neglected to shape up properly till this point. Then they sauntered drunkenly up to The Blue House, with arms over each other's shoulders. Finishing up about 2:00am, very pleased with themselves.

They both agreed. What's the point of money, if you ain't got mates?

'Still, it's only a laugh anyway, innit?'

*

25. The Double Act.

Laurel and Hardy & Abbott and Costello

Versus

The Two Ronnies & Morecombe 'n' Wise

    The 'Double Act' when executed properly is one of the most powerful and rewarding combinations.
    Dean Martin and Jerry Lewis can thank their huge fame and fortune for this. When their paths crossed in Atlantic City and Jerry Lewis, under extreme pressure, took drastic steps. Literally risking life and limb, with Lucky Luciano breathing down his neck, no less. They went on to become the Double Act of the Century, but as per usual it all ended in tears. With the same old faces showing up to cause the reasons for their inevitable demise.
    Money = Greed, Success = Jealousy or Power = Control.
    But back to our headliners for now.
    Notice how the two leading combinations from both sides of The Atlantic present themselves. Both are similar physically, Fatty & Skinny v Big n' Small. Then we have Straight Sensible Fellah with Simpleton come Idiot v Friendly Stooge with Funny Man & Piss Taker.
    Yet by virtue of titles alone the English guys are much more loveable and approachable because they are presented as a team which we can be a part of, if we choose. Whereas the American counterparts are just two blokes working together to try and get a laugh.
    This representation was invaluable 'On The Knocker' and once a couple of Brighton Boys melded well together, well, there was no stopping them, and the world was their oyster.
    The top combinations, once again can be up for a matter of debate and someone's always going to have a different opinion. Anyway the next few tales are examples of such recipes for success, without even knowing the ingredients before they started.

A Lovely Pair of Knockers

*

I have already divulged how Frankie and Barry 'The Buzz' Bubball, found fame and fortune together. Other occasions were just as funny, if not as profitable.

They were once given a call, by Bingo. It was a widow in Hurstpierpoint, so not exactly an expedition. There was an old oil painting in the hallway evidently, that if confirmed original, could well be worth in the region of two bags. A lot of ifs, buts and maybes admittedly, but eight miles out of Brighton, worth a morning of anyone's time. Off they go, with no mention of strategy.

The Buzz, knocks the door and the sweet little thing invites him in. Admiring the picture in question, she remarks that she has had a number of people enquire as to how much she would take for it, over the past few months.

"Well," he says, "My friend in the car outside would surely be able to advise of its true value." If she were interested, of course it was entirely up to her.

"Invite him in then," she answered. Given the nod, Frankie enters the arena. Barely through the threshold, he takes a step backwards, and compliments the lady of the house on the bright shiny brass doorstep.

"Thank-you for noticing, people show small regard for the rigours of good housekeeping these days. When I lived up in Whitechapel, it was deemed shameful if the doorstep was not kept bright and shiny. Who knows who might call at any given time?"

"My sentiments exactly," came the reply.

"Now, this painting," admiring closely with both fists on hips, "Do you mind if I take a closer look?" Not waiting a second for a reply. He reached up and removed the picture from its hook. At the same time he placed his thumb in the furthermost right hand corner of the canvas, then with no apparent pressure, pushed his thumb straight through it, creating an immediate hole of ¾ of an inch.

"Oh that is very inconvenient, it must be quite ancient. I can't believe I have done that. Now what are we to do?"

A Lovely Pair of Knockers

"Well," exclaimed The Buzz, "Whether it was worth anything in the first place, it's certainly not worth sod all now. Put it back where it was. You clumsy oaf."

"But I cannot damage this lady's property and not suffer retribution. I realise I have desecrated this piece of art, so surely we must offer her some kind of compensation?"

"Don't you worry about that pal. The thing no longer, if it ever did, has any value, now that you've ruined it. Put the bloody thing back where it belongs."

Then The Buzz snatched it from Frankie. Frankie stood back, startled. Then leant towards Barry and looked over his shoulder, The Buzz turned his head looking back over his own shoulder naturally. This enabled Frankie, to grab the painting back from him. Then stepped back three paces and ordered Barry not to try that trick again.

"Now, Mabel, what sort of sum could I offer you, so that you are satisfied I have done you no wrong. Shall we say fifty pounds?"

"Well I don't really know. The most I have been offered was forty pounds. But of course, that was before that damage was done." Pointing at the hole.

"Listen to me now," shouted Barry in a most irritated tone, "We cannot possibly waste that kind of bish-bosh on a ruined smudge, that hasn't even been seen by anyone who has a danny what it's Rita is."

Mabel, not having a clue what had just been said, declared that she no longer wanted the painting in it's present condition, and how much might it cost to repair. Frankie insisted, it was beyond repair, so she should take something for it. Going into his pocket and taking out a ten-pound note.

With that The Buzz dived towards him, like Gordon Banks, and managed to disengage the note from his fingers without tearing it, exclaiming,

"You know darn well that is my week's rent money, and I want it back." He did not lose balance for even a split second, it was like watching Rudolph Nureyev himself, the way he landed so lightly on his feet. He did, however, now have his back towards the pair of them.

Frankie had instinctively stepped aside, so was in an advantageous position.

225

A Lovely Pair of Knockers

"If I were not raised to be the gentleman that I am, I would surely teach you a lesson you would never forget. However with ladies present you can think yourself lucky. Now, Mabel, please tell me, honestly, how much it will it cost to rectify this terrible situation."

Barry was straight on the ball, "I have already told you, we do not have any money, as such. We were merely stopping by to give a rough guide to that picture's value. You have single-handedly put that plan into disarray. We'll be lucky if she doesn't call the Cossers on us."

"Now, now boys," interrupted Mabel, "This has gone far enough. Take the bloody painting with you and don't bloody well come back. I do not usually use bad language but you two have driven me to my wits end. Come on, the pair of you, out with you." She shooed them both out the door, then gave them a fond wave as they walked down the garden path.

They pretended to shove each other, then looked over their shoulders and waved goodbye. Out of sight they started laughing. None of this performance had been rehearsed or spoken about, it just came naturally.

The painting was not difficult to repair, as the top right hand corner was part of the skyline, not unusual. That cost £35. They took a chance in the salerooms, as Peter Terronni, in Prince Albert Street could not be sure. He was certainly sure he made a mistake though, when Frankie and The Buzz split £22,000 after the auctioneer took his cut.

Worth working on a Monday morning after all. They chipped in £2,000 each for Bingo, for putting them in it, and still managed to have a nice Monday Club drink in a few of the Pubs and Clubs.

*

The Widdy Brothers were not only a great double act, but sometimes also worked as a threesome. On one occasion they were working a renowned street in London's Mayfair District.

No toes Widdy was in charge, he had lost his three smallest toes as a youngster in a traffic accident. This gave him a great advantage in the summertime as he always wore flip-flops to

A Lovely Pair of Knockers

accentuate his disability. Immediate sympathy came his way and he played it like a concert pianist.

Straight knocking was the order of the day, which means no bills had been dropped in advance. The youngest; Sean, knocked a door and saw behind the lady, when she answered, what looked like a collection of China Dolls. She told him however that she could not allow anyone in as her Husband was away at sea, and maybe he could come back tomorrow.

The next person to answer gave the same reply, he ventured that their neighbour's husband was away and he would be calling tomorrow, so could he make an appointment for tomorrow at 11:00am, once he had finished that engagement,

"What are you talking about?" Questioned the man.

"Her husband has been dead for twenty years, and she's nuts, off her rocker she is."

Once conferring with the other brother Stan, they all decided to give it a go, no toes was first at the door,

"Your husband has decided to sell some of the furniture and fancy goods you have in this flat Madam, and has instructed me and my associates to value the said goods and forward an estimate as to there value. Would you please make way, so that we can make haste and sort it all out as soon as possible? Come on, chop chop."

Then pointing to Stan, advised,

"He's in a hurry, and wants to get on and have a Donald in Soho." Perplexed and unaware of the situation she allows them to enter. Within forty minutes everything was accounted for, packed and shipped out. The Lady was very grateful, and thanked them kindly for their prompt and efficient manner, even tipping young Sean a tenner for his trouble.

There was a choice selection of pressed bisque dolls, French circa 1880, with open/closed mouths, fixed blue glass eyes, with jointed wood and composition body, about 15in high, the best of the bunch, making £42,000. Others of similar period and style but not in quite such good condition had to go for £13,000, £14,400, £11,100 and £10,500 respectively. The rest of the collection was sold as a job lot for £7,350. The cabinet they were kept in was of no use, obviously, so they gave £45 for it. It was a French kingwood vitrine, Paris, circa

1900, in Transitional manner, with three shaped glazed doors and side, 175cm wide. It made £12,000 in 1994 at Sotheby's.

They cleared £97,000 after the Auctioneer's commission. They then went for a few drinks and a nice lunch in Chinatown. No toes had to foot the bill, no pun intended, after Sean and Stan got into a fierce argument about who had paid the £45 for the display cabinet. It got completely out of hand, so they were both arrested and carted off to the nearest cop shop, at Cannon Row Police Station. You just can't please some people.

*

One such partnership, that never even got started, yet could still be deemed extremely successful. Ray Comfort convinced Perry Bowels once that it would be a good idea to try working a Bank Holiday.

They went down to Torquay on a Sunday, and started dropping bills early Bank Holiday Monday. At 6:30 am whilst getting a few through the letter boxes, an old boy opened his window and enquired after Ray, what the bloody hell was he doing at such an early hour?

Ray explained the situation and showed the man his leaflet, from the pathway,

"Well oim an oily roizah too, yong man. So you bess cominn yong fellow. Oy may well have' somptin of interest to you."

Twenty minutes later Ray emerged from the gaff with the most amazing pair of Viennese enamel, jewelled and silver gilt mounted vases, circa 1880, 22inches tall in fitted cases. Fortunately Ray was holding the stock money and laid out every penny he had on him, £325.

He found Perry as soon as possible, telling him there was no need to bother dropping any more bills as they no longer had any cash to buy anything. Mr Bowels was none too pleased with this information and stormed off, back to the B & B, with the right hump.

"It's a bloody good job I've got thirty quid for the petrol home, or we'd be right up the creek, you silly sod. What with the Banks being closed, we would have had to sit around all day, in this shithole running up a bar bill, till tomorrow. Come on let's get home, and I'm never working with you again."

This statement was rescinded when the vases in question were sold at Auction in London. A connection of Ray's had inspected them, and advised accordingly. The £42,000 price reached, after two prospective buyers had battled for them, cemented Perry and Ray's friendship for many years. But they never actually worked on the door together again, had plenty of other deals though.

*

On another occasion, old Jimmy McCue, who was well known for his dressing up regalia. Today he was a man of the cloth, and was waiting to be seen by a well to do Gentleman, who was known to have a religiously fuelled guilt complex. Sitting in the foyer he sees a beautiful Longcase Grandmother Clock. Right by what looked like an outside access door. Lo and behold after easing the door ajar it is as expected, on top of that there is a wheelbarrow just a few yards away.

Directly in view are Frankie Slimtone and Barry 'The Buzz' Bubball, who have taken him to the call. He has done no less than grabbed the barrow, tilted the Clock onto it and slipped outside giving the thumbs up sign that everything is okay. Frankie was astounded how quickly he had bought such a nice piece, then Jim told him it was without consent and panic struck.

"Come on you stupid prick," cried Frankie, "Let's get the hell out of here lively. I don't believe it. Buzz, get this motor moving."

They managed to get away unscathed, and to be fair the walnut Longcase Clock, with 10in brass dial, with silver chapter ring signed Daniel Quare, London, circa late 17thC did return £9,000, so they got £3,000 each. The buyer was able to sell it on years later for twice as much, but it was hardly a sellers market under the circumstances.

*

David Le Bloom and Cauliflower were another successful partnership. Cauli had played Rugby at County level, so his ears had suffered accordingly due to the scrums. They enjoyed each other's company and worked well together for some years. Then came the big'un. They were knocking a block of flats in London, and Cauliflower appeared at one stage with a Sainsbury's trolley, fully laden with what looked like costume jewellery. Upon further inspection David declared he fancied the Tom as right stuff. Tony Barnes confirmed his hunch once they got back to Brighton.

The actual spoils received are somewhat cloudy, but David Le Bloom invested his share into a Jewellery shop somewhere in The Lanes. He has continued this career choice ever since and has recently opened up at a new and fresh venue, but still in the Lanes which he prefers. As always a perfect Gentleman and pleasant company.

Cauliflower invested his share with a couple of reliable pals, William Hill and Victor Chandler, they will never let you down. Time after time they will continue to take every last penny you are willing to invest on a scrappy piece of paper bearing their name at the top.

*

Everybody is entitled to their opinion on Double Acts, but during the course of the next chapter, which is a tad longer and needed to be broken up into three parts. As did The Godfather Trilogy, you will witness the best Double Act of all time. Not as famous as the ones at the beginning of this chapter, but that was in fact their greatest achievement. Nobody knew about the pair of 'em. Not until now that is.

*

26. The Longest Day.

The Forest Road was legendary as one of Dick Turpin's favourite haunts, now known as Houndhurst Road.

I always referred to it as Sherwood Forest when taking this route with my Dad. I imagined in my world of fantasy that, Errol Flynn in his role as Robin Hood would jump out from the thicket at any moment, to hold us up with bow and arrow, and behind him Little John and his band of merry men. We travelled down it many times over the years but my wishes were never granted. The great 'Tasmanian Devil' Errol was long since gone.

*

I was now heavily pregnant and had not been out of the house for a couple of days. Grace had popped in with some home-made carrot cake which went down well with fresh coffee. Then, out of the blue Dad pops his head through the door, at precisely ten o'clock, and announces we are going on a little 'Road Trip'.

"I don't want any nonsense from the pair of you," he requested, "I've got a quick errand to run in town and I shall return at eleven thirty prompt and expect both you and Grace to be ready. It's only up the road to Weybridge and we can have a nice little light lunch up there, take care of some very important business, and then, maybe stop off at that nice Country Hotel you like, on the way home for Afternoon Tea, how does that grab yah?"

This immediately felt like one of those occasions when to oppose the proposition would be a complete waste of time and energy. He had obviously planned meticulously the events for the day, and no doubt, had already cleared with Grace that there were no other previous engagements to intrude upon.

Grace and I glanced at each other knowingly over the next eighty minutes, both of us equally excited and intrigued as to what lay ahead. Grace was saddened of the news that Fred Astaire had died of pneumonia yesterday, aged 88. He was one of her old favourites.

It was June 21st, and breakfast TV plus relevant weather forecasters had already declared on numerous occasions that this was officially the longest day of the year. Boy, were they right!

Arriving back outside the house at 11:25 am, always early, never late, Dad helped Grace with the umpteen bags I now felt necessary to travel with in my delicate condition. The last scan had revealed twins were on their way, and they had both started kicking within seconds of each other. Pillows fluffed-up in the back of the Bentley, Grace neatly and primly sat up-front, he turned round to me with that all too familiar glint in his eye, winked and asked, "You alright my little treacle? We are going to 'ave a day to remember my little darlin'!"

He had no idea how right he was.

I now resided in a detached house in Langdale Gardens, off New Church Road, so we took the route up Sackville Road, and over snaky hill to the A23, in what seemed like minutes.

Now was the cue to enquire about our impromptu journey.

"So pops, what's this all about then?" I ventured, as we passed The Plough, now safely out of Brighton City limits. We were not actually deemed a City at the time, but it just sounded right.

"Yes Robert," added Grace, "What's the apple for Christ's sake? I've been itching to tell Stephanie of your plans, but you made me promise you devil. We haven't had this much cloak and dagger since that awful Murder Mystery evening at The Ramada last Christmas. I sincerely hope it will turn out to be more entertaining than that load of crap. I know you meant well, but let's be fair, it was an absolute shambles, and for what it all cost. Then there was the wine- oh the wine- the wine was...."

"Alright, alright Grace, you are never gonna let me live that one down are you. Forget that old nonsense, today is a bit special. No girls, today is a very much, long awaited occasion. That although, could only come about by some bad news, it is also the final piece of a puzzle that is about to complete a very nice picture. A very nice picture indeed, I might add."

*

He had a kind of smirky look on his face that was reminiscent of the time I had asked him about a property situation many years ago. That was when Georgie Balcock's Mother had passed away, and it appertained that Dad owned the house. He had all the paperwork sorted and the deal was that once she died, no other family members had any rights to it. The house now became part of an independent portfolio of an offshore company.

It had been one of the first of a long line of properties purchased by my Father at a delicate and vulnerable time. Council houses were being sold off, with the tenants being offered first refusal, at heavily reduced market rates. Very few though, had the 10% deposit required, 3 years books, or proof of regular income to consider such a huge responsibility. So he had propositioned many households, with the option to allow him to buy the place on their behalf. He also proposed to renovate the place and set a reasonable rent for the rest of their lives.

Rumours were rife of rogue Jewish or even Arab landlords, who were sitting pretty and ready to pounce on the situation; buying up all these properties and tripling the rent, or even kicking tenants out on to the street. Terrifying.

Can't for the life of me, imagine who spread those vicious rumours.

In those days this sort of behaviour was common practise. If nobody came forward, the properties went to auction.

The tenant still had the responsibility of the Rates, now known as Council Tax, once the house was purchased, and many saw his offer, as the work of a hero and saviour.

That smirky look on his face, years ago, was all about the realisation that a cunning plan was now coming to fruition. His patience was to be rewarded and also a kind of retribution for undeserved happenings, through no intentions or fault of his own.

There was also an undetected vengeance being perpetrated, against a small faction of Brighton. Brighton's Knocker Boys.

*

Anyway, back to the journey.

"You pair just wait a wee while and all will be revealed," he teased. By Hickstead I could stand it no longer, the babies were kicking well and I just wasn't in the mood for all this bollocks.

The sun was blistering into the back of the Bentley, and I surprised even myself with the outburst,

"Oh come on Dad, stop all this bloody nonsense, where are we going and what the hell is going on?"

"Okay, okay," he said, "Well. A long long time ago. Barney and I."

"Get on with it Dad," I interrupted.

"Yes, come on Robert," added Grace sharply, "Let's get to the point, and what's my dear old Barney got to do with anything. For Christ's sake man, out with it."

"Here we go, I'll spill the beans, no pun intended," we both glared at him, and I kicked the back of his driver's seat.

Now he just started laughing, which infuriated the pair of us so much he decided to turn off at The Bolney Stage.

"I'll tell you what we will do, let's stop off at South Lodge first instead and do the light lunch there, out on the patio, it's a nice enough day. Then I shall explain everything. But we can't hang about, I have to be in Weybridge for three o' clock sharp. And today ladies, time waits for no man."

As we came into South Lodge in Lower Beeding, he said to Grace, "I had this booked for 4:30 pm, afternoon tea, but it shouldn't be a problem. They are very accommodating, true professionals at this gaff."

I then realised that Grace had only heard of this place and so was not surprised when I saw her glazy eyes as we approached.

"Tell you what Dad, instead of going to the car park, drop me off at the door, and let them park-up for you."

"Good idea Minnie, didn't fancy clambering all over the place with all this lumber anyway."

Rodney greeted us at the door, in morning dress and grey gloves. We explained a change of circumstances and went straight through to the veranda at the rear. Rodney didn't seem in the slightest

A Lovely Pair of Knockers

bit surprised and helped with the bags accordingly. I did, however, have to get up immediately for the powder room, Grace followed.

When we returned, Dad was browsing, the lunch menu,

"Do you fancy a game of croquet before we eat?" He asked cheekily, "Nah, neither do I."

A selection of sandwiches, house special coleslaw, French fries to share, sparkling water all round and tea for three were promptly ordered, Grace and myself were now starting to get irritable.

"Right then," he began, "Now I know you two are getting a little bit tetchy, but I have been waiting for this day, since nineteen sixty fucking five. So spare me the daggers and grant me some degree of courtesy while I savour the moment, so to speak."

"Well?" we both demanded in unison.

"Steph, you know every Christmas, we get a card from Mrs Vivian. To Bob, Barney, family and friends?" I just nodded, not wishing him to stop.

"Well, she gets a card from me every Christmas as well, the difference is, I always send mine on November 25th. On the back of the envelope, I write my current address or the address to send her card to so that I always get mine by the 22nd December. You once asked, 'How does she know that we have moved when we never ever see her?' There's your answer."

He then continued, in a now serious mood.

"Now you know I always said it was someone I had done some work for, it was a bit more involved and complicated than repairing a flint wall. She was a very well to do Lady, by title not just manners. Her husband Sir Terence Willoughby was awarded the Victoria Cross in World War II, he died earning it mind you. So although still a beautiful woman she was also what you might call a spinster. Due to her bloodline there was never the option of remarriage. She was clearly devoted to El Tel as we called him and loved him dearly. He was badly injured at the Battle of Stalingrad, managed to get home, but died in hospital with Vivian holding his hand."

"Her big house in Cranleigh had grown into disrepair. Despite the efforts of her devoted Butler, Housekeeper and Grounds man. It wasn't because she was skint or anything, she just didn't have any enthusiasm."

"Anyway, it was springtime in 1958, me and Barney were casing a joint, down the road in Manning's Heath. During a Pub lunch in Cranleigh at The White Hart Pub in Ewhurst Road, we somehow started talking to this posh bloke Wilfred."

"It turned out he was a Butler, who was taking a day off on strict orders of his boss. We threw a few extra drinks his way and it seemed he was able to take the weight of the world off of his shoulders, by sharing his troubles with a couple of polite strangers. They were not even his troubles, just the poor plight of his mistress, the lovely Lady Willoughby, as he referred to her, all in the strictest of confidence of course."

Both myself and Grace were now completely captivated, practically ushering away the waiters as they presented the most marvellous array of sarnies you could ever come across.

Slightly distracted for a brief moment, Dad remarked how lovely it all looked,

"Nice touch the little triangles, crusts all cut off an' all."

It did all look very splendid, but our attention was focused on one thing and one thing only.

"Will you please get to the fucking point, please Dad," I said, completely forgetting any decent education I had ever been the recipient of.

He nodded and continued in his sombre tone.

"So, after our little meeting with Wilfred, and hearing of the dire position of his dear employer we decide to take a jolly up to the house, and offer our services, as to any significant repairs to help get the place into shape. I scribbled the number of the B & B me and Barney were staying at and asked him to let the Lady of the house know that we would be calling the next day. To which he readily agreed."

"Quite happily he put on his hat and coat, and had a spring in his step, that he had undoubtedly not felt for years. Then jumped into his Morris Minor and drove off up the frog. A little zig-zaggy if we were to be honest, still drink-driving was not really an issue in them days."

"So, what's all that got to do with what's happening today for God's sake," I had to stress.

"Listen to me," he said sternly, "If you could shut the fuck up for ten poxy minutes, you'll find out wont'cha?"

I had been put in my place, but retorted:

"I'll have my twins before the story is over at this rate, it's like Hans Christian bloody Anderson."

"Well, I have to be fair, he was a good storyteller old Hans, but he never had one like this. And like I said earlier, I have been waiting 22 sodding years to tell it. So calm down and stop inter-ruddy-rupting. Try that rare roast beef and horse radish, it's lovely."

"Ham and Mustard's not too shabby," piped in Grace.

"Gone off cheese the last few months myself," I shared.

We were all getting each other at it now. Dad took off his jacket, to reveal some quite distasteful bright yellow paisley braces, obviously Liberty's of London, over his coral blue with white-collar shirt. The navy and yellow spotted tie did not complement his Saville Row Pin Striped suit whatsoever, but I'd given up on his wardrobe years ago.

I know I've wandered off at a tangent again but it does help to share the complete helplessness and anxiety that I was feeling at the time.

Are you feeling it too?

Good.

Here's the rest of the story without any further ado, as explained by my Dad.

"So, we call the next day and Wilfred, after short confirmation with Lady Vivian, agrees to receive us at 11:30 am, to discuss the possibility of some minor restoration at the property. We of course are bang on time. He answers the door in full Butler attire and leads us to a waiting room."

"Two minutes later, with a glint in his eye, 'Lady Vivian Willoughby will see you now. Tea will follow in exactly 15 minutes as requested by her Ladyship.'"

"This little scenario had already been explained by Wilfie. We had 15 minutes to present ourselves, put forward any proposals, be sure to mention financial commitment and stay polite at all times. Once the Tea was served, we were not to speak unless spoken to. Her Ladyship would delight in serving Tea, and whilst enjoying cake and sandwiches she would be calculating in her head whether she did or did not wish to go ahead with any of the proposals mentioned."

"Good day Gentlemen, I trust you are both feeling well."

"Thanks Ma'am," I said, as I had been deemed spokesman, and Barney would only speak if and when directly asked a question. Then he would only refer the question back to me anyway."

"She had a very smooth silky voice, that was not lacking in authority.' I take it you were the two gentlemen inspecting the grounds yesterday. Although you could not have possibly done a thorough job as you seemed to dash around all over the place in a very short period. However, what do you think are our main concerns?'"

"Well your Ladyship, I think………."

"At that very precise moment, all our lives changed, forever. Raising both her hands in the air she said:"

"Hold on right there. Now, I may not have ever had to hold down a job, or perhaps even do a weekly shop at Waitrose, Marks & Spencer or wherever, BUT, I am not a fool, or for that matter a stuck-up toffee-nosed snob. My staff are very loyal, and I understand concerned for my well-being."

"Hence the attendance here today of you two scallywags. I am a Lady, as you probably know a widow, but also a lonely person of my own volition choice and standing. You will not call me Ma'am, Ladyship or any of those other tawdry titles to which I have had to surrender to these past years. You may call me Mrs Vivian."

"Now, let's get on with it, what do you propose? How long will it take? And what will it cost?"

Dad explained how he went straight into selling mode and after what felt like an hour; Wilfred came in with the tea.

Due process was then followed.

Wilfred came back 15 minutes later and cleared the tea, and gave them a solemn nod of his head as he turned to leave, this was the sign that they would soon find out their fate. She would either invite them to remain and discuss details or simply thank them for attending and wish them a good day. Dad began again,

"I says, so Mrs Vivian, what do you think? Is it a goer or not?"

"Well, she replied rather tartly, you have both conducted yourselves as I would have wished. Although, that is the first time in my whole life I have ever had the displeasure of being addressed as 'Mrs Vivian', it was, after all, at my request, and now that it has sunk in, I find it quite refreshing."

"Please do not be offended, but I have never before acquainted myself with gentlemen of your demeanour. My late husband was a little older than myself and had such men under his command in both Wars."

"We will not tittle-tattle too much you understand but I feel it necessary to explain a little of my circumstances and myself so that we are all batting off the same wicket, as they say."

"She then raised her right arm slightly, in anticipation of a reply, so nothing was said."

"I married quite young and in retrospect did not gain from matrimony all that I should have. My husband was a truly patriotic soldier and although I feel he loved me dearly, his heart was always for King, Queen and Country. A poor second is all I could ever bequest or hope for. He travelled far and wide, without so much as a sidewards glance."

"There were of course opportunities to accompany him on such journeys, but I felt that I might distract him from his duties and responsibilities, and thus not allow him to fulfil his true potential. Who knows?" said with a shrug of her shoulders.

"He had high office in Russia at one time, before the Revolution. He had advised that the arrival of that dastardly Rasputin fellow and allowing him any authority was a grave mistake. But they paid him no heed and Alexandra developed some underlying feelings towards him. She was at first sceptical, then intrigued and eventually mesmerised and captivated. He reiterated of course that she was never unfaithful to her husband, The Czar Nicholas, whether true or not Sir Terence would never betray their confidence."

"This was the beginning of the end as far as my husband was concerned. The Romanov's always promised to visit him on his own soil one day, if only to meet his wife, of whom they had heard so much. He sadly left them under tragic circumstances but did not leave unaware of their gratitude for his services and loyalty. One of the items presented to him upon his departure I hold in high regard and has supreme sentimental value to me. I do believe it is also of some exorbitant financial value into the bargain."

"One other sad thing in my life is the subject of children. During the First World War, my husband led some of the charges during The Battle of the Somme. Of course to come back in one piece was a gift from God in itself, but unfortunately there was one piece of him missing. Sadly left on the battlefield, and never to be retrieved. The one piece, that if not functioning properly, meant that our next generation would not be from the loins of my husband at any rate."

"The usual arguments took place, he wished to divorce me on the grounds that he had committed adultery, whilst away from home. He therefore deserved nothing other than the French Foreign Legion, he would have done it as well, mark my word. I felt this was an absurd attitude to take, but as it was common knowledge when such things occur, by some miraculous fate the woman somehow became pregnant."

"I could never imagine being unfaithful to my husband, and would not lie with another, whatever the consequences. We eventually agreed that our marriage vows were sacred and our lives governed by them accordingly. Eternally barren the both of us, for better or worse, so be it."

"I do not know why I find it necessary to divulge any of this to you two, but maybe it is time for me to confide some of my more pertinent lifetime events. Also of course with the knowledge that no other living soul ever be aware of the same knowledge that is shared and talked about in this room today."

"Then comes the guillotine moment. That is capable of scaring the shit out of anyone on this Earth. She says to us both, "So Mr Bob, and you Barney. What have you to share with me? So that we both have shared dark secrets that no-one else should know, for fear of retribution and absolution."

"Me and Barney look at each other and for the only time ever, genuinely, didn't know what the other was thinking. Lucky bastard Barney, he immediately kicks into gear and follows instructions.

"Well, Mrs Vivian. As you have probably already presumed, Bob here is our spokesperson. So whatever he decides to share is okay by me". Then raising both hands simultaneously, expresses his side of things,

"Whaddayassay, Bob?"

"Done me like a smelly kipper he did," explained Dad proudly.

"But if you make a plan, you make a plan, and so you gotta stick to it. Talk about the ball's in your court. This was one situation that certainly doesn't come around too often. This Lady, quite unexpectedly, has just opened her heart to two renegade strangers. This was, however, one clever woman. No doubt the Butler had hinted that we were not just a couple of travelling opportunist builders, but had more to our make-up, and promise, than met the eye. Therefore advising to instigate some sort of unbreakable trust, he had undoubtedly picked up on the fact, me and Barney were like blood brothers and his information had been totally absorbed by Lady Vivian."

"She had in fact, spent all night deliberating whether to get back in the game of life, or not. So, in these seemingly few minutes, she had taken the bull by the horns, and laid out a scenario, that we could be a part of, or runaway forever. All the while, with the hunch or sound knowledge that we were not the type to run from anything."

"Still, the fact was, she had made this most gargantuan decision and assumption in the space of fifteen minutes, while I was giving all the spiel, and then decided to go ahead during the quarter of an hour it took for tea. In-fucking-credible."

"Now, let's be fair. After spending thirteen years mourning the death of your husband, looking forward to God knows how many years doing sod all. Attending fetes, Garden parties and suchlike, to make such a magnanimous decision in half-an-hour? She sure was some Lady, and this just had to be respected, then grasped in it's entirety, and appreciated to it's full worth."

Dad continued in the same rhetoric, Grace and I were completely transfixed,

"Sometimes the easiest and the hardest decisions have to be made instantaneously. It would be true to say Barney was behind me all the way, but then he could always say I was a stupid silly idiot later on, if it all went pear-shaped."

"But this was a classic case of 'No Brainer'. She knew instinctively what we were all about. But nevertheless, she had really and truly bared her soul like never before, so this was sensationally someone's life-changing moment up for grabs, if we had the balls to grab it."

"We are in," I said. "If, what I think you are proposing is correct. We tell you exactly what we are all about and a team is formed, whereas we can cross the divide and share the spoils. I will tell you this now, and never have to mention again. If and whatever we gain from our exploits in the future, we will share evenly amongst the pair of us. Me and Barney, you and your household, two even partners, how's that for starters Mrs Vivian, before I declare any more information."

"Not quite what I was looking for," came the reply, "But, to make life easier, let's put it like this. Whatever knowledge you gain from my acquaintance or any other people that I may deem appropriate to introduce you to, is entirely at your discretion."

"If for instance, some shares trading information, were to be accidentally sent to the wrong address, what business is that of mine?"

"Upon such a fateful event. If you were to benefit, by let's say for the sake of an argument, £45,000 and you decided to donate £17,500 to build a new wing, to include a much needed new kitchen, at the nearby Cranleigh Orphanage. I would be more than happy to cut the ribbon at the opening ceremony."

Dad was loving every minute of this and carried on with more fervour than I had ever witnessed. It was catching though. His captivated audience, had stopped interrupting, that's for sure. More tea was requested and he continued even more excitedly,

"She certainly wasn't messing about, she really meant business. It seemed like a dormant Volcano had suddenly been awoken, and Mrs Vivian actually seemed to be getting younger by the minute as we spoke."

"So a major plan was afoot. I explained that in reality Barney and I were like a pair of Raffle tickets. Not so much as in buy a ticket maybe win a prize, but let us know where and when some valuable prizes might be vulnerable, and we go in and nick 'em."

"I also advised at this stage that we had a nice little earner in Sussex. Whereas an arrangement had been agreed upon, with a trusted and honourable friend of the family. Who just happened to be a copper and helped out now and again with some valuable information. This ensured nobody got hurt or suffered a wasted journey. He was sincere and could be relied upon, but his identity would never be revealed, as in the same confidence assured to her Ladyship......oops sorry, as Mrs Vivian."

*

You can obviously imagine how the hairs on the back of my neck stood up when this information was revealed. I sat up rigid, but somehow managed to play it down, and moodied that the twins were kicking. So much for no more secrets.

*

There were some Golden Rules that needed to be strictly followed and should never be broken, under any circumstances whatsoever.

They never reneged on a deal, ever. No-one ever, went back to the scene of a crime. If someone was not happy with the situation, it made perfect sense to terminate the agreement, without prejudice. Or, if at some time, the arrangement was in danger or jeopardy, there was no point in arguing the toss, close it down, for fear of discovery. This was something that nobody was prepared to risk anyhow. And if they were willing to take that chance, well, then they were out on their arse anyway.

Mrs Vivian did not seem at all surprised or shocked by any of these revelations, in all credibility, none of it evoked much emotion from her whatsoever.

"Okay then chaps, back to our first event let's call it. What first and foremost is the most important factor in the renovation of Willoughby Manor?"

Purposefully, Dad had advised, the flint wall at the rear of the property, not only looked dishevelled, but also invoked security issues.

"If I was gonna screw the joint, that's exactly where I would get in and get out, sharpish," was Barney's unprovoked input. With glares from both Mrs Vivian, Dad, and even passer-by Wilfred, Barney did not utter another single solitary word, for fifty minutes, and that was only to nod his head and say goodbye!

"The flint wall is a serious issue, I advised, now it's not just a case of repairing, but more a matter of dismantling and rebuilding. My thoughts, however, are of a different nature. Let's take down the wall, keep all the flint, obviously, and build a 10ft high screen wall, right around the whole of Willoughby Manor. You do understand of course that Barney and myself will only oversee the work, with our network of associates no job is too big or too small, and will only ever invite trusted people to the Manor."

"This will, I must admit, give a totally new modern appearance to the place. But, with red bricks and a few fancy patterns in Blue Staff's, and a complimentary soldier course right across the top, with numerous intermittent piers to break it up, it will look classy, secure and add value to the property."

"Now, I know full well, that you have no intention of selling the drum anyway, but it still gives the impression of prosperity, and well, if you ever needed to access some extra Johnny, you could always borrow against the value of Willoughby Manor."

Mrs Vivian began to speak, but the old man now had the floor and copped for the raising of the hand ploy, that she had played a few minutes earlier.

"I know, I know. You would never need to borrow money, but it's not always all about borrowing money these days, it's just having the option of not having to liquidate other assets that you have at your disposal. Let's say for instance, your husband had a coin collection, that held some great sentimental value, but not to you."

"Then you decide to go on a world cruise some time in the future, for instance 1975, and it's going to cost £3,500. Instead of selling the coins, you let the Bank pay for the cruise, 'cause you have got a lovely secure red brick wall all around your house."

A Lovely Pair of Knockers

"With a glowing smile Mrs Vivian says, 'I like the way you're thinking,' then with a slight pause, continues: 'But the coin collection, it will, not under any circumstances, well, it will never be sold.'

This caused a couple of pensive moments, but Dad cracked on.

"Now, by utilising all the flint, I would like to propose two 14ft pillars, creating a grand entrance to the property. There is definitely enough flint, and it will add to the stature of The Manor. Then, I think it would be appropriate to have some kind of symbolic statue atop of each one, maybe a lion or horse, whatever. Then we will install electric gates that can be operated by remote control from the Rolls or inside of the house."

It was agreed that nobody needed to know about the side entrance that Wilfred took when driving the Morris Minor, and covering that would be state of the art surveillance cameras. Now, none of this would come cheap, they were delving into the James Bond world a little bit, but in a few years time it could easily be upgraded, at very little expense.

"Very little expense, sounds very expensive," commented Mrs Vivian.

"Well replied," said my father, "However, if you were able to confirm precisely when the Hunter-Smith's of Faversham Hall are taking their annual holiday, we could safely say that there will in actual fact be no expense whatsoever."

"I seem to recall, that I need to visit a stonemason in Glastonbury, between 17th - 31st of May," was her reply.

"The finishing touches should be a Unicorn's head design that I had in mind."

"True to form, Faversham Hall had very little security when visited during that time. By July, two magnificent Unicorn heads were placed at the entrance of newly secured Willoughby Manor, one on each of the towering and imposing flint pillars."

"And so began," continued Dad, "One of the most unusual partnerships you could ever imagine. Two crooked East Enders with no malice aforethought, and a fine Lady of the finest breeding with absolutely nothing but malice. She gave us jobs we would never have dreamt of, and sometimes even instructions as to the best way to pull off the heist. We were responsible for selling the booty, although she did offer some valuable advice from time to time. It was agreed that everything was split fifty-fifty and we never had rhyme or reason to sway from this arrangement. Mrs Vivian sure was a class act, not once did she ever question the resulting dividends on her end."

"On one occasion she was attending a Grand Ball in Buckinghamshire and unusually requested Barney to drive the Roller. The neighbouring estate housed one of the most prestigious collections of Tiffany lamps. Yet of the huge collection only 8 were of significant value, they all went that night, into the boot of a pristine 1958 Rolls Royce Silver Cloud."

"A man dressed all in black had a brief encounter with Barney, before cycling off and left his borrowed bike at the nearest train station. The driver of the Silver Cloud smiling all the way back to Surrey, and his passenger in the back, smiling that sweet smile of revenge."

"The Rollinson's had failed to appear at Sir Terence Willoughby's funeral, with some lame and pathetic excuse. Conscientious objectors to the War or something."

"Christopher Rollinson had attended Eton with Terence, playing Rugby and Cricket alongside him. Rollinson went onto Cambridge whilst Terence attended Oxford, purely on family tradition reasons. They had even attended together the 1912 Boat Race, and made a wager of 25 Guineas, as to the winner."

"It was the 69th running of the race. It was to be held on the 30th March, with a re-row on 1st April, what kind of fool am I? I hear you ask? But genuinely, Cambridge were sunk and Oxford waterlogged. Former Oxford president Mr I. Pitman, the appointed Umpire declared, the competition null and void. Oxford won by 6 lengths on the following Monday, in 22 minutes and 5 seconds. Taking their lead in the event to 38-30. Although it was the 69th, the dead heat of 1877, was the cause for not adding up correctly."

"Rollinson had welshed on the bet, declaring that Oxford had not won 'On the Day, of the Wager'."

"Sir Terence, had not made a song and dance about it, but within their circles, Christopher Rollinson was now regarded as a cad and charlatan. It was rumoured, that this episode cost him a knighthood."

"Lady Vivian had never forgotten or forgiven them for the blatant public rebuff, but now felt the score was settled."

"So, about how many jobs did you do with each other?" I was compelled to enquire.

"Well," he answered, not being offended in the slightest by the intrusion, "The whole Manor was gradually refurbished, a new roof, Greenhouses added, an East Wing, all the windows replaced. Even all the chimneys cleaned, so they could be put back to work. Bitch of a job that was. Old Phil Chapman the chimney sweep from West Ham said it was the last job he would ever do. Still, considering we paid him £3,400 he never had to. We took care of everything and Mrs Vivian never received a bill. Central Heating was installed, then of course..........."

"Oh I am so sorry to interrupt sir," came in Rodney from nowhere, "But you have an urgent personal call at the front reception desk, please follow me sir."

"Be right with you Rodders," he replied.

"Get yourselves ready girls, it's time to make a move."

We both looked at each other in sheer astonishment as he added,

"The car will be out the front in six minutes, giving you plenty of time to visit the powder room. Rodney will see to all the bags. And as I said earlier on, today time waits for no-one. So get yer skates on."

*

He was already in the driving seat when Rodney started to help with the baggage and not until we joined the A23 did anyone speak.

Dad kicked off, "Well, come on, let's be fair, I knew full well I wouldn't be able to fend the pair of you off till soppy Surrey could I. You know what you're like the pair of you. What's happening? Where are we going? Who's died? So anyway before either of you go into one, there is still just about enough time to finish most of the story. If you want to know, of course?"

The silence said it all.

He got the message.

"So things were going nicely. Then, as always, life takes it's turns. Barney finally decided to make an honest woman of Gracie here, I was best man of course, but we were both disappointed when Mrs Vivian declined her invitation. Wilfred drove 'em both in the Roller of course, and with the wedding card were two tickets for The Queen Mary. Where did that cruise go Grace?"

"You know very well that it went round the whole sodding world Robert," she quipped with an embarrassing smile, "I always thought it was you who gave us that cruise," she added pensively. Already casting her mind back to that wonderful time she had shared with her Barney.

"Like I said," he carried on, "That trust was never ever questioned or even slightly doubted for nearly thirty years now. That's the whole thing see, I got word last week that Mrs Vivian passed away. And that strict instructions had to be adhered to. It was not deemed favourable for me to attend the funeral and knowing Mrs Vivian it would have been for all the right reasons. She was a staunch and gracious woman."

"After Barney and Grace got hitched," he was now addressing me on a much more personal and private manner, "I met your Mother and the same procedure followed where Mrs Vivian was concerned. 'Unable to attend but please allow Wilfred to drive you to the service and subsequent celebrations.' The wedding card contained 1st Class tickets to Los Angeles, 7 nights at The Roosevelt Hotel, Hollywood Boulevard. Incidentally that was where they held the very first ever Oscar Awards."

"Then there was a Limousine transfer to an upcoming place in her opinion, it was a bit of a drive, but well worth it. That was Las Vegas, staying at The Sahara, where tickets had been reserved for a show featuring some bright young stars, nick-named 'The Rat Pack' would be performing. She really had it all sussed did Mrs Vivian."

"After five days in that 24 hour place we flew to New York City for three nights, staying at The Waldorf Astoria. We did a bit of shopping, Macy's, Bloomingdales, Times Square, Statue of Liberty and The Empire State Building, were all visited in a manic fashion."

"We even managed to do a spot of ice skating in Central Park. It was magical, and I would like to say that it was at one of those locations that you were conceived, but it wasn't. After all it was our honeymoon."

Realising a slight faux-pas, he petted her knee, saying, "Sorry Grace."

"Oh don't be so silly," she huffed.

"It was over before we knew it and we were soon on the plane back home to London. One glass of champagne and we both slept nearly all the way home. This was her way of divvying up the spoils in a more equal manner. Instead of fifty-fifty, this made it closer to a three-way split. Wilfred was there to meet us at the airport, and after we had babbled on and on how fantastic it all was, he advised all would be relayed to her Ladyship. As he dropped off the last of the luggage he handed me an invitation to lunch for myself and partner, meaning Barney of course, at Willoughby Manor, Sunday 24th January, 1965."

"Both excited at the invite, we were both wondering what her latest acquisitions might include. The pair of us were all suited and booted, but on this occasion, we were both also slightly apprehensive and felt something special was about to happen. So we had decided to let one of the boy's drive us down to Cranleigh. Derek dropped us off at The White Hart, while we waited for Wilfred to pick us up in the Roller, as arranged."

"Wilfred was already there when we arrived. He was now in charge of the recently delivered Pale Yellow Rolls Royce Silver Shadow, courtesy of one of our latest projects. It was ten to twelve, but a quick wrap of his knuckles on the Pub door saw it swiftly opened, and we were led to a table. A little bit of banter but nothing of any consequence was discussed, as always Barney moaned about having done £65 on the horses and we both told him gambling was a mug's game. This then led to me explaining the rudiments of craps as per Las Vegas. It all went completely over their heads but I was oblivious."

At this time I felt the need to interrupt.

"Dad, I know you like to prove to everyone that you have a terrifically good memory, and indeed it is commendable that you can recall the intricate details of a meaningless conversation from over 22 years ago, but, for crying out loud, what's it all got to do with this pantomime today? Please get to the point will you. For goodness sake, come on do me a favour, please."

"Sorry Steph," he moaned, "I must admit I do get a bit carried away sometimes. But you have got to understand that this is the only time I have ever had the opportunity to tell this story. Anyhow, we rolls up to the house, in the Rolls."

Neither of us paid any heed to the pun, so he sheepishly continued.

"Okay then. Lunch was sumptuous as always, yet instead of tea in the sitting room, Wilfred was instructed to lay out Coffee, Cuban cigars and some vintage Remy Martin V.S.O.P. Brandy in the Study. As we followed Mrs Vivian through, we both knew something was seriously afoot."

"We all sat down and made ourselves comfortable, then after lighting our cigars, sampling the velvety Brandy and sipping our coffee, it was time to reveal the true purpose of our invitation. Like I said before, this Mrs Vivian was a classy Lady."

"At this time Mrs Vivian instructed, in her most authoritative tone, 'Now now boys, this is no time to be polite. Drink up that Brandy. I will join you, and that bottle needs to be finished, before you leave this day.' She had picked up a few of our phrases over the years, but still felt slightly awkward when she chose to copy our euphemisms."

"Please don't see this as a negative day, but today I am terminating our arrangement and 'The Firm', is being put into liquidation from this day forth. Amazed, we both gulped down our Brandies in astonishment, and she merely, in the most casual of ways, took another sip."

"Mrs Vivian opened the drawer of her Bureau. Tasty bit of furniture, that was, I'll tell you, must have been circa…"

"Don't bother starting to explain about the furniture at this stage please Dad," I curtly interrupted.

"Sorry about that, Steph. Yeah. So she starts laying out some papers on her desk, then rings a delicate china bell. Wilfred enters on cue, coming in with one of them Tea Trolley things, fully loaded up with an assortment of boxes and on top, a collection of leather bound, what I thought were Encyclopaedias."

"Wilfred turned swiftly and left the room after pouring some more Brandy and coffee. Mrs Vivian was in full control of the situation, so continued, 'This document, or these papers, or whatever, are my last will and testament.'"

"We both lurched forward as one, but she soon calmed our reaction with a dismissive wave of the hand."

"No, don't start getting excited, I'm not going anywhere, not just yet anyway. There is nothing wrong with me, I assure you both. It's just that life has taken another turn for us all, at the same time. You are both now married, probably looking forward to starting your own families, and I feel it is my duty to allow the pair of you to start afresh. My position is the same, and whilst I would clearly enjoy observing how your lives progress, I sense that my own fragility may suffer as the years go by."

"Please do not think me selfish, but whilst witnessing the joys of marriage and children can be rewarding, I find myself feeling a tinge of bitterness, as I was never able to experience such things myself with my husband. I trust you both understand."

"As elegant as a prima-ballerina, she rose from her desk and approached the tea-trolley, announcing, 'The boxes below are labelled accordingly, and will be held under lock and key, in safety deposit boxes, at my Bank, until the appropriate time. In due course you may both inspect them, and then we will enjoy our last conversation together.'"

"That was when I had something serious to add," said Dad, "Well Mrs Vivian, you know me well enough, I always speak my mind."

"Of course you do, Mr Bob. I expect nothing less."

So I say: "Well, if that's the case, and I know once you've made your mind up, it is not to be detracted from."

"Don't try and speak as I do Bob, it doesn't become you," she countered.

"Oh alright then, well if this is to be our last encounter, don'tchafink we should invite Wilfred in, to join us for a couple?"

"Certainly not, what a ludicrous suggestion." she barked,

"Whatever would the world be coming to. Absolutely preposterous."

"That said, I had to take the high ground didn't I. Okay, but I don't think the one bottle of Brandy is gonna be enough, and we will certainly be requiring another cigar and a couple to go, if that's to your liking, Mrs Vee."

"I must confess," she countered, "That I had a feeling you might both get slightly emotional at such news. So, readily prepared in the back of the car, is a box each of the Havana cigars for both of you. Also a bottle of Brandy apiece and a case of vintage Dom Perignon Champagne, which I would request, if it is not too pertinent, are reserved for those special occasions of which I will not be available to partake."

"Both me and Barney were of course, indeed very emotional, and Barney chose this moment to excuse himself for a couple of minutes, while he visited the Cloakroom."

"Mrs Vivian smiled knowingly at me and whispered in the most gentle of tones, 'I knew he was the softy.'"

"She then continued, in a now more assertive manner."

"Now Mr Bob, as we agreed many years ago, we are all equal partners. What a crock of old shit that was, if ever I heard one. You and I are both, more than well aware of each and everybody else's worth. Yet the pair of us both feel it appropriate to share on equal terms. This I have honoured over the years, and we, all three, shall speak more about that later this very afternoon."

"That was when I told her not to try and talk like us as it did not become her. She then smiled that wicked smile of hers that needed no interpretation. Beautiful moment that was."

She continued, "To my right, *pointing at the tea trolley,* are all the worldly goods of which I rest any sentimental value with. Upon each and every single item, are the soul beneficiaries, and instructions as to there disposal as they see fit. You Mr Bob, are to be the trustee to all my charitable organisations and the sole executioner of my will. If, and only if, by some dastardly event, should it appertain that you were to meet your demise before myself, then be rest assured, I will duly make other arrangements. Regrettably of course. I sincerely hope, that that will not be the case."

"Barney returned at this point, with his hankie having just been returned to his jacket pocket. Once he was settled, we all had another sip of that delectable Brandy, that was now going down smoother than a £1,000 a night hooker. Sorry for the unseemly reference girls, but it seemed the most appropriate thing to say, thinking about it. Let's be fair, man cannot live on bread alone, and since your Mother died, I swore to never enter into another meaningful relationship, but I'm no Mrs Vivian."

"Alright, alright Dad, spare me the gory details," I said, "I realise you are no Trappist monk, if a situation presents itself, what are you supposed to do. But there is no need to go into all that right now."

Point taken.

This was now becoming quite complicated, one minute we were referring to 1958, then 1965, then years in between and all the other conversations and personal feelings, it was getting a bit messy. Fortunately we were now approaching Weybridge and our destination was in sight.

"So, what's the apple then Dad, what's going to happen now?"

"Well," he began, "I am going to park up in The Old Crown Pub, in Thames Street. It's situated beside the River Thames, at the point where it merges with the River Wey. Then buy a bottle of wine for you two, I know full well that you will only have one glass Min. While I have a pint and then continue with the story before I go next door to the brief. Grace is more than capable of finishing the rest of it, I can assure you."

As promised, that's exactly what he did. Grace went for the Merlot on offer, a glass of which I treated myself to also, while he had a pint of Bitter which he had no intention of finishing. Once settled down, he began again, to attempt finishing the story.

"Back to Willoughby Manor. Where was I? That's right, the old Tea trolley. So on the top, was not a load of Encyclopaedias as I first thought, but one of the most revered private coin collections in British History. The hypothetical coin collection that I mentioned many years ago."

"This, declared Mrs Vivian, "Is yours to take away today, Mr Bob. Do with it as you wish, remembering of course, my words of yesteryear that it would never be sold. Not by myself anyway. Here is another interesting piece, with a little note."

"Reaching to the under-shelf, a 15 x 15 x 10in box, covered in Navy Velvet, with the tiniest and sweetest of hatches fixed to the lid appeared."

"As the enclosed note suggests Bobby Boy, this is for you to present to the person you love most in the world, when it becomes yours to give. I only hope that you have someone other than yourself, when the time comes. I am confident you will have."

"Next up comes a similarly designed box, but of differing dimensions. 20 x 20 x 4in, with the same 18k gold latch."

"This will be yours Barney, with the same sentiments attached. They are just presents really you understand. I hope the recipients are pleasantly surprised."

"We all took another large swig of the Brandy and Mrs Vivian tinkled the little bell once more. Dead on cue, Wilfred came in with fresh coffee, and what looked like another bottle of the cherished Brandy."

"She had it all sorted, right down to the finest details." Dad said proudly. She then went on to explain that Wilfred had requested nothing, so had got the most. A nice little Cottage in Poole, Dorset, right on the shore, very popular with surfers evidently. Sandbanks it was referred to.

"There were enough shares in various companies to see him to the end of his days. These being calculated at 100, time to receive a card from the Queen. If he surpassed those years, he could sell off the shares and be comfortable for another forty. Point taken."

"Housekeeper, Mrs Bollingbroke, was more than happy to retire to the Isle of Wight with her husband. Then see out her days in the Summer House, attached to her daughter's Hotel. Another generous gift from her Ladyship, some 15 years previously."

"The Grounds man, Horace, had preferred to stay in his little Cottage at the back of the Grounds, and spend the rest of his days doing what he knew and loved best. For who or whatever took over The Manor, when Lady Willoughby was no longer around. His wages would be covered by the Estate, for as long as required."

Dad looked at his watch realising the moment was upon him.

"Well then", he announced, "Now it's time. Exactly 2:55 and I'm off next door to find out the whole shit shot and caboodle."

"Hold on a second," said Grace, "What else do you and Barney share then?"

"Have you not paid any attention at all Gracey? I don't jolly well know yet do I, and as I have stated twice already today, 'Time Waits for no-one today'. So I'll see you two clowns in about half-an hour or so. Adios amigos."

And there he was, gone.

*

27. The Longest Day Part II.

Grace and I didn't really say that much to each other over the next 45 minutes, but Dad was right, she did manage to finish the bottle of Merlot. I stuck to the one glass, against Doctor's orders I know, but this was turning into a very interesting day indeed.

When he did return, at exactly 3:45 pm as predicted, he looked like he had visited the hereafter, instead of the Solicitor next door. He was indeed a whiter shade of pale, and completely devastated. We both asked at exactly the same time what had occurred.

"A large Brandy please, the best in the house, and a nice bottle of Champagne on ice also if you don't mind please bartender."

"Remember you're driving Dad," I informed him.

"Don't worry about that Stephanie my little darlin', we are not going anywhere for an hour or so, and I fancy the occasion warrants it."

No contest.

With the drinks sorted, he began in earnest,

"Well, The Manor House, as to which it is now to be referred to, is to become a charitable trust, for one of three different purposes. Left to my discretion, and I might add responsibility. Although I am at liberty to engage all and any staff that I deem necessary."

The distraught look on his face, displayed the full knowledge and recognition of the huge responsibility he now had on his shoulders. The realisation of it all, was in reality a burden he had not been expecting, obviously. It tickled both Grace and I at the same time, and as non-poker players he sensed it straight away. Still, he had in his past, been responsible for the safety and well-being of a whole crew of villains, not come unstuck, and taken it all in his stride.

"It was quite a long two minute walk from that Solicitor's. A man of my new found position must make important decisions, not rash ones mind you. Such a decision has been made. I fancied, with this new dilemma placed upon my shoulders you two might find it amusing. So let me tell you both, you are now duly appointed trustees and members of The Board. So will be able to share this delightful responsibility with me. Welcome to the Club."

Then holding his hand up as if to initiate or offer surrender,

A Lovely Pair of Knockers

"Don't bother trying to wriggle out of it. You will only be in advisory positions, but I know I will be able to rely upon you both to help with the usual fundraisers, fetes etc. etc. it's all women's work you know."

All of a sudden Grace and I were colluded into the events of the day. He continued with a revitalised glow in his cheeks,

"We can all three of us sit down in the near future and decide what to do with the place. There is a year long deferral or deference period, before we make any final decisions and forward the relevant proposals to the local Council, for approval. Whaddayassay?"

As if we had any choice, in the matter.

"So while we are all cosied up in this little boozer, before it all goes out of my head, I'll finish describing the rest of that memorable and delightful afternoon. Just before that though, excuse me please Bill, can I get a large Ploughman's to share please, and three packets of crisps please? That'll help soak up a bit of the booze."

"With all the niceties taken care of, Mrs Vivian asks us, 'Do you remember when we were first acquainted chaps?'"

"Of course we do," answered Barney, "No that I had much to say on that fateful day."

"You've not had too much to say for yourself at all, over the years really," she commented, "Still, we all have our roles to play, and Bob here has had to go the extra miles and stick his 'Boat Up' more often than not for the cause, as they say."

"She had shown us so many different ways to play the game. In the summer of 1962 she suggested to The All England Club that an anonymous sponsor would treat all the Wimbledon Ball Boys and Girls, to a special Gala Dinner at The Savoy Hotel."

"She would gladly present each and every one of them with a commemorative medal to mark the event. Of course all the top committee members were invited at the Top Table and the Master of Ceremonies toasted each and every one of them by name. A framed certificate was issued bearing their name, as an official keepsake."

Shortly after this Dad received his All England Club membership, and has had Centre Court tickets for every Wimbledon Championships since. The tradition still continues, but the venue changes from year to year.

A Lovely Pair of Knockers

Dad proudly explained how, using her guile, Mrs Vivian hints at an early stage of the season, the possibility that the Wimbledon Gala Dinner may befall a different reputable establishment, which was in with a chance this year. Then miraculously, hey-ho for a mere £5 per head, top Hotels would be offering facilities, within weeks, hoping to become host to such a prestigious event.

*

A similar tactic was taken in 1964, when their beloved Hammers made it to the F.A.Cup Final. Although she had little interest in the sport, Mrs Vivian invited two prospective investors to a fundraising Luncheon at The Dorchester. The donation of £3,000 to The Royal Variety Club, ensured 4 tickets for the match arrived three days later in the post.

They had a great day with 'The Hammers' beating Preston North End 3-2. John Simmons, Geoff Hurst and Ronnie Boyce getting the goals. Sir Geoff would return to Wembley a couple of years later and score that historical hat-trick against the Germans.

West Ham United's lucky number was three that year, all through the competition. Check the statistics;

First game in round three, 3-0 against Charlton Athletic.
Second game round four, 3-0 against Leyton Orient, on a replay.
Third game in round five, 1-3 away to Swindon.
Fourth game in round six, 3-1 to beat Burnley.
In the semi-final it was, 3-1 again, beating the fancied Man United.

This match was held at Hillsborough. Where some years later Liverpool fans would suffer terribly at the hands of the F.A. Due to their bad organisation and terrible distribution of ticket allocation.

The police didn't help of course, but who am I to say? It was a bad day for Sport altogether, but Liverpudlian's especially, who still carry the torture and mental anguish that they will never forget.

To this day you still cannot buy The Sun Newspaper in Liverpool, due to their awful biased coverage of events after that sad day.

A Lovely Pair of Knockers

With their tickets, there was also written confirmation that two tickets would be available to Bob and Barney, available for collection at a special gate, for every England International match thereafter. As well as all the F.A. Cup finals.

Dad and Barney particularly enjoyed surprising a couple of old pals when the situation arose. If they couldn't make it themselves, or were not particularly interested, they ensured those using the tickets behaved immaculately. They were never let down.

The stories rumbled on.

Mrs Vivian revelled in how she had 'sculpted' the pair of them, and groomed them to perfection. She also marvelled at the way they had adapted themselves into honest businessmen, without forgetting their roots. She felt no compunction to pull them up on any of their mannerisms or of the formal behaviour expected.

She would always have forewarned any fellow guests that might take exception that they, Bob & Barney, were her pet project.

"So please make allowances," would be requested. Followed by the foreboding words, "You would not wish to embarrass me, now would you? That I can assure you would be a grave mistake."

Few made the mistake, and those that did, suffered badly.

One such occasion happened at the Races. Invited to Ladies Day at Royal Ascot, Mum, Dad, Barney and Grace were enjoying themselves in Mrs Vivian's Private Box. A very rare occasion, as this was to be one the last occasions they would mingle in Public. Mrs Vivian had instinctively sensed this was the time to part company. They were sniggered at by Lord and Lady Ashfordly, for not knowing what Oysters Fitzpatrick were. When they all decided to settle for 'normal' ones instead, with Champagne.

Mrs Vivian, visited her stonemason for two weeks in September. At the same time Ashfordly Hall, was visited one night by uninvited guests. An estimated £85,000 of Silverware, a John Constable Painting, and jewellery to the tune of £210,000 was amiss, never to be recovered.

That Christmas, two large Great Danes, were placed either side of the front door at Willoughby Manor. The Great Danes were to be a pertinent point. Mrs Vivian had had the stables converted into kennels by now. She proposed to breed Great Danes and had engaged a very enthusiastic gay couple to help with the hobby. Jimmy and Johnny were very enthusiastic, heard of these two before somewhere, turning up like a pair of unwanted Jacks at a poker game. This was one of the reasons she now expressed her wishes to venture to pastures new. Hence also the need for the newly constructed East Wing in which the happy couple could reside in privacy.

The kennels had come courtesy of the interminably rude Lady Middleton, of Sudbury. The unfortunate loss of family jewellery, stolen in a dawn raid one summer night. By some chancers, had said the Police. The fact that she was known to partake in far too much Gin on a Saturday night, and not lock the doors properly, did not help with her subsequent insurance claim.

The Annual Stable Lads Boxing Finals was another similar Sporting coup. Another extremely prestigious affair, at The Hilton Hotel, Hyde Park corner. Not one attended by Ladies though, not in those days anyway. They found themselves getting into the atmosphere quickly, and so donating generously to the fund for retired jockeys or stable-lads who had fallen on hard times.

This was a weird kind of turnout, as all the distinguished owners and trainers of the time were in attendance. They spent copious amounts of money and donated extravagantly. Raffle tickets alone came in at £50 each, but the two main prizes were a Rolls Royce Car, and a World Cruise on the QE2.

You couldn't help thinking, why didn't they just pay the jockeys and stable-lads more when they were riding?

Anyway, this led to Dad and Barney becoming fully fledged members of The Jockey Club. Now a simple phone call prior to the relevant meeting, names given, and entrance to the Owners and Trainers Enclosure was assured. This applied to any course in the UK, the very next day. Glorious Goodwood was their favourite, with Epsom a close second, just by a short head, all taken for granted. They invariably got wind of a nice few winners, as they were considered insiders. The usual comment being, 'I think she will run very well today', or 'good value at the price for sure', that was usually information enough. Neither Dad nor Barney were big gamblers any way, in any aspect of their lives.

A Lovely Pair of Knockers

He explained that after getting through far too much of the Brandy, Mrs Vivian still had all her senses about her. Unfortunately he and Barney were now three sheets to the wind, and upon her instructions, Wilfred gathered their things together and placed them in the Car. Then dropped them off at their pick-up point where their own driver would finish the job and take them home. The Coin Collection had it's very own impregnable steel container, only Dad had the combination.

As cordial as ever, despite all three having consumed far more alcohol than anticipated, the farewell was considerably restrained. They had promised never to try and get in touch with her again, and the only method of contact would be via Christmas cards. This was all very exact, as one would expect.

Bob would send his on the 25th November; it would include a short yet courteous note so that any relevant news could be conveyed. Once read it would then be destroyed. Mrs Vivian's card would arrive by 22nd December; any note included would suffer the same fate. These were her specific conditions, not to be detracted from.

They kissed the back of her hand in turn, then put their arms around each other as they made their way to the waiting Wilfred. She escorted them to the door, then Mrs Vivian, turned and didn't look back, and neither did they. And that was that.

"But Dad," I implored, "Didn't you ever want to go and visit her again. You know, when she was a bit older."

"Of course I did Min, but when sticklers like that, give such positive instructions, if you went against their wishes they would feel totally devastated and yeah I suppose, well, betrayed would be the best way to put it. With that sort of relationship why would anyone in their right mind wanna ruin it? A couple of years ago, her little note with the card, informed me that Wilfred had died a few months earlier and it was a shame I couldn't be there. That old Stiff-Upper-Lip is one hell of a thing you know."

"What do you think she felt like, when my little note in 1968 included the news that your Mother had died. My Christmas Card that year had a Robin on it, with a tear on it's cheek, and the note said, Very sorry for your loss. I pray for you and your daughter. Love Mrs V. That was the toughest letter I ever threw on the fire."

"Of course, then there was that other terrible year when I had informed her of Barney's Cancer discovery, and terminal condition. True to form, her card arrived promptly. The little note expressing deepest sympathy for all concerned, and sadness at the awful news of a much-trusted person. May his pain be short and the ending be swift. Mrs Vivian. Even under those circumstances, she would not consider going back on our arrangement."

"Then, right out of the blue comes this strange message by telegram. Requesting me to lunch at The Royal Garden Hotel, Kensington, with a Mr Smithson at 12:30 pm, Friday February 12th, 1972. To discuss a proposition to which all conspirators would benefit. It had that hint of Mrs Vivian about it."

"I attended accordingly and was led to a corner table, after enquiring the whereabouts of Mr Smithson. A fellow came and sat opposite me at the table set for two, he was unremarkably indescriptive. He introduced himself as Henry, he then ordered a Caesar Salad with a bottle of the House Chardonnay. Upon tasting it and agreeing it was a fine vintage, he excused himself to go to the Gents. I never clapped eyes on him ever again."

"He had, however, left under his side plate, a small envelope. Which he had indicated with a flick on the side of his nose when departing, was for my attention. I had his Caesar Salad with my Gammon, Egg and Chips. Finishing the bottle of Chardonnay that had been left. Lovely lunch it was. Then when I asked for the bill, was told my Gentleman friend had been called away on urgent business and had already settled the account. Even lovelier then I thought."

"Come on Dad, you're starting to slip off the track again," I advised, "You were doing quite well there for a while, don't spoil it all now." This would be his last reprimand.

"Right," he agreed, "I scanned the instructions very carefully. It was all typed out. With the full knowledge that it should be destroyed once read. It seems that there was about to be a disastrous fire at Windsor Castle. This was to be a terrible event and many very valuable paintings, sculptures and works of Art would be lost for eternity. Unless, by some strange coincidence they could be moved prior to the tragedy."

"This is your last job. Don't let the side down. That there resembled a familiar tone."

"Then go out and enjoy being the unknown Talk of The Town. Best Regards. Then as an after thought on the part of the sender, was typed: 'If of course you or any of your associates should be caught during this operation, nor I or anyone else known to me will have any knowledge of your existence.'"

"There was no return address to send a reply to anyway. But I knew damn well where it had come from. She just couldn't leave it, could she, I thought to myself. It was all a bit Mission Impossible I know, but needless to say there were a lot of comings and goings at Windsor Castle that following week."

"Barney was not well enough to take part but masterminded most of the operation. It was his swansong job and at times he really did look like he was getting better. He deteriorated quite rapidly once the haul was stashed."

"Posing as an Art Historian, commissioned by Lloyd's of London, the insurers. With some brilliant forged identification and appropriate authorisation. Barney even engaged the services of a top make-up artist from Pinewood Studios to disguise me beyond all recognition. You would have walked straight past me yourself Steph. You and all, Grace."

"We logged and chogged some of the nicest and saleable items with consummate ease. A few pieces also needed minor repairs and were taken with all the relevant receipts issued. It seemed three oil paintings were also in need of slight restoration."

"Quite a few bits of Silverware needed professional polishing to restore to its full effect and glory. I complimented some of the staff on their excellent work, but explained after a hundred years or so, some pieces just needed a little bit more than the old Brillo, y'know."

"The haul was quite delicious to look at, once all collected and safely stored at Shoreham Airport in the secretly acquired hanger. In a very well secured office we had a huge safe that Barney had said even he wouldn't even attempt 'to blow the bloody doors off'. Of course if it was warranted, he'd have a go at anything."

"It was in fact, the last one of seven made by The Hayman Safe Company, of USA. They were all originally allocated to major branches of The Midland Bank, in various parts of the country. There had been a Union issue over health and safety regulations at the Coventry branch, so the refurbishment there, was way behind schedule."

"The last vault had been left undelivered due to parking space availability. So, tipped off by one of our mates down the docks, we had quite simply just loaded the container it was stored in, onto a low loader. Driven it down to the airport, then unhitched it neatly in the far corner, and that was it. The low loader was driven up to Gatwick, parked up, cleaned up and then reported stolen."

"Some soft furnishings were installed in the container, along with electricity and water supply, for making tea and coffee. And there you had a pretty much impregnable office."

"Being accustomed to relieving others of their valuables, we were certainly not willing to take any chances of the role being reversed."

He then sniggered to himself, muttering under his breath, "Me and my mate woz no fucking mugs, that's for sure."

Grace gave a knowing smile and whispered to the pair of us,

"Make you right there, you slippery couple of bastards."

Dad continued:

"Curiously there was no news coverage or mention of the Windsor Castle incident in the papers. Proof enough that the Royals have more control over the tabloids than people give them credit for. And the Public only get to know what is deemed appropriate, by the powers that be that is."

"I'd liked to have been a fly on the wall when the penny dropped at what had occurred. One moment the staff are devastated about the small fire. Then relieved beyond belief that quite a few items were being restored, and so were not on the premises at the time of incident. Then when contacting the relevant companies, that had been fortunate to call just days before the tragedy, another bombshell. I'm still not sure who fared the best out of the whole scenario."

"Did Lloyd's, who were surely the underwriters, fork out for the missing valuables or not? You could hardly accuse the Queen and Prince Philip of trying to fiddle an insurance claim. Like some kind of commoner, now could they? Or would they? Just another little storm

A Lovely Pair of Knockers

in a teacup for the Royals. Oh that reminds me, did I mention there was a 48-piece Royal Doulton Tea Service that was having a much-needed touch up too. Very carefully packed up in its very own Tea Chest."

"It really did feel like the nearest thing to nicking 'The Crown Jewels'. But as none of it was so sensationally well known about, was not so hard to offload. Tell a Texan Billionaire that something had come from Windsor Castle and you practically had a blank cheque thrown at you. Let's just say there were plenty of zeroes anyway."

"Most of it went to private buyers in the States. But also, there was an Egyptian fellow, who took a shine to a few bits and was only too happy to pay well over the odds. He'd just bought a corner shop somewhere in Knightsbridge."

"Twenty years later there was to be a much more serious fire at the Castle, practically gutting the place. Maybe they recouped the losses from the previous misdemeanours, on that one."

"Due to the unusual circumstances of 'The Big One', as I like to refer to it. I just sat on the money till Christmas, feeling sure the accompanying note, with the card, would reveal all. It did really, but in a lovely way. 'Crufts having slight difficulties with major sponsor. Any Ideas?' A cheque was made out to the Kennel Club for £150,000 from one of my offshore holding companies, along with the request that it should remain anonymous."

"This was my big chance though, I thought to myself. Mrs Vivian, now seriously involved as a judge in these doggy doo-dahs, was bound to be there. So I could get to see her one more time. She beat me to it though. A postcard arrived on Valentine's Day from Monte Carlo, and the familiar handwriting stated, 'Please do not spoil my Crufts experience'."

"Mrs V. had obviously felt the same sentiments, and did not wish for any unexpected people to turn up. I conceded, of course. That's one of England's great traditions to which I will never attend. I might do now though, after all I send 'em a nice little cheque for £10,000 every bloody year. Should be entitled to decent seats, dont'chafink?"

"Of course the Christmas tradition continued and when I informed her of Barney's demise she sent the same card with the weeping Robin on it. The little note just said, 'So sad, but you must stay strong for those around you. Another trusted friend is gone. Mrs V.'

"That's about it then, he declared. Mrs Vivian, in her own cunning and loving way, has seen fit for us to pave the way forward. I guess we should be honoured. A few distant relatives have had their meagre donations applied and it appears the rest is now up to me. Only a couple of minor finishing touches to deal with on the way home, so let's go girls."

He then jumped up, downed a glass of champagne, passed a glass to Grace and promptly whizzed around the Pub, giving away the champers till the bottle was drained.

Ushering us both into the back of the Bentley, he took off at a moderate pace. He'd only had the large Brandy and a glass of Champagne, but as he said, even without anything to drink he would still be flying.

*

The Forest Road was legendary as one of Dick Turpin's favourite haunts, now known as Houndhurst Road, but I already told you that.

It was at many points not wide enough for two vehicles to pass each other, so we now cruised at a steady 30mph, with intermittent stops for oncoming traffic. It was a beautiful day for more than one reason. The sun filtered through the trees in a mesmerising fashion.

With a few packages on the passenger seat he asked:
"Well, Grace are you ready for it?"
"Ready for what?" she asked.
"You cannot possibly believe I was kidding after all this time surely?" he answered quite indignantly.
"What on earth are you going on about Robert?" Grace was now genuinely puzzled.
"This of course," he bellowed. He then raised a package containing a navy coloured Velvet covered box, approx 20 x 20 x 4in, at which Grace gasped in amazement, before he slung it straight into her lap.

A Lovely Pair of Knockers

"What's in this then?" she asked. Dad was beside himself.

"For crying out loud Grace, knock me down with a feather, for the last time. Have you not listened to a single solitary sodding word I have bloody well said? This is it. The gift to Barney, from Mrs Vivian. To give to the person he loves most in the World. If he was still here with us now, he'd most definitely give it to you, now wouldn't he? So here it is. I do not have a clue what is in it so please, please me, and put me out of my misery."

Tentatively glancing in my direction, Grace tripped the latch, and looked inside the case. Then she just fainted. Dropping the box on the car floor.

"What's happening? What the fuck's going on?" shouted Dad, "Sort it out Steph will yah?"

All the excitement and the couple of drinks were now taking their toll on all three of us. But I remained calm, took a bottle of Perrier water from my Hermes bag and threw it over Grace's face rather ingratuitously. Then out came the baby wipes and I dabbed her forehead. As she came to, she instinctively grabbed at and retrieved the velvet box, like a street beggar snatching at a stray five-pound note. Then came the glow on her face that was equal to The Good Fairy of The West, from The Wizard of Oz.

Opening the case again, she proudly revealed a 20in necklace that held 10 six-carat sapphires each surrounded by two carats of diamonds, with matching earrings. Stunning and surreal is surely not enough to describe it.

"I can't believe it," she finally managed to blurt out, "There was I, thinking all along this was another of your pranks or fairy tales Robert."

"When have I ever told you porkies, or led you up the garden path Gracie baby? Everything I have told the pair of you today is the Babe. Now I know Barney is not around to help out. To share out in a friendly way, our newly acquired responsibilities and problems. But we must be sure to honour him and do the best we can, dont'chafink?"

"I suppose so," she replied, in a docile way that I had never witnessed before.

Looking at me now, in the rear view mirror,

"Well then," he carried on joyously, "Here it jolly well is."

"Here is what?" I enquired.

"The very last piece of the puzzle my little darling. The last piece of the jigsaw, to complete a lovely pretty picture."

With that he tossed a navy coloured velvet box 15 x 15 x 8in, over his shoulder with the accuracy of a fly fisherman. It landed right smack, bang, in the middle of my lap.

"Oh well," I remarked, glancing across at Grace, and catching Dad's eye in the mirror, "Here goes."

He winked, smiled and then sticking his thumb in the air said, "Here's looking at you kid."

Slightly nervous and a bit shaky, I teased the latch and then the lid open to take my first glimpse of the contents. To my amazement, inside was the most fantastic, and yet, delightful Fabergé Egg. Gold and purple with, with…….. then exclaimed

"Oh fuck, goodness gracious me My waters have just broke."

*

28. The Longest Day Part III.

The back seat was sopping wet and I suddenly had this feeling of complete helplessness.
"Oh shit," cried Dad.
"Don't worry, don't worry," insisted Grace, who had no experience whatsoever of this situation.
"Right, don't panic, don't panic," Dad screamed. "Fuck me I sound like Corporal Jones, from Dad's fuckin' Army. As it happens, really and truly, don't panic. Two minutes up the road and there is some sort of Scout Camp or something. I'll pull in there and see what sort of help we can get. They'll be sure to have a phone and be able to call an ambulance, or at least tell us the best Hospital to head for."
My turn now, "Well, I've never done this before Dad, but I have a funny feeling we do not have time to wait around for a poxy Ambulance, or take instructions and soppy map readings to see which bloody Hospital is the most convenient."
Then a magical line that would stay with us all forever,
"Hold on to this Egg for me Grace, I think I'm hatching myself today."
As we pulled into the dirt track that led up to The Scout Hut, as he described it, there was a vague resemblance of a building. I then came over all dizzy, and wished I hadn't had that one glass of fizzy. We were all poets by now of course, another one of the many traits I had gotten into, since meeting them sodding Brighton Knocker Boys.
The next few hours are all a bit too hazy to even bother recounting. You ladies that have shared the experience need not to read all about it, because you have been there, done it, and bought the T-Shirt.
For you fellahs reading this. It's really not worth trying to explain what we go through, because you simply cannot coerce or understand in the slightest what it's all about. For those girls who have yet to experience childbirth, I say, your day will come soon enough. No need to spoil it for you with T.M.I.

*

Needless to say the experience was, as with every Mother, a life changing moment. The boy came first, at 11:05 pm, last orders, and her highness arrived 15 minutes later, just before closing time at 11:20.

So, he was on time and she scraped in at the last minute, a trait that would follow them for their entire lives.

He was quiet at first, but she came out screaming. Undoubtedly they had been fighting inside of me to see which one could get out first. This for the next five years would be a bone of contention between them. They were to do everything else in life simultaneously. All the lovely things, and all the worst things, but I'll come to all that, a bit later.

They were certainly Babes in The Woods, as far as we were all concerned, Dad for some strange reason was really conscientious about me not giving them names immediately. Of course I had ticked over in my mind many possible names, popular at the time, but these circumstances, now had a totally new perspective.

One of my pals had already advised that when you have that automatic unconditional love that you are encapsulated with, once having a child, or two as in my case. It is only then that you should choose a name that will stay with you, and the child naturally, forever. Quite a big responsibility really, and too be fair I was absolutely knackered and wanted to sleep for a week. Yet couldn't bear the thought of missing one incy wincey second of staring at these two beautiful little things, that were so contentedly nestled next to me. Their Mum.

Nevertheless, I drifted off from 12:15 am to 2:45 am, then, woke up in a blind panic. Alone in a strange room. I flew out of the bed and ran into a common room, and there proudly, sitting in a comfy looking velvet Chesterfield sofa was Dad, cradling the pair of them. With Grace standing behind cooing like a Mother Goose.

"What the hell do you think you are playing at," I demanded. "Ain't babies supposed to be kept with their Mother's at this time? Bonding and all that shit."

"Of course Steph" he smiled lovingly, with a glow in his face that I had forgotten about, "But don't you think it might be wise to make yourself a little bit more, let's say, presentable luv."

A Lovely Pair of Knockers

Looking down, I realised I didn't have a stitch of clothing on, so sheepishly pointed a weak wavering finger at him and said:

"I'll see you in a minute."

"Okay sweetheart, you just get back into bed, then me and these two little cherubs will be straight in."

Grace had quickly covered me up, having snatched a lovely soft 'throw-over', from off of the couch and wrapped it over my shoulders. Also sparing my dignity, by covering other bits, don't mention tits.

"Come on Steph, let's sort you out babe. It's been a long day."

"Long day," I shouted, "Long fucking day. Them prats on Breakfast telly, were certainly not bloody well joking, when they said it was the longest day of the year, were they Grace?"

She moved her head from side to side and agreed with me, "No, they were definitely right about that one Steph."

Dad popped his head around the door, to let us know he was going out to the car, and did we need anything.

"A genuine Fabergé Egg would be nice," I could not resist mentioning.

At that point Grace's jaw dropped and her eyes literally popped out of her head. She went extremely pale, and for that split second I thought something bad was about to occur.

When he came back with three nice mugs of Nescafe, he sat down and mockingly mopped his brow, in a most exaggerated fashion.

"Well, you certainly know when your luck's in, that's for sure. Some chancer could have nicked the Bentley outside, while you were in labour. Well possible I might add, because I never bothered to lock it, and even left the keys in the ignition."

"I know we are off the beaten track an' all that, but you never know. They would have had a nice ride for a few miles, then discovered on the back seat, a priceless Fabergé Egg. And a necklace with matching earrings worth about a million quid."

Grace reacted in astonishment, but I could tell she was aware of her mistake and I knew she was guilty.

"Oh no, Robert, I didn't did I?"

"Yep, you certainly well did Grace. Mind you, what with all the commotion, it's no great surprise. But no harm done. Here we go", and with that he pulled his jacket open to reveal both of the velvet clad boxes with contents intact.

Then he decided to ask the all-important question,

"So, what are we gonna call these two herberts then. Hansel and Gretel would be fitting dont'chafink?"

They certainly were 'Babes In The Woods', I agreed, but let's just take a little while, before I decide.

The pair of them, then began to explain what had happened. Gradually it all came back to me, as they recounted the events of the previous evening.

As we had arrived unexpectedly, the Chief Scout Master, or whatever his position at the time, had heard the car approaching and had rushed to the door.

Known as the Bentley Copse Scout Camp Site, it was quite ironic as we actually arrived in a Bentley, would you agree?

He feared the worst at first, down to the extremely agitated look on Dad's face. But then sprang into action, once he was made aware of the predicament at hand, and called emergency services, for an Ambulance. Amazingly, the telephone operator who took the call, was also a local nurse, and advised she would contact Sister Mary Sledge at the nearby Rectory in Cranleigh. She would be sure to arrive sooner than any ambulance, so long as she was in the vicinity.

Checking that there were appropriate supplies and necessary tools of the trade available so to speak, she advised that everything would be okay, and all of you try and keep as calm as possible. Ringing off impatiently and with a curt attitude, Dad had been very concerned how things might pan out. He was of no bloody use, as far as he was concerned anyway.

The poor sod was totally bewildered by everything that was going on around him. All he could do was pace up and down with the proverbial cigar gritted between his teeth.

Then within just two flat minutes, the very same girl called back. Advising that Sister Mary was on her way, and would arrive in approximately 12 minutes, and take charge of the situation. And that was exactly how long it took before the delightful Sister Mary arrived

A Lovely Pair of Knockers

and rang the doorbell. Her entrance was all very prim and proper. Resembling Audrey Hepburn, in Sabrina mode, certainly not inferring she might be any Holly-Go-Lightly, I might add.

Her habit was removed upon entry of my allocated bedroom, and all of a sudden a warm calmness overcame everyone present in the house. Her soft, soothing voice was like an angel from heaven. She asked at first all our names, then slipped over casually on to how often the contractions were coming.

She then opened her handbag, removed a packet of chocolate digestives and declared,

"That's all very good then, now why don't we all have a nice cup of tea? Shall we?"

Whilst sipping her tea, reminiscent of Mary Poppins interviewing potential clients, she gave what seemed to me, a barrage of questions that bordered on Gestapo interrogation procedures.

But of course they were all relevant to the situation at hand. Easily answered, and obliviously, also distracted me from the terrible pain I was feeling. When the ambulance finally arrived at 6:30 pm, she simply signed a prescription for some painkillers and packed the paramedics off. Instructing them that everything was fine and in good order.

She would supervise everything at this stage, and it was clearly inadvisable to move the expectant Mother. She was satisfied at present that things were taking their natural course. If there were to be any unfortunate complications she would advise accordingly, but at the present time this was not anticipated. Praise the Lord, My Sweet Lord.

Without any prior knowledge as to how these things pan out, I can only presume that she carried out her duties in the most concise and impeccable manner.

As I was now in possession of the two most beautiful little creatures in the whole wide world. I knew that somebody up there liked me, but even so, a Fabergé Egg could come close. Of course, there was indeed, one very close by.

I had decided on their names, but felt very strongly about the occurrences of the day.

There was an imploring compulsion to include the surroundings in this most memorable of moments. So I had finally devised a way in which to commemorate both this Godsend of a place, and all those that were a part of it.

The circumstances and the logistics just had to be recognised, so I began,

"Okay Dad, you know exactly how I feel about this road, and although I was unaware of this God forsaken place we find ourselves in now. I still need to honour my first hopes and wishes, from many years ago."

Holding up my two gorgeous and delectable little miracles, I announced,

"Here we have Will & Scarlet. I fancy my original choices of Billy & Tillie will bode as pet names. As a family we have always used them ourselves, so I see no need to discontinue such a family tradition and practise at this stage. Will, as in William, is shortened to Billy, and Scarlett exaggerates the T's into Tillie. If they both decide at later dates, or stages in their lives, to be addressed as Will & Scarlett, well, if and when the issue arises, they will be old enough to make up their own bloody minds anyway. Or mind their own make ups, or, oh shit, I'm going all dizzy again," then I passed out. Again.

When I was aroused an hour or so later, everyone seemed really pleased to see me. Evidently, the fainting bit was only natural, but I had not responded to the usual practises of regaining consciousness. However, my Father had created merry hell as to why the fuck I was not coming back to the land of the fucking living, and if I was not brought back within the next five minutes, there would be severe repercussions for all concerned.

A bit dramatic I know, but he thought at the time he had lost me. How sweet, that he cared so much.   Bless Him.

Once I was back in the land of the living, I had a quick shifty with Grace to check-in where I had checked-out, so to speak.

Attracting everyone's attention, I decided to continue with my reasoning for the kid's names.

"I and I alone am responsible for the names of my children, explaining the whys and wherefores is of no consequence to me at this present time, but here goes anyway. Will's middle name will be Stephen, and Scarlett's will be Mary."

*

After all my Dad had nicknamed me Minnie the Minx as a child and this had been shortened to Minnie as the years went by, with anyone worth their salt being aware of the connotation.

*

Sister Mary had been phenomenal. Strong when required and extremely pleasant despite the unrequited and blasphemous outbursts of complete strangers that she had no previous knowledge or commitments to or from. She had also shown an unbelievable tolerance for the likes of us, under such demanding circumstances.

She probably expected to meet a different type of group when entering the scout camp, what with the Bentley parked outside. On top of that, she brought untapped strength and a tremendous sense of camaraderie amongst us all. Sainthood was deservable, but I was not in a position to grant such an accolade. The Pope's gotta do something for his bloody money.

"You certainly have been a busy girl," remarked Dad, sitting right next to me and my Babies in bed, rubbing his chin,

"I can't say anything you have said is at all unreasonable, and even if I did it's not my call. There is one little thing niggling in the back of my mind though, but I'm sure it can wait."

"Dad," I shot back at him, "I reckon we have had enough news today. Now is not the time to start leave anything else unsaid. Dont'chafink?"

"I reckon you're right there Min. So here goes. Well, what about the Father? Is he not entitled to be made aware of the existence of these two beautiful little babies? And although I am more than willing, honoured in fact, to help in any way that I can, they do also have other Grandparents. They may also wish to care and share in this joyous occasion."

Time to explain my take on the situation. I had pondered this inevitable scenario, many times over in my head during the last few months. He was always on my mind, but no part of any future plans.

"I have not taken this situation lightly Dad. Let's get serious, if I put my mind to it, I know full well I could find him and let him know of the particulars at hand. Lovechild could be bandied about, but it really would not be fair to any of those concerned. If and when he returns, from wherever or whatever he's doing, the situation will be reviewed and all things taken into consideration. Until that occurs let's just keep schtum. Anyway, as Will's middle name is to be Stephen, I reckon that that is confirmation enough as to paternity issues. His name will also be on their Birth Certificates."

"I appreciate your concerns for his parents, but I've never met them, and I'm not about to start turning up on their doorstep. From what I can gather as far as this sort of thing is concerned, it is not their responsibility. Then, of course, it puts them in an unenviable and very awkward position. How can they not tell their son he is a Father? It is up to me to do that, and at this stage I think I have made my thoughts clear enough. I do not wish to discuss the matter any further, to quote wise words of a much respected Lady."

He nodded affirmatively and the subject did not arise for another six years.

Sister Mary had some lovely crocheted shawls that adorned my lovely babies. She even produced an ancient Polaroid camera to capture some of those first hours for eternity. There were no great expectations of the resulting photographs but they turned out to be sensational. Unforgettable.

I know we are creeping into the next day now, but I'm sure you will forgive me, due to the extenuating circumstances.

Nobody was particularly tired but, some shut-eye was definitely needed by all, so we still managed to get a few hours kip. Then at 7:30 am Grace called the Cranleigh Community Hospital, as advised by Sister Mary, to have the 'Babes in The Woods', fully checked over.

We got back onto the Road, passed Cranleigh Golf and Country Club, then veered right on Barhatch Road which took us down to the B2127. Then along till St Nicholas Church right opposite the Hospital.

This was just common practise, and to register them officially. Sister Mary had not overlooked the matter of Birth Certificates; she merely had none on her person at the time she was first contacted. She had of course duly signed an affidavit to confirm Dates, Weights and Times of Birth. Will had weighed in at 6lbs 7oz, whilst the slightly more petite yet perfect Scarlett was recorded at exactly one pound lighter.

In all fairness I was about to make an out of character impulsive gesture, but would never regret it. Nobody else could understand or even contemplate how important this decision was to me. Or possibly, from another perspective, dastardly unfair treatment of an indefensive tiny little baby girl. I knew though in my heart that when the moment of truth did arise, that my little treasure would see the funny and affectionate side of the story, hopefully anyway.

But what can an indefensible little baby do about their circumstances when delivered into this world? The same had applied to me after all. Do you remember? Spoon / Toothpick.

When the registrar asked for my details, to be recorded on the Birth Certificate, without the slightest glimmer of humour whatsoever, I instructed all the names as discussed. But then an uncontrollable urge and feeling of inconceivable mischief came over me, and I could not resist the temptation put before me. When it came to the second born, I instructed that the official name to be recorded should be Scarlett Bloody Mary Marchant. He smiled ruefully and did as he was told. It had a ring to it, don't you think?

Once all the official stuff was taken care of, it was all plain sailing. I couldn't give a toss what anyone was up to, so carried on regardless.

They never even looked similar to me. Although some say all newborn babies look the same anyway, but as far as I can recall, nobody else ever mistook one for the other. Obviously Billy was in Blue, Navy and sometimes a cool shade of Green. Scarlett in White, Pink and Lemon. This immediate colour clarification surely helped everyone distinguish the difference, but even though it was unintentional, it was probably some subliminal conscientious decision on my part. To give them both their own identity, and individuality.

Everything was in order at the Hospital. They had been well pre-empted of our arrival and it was practically a supermarket sweep. Every department had been awaiting our imminent arrival and things had gone as smooth as my two little baby's bums, as warranted. I was assured, in no uncertain terms, that not a single living soul, would wish Sister Mary's latest arrivals to have anything other than 100% service and attention. She undoubtedly had a lot of clout at this particular establishment.

*

It must have been about 10:30 am, when we finally began our journey back home to Brighton. Dad now also had a place in town, and conducted most of his business from my Offices, in Hove actually.

As we pulled onto the A23, Dad made his first grand gesture of the day,

"I expect you'll be visiting Mothercare on a regular basis over the coming months, and years won't you?"

My sarcastic reply was to be regrettable:

"I dare say that is a likely assumption. Hardly worthy of Mastermind or Pub Quiz stature Dad. What the heck are you getting at now?"

He then fished out of a previously unnoticed nondescript briefcase, a pristine leather bound folder and gently passed it carefully over his shoulder for my consideration, adding:

"I don't know exactly how it works out for any discounts, but that there represents about two million quid's worth of shares in Mothercare. They should have gone to Wilfred, but hey-ho the company is pretty solid. Mrs Vivian, of course, had never stepped across the threshold of any stores, but found it sort of comforting, what with not having kids an' all that. Them two herberts will be the only two kids in the shop who could actually buy the whole sodding lot. Absolutely fabulous, they can have everything that they look at. Funny old game innit?"

He then started to chuckle to himself for the next ten miles or so, then came out with a classic comment:

"That's not too shabby is it? How's that for a little kick-start in life. A million quid each, and they ain't even got indoors yet, bloody marvellous. Oh yeah, plus I will throw in a little Holiday Home down in Poole, Dorset, just for laughs. The Sandbanks are reputedly the most expensive and exclusive bits of Real Estate in the whole country. She knew her stuff did Mrs Vivian, it's like The Hampton's of England it is. Somewhere to go, in the summertime, when the weather is fine. Old Wilfred won't be needing it."

He was no singer, but we could not resist joining in when he began chanting,

"Who wants to be a millionaire? They do. Have lots of fights and greasy hair. They do."

During the final stages of the journey home, both babies finally relaxed and within minutes, both of them slept soundly. I could swear every breath they took was totally in sync.

"Dad," I whispered, "What happened to the Copper you mentioned earlier? The one that got the gooner when you met Mrs Vivian?"

"Oh old Ted, well he karked it late in 69'. Some sort of traffic accident or something. It was all a bit of shame that. He had been quite useful to me and Barney. We earned some good money with the old umbrella. He didn't actually get the gooner though, he was just taken down the pegging order so to speak."

"We had a nice tight little crew sorted, so any of his clues, still got proper attention, and his end was always given respect. He kept earning till the day he died. He even got a nice drink for some jobs that had nothing to do with him. It was truly a case of honour amongst thieves wiv' the old Bethnal Green Berets, babe."

"It was all down to our Dad's really. They had actually rescued him in Dunkirk, and we felt he kind of enjoyed our little soirees. He had a couple of dustbin's of his own, but was able to be more of his real self with the pair of us scallywags, as he always referred to us two."

"We always reckoned his missus wore the trousers. But once we approached him with our little scheme, it kind of gave him a new lease of life. It was all a bit cloak and dagger, but he loved the secrecy of it all, did Ted. He got well looked after an' all though. Don't you worry about that. Why do you ask? Of all the things I have talked about, why does that particular subject stick in your nut?"

"Oh nothing really, I just wondered if you went back to see what happened to all his share of the booty. He must have copped for a fair bit of gear over those hungry years, surely? Were you not inquisitive to see what happened to it all?"

"That's just one of The Golden Rules Stephanie, my little love. Never go back to the scene of a crime, unless you fancy doing time. Now no one in his or her right mind wants to do that. Now do they?"

"Not that any crime was ever committed at his gaff. But nevertheless, we could still have got a tug if we started sniffing around the village once he was gone. No gain. No profit. No point."

*

We finally got around to discussing the Fabergé Egg. Mrs Vivian had assured him that it was the real McCoy. Karl Fabergé had originally made 150 of the treasured eggs, with only 148 accountable for. Two had never been delivered. My egg had been given to Sir Terence at the breakout of the Russian Revolution, by one of the Romanov's as recognition of his honour and loyalty. Any and all historic references to this subject will report the same story, none of which though can account for the whereabouts of the 'The Two Missing Eggs'.

The truth of the matter being that the Russians, when communism took over, sold most of the eggs. It is common knowledge that the likelihood of finding the whole collection would be impossible. With seven or eight rumoured to be somewhere in Europe, England at the top of the list.

"Your one is safe and sound, and For Your Eyes Only," announced Dad very proudly.

"If you ever contemplated trying to sell it though, there would be a hell of a stink. God knows who and his brother would be asking more questions than Magnus Mastermind Magnusson. But that should never be necessary, so just enjoy it."

Then adding, "Of course if you found yourself short of twenty million quid one day, you've always got that to fall back on."

Who was I to question such a plain and simple outlook?

*

He then began to reminisce,

"1966, that was a special time, winning the World Cup. Of course Barney and me had tickets for the Final. Your Mum and Grace didn't wanna go so we treated a couple of the lads. The two herbets from Southend had a great old time."

"That very same day Charlie Richardson and all his gang were collared. 'Mad' Frankie Fraser, was already banged up but still got a few years added to his sentence. Eddie got sent down as well, and it left things all clear for the Twins to do as they liked. Not that they gave a flying fuck in the first place. We kept a safe distance from them but there was still an element of respect between us. They called upon our services a few times, but we never needed theirs."

"It must have been 1966 when we first got involved with that bunch of toe-rags from Brighton, they called themselves Knocker Boys and could get in anywhere. They earned good money, but always came to us when the prize could not be prised, from some stronger willed folks."

"Barney was approached first, so he dealt with them exclusively. So I didn't know them and they didn't know me. Just how I wanted it. We earned decent money out of their clues as well, but then of course when the business with your Mum came to light. Well that was when I lost the plot and severed all ties with them, and swore to make their lives not so shiny and bright. The last load of jobs I sorted, I refused to give them their cut, and so that was that."

"I still reckon I got the short end of the stick, but hopefully we can move on now, and look forward to a bright and happy future. Whaddayasay?"

"Absolutely Dad, abso-Brighton-lutely," then I tried to doze off, but could not take my eyes off the two little bundles of joy in my arms.

Grace was sound asleep next to me, we won't mention the snoring. Too late. Sorry Grace.

He then carried on with his curiosity, which was now poignantly aroused,

"Anything else attract your attention then, over the last day or two then Min? It's best you ask me now, coz this little window of opportunity is about to be shut for all eternity. And will not be opened again for a very long time."

"No I think I'm okay for the time being. Just don't be so secretive or reclusive in future. I'm just interested in the family history that's all. If there are any more adventures that should be revealed that is, after all we did say no more secrets, didn't we?"

I settled back into the comfort of the Bentley, and smiled knowingly to myself. I now had the fourth and final side to the Forest Row saga, and it sure felt good.

*

This is already the longest chapter about the longest day, and of course I could ramble on for many more pages. I'm sure you can understand, but let's not detract from the main issue and get back to the subject at hand.

What else happened on June 21st 1987, and is relevant to Brighton's Knockers? So begins Part IV.

*

29. The Longest Day Part IV.

Frankie was to go on and break another Golden Rule himself, on 21st June 1987. When he received a letter from Arkwright & Partners Solicitors in Norwich. It seemed he and one other, were the sole beneficiaries in a will, and could he please attend their offices at his earliest convenience.

Scene of a crime, I hear you mention, 'Don't Go Back to the Scene of a Crime'. Surely.

Even the clever ones, can do the silliest of things.

He could not resist it, and contacted the Solicitor, arranging to meet the following Monday. But something else was to happen that day, and he never attended the meeting.

*

On that very same day, Barry 'The Buzz' Bubball was about to break one of the sacred Golden Rules as well.

Another one 'Going Back to the Scene of a Crime'.

Why was my Dad the only one who never broke these sacred rules? That's why he was never nicked. Being the answer.

He had met a little tart in a little Pub at the end of Western Road. This should have sounded alarm bells in itself. One of the seedier boozers in Hove, and with one of those inhospitable guvnor's you tend to come across from time to time. There are a few landlords, and landladies for that matter, in Brighton & Hove, other Towns and Cities as well I suppose, who have for some unknown reason just managed to choose the wrong vocation.

Anyway 'The Buzz' thought he was onto a good thing and although he was still married and quite happy with Eileen. He was still an untamed entity, who didn't mind straying from the straight and narrow when it suited him. The bird suggested another venue so off they go to Hangleton, and into The Grenadier.

A Lovely Pair of Knockers

Territory Barry had sworn not to venture into ever again after a tricky situation a few years previously. As luck would have it, the same muggy mob from the previous incident were holding court in the Public Bar. The Buzz, was no chicken, but he should have just clucked and knocked off, that particular day.

He challenged one of the motley crew to a game of pool, insisting twenty quid each was wagered, then proceeded to absolutely humiliate his opponent. Taunting him with backhanded shots, doubles, one-handed shots, then one-handed no looking. Then topping it all off and really rubbing him up the wrong way by potting the black one handed, no looking and standing on one leg. The geezer was severely agitated, embarrassed and pissed off, all at the same time.

The Buzz had only been in the place for forty-five minutes, and it looked like World War Three was gonna kick-off. Fortunately there was a mediator in the frame, Chris O'Dwyer.

A big strong Irishman who had recently started using the Pub, knew both parties and suggested a smoke outside in the car park might calm down the situation. Barry was only too happy to oblige, and magically produced some fresh Paki Black he had scored earlier in the day. Things seemed to come to equilibrium between the two factions, after sharing a couple of spliffs.

Barry agreed to join them for an impromptu party and played the big shot. Going into the shop opposite on the small shopping parade, he bought a case of Fosters, bottle of Vodka with some Orange juice and four bottles of snide wine, as he referred to it. Everybody considered this generous and gladly welcomed him into the fray.

Things were apparently going okay, but all was not as it seemed. Barry's drink was spiked with a couple of untested Jubilees, and he passed out. He had indulged in various other bits and pieces already that day, as well as having had a fair amount to drink.

They tried to wake him, at around about midnight, realising that they had gone too far. An ambulance was called. Alas the paramedics could not resuscitate him, and pronounced him D.O.A. once reaching Sussex County Hospital. The bubble had finally burst on Barry 'The Buzz' Bubball.

A Lovely Pair of Knockers

Nobody was charged over the incident and the coroner recorded a verdict of death by misadventure. Research had gone into his lifestyle, with a few people describing his lavish habits, and not surprisingly, his drug use had come into the picture. It was not unusual or any great surprise when the coroner summed up at the end of the brief inquest. Pronouncing him a victim of his own excesses, then adding that ironically, he was born with a smile on his face and went out the same way.

*

Frankie Slimtone was devastated when he heard the news. He consoled Eileen who had been visiting her sister in Burgess Hill, at the time, due to Barry's latest bender. Their marriage had been a bit rocky at times, he was a nightmare to live with but she loved him, and they always got back together. Not this time though, and she was having trouble coming to terms with the tragedy. Frankie had been best man at their wedding in 1982.

They had not worried about getting married when Eileen first fell pregnant years earlier. Then whilst dancing to Dexy's Midnight Runners down Sherry's one night, Barry had gone down on his knees and proposed. They got married within a month and had a nice small reception at The Ladies Mile out in Patcham. Their first dance was to Dexy's obviously, but everyone joined in when Wham, ABC, Madness and Culture Club were all given a go.

Frankie was also the Godfather to their son, named Robert. Barry had a sick sense of humour, so Bobby Bubball had been too tempting for him to resist. When people criticised the name choice, The Buzz said at it would be character building for his boy, and make a man of him. The Buzz unfortunately never got to see how that panned out.

'Would he make 50?' was asked at the start. He was 39 years of age, so he didn't even manage 40.

*

30. Adios Amigos.

The Funeral was nearly a very sombre affair. But The Buzz managed to get the last laugh on them all. Due to his wayward lifestyle he had actually made a will, which Mr Ragsby produced when hearing of the dreadful news. It was not complicated, as everything went to his wife, naturally.

He had a few stipulations though. The first being that his trademark song was to be played and everyone was to sing and dance in the Woodvale Chapel, where he was to be cremated.

He had certainly given this event some serious thought.

As people entered the Chapel, the theme tune from 2001 A Space Odyssey was played, the same tune that started Elvis's concerts in Las Vegas. Absolute classic, this was also the best music to enter a boxing ring too, as far as Stevie Martin was concerned anyway.

So he told me.

It was the first time anyone had experienced an Agnostic service, including myself. So when the lady conducting the service added that, Barry hated it when the Hymns came on at funerals and nobody sang, people got the message. She also mentioned that he wanted everyone to be laughing and dancing not crying 'cause of dying.

This at first was pensive, but once the first chorus of Always Look On The Bright Side Of Life, from Monty Python's Life Of Brian came round, everyone just burst out laughing and started to move about rhythmically on the spot. Singing their hearts out like the Welsh Male Voice Choir.

When Come on Eileen, by Dexy's Midnight Runners got into swing everybody was having a whale of a time and dancing in the aisles, it was all very uplifting and life-affirming.

By the time Frankie got up to deliver his eulogy, it was tears of joy and happiness rolling down his cheeks rather than sadness. The likes of Coco and Bertie Collins, Phil Decanter, the Nearly, Bowels and

Missin Brothers all under the same roof without any aggro, all resulted in making it the most memorable of funerals.

Eileen had a short speech, then, I Will Always Love You, by Dolly Parton was played. This encapsulated the moment, and everybody hugged one another and then just simply burst into tears. Extremely emotional, and enjoyed by all.

Tommy Barnes happened to be in town at the time and showed his respects; in the most deliberate of ways. As Dolly came on he discreetly passed a few small bottles of Liquid Gold, which were passed amongst the congregation. Some started to laugh, others looked puzzled and refused the gesture. Then bundles of people just started to hug one another. It had been at the request of 'The Buzz', and he had travelled from Majorca to carry out the chore. He was honoured to carry out these last wishes also. Frankie just laughed and joined in. Absolute classic.

The soul searching, and feeling of total unity, amongst everyone in the moment, was undeniably incredible.

It did get slightly out of hand when Lonnie Donnegan's version of My Old Man's A Dustman came on. It had everyone dancing in the aisles and kicking their feet far too high in the air, like absolute nutcases. But it soon calmed down for the last eulogy by Phil Decanter. Short and sweet, but extremely poignant at the time.

You really and truly had to be there to appreciate it.

The two Eds were in attendance and could not quite comprehend what the hell was going on, but joined in anyway. Rosie had chosen to stay home with the kids. This was a wise decision, as they would surely have been severely confused by the way an English funeral was conducted. A culture shock for sure.

The last song by Elvis, If I Can Dream, got everyone crying and hugging one another. Now that was emotional.

Then of course came the Grand Finale.

They all danced out of the Chapel in a Conga Style, to Culture Club's Karma Chameleon. The small liquid bottles had been distributed in the most discreet fashion, but anyone who fancied a hit had been accommodated. Fantastic!

The looks on the faces of those waiting outside for the next service, was something to behold, as no-one could control their laughter. It must have looked so disrespectful. All thinking the same thing though, 'Only The Buzz, could have pulled it off'.

Immediately after the service, everyone was to have Fish & Chips at Bardsley's in Baker Street. They would be closed for the private function accordingly, so that Beer and Wine could be served. (They didn't have a liquor license in those days) This would have allowed time for his ashes to be presented, which were to be taken immediately to the Pier and scattered over the rails and into the sea.

It can take up to six months for the ashes to be presented as a rule, and the definitive identity of the ashes can never be guaranteed. It is rumoured that up to six people at a time have been removed from their coffins and cremated. Frankie slipped one of the staff a bag of sand to ensure this was taken care of. Let's all just hope this honourable gesture was not betrayed.

A little note attached to the urn read; 'I was always off the rails in life. So now throw me over them in death. Love 'The Buzz'.

Horatio's Bar at the end of the pier would be expecting us all by this time, and so the wake would be held there. A free Bar had been arranged for one and all. There were also a few DJ's in place, Paul Clarke and Mickey Fuller were well popular at the time, accompanied by an up and coming kid; appropriately his stage name was Peter Pan, who had been strictly instructed to play dancing and sing-along tunes till everyone was completely knackered.

Motown was predominant, Dexy's of course, The Jam, Madness, Culture Club and George Michael Whamming it out, with The Who and Rolling Stones classics. Don McLean's Bye bye Miss American Pie was sung and danced to by everyone, along with Elvis and Tom Jones.

The DJ's got right into it too, so asked new kid in town Mickolos to help out so they could join the revellers on the dance floor.

Edwin Starr giving Eye-2-Eye contact, McFadden and Whitehead were not gonna be stoppin' us now, and if anyone wanted

A Lovely Pair of Knockers

to stop Donna Summer, Lovin' to Love You Baby.......... well why the bloody hell would they?

Memories of the Great 1970 Derby Day Out were fondly brought back to their hearts. Barry's embarrassment top of the list,

"I said he'd never live it down. Not even when he died," commented Eileen. This brought tears of laughter all around.

Frankie could hardly contain himself when he reflected on a conversation he'd had with Barry a few years earlier. Explaining how on one occasion 'The Buzz' had enquired as to their finances.

"It's all in the book Buzz, don't you worry, I told him. Then he insists on seeing the book. The famous lost book? I ask him. What do you mean? Says Barry."

"Well I tell him; it's all in the book, The Famous Lost Book. He wasn't impressed but saw the irony. Never asked to see the books again after that."

I even took centre stage myself at one time, and recounted the time they had told me about the Benny Weakes fiasco. This had been one of Georgie Balcock's favourites and he could rarely recount it without going into fits of laughter. Vince Nearly had bet some of the other knocker boys that his protégé could eat 'X' amount of pork pies within a certain time. He had then spiked the pies with hot mustard and bunged Benny ten bob to carry out the challenge. Benny came up trumps, but was then accosted in the pub by a busty bird who had nye on suffocated him within her assets, and he had lost all control of his bodily functions. Both ends had expunged their contents and he had been frog-marched out of The Basketmakers where the dare had taken place. Everyone knew the story but revelled in hearing about this escapade once again, true blue knocker boy stuff.

Champagne was plentiful; food was available but not really required. Only Manny Marks did it justice, but granted, he had missed out on the Bardsley's Fish & Chips. The staff were all great, and even neglected to mention when they were supposed to have closed. They did have to vacate before twelve though or the seaside patrolling police cars would have been aware. The last thing anyone wanted was another disaster on the Pier, it can get pretty dangerous late at night, as the lighting was not too clever at the time.

I had intended to leave early, but got caught up in the unbelievable atmosphere. Only a Brighton Knocker Boy could go out in such style. This had been my first night away from the twins, but Grace was looking after them. I felt guilty, yet exhilarated at the same time when I checked in on them, before finally crashing out myself. Partying and Motherhood did not mix, in my opinion.

All in all he had a bloody good send off. It's when it all sinks in to those left behind, that they then begin to suffer.

*

I would also like to mention at this point, that I would wish my funeral to be conducted in the same way. All the same tunes, but swap Dolly Parton for Put Your Arms Around Me, by Texas. I only hope that there are as many people able to attend, when it is my time to go.

Fortunately I also have the funds, in place, available to cater for such a proposal. Hopefully there won't be too many free loaders on the firm. Can't be helped though, when you have sold thousands of books, which announce and declare such an event.

Hey ho, and away we go!

*

A Lovely Pair of Knockers

31. The Golden Rules.

The whole of the Knocker Boy community was shocked at the passing of The Buzz, but as in many similar cases, it was all forgotten in a seemingly short while. Things were soon back to normal, so it was back to the old drawing board and work as usual.

Frankie, however, could not seem to motivate himself to get back to work. The shop he and The Buzz had rented was long since gone. Perry Bowels, had taken it off their hands, and was going great guns, shop owner status suited him well. By this time all the pioneers had their own premises, whether shop, warehouse or yard.

Others had decided to pass their knowledge on, and had well organised teams of young knockers who were keen to learn the game. They were trained to 'Get In', first and foremost. Then if there were some interesting items, they would call on the 'Expert', to give a fair and honest valuation. This usually worked well for about six months. Then the 'apprentice' would tumble that they were being just as manipulated as the people they approached, and decided to 'Go It Alone'.

*

It was one Monday morning whilst having a little tidy up that Frankie came across the Solicitor's letter that he had received back on that fateful June 21st. He had completely forgotten about it, due to all The Buzz business. He was also aware by now of my unusual childbirth episode, at the same time. He called and made an appointment for the following day.

Still slightly puzzled how they had tracked him down, Frankie enquired accordingly. The person on the phone advised that they had employed specialist researchers to find his exact location. This gave Frankie a sense of security, and so was not suspicious or wary as he made his way up to Norwich, in the Roller, the next day.

Once the deal had been done those few years ago, Frankie, against the wishes of both Murphy and Giles Capshaw, had still decided, after a couple of months, to write to the Crowns and tell them he had rescued his Brother, and they were both safe and sound. His take on the situation was that they would be happier in receiving some confirmation of events. Then they would feel that their generosity had been deserved. He regarded this as more like sending someone a postcard from their holidays, rather than a Dear John letter. Or even worse still, nothing whatsoever.

*

    He was feeling optimistic as he drove up casually to Norwich in the Rolls Royce, he had grown ever fond of.
    He was early. So once he thought he was pretty close to the vicinity, he parked up and popped into a Pub for a pint.
    When he arrived at the address on the letter headed paper he was quite was taken aback. It looked like a condemned building from the outside and was not much better when he entered. He pressed the appropriate buzzer and was let in by someone over the intercom. As he mounted the stairs, as instructed, he felt a tingle down his spine. He entered an upstairs lobby, and was suddenly wary of prying eyes all around him.
    A tall man in his fifties came out of one of the doors and offered a filthy hand that looked like he had just cleaned the toilet with it. The grubby black fingernails repulsed Frankie, so he just put his hands in his pockets and asked to whom he was speaking. Not particularly polite, but this just didn't seem right.
    The skinny leather clad man, gave no answer. Frankie momentarily panicked, but then the hallow face smiled at him and he was suddenly at ease. He was led into one of the offices and asked to wait. It was all quite surreal.
    He was offered a seat at the desk, placed in the middle of the empty room. The man gestured for Frankie to sit, and he pointed to another door as he left. There were a couple of swivel office chairs the other side of the desk, indicating someone would join him soon.
    After two minutes the same man returned, accompanied by a similarly dressed chap, only he was short, stocky and bald. They both sat down, pursed their lips, frowned and folded their arms.

"Cor Blimey," said Frankie, trying to break the ice, "Laurel and Hardy without the laughs you two."

"There will be few laughs in here today matey," said the tall one. "You are in a right shitload of trouble my son. So I suggest you shut your fucking mouth and listen very carefully to what you are about to hear."

"Where is the Solicitor?" protested Frankie, "Because I seriously doubt that you are the person who requested my presence here today."

Both of them stood up, parted their long leather jackets and allowed Frankie to see that they were both carrying handguns, and had machetes tucked into their belts. The pair then put their index fingers on their lips. This needed no further instruction. Frankie got the message loud and clear.

*

Frankie would never get to find out their names or true identities. The fear of God was put into him that day. On the rare occasions when recounting this terrible ordeal, he would refer to the tall one as Bill and the short one as Ben. When I say tall he was 6ft 9in, and resembled lurch from The Addams Family. The short one was 6ft 3in and weighed about 24 stone. I will refer to them both in the same way.

*

The short one, Ben, began:

"Well, at least you've got something right. Mr Arkwright will not be present today, and it is very doubtful you will ever have the pleasure of meeting him either. He has, well let's just say, he has deemed it necessary to be elsewhere."

At this point Frankie knew he was in serious trouble. The unfortunate visit to the Pub caused him to lose control, and he began to pee all down his trousers. This bodily malfunction bought no reaction at first to his two captors. They looked at each other and smiled. This did nothing for Frankie's hopes in this now seemingly very dangerous situation.

He sounded a bit pathetic when he eventually managed to say something, but blurted out, practically in tears,

"Well, I don't suppose I can be excused while I go to the bog, can I? But can you at least tell me what the hell this is all about?"

The three minutes it took for them to ponder the situation were the longest he could ever possibly imagine.

Bill began, "Now Mr Slimtone. Do you remember Mr Thomas Crown, of Hunstanton? Don't bother answering that. If you say no I shall break both your kneecaps here and now, and that will just prolong things and make this process, much more arduous than necessary. In fact, do not attempt to agree or disagree with anything I have to say at this present time. Do I make myself clear?"

Frankie just nodded. Tears now welling up in him. He had never experienced a call coming on top, in such a dramatic fashion. At least you knew where you stood when the Old Bill nicked you. This was getting scary.

"Well the thing is this. Mr Crown was unaware of the two of us here. Being his long lost distant relatives, and all that. Due to circumstances, that is none of your fucking business anyway. I shall deliberate on that no further."

"Imagine our surprise when we made our annual visit to the property, albeit without their knowledge. We just kept an eye on our inheritance, so to speak. To find out, that some slimy little bastard, from Brighton, had wormed his way into their affections years ago and we knew nothing about it. They both passed away within days of each other under mysterious circumstances, that also, is none of your business. Needless to say you could easily go the same way if you don't play your cards right. That's the old Brucie coming out in me, funny that, eh?"

Frankie could see no humour in any of these proceedings.

"Now, this is the situation. Mr Arkwright has been fully briefed on the situation and has given us the use of his office to conduct the business at hand. Whilst he has taken a much needed break. I won't tell you what sort of a break, but I'll leave that to your imagination. Are you getting the picture Frankie? You don't mind me calling you Frankie do you? Nah, course you don't."

Ben took over, in what seemed a more sympathetic manner, "See, the thing is this Frankie. You had it away with a nice bit of Tom from that gaff. We know, because we put most of it there. For safe-keeping, so to speak."

"So you can forgive us for taking drastic steps to find the wanker that got their thieving little hands on it. We don't feel too clever about it at all, but we are not bloody stupid. We don't exactly expect you to be in a position to return the said goods. Or can you? No, don't bother trying to answer that either. You will only start to upset me if you try and give us any bollocks. What's done is done. We are all men of the world."

"What will be done, well that's another question entirely. This is where you may have some influence on your fate, and be able to rectify the situation."

"Now, we may not come across as the more eloquent types, but we have had some time on our hands to do our homework. You are not exactly skint, now are you? The thing is, how much cash can you lay your hands on in a short time? Then we have the problem of you keeping your gob shut. Will there be any comebacks? You do see, don't you that there are quite a few questions that still need to be answered. They are all to be sorted out in the next couple of days. Sooner rather than later, but only with your full co-operation, of course."

Bill then removed a small Hessian sack from one of the drawers in the desk. He came round the desk towards Frankie and gestured for him to put his hands behind the chair he was sitting in. It was hardly worth arguing under the circumstances. Handcuffs were attached to both his wrists and ankles.

His wallet and keys to the Roller were taken at this point, along with the snidey little comment,

"You won't be needing these for a while."

Then a length of rope was wrapped around his body securing him to the chair like a second skin. A damp tea towel then got wrapped around his mouth and then a towel over his eyes. Then he presumed it was the sack placed over his head.

Bill now finished their first meeting with these wise words; "The thing is Frankie, we have got you exactly where we want you. We are now going to leave you in peace to think about all these problems that we have. When we return, I hope you have come to a sensible and reasonable solution to these problems. That we can all agree upon. There is no point shouting or wearing yourself out, the building is empty. There are no neighbours to speak of. It is only fair to give you plenty of time. So we will return this time tomorrow. You won't starve or anything like that in such a short time, so use it wisely and come to the right decision. See ya."

With that they both left the room. He heard the front door slam and was resigned to spend the next 24 hours in solitude.

With no food or drink.

That was exactly what happened.

*

Of course, Frankie had expected to get a visit within a couple of hours. A small drink or even a morsel of food. Not a chance.

His bodily functions were not aware of his predicament, so there was no point trying to hold it in. Very unpleasant experience altogether.

It was in fact a couple of hours before he even began to think how he could get out of this unscathed. Then, once it all sank in, how serious the situation was and would he even survive this ordeal? How could he guarantee to Bill and Ben's satisfaction, that there would be no repercussions? Would they even consider giving him the chance to prove himself?

Needless to say he didn't get much sleep. He did doze off for a few moments at a time, but it was merely minutes. When he finally heard the doors opening, he realised now was the biggest test of his entire life. When it came to thinking on your feet.

A Lovely Pair of Knockers

Bill and Ben strolled in casually, as if wandering around a department store. They were not new to this caper. They brought with them some air freshener, and sprayed him generously before undoing his head wear. For one split second he even imagined the Police, or some heroic figure might be rescuing him.

That soon diminished once he regained focus, and recognised the two menacing figures standing in front of him. They were as smug as you like.

Yet there was also an underlying resentment brewing inside Frankie. The thought of actually calling their bluff had crossed his mind at one stage. But the potential disastrous results of such a bluff far outweighed the benefits. One chancy call too many, and you'll find yourself next to 'The Buzz', he reassured himself.

Ben kicked things off, his voice was reassuringly menacing,

"So, Frankie Boy. How do you wish to proceed? We will give you the one chance to propose a solution to our problems. If it is not acceptable, we will give you our demands. If that does not suit you, then you will be getting fitted for a wooden overcoat. So, what's your opening gambit?"

Frankie took a deep breath, and began the most important deal he would ever make.

"Right then chaps, here we go. If you take the Rolls, I will have to sign the paperwork. Then make some story up for my partner as to why I have taken such a big decision without consulting her. Now we all know that this arrangement needs to be taken care of without anyone else raising an eyebrow, let alone suspicion. Would you both agree?"

They both nodded and turned their bottom lips up.

"Good. I'm glad we have that factor clear from the start. Now I know what I can leverage within a week, and what I can get in a month. Please help me out and give me a ballpark figure. How much are we talking about? Remembering of course that I would not have got anywhere near retail value for the said goods. Plus, I am sure you have given me a little credit, for not denying the whole thing in the first place. Sorry about that. But you must admit a lot of people would have played that card."

Bill's turn, "Well, Frankie. That card, as you referred to it, was never yours to play. You greedy little shit. You, my son broke one of the Golden fucking Rules. Didn't you, you little prick? You returned to the scene of a crime, and that sealed your Fate, Mate. You are guilty as charged and that is all we care about. What did we reckon?" Looking at Ben.

Ben held up three fingers.

"Okay, okay," said Frankie, "That's a bit more than I was expecting, but hold on, don't get excited. I wouldn't want to upset you now, would I?"

This made even Bill and Ben snigger a little bit. Even though it was not the desired effect Frankie was looking for. After all he was hardly in a strong bargaining position.

Having tickled them slightly, under such pressure. Frankie felt he might be in with a fighting chance now, so added,

"I take it that was three fingers for three hundred grand, and not thirty thousand, can I?"

When Bill advised not to start trying to take the piss, or things could get out of hand. Frankie re-grouped and got down to business.

"Here's what I can do straight away. I will leave the motor as collateral. Then once I have had a chance to clean up, at, let's say at The Laughing Cavalier Hotel. You can watch me go to the Bank, and withdraw as much as I can. I will then make arrangements for as much cash as I can to be transferred the next day. This can all be observed by you both, at all times."

"On top of that, I promise not to try and inform a single soul about any of this nasty business. You knew that bit anyway, so no surprise there. I reckon I can get my hands on about sixty five grand, in cash, by the end of the week."

Frankie now had an audience he was comfortable with. It was after all one of his best attributes. Getting someone's full attention. Never before had it been so important.

Bill and Ben made no comment, so this in itself was a mark of encouragement. Frankie was still in the cuffs, wrists and ankles, as well as wrapped in the rope. They had still not offered him anything to eat or drink, so he was by no means out of the woods just yet.

A Lovely Pair of Knockers

"Now, obviously I need to get out of these shackles at some stage. This clobber is never ever going to be needed again for the rest of my life, but I will need something to wear in order to book into the Hotel. What did you have in mind? Some kind of nudist camp or something?"

Bill left the room for ten seconds. Returning with a local sports supplier's carrier bag. It contained a grey tracksuit, trainers, boxer shorts and white socks. He threw them at Frankie's feet and moved towards him.

Frankie cowered away as much as his restraints would allow.

"Don't start getting scared now Frankie," he warned, "You have passed the first test. It should be plain sailing from now on. You just keep to your word and this might not turn out as bad as you first imagined."

He unlocked the handcuffs, and threw a damp towel in Frankie's face, stepping back and admiring his handiwork, he said, "Now. You clean yourself as best as you can. Don't worry about the smell too much. We know the Hotel you mentioned and are okay with that. Before you get too excited though, where is the rest of the money coming from?"

"Well," began a relieved Frankie, "I feel so much better now. Right then, to the point. I will have to sell off some of my more sentimental bits, that I have sort of kept for a rainy day. I can safely say, that the weather forecast, predicts an enormous fucking thunderstorm is coming my way. So I do not have any qualms about that, and what I need to do."

"These bits will have to go to the auction rooms. You will be informed exactly where and when they will come up for sale, and you can attend. Not standing next to me though, I'm sure you can appreciate that. As soon as a cheque is issued, I would have put in place, an arrangement with a local Bank, and they will cash all the cheques straight away."

"Now for sake of an argument, I reckon the bits I have in mind, should fetch in the region of £215,000. So I will need one more piece. I have already thought about it and am confident in being able to secure that particular article. That lot should come to......"

At this point Ben, who raised his hand for Frankie to be quiet, interrupted him, and ordered Frankie to hurry up and get himself dressed.

They didn't leave the room, however, and Frankie was further humiliated when he had to remove all his soiled clothing, right in front of them. These were for sure, two right horrible bastards.

They gave him a bin liner to put all his clothes in and instructed him to tie a knot at the top. He then noticed they were both wearing thin plastic gloves, like those from a Petrol Station, so had not touched anything of his belongings. Or left any clues as to their identity or presence in the building.

Ben left for five minutes, came back and whispered in Bill's ear. This was of some significance, as Bill nodded in agreement.

This indicated they were ready to leave.

They escorted him to his car. Bill threw the keys at Frankie, and then enquired, "Do you know the way?"

The fresh air was exhilarating, but Frankie realised that both men beside him knew the relief he was feeling. So there was little point in making idle conversation. He was well aware there was still a lot more ground to cover, and he had to toe the line.

"Where to? San Jose? Leave it to me," replied Frankie, "You can show me the scenic route if you like."

The journey to the Hotel was uneventful. As they left the Rolls in the Car Park, Bill clicked his fingers at Frankie, demanding the keys. Frankie handed them over meekly.

When approaching the reception, a young girl appeared from nowhere, catching Frankie unawares. She was brassy to say the least. The first thing you saw was the cleavage. The low cut chiffon, purple flowered, gypsy dress clung to her narrow waist, and was cut just short enough to make you sneak a peek for her knickers.

Her auburn hair was tied in a scruffy bun, adorned with a totally inept yellow plastic rose. She had full red lips, too much peachy blusher and big black false eyelashes. Large hoop gold earrings fell from her delicate ears. The nails, on her long slender fingers looked

A Lovely Pair of Knockers

like the talons of a Tiger, and matched her ruby red lipstick. The long bronzed legs, finished the look of a beauty queen on parade. Tucked neatly into black patent leather four-inch stiletto heels.

Recognising immediately the two either side of him she casually remarked, albeit with a knowing come-on sexy grin,

"Hello, you must be Mr Thomas Crown, we have been expecting you."

She produced a brand spanking new register, opened it in the middle and instructed Frankie, "Please sign here sir."

This was all part of a master plan, and well, staged thought Frankie. Still, The Laughing Cavalier was his idea; it was no surprise that they could sort out this kind of arrangement in such a short space of time. It was no different to sorting a similar thing at The Bowthorpe with Maxy; it was just a bit more upmarket

"Here you go Frankie," said Bill as he handed Frankie £20, "You can have a few beers in the Bar here tonight. Anything you order to eat will go on your bill obviously, but please do not try and leave, will you? Be aware; be very aware, that your every single move is being watched. So don't be silly, now will you?"

"I've got the message, loud and clear," answered Frankie, "Will the phone be tapped as well boys?"

"Nice to see you haven't completely lost your sense of humour Frankie," said Ben, "And yes, of course it fucking well is." Then added in a sinister way, "We've been more than generous to you so far Frankie. You have been given a very rare opportunity here. We usually just wipe our mouths and count our losses, in such cases. It usually ends with someone getting killed, in an extremely horrible fashion, so don't cock it up. Old Thomas should have given us the right information a bit quicker. Then he might still be here himself."

Bill piped in, "You just go and clean yourself up. Try and relax a bit. Make sure you make the relevant phone calls to Brighton. Have a few drinks and a nice meal. Then, you never know. Young Bridget, the temporary Receptionist over there, might even keep you company in your room tonight."

The wicked grin and knowing wink did nothing to arouse Frankie. She was obviously his babysitter, and the invitation was certainly not R.S.V.P. Still it could be worse. Couldn't it?

*

Once cleaned up and settled in his room, Frankie called Eileen. He explained he was in a bit of a pickle, and that if she was not too attached to it, could she let him have that old mirror in 'The Buzz Bar'. He would get a decent price but he really needed it this week to get out of the trouble he was in. She couldn't give a toss about the mirror, and assured him that if Barry were still about he would not think twice.

She finished the conversation off with comforting words,

"So consider the thing yours and pick it up as soon as you like, and don't even think of offering any money for it. Not after all you have done for young Bobby and me. You take care of yourself Frankie, and we'll see you soon. Bye. Bye bye now."

As he was about to hang up Frankie hesitated, then heard the click on the other line. Ben had not been kidding about his every move being monitored.

*

The evening that followed was totally incomprehensible. Under such extenuating circumstances of course.

Bill and Ben were waiting for him when he came down. It was now two thirty, so they had to get to the nearest Barclay's A.S.A.P. Looking pensive they led him out to the car park, then advised it was quicker to walk than drive. They were not wrong. They marched like paratroopers on parade, with an arm each under Frankie's; his feet hardly touched the ground. Within six minutes they reached their destination.

Frankie approached the teller, well aware his every move was being scrutinised. He also knew he had to do things right.

"Hello darling," he began, "I wonder if I might be able to see a personal Banker. It's not that I have no faith in you, but I will be

A Lovely Pair of Knockers

making a few special requests at this branch over the next couple of days and it might be easier for all concerned. It will also be greatly appreciated by myself, as a long and well-respected customer of The Bank. Whaddayasay?"

The girl took an instant shine to Frankie. Her eyes lit up, and she gave the most unexpected of replies, in a most confident and friendly manner, which for a moment caught him off guard,

"Well Sir, if that is the case. Due to the time of the day, I am a personal Banker myself. I can close this position straight away, and deal with all your needs immediately. Please follow me."

With that she closed her till and ushered Frankie to a private consulting room.

In the most professional and speedy manner Frankie explained himself. Not only was it necessary for him to commit most of his Business Account funds to an unexpected, yet hopefully profitable project. He would also be transferring some large cheques from reputable business's that required cashing in at their earliest convenience.

Within the next month or so, some three hundred thousand pounds would be involved, and he did not wish any alarm bells to start ringing. Forewarned is forearmed he reassured her. Relevant Business Account charges would be levied, of course, and if all these transactions could be administered, with the least attention it would be greatly appreciated. There was also some Government involvement, but he was not at liberty to divulge any of these details, and trusted she understood.

Poor little Sylvia, she was captivated by his sparkling eyes as soon as she clapped eyes on him. Once he had given the spiel, then slipped in the Secret Service bit, she was swept off her feet. Frankie was unaware at first, but once Sylvia assured him that he should deal with her and her alone from this day forth, he suddenly realised that this terrible predicament could possibly include a cloud with a silver lining.

Mr Slimtone was able to withdraw £5,000 there and then. He'd clocked there was no ring on her finger. Frankie thanked Sylvia and said he was looking forward to more dealings with her branch, and maybe getting to know her better. He would be in the area for the rest of the week, so maybe they could meet outside business hours, if she wasn't otherwise engaged. The smile this got assured, him no one else would interfere with this little parlance. The chemistry between them was electric, Sylvia was excited and Frankie physically aroused, it had got a little awkward at one stage, but they got over it.

Sylvia was delicate. With a slender body she had what seemed like an impossibly slim waist, her statistics were Playboy legend, 36-24-34. Enough bosoms for anyone, you could get your hands around the waist, and a bum well worth patting. She had shiny black shoulder length hair with a classical touch of a Vidal Sassoon bob style.

Dark brown almond shaped eyes with sixties style thick eyelashes. High cheekbones surrounded a perfectly shaped nose, with a little tweak at the end that gave her an impish look. Her full-bodied lips were never without max factor pink or orange lipstick. That was the bit of Jewish heritage she was endowed with. Her legs were long and muscular, due to her strict athletic regime of a five-mile run every single day. She was fit, and that simply was all there was to it.

"Things can only get better; only get better, now I've found you!" Said Frankie, smiling to himself as he left the building.

As he came out Bill and Ben approached, having been standing guard, looking for the first time, somewhat concerned.

"What the fuck are you up to Frankie," demanded Ben, "What's with the smug look on your boat? If you think you're gonna turn us over twice you are the stupidest soppy little twat I have ever come across. Come on what's the game?"

"Calm down. Calm down. Don't get out yer pram. If you honestly think I have tried some slippery move after what you two arseholes have put me through, you deserve everything you ain't got coming. Whassamatter wiv you two?"

Bill jumped in, "Well, you don't exactly look distressed Frankie. You have also developed a smarmy sort of look about you that makes us both feel a little bit uneasy. Explain yourself?"

"Well," started Frankie, "Not only have I secured a nice reliable contact in the Bank, that will not jeopardise any of our dealings over the next few weeks. Not only have I secured your first five thousand poxy pounds. Not only that, I think I have fallen in love."

Bill and Ben just shrugged their shoulders in disbelief, and simply frogmarched him back to the Hotel. This time it took eight minutes.

Bill and Ben were resolved that they were indeed dealing with just as much of a nutter as they deemed themselves. They instructed all concerned to keep a good eye on the little toe rag and inform them immediately if anything was in the slightest bit suspicious. Their crew was fully trained and knew what was expected. Nothing much really, just keep their eyes peeled. The evening was to be uneventful. Yeah right.

*

32. Making The Best Of A Bad Job.

Once back at the Hotel, Frankie understood he was under house arrest, but what the heck. All he had to wear was the shitty tracksuit provided, but he now knew he had a bit of leverage and tomorrow would be another day.

He resigned himself to a night in The Laughing Cavalier, how funny would this work out. To some degree, he was the safest man on the planet. He recognised at least four shady characters in the Bar, there for his benefit alone obviously. Why not make the best of a bad job?

It was now 4:00 pm, so he went up to his room to take another shower. As he was undressing there was a knock on the door.

"Hold on a sec," he advised. None of it. Bridget opened the door with her hotel skeleton key, and entered. To be fair she did at least have the flimsiest of negligees on, and to say anything would just quite simply have spoiled the moment. She kicked off her slippers and sidled up to him in the most passionate of embraces. Wrapping her arms around his shoulders, and then hopping up so that her legs squeezed him round the waist like a boa constrictor. Terrible. Poor Frankie. She then thrust her tongue down his throat like she hadn't eaten for a fortnight.

"I strongly recommend the room service." Was all Frankie could bring himself to say.

Imagination is the best form of description, so I leave the rest to you on this particular situation. Take as long as you like!

The shower session took much longer than Frankie had anticipated, but he was not complaining. For some strange reason he felt a slight pang of guilt. He had no strings attached, but that Sylvia at the Bank had been on his mind since his recent sexual adventure. He was puzzled and intrigued why this should be.

Anyway he went down about six-ish. He entered the Bar and ordered a pint of Foster's Top, with some extra pound coins in his change to have a go on the Fruit Machine.

It was nowhere near as good as his first encounter years ago. Next was the dining room. Bridget, funnily enough was the waitress. Looking really good in French Maid uniform too, showing that hint of stockings and suspenders below the hem of her short black skirt.

"How many outfits have you got then Bridgie Baby?" Frankie could not help asking.

"Don't you worry Frankie baby. You just order tonight's special and all your dreams will be answered. The Fairy Godmother will give you the night of a thousand nights if you play your cards right. Ooh, that's the Brucie coming out in me."

This turn of phrase sent a chilling shiver down Frankie's spine; he immediately ordered a Bottle of House Red Wine and a large Brandy. Along with a prawn cocktail and whatever she recommended for the main course. He broke out in a sweat, but then put it down to the strenuous day that he had undergone.

The food came and went, he could not even remember devouring the Goulash and Mash. Twenty minutes later and he was chatting with some locals in the Bar. Still well aware that there were beady concerned eyes still focused on his every move. Being Frankie, it was not long before he got into the swing of things. A few jokes, anecdotes and various educational queries came into the friendly debate.

One of the locals quoted the classic verse; 'The Quick Brown Fox Jumped Over The Lazy Dog', claiming that it was the shortest sentence to contain every letter of the alphabet, with only 9 words.

Frankie then could not help but take centre stage,

"My mate was in a little afternoon drinking Club, down in Brighton, when someone mentioned that particular fact just a few months ago. His name was Barry, referred to by most of us as 'The Buzz',

He gave us his own version; 'I'm in Xanadu, Pick Up Crazy Violet, Request Blow Job, She Says Go Fuck Yourself'.

"Now to be fair that is a couple of words more, but for sure is much more enjoyable. Oh, and by the way, that should be jumps, not jumped, otherwise there is no 'S' in the sentence. Just be sure to remember that me old carrot cruncher."

Most of them laughed but a couple took offence. Upsetting a couple of locals in a Bar was the least of Frankie's worries. Anyway young Bridget had started giving him the eye, and that was certainly not to be ignored. He did his usual and ordered drinks all round, announcing,

"Come on, I'll have one more drink. Before I have another one. Who knows what tomorrow might bring?"

There was never a truer word spoken.

The night was not short and young Bridget put Frankie through his paces once again in the Bedroom. The morning came too soon. Had he had a good bad or ugly experience, he still could not tell. When he went down for Breakfast, there were two familiar looking figures, loitering in the hallway. It certainly was not good, but the bad and the ugly were most definitely in the picture.

They joined him for Breakfast. Not a single word was exchanged. When that was done with, it was 8:50 am, so it seemed only polite to stroll around to the Bank. As they neared the building Frankie perked up a bit at the expectation of seeing young Sylvia once more.

As he entered Sylvia acknowledged him and guided him straight to the same Private Office as yesterday. Everything was in order and the cash was ordered from the vault. Whilst waiting, Coffee was served and some idle chitchat ensued. Frankie was more embarrassed than Sylvia, probably due to the shenanigans of the night before. They arranged to meet after she finished work for a coffee. Alas this was not destined to be.

Upon exiting the Bank, Bill and Ben were straight on him. They marched back to the Hotel and went up to Frankie's room. He thought things were going to plan, but as soon as he opened the door they pounced on him like a Leopard on a Gazelle. Straddling him onto the bed and holding a knife against his throat.

"Right then," said Bill, "So, you have shown good faith up till now sunshine. It's Thursday morning; here is a return train ticket to Brighton. Get yourself down there, sort out the motor, put things into motion for the stuff in the auctions, and get yourself back as quick as humanly possible. We do not want to have to send out a search party.

Because if that is deemed necessary, it will be a search and destroy mission. Do I make myself clear Mr Frankie?"

"You certainly do. Here is the thirty grand, and there will be the same amount tomorrow. That clears out all my cash. Still, I will need some moving about money, and people down my way do not expect me to wander around potless. I am still shit scared of the pair of you, as you can appreciate. But, if you don't stop acting like a couple of schoolboy bullies, someone is gonna tumble. So let's start being a bit cleverer, shall we?"

"Point taken Frankie," said Bill, "Now you just do as your sodding well told, and leave the rest to us. Here is a ton. Now get yer skates on. There is a Taxi waiting to take you to the station."

No more needed to be said.

*

33. Wake Up And Smell The Coffee.

Frankie was well aware of being followed every step of the way to Brighton. They had already told him that they were well aware he had to change at Liverpool St Station. Get the tube on the Circle line to Victoria, then the first Train to Brighton. There was a possibility he would be contacted by an associate in Brighton, but this would only happen if there was anything fishy going on.

When he finally got back to Brighton, his first call was to his pal Raymond Pilch, at Graves Sons & Pilcher, Estate Agents, along Queen's road. Fortunately he was available and they took a short walk to The Quadrant Pub near The Clock Tower for privacy.

It was a bit early, but Ray never refused a free pint and was all ears as Frankie sat him down. His words were few and serious;

"Right then Ray, here we go. Just listen to what I have to say, nod your head and do not interrupt. There are people watching and listening to my every move. I have not lost the plot, but I need you to be a friend rather than a business acquaintance on this issue. I am placing my full trust in you that you will carry out my wishes to the letter. I want you to sell the house in Dyke Road Avenue sooner than possible. That does not mean as soon as possible, it means what I say. I am not interested in market price, profit margins, or any other Estate Agent bullshit."

"I know you have certain clients that have access to funds to acquire attractive properties at short notice. This is one such occasion. I want it sold by Monday."

"You will receive a special bonus from me personally for this sale, so don't worry about hagglers, just get rid of it. I do not have time to explain the details, but trust me, it has got to go, and I no longer wish to live there."

"There are no dead bodies at the moment, but if this matter is not dealt with immediately, I fear for my life. Can you do it, yes or no, it's as simple as that? Can you help me?"

"Well Frankie, I'm not so sure I understand."

Frankie jumped straight on him.

A Lovely Pair of Knockers

"Don't mess me about Ray. Can you do it or not? With no questions asked."

"Yes Frankie, I can. Now how much are you looking for?"

"You're missing the point Ray. Can you please just sell it?"

"Yes, leave it with me. When can you drop some keys round?"

"Meet me here at 3:30 pm, and I'll leave it all to you. Is that good enough? If you can sell it by then, I'll be a happy chappy. See you later mate. I'm relying on you. See ya."

With that Frankie finished his pint and bolted. Raymond was slightly perplexed, but understood that chances like this, completely out of the blue, didn't come around too often. There were a couple of punters he knew that would jump at this unexpected opportunity. He already had a couple of phone calls to make, and couldn't wait to get started. He still took a few minutes to finish his pint though.

Frankie went straight round the corner at the end of Ayr Street to Queen's Square and jumped in a Cab. First to visit Eileen and pick up that Queen Anne mirror that Barry had kept from The Forest Row coup. He fancied it around forty bags, and that would be enough to keep those two horrible gorillas from topping him.

Whilst there he also picked up a little Transitional ormolu mounted tulipwood and marquetry gueridon, 14in diameter.

These he took with him to his next stop. There was a yard in upper Gardner Street, mostly overseen by Bubbles and Basher Drawers. He was well aware that Steve, a guy that used to drive for Tommy Barnes, operated out of the premises. He was bang on.

He took Steve to one side and arranged to meet in ten minutes time at the Brighton Tavern. With the full knowledge that he was trustworthy, beyond reproach. Frankie gave him precise instructions.

He took Bubbles to one side and left the little table with him, agreeing £10,000 was owed. Bubbles already had a punter for it, so would earn handsomely. Frankie did not need the readies at the present time though. Nod and a wink ensued. Sweet.

This ensured sufficient readies would be available when needed.

When he collected the ten bags he would give Eileen half, amidst protestations, but she finally accepted with hugs all round.

He met Steve as arranged, "Now, let's get to my place in Dyke Road Avenue, and take stock," instructed Frankie.

Frankie, during his time on the train had made his mind up. Sell absolutely everything, have a clear out, and come away with as much as possible, while he still could.

Once there, it was easy. There were a few items to be taken to Sotheby's in London. Those that Bill and Ben would be aware of. The rest was to be divided between Gorringe's in Lewes, and the Auction House in Billingshurst. Steve was no mug, and understood exactly what was required.

Frankie took this opportunity to throw some aftershaves, shoes, underwear and socks in a small kit bag. Then put three suits, and five shirts with ties in a suit carrier.

He then made a couple of phone calls before jumping in the shower. The best he'd felt for God knows how long. Feeling refreshed he joined Steve in the Dining Room.

"By the way Steve," advised Frankie, "That Louis XVIII ormolu gueridon, with the inset porphyry top with beaded gadrooned border. It's about 45in diameter, well, I reckon it about £100,000. Do me proud, and we'll go halves on it, whaddayasay?"

Steve never said much, so he just smiled, then replied, "You've got it Frankie. Just leave it to me. I won't let you down."

That may seem an extravagant gesture, but Frankie was putting his life in Steve's hands here. There was no better way to guarantee loyalty and a proper job, than the promise of a nice lump of money.

*

After all, Steve had got a nice chunky deposit for his house in Surrenden Road, a nice respectable area in Brighton, from Frankie's generosity back in 1970. The Forest Row job. So he was familiar with some of the furniture anyway. This deal would pay off the whole of his outstanding mortgage, and finally he would finally be able to take that family holiday to Disneyland, California. The missus would enjoy lazing by the swimming pool in Palm Springs, and they would all marvel at the Grand Canyon. His favourite part of the trip would be Las Vegas, Mum and the kid's entertained full time in Circus Circus, leaving him to get familiar with Texas Hold'em Poker. They all enjoyed great meals together wherever they went, happy days. Cheers Frankie Slimtone.

*

"That's sorted then," said Frankie, "Give me a call once it's all sorted. You know the score. This is where I can be contacted. Room number nine. If I'm not there just leave a message. Take care my son." He passed him a card with the details of The Laughing Cavalier, and that was it.

Frankie bade farewell to his treasures, left some keys with Steve. Then asked him to drop him down at The Quadrant so he could give Raymond the other set.

Arriving a bit early, Frankie actually relaxed, sat back and looked back at what he had achieved in just a couple of hours. Ray was bang on time and informed Frankie two interested parties would be viewing the property later in the day.

"Knew I could rely on you Raymond. Don't sell yourself short mate, charge what you would charge anyone else."

Then laughing, he added, "If you still charge me the going rate after making such a killing, well, I'll see you in hell my son. Coz that, my old son, would be a diabolical liberty, for sure. No, don't worry about it; just get rid of the gaff. I shall see you some time next week. You take care; I have other pressing business to attend to. Here's my contact number in Norwich. Room number nine. Leave a message if I'm not available."

"Oh, and by the way, all the relevant deeds and paperwork are at Mr Ragsby's in Marlborough Place."

Kissing him on the cheek, Frankie stood up and left. Clocking in the mirror to his left, a shadowy figure that he had noticed more than once that day. He marched along the road to the Station, fully confident that not only had he done as much as he could to satisfy his predators, but also covered his own arse into the bargain.

As he strolled along Queen's Road he was absolutely buzzing. Then the harsh reality of what he was going back to dawned on him, time for another drink.

At the Bar in the station, the mysterious follower in the Burberry raincoat and Trilby Hat sidled up beside him.

"I'll have a Vodka and Tonic thanks Frankie, the next train to Victoria is not for another twenty minutes so why don't we get acquainted? My name is Vernon by the way. You knew I was tailing you anyway, didn't you?"

"Course I did. Do you think I'm some kind of lemon, or what?" then speaking to the barman, "Cheers mate, make that another Large Vodka and Tonic please. Ice and a slice would be nice. Okay by you Vern?"

"That's fine thank-you. Why don't we take a seat?"

He explained in no uncertain terms that he had indeed been keeping an eye on Frankie's actions in Brighton. He was connected to The Brothers Grimm, as he referred to them. As far as he was concerned everything was in order, and he would call them confirming these feelings, as soon as Frankie boarded the train.

"One last thing though Frankie. You have been very fortunate up till now mate, in my humble opinion. Previous dealings with those two herberts don't usually end under amicable conditions. So watch yourself. If I bump into you in the future down this way, I hope we might become friends. You seem like a good geezer to me. So, 'Be Lucky'. Cheers."

With that off he went, smiling and saluting. Then pointing to platform five, "That's not a train you wanna miss me old son."

Frankie was resigned. His situation was dire. There was, however, a light at the end of the tunnel. He was now assured that not every single person connected to his two adversaries, was an absolute nutcase, determined to cut his balls off. He needed to create an angle, so that he was not constantly at the beck and call of his two mercenary captors.

*

A Lovely Pair of Knockers

    This was certainly no time for sentimentality. Frankie needed some serious money to get through the next week or so. He knew the gear going into Sotheby's would need to be catalogued. They would not rush such rare pieces without getting the right kudos, and that would take time. He was still confident that Steve would try his darn best to get them in the earliest possible sale, but that might still make Bill and Ben a bit twitchy.
    He went straight past Liverpool St. on the tube, getting off at Farringdon. Just a ten-minute walk to Hatton Garden, to see one of the people he had called two hours ago.
    He had on him two very valuable items. Jimmy the Jew, had once offered him £50,000 for the Patek Philippe & Co Geneve bracelet watch. No.861245, 3.4cm and it was still in perfect condition. Frankie had told him to have £45,000 in cash and he had a deal. He was expecting a haggle, but the guy came through, and had the readies ready.
    Jimmy Jacobs had rubbed his hands together after Frankie's call. He had a Norman Hunter primed and ready for that lovely watch. One quick call and it was sold for £60,000. No wonder he didn't bother to haggle. Just for being at the end of the phone at the right time, fifteen grand. Business is business, as they say.
    Frankie then decided to keep the gold Grande Sonnerie keyless lever clock watch, A Lange & Sohne, circa 1910, 5.5cm. It was also worth £40,000, possibly more at auction, but let's not be hasty he thought.
    He got back on to the Circle Line and headed for Liverpool Street, sharpish. Fingers crossed there were not too many pairs of eyes on the lookout for him. There was a calming sense of security about having that amount of cash on him. Just hope they don't frisk me, he thought to himself. This was the ace up his sleeve if he needed it, and it made him feel so much better. There was this feeling of vulnerability, and nakedness about having no money on you, especially in such an unpredictable and potentially explosive situation.
    When he got to Norwich it was just gone seven o'clock. Slightly behind schedule, but nothing to get excited about. There were no eagle eyes about, as far as he could tell. Then Bill and Ben were

waiting at the gate. Frankie, however, was no longer shitting himself every time he clapped eyes on them. He actually smiled and welcomed them both with open arms. This made them both feel decidedly awkward, and ill at ease. Exactly what Frankie intended.

"How's things then me old Bed & Breakfast boys?" he exclaimed. This brought no reaction, and it was straight round to the Hotel. The Rolls was ready, with a new face in the driver's seat. Frankie had by now, resigned himself to losing the car anyway, but was not going to let it go without a fight.

Once back at The Laughing Cavalier, he quickly went to his room and hung up his freshly acquired clothing. He joined Bill and Ben in the Reception area and they adjourned to the Bar. It was not particularly comfortable, but they eventually began to converse.

Ben began, "Right then Frankie. We have had some sound information, and therefore solid confirmation, that you have actually conducted yourself in a right and proper manner. How are things shaping up? Don't bother to fanny us about too much, now will ya? Just give us the full monty."

"Well, before I make any guarantees, I am waiting for two important phone calls this evening. I've told Bridget to get my attention here or in the Dining Room straight away. Its 7:30 now and I expect to be called within the hour. So you will both have to wait and be patient. That's all I can say for the time being."

"Wait and be patient," exclaimed Bill, "What do you think we've been doing for the last thirteen fucking years, you cocky little bastard."

"Take it easy mate," interrupted Ben, "Let's just see what happens in the next hour or so. Anyway, I take it you can still get another thirty grand tomorrow Frankie?"

"Yeah, yes of course I can. It's all sorted. I told you both that. I'm not about to go and cock it all up, now am I? Come on get us another pint, it's been a bit of a long old day."

Right at that moment Bridget came into the Bar to inform Frankie there was a call for him. B & B both acknowledged this was a good sign and he went straight to reception. There was no point in

A Lovely Pair of Knockers

trying to hide any of the conversation; everyone was in the loop, so to speak.

It was Steve the driver. He'd had a blinding result at Sotheby's. Frankie was just about to explain the next chain of events to Bill and Ben, and Bridget interrupted with the news that there was another important call for him. They both looked on with favourable gestures. This time it was Raymondo, and he had equally good news for Frankie, but this was of no concern to the Brother's Grimm as far as Frankie was concerned.

When Frankie finally joined Bill and Ben in the Bar, he was feeling quite elated. He informed them that his man in Brighton had managed to get all their stuff in the next auction, this coming Thursday, and it would nearly all be logged in the official brochure with photographs included.

This was a real bonus, with estimates in the catalogue looking very healthy. The auction would be held from 10:30 am Thursday, at Sotheby's of London, 34 – 35 New Bond Street. Viewing was available on Tuesday to the trade, whilst Wednesday was open to the general public. Steve had certainly done the business.

The pair seemed to be quite satisfied. Now was Frankie's opportunity to try and get an upper hand, or at least a say in the following proceedings, happening the following week.

"If it is not too much of an issue," he began, "As you have both conceded. I have done nothing other than tried my utmost to do your bidding. The thing is this though, I really don't fancy, in fact I can't bear to think of myself, being locked up in this shitty little dive for another week. It kind of leaves a bad taste in my mouth."

"I'm not gonna stay up 'ere like the Prisoner of fucking Zenda. The Man in The Iron Mask had more freedom than I've had the last few days. What I suggest is this. I don't necessarily know anyone there, but I would much rather spend next week in some more friendly surroundings. Just down the road in Great Yarmouth, for instance, whaddayasay?"

They looked at each other, Ben nodded, and then Bill agreed that this would be acceptable. They actually had a place there

317

themselves, and so would be within a stone's throw from wherever he suggested to be plotted up.

"That's all fine and Dandy then," announced Frankie, "I shall make enquiries tomorrow, as to my desired residence. I take it you were not expecting me to go back down to Brighton, were you?"

"Certainly not Frankie," replied Bill, "We'll leave you to it for now. Don't get any clever ideas, you are still being watched. See you in the morning for Breakfast."

With that the pair looked at each other, sort of checking nothing more needed to be said, shrugged their shoulders and left.

Frankie did more of the same, enjoying Dinner and then having a few drinks in the Bar. Bridget did not visit, which Frankie was quite happy about. He could now concentrate on Sylvia at the Bank. She may well have some advice on the location in Great Yarmouth; it must surely be a bit livelier than Norwich.

Things went to plan. When he got to the Bank Sylvia was waiting, and they followed the usual procedure. Frankie changed the arrangement, however once they were in the Private Office. He had a much more confident air about him now, due to the fact he was now wearing his own immaculate clothing and shoes.

"I won't actually be needing the cash today Sylvia, but if you could do me a great favour I would really appreciate it."

"What might that be then, Mr Slimtone?"

"What I need to do, to satisfy, my accountant. Is to withdraw all the funds, so that I can then show a receipt of zero balance in my Business account. Once you have provided me with that, I will be making a deposit of £35,000. So in fact I am depositing five thousand pounds today, rather than clearing out the account. Do you think you could manage that for me Sylvia?"

"Well that it is slightly unethical, but I don't see the harm in it. As long as you are not in a rush, I'm sure this could easily be arranged."

"Great," said Frankie, "Now, Howsabout you tell me what time your dinner break is, because I have something more personal to ask you, and also buy us both a nice bit of lunch while we discuss it. Whaddayasay?"

A Lovely Pair of Knockers

"That would be most appreciated Sir, I take a break at 1:00 pm. We could go to Vamos A La Playa, just a couple of Streets away. A very pleasant little Spanish Bistro, a family run place, all the staff there are really nice and friendly."

"Great," beamed Frankie, "I'll see you at one o'clock then."

"Just before I go, can I make a couple of important phone calls, of a private business nature? You do understand don't you Sylvia?"

"Of course. You take as long as you like Frankie. By the time you have finished, the relevant paperwork will all be ready for you. Just dial nine for an outside line. Oh, how poetic that sounds." Smashing.

The next couple of hours were crucial. His first call was to Raggers, to confirm that the £225,000 on the table, was more than acceptable for his property in Dyke Road Avenue, and to be nothing but amicable with all Raymond Pilcher's demands. Ragsby was totally okay with all this, and confirmed everything would go as smoothly as humanly possible. He told Frankie to make sure wherever he was staying had a Fax machine, and then everything could be done in his absence. At a price, of course.

He then called Steve the driver to make sure all his other worldly goods had got to Lewes and Billingshurst. He confirmed everything was okay, and asked when he would be needed next;

"Just chill for the rest of the week mate. Let me know when the other stuff is due for sale and we will make all the necessary arrangements. You can come up to Sotheby's on Thursday if you like, but that's entirely up to you."

He knew darn well Steve would be up for it, as they had put the Louis XVIII Table in that sale, but obviously under a different name. Evidently it had attracted a lot of attention.

x

Back to the situation at hand, and into the fray once more.

Frankie informed Bill and Ben, after giving them thirty large, that he would divulge his intentions for Great Yarmouth, at three o'clock sharp, at the famous painting. They both looked at him quizzically, so he knew he now had the edge, the edge he had been hoping to get, for some time.

One of The Brighton Knocker Boy's, most advantageous assets, was their secret coded language. Cockney rhyming slang had nothing on these herbets. As soon as any little move had been made or secured, they went into auto-mode of secret language. Hence the famous 'Haggerty' expression, no one, other than a Brighton Knocker Boy would have a clue what a 'Haggerty' was.

That is of course, why there is a Glossary at the back of the book.

Even when on your Jack, this method of saying something, that the person you were talking to, did not have a danny, what you were referring to, would give them a sense of superiority.

This also probably reflected on the fact that most of them had not been particularly successful at school, academically that is.

On top of that, their Dad's were old school working class and ill-educated themselves. So hardly encouraged them to complete their homework in a diligent fashion. What chance did they have?

The two recent examples. Bed and Breakfast boys and the famous painting, gave Frankie some much-needed confidence, but he still needed to have all his wits about him, and make sure he didn't get too cocky.

*

Back at the Hotel, he got all his gear ready for a quick escape. Well aware he had to inform the Brothers Grimm of his intentions, he still didn't need their constant and intimate observations at all times, unless of course they agreed to one more of his conditions.

He juggled with his time for an hour or so. Having a pint too many in the Bar, if he was honest with himself, but what Sylvia did not know would not harm her. This was still a very precarious situation, whatever way you looked at it.

A Lovely Pair of Knockers

He met and walked with her at one o'clock as arranged. They sat down and ordered some tapas, along with a bottle of the best bottle of red in the house. All fine and Dandy, and he was certainly feeling randy.

It appertained that Sylvia lived with her parents in Great Yarmouth, and although they were Jewish, she did not share their strong beliefs. She knew of a very discreet Hotel on the Sea Front. One that would not divulge of her co-habiting with Frankie, that is, and as far as she was concerned, that was paramount, especially at this stage of their relationship. If, of course there was to be one.

You're bloody right there is, affirmed Frankie.

Let's go for it.

Bill and Ben were at The Hotel for three, and joined him in the Bar. They resembled The Blues Brother's today, as they were both in black suits with white shirts and thin Black ties. The black hat and sunglasses as accessories had been neglected.

"I intend to reside at The Kensington Hotel for the foreseeable future, if that's acceptable to you both. It is nothing fancy and my stay shall be discreet. Having reviewed the estimates on the bits with Sotheby's, there may be a slight problem with all the cash once each cheque is cashed. It's nothing to worry about though as I have a proposition for you. I really don't want to give up the Roller, and want to know what your plans were for it?"

"We have discussed it and don't really have the need for it Frankie. It has attracted much more attention than we had anticipated, but we've still got to take it, on account of family principal," said Ben. Admittedly though, this was in a sincere and apologetic manner.

"What sort of reason is that, for Christ's sake?" asked Frankie.

"On account you shagged my Sister Bridget," he replied.

Frankie did not quite know what to say at first, so quickly mentioned in his defence that he had been seduced, so who could blame him.

He then requested of Ben to, "Keep your hair on." As a tester

"Well she is a complete nympho, I know, but there must be some kind of remuneration for your actions. That's just how it is. We promised her a nice drink for looking after you. She just took it a bit more literally, than we thought she would. You're the clever bastard, what do you suggest? After all you have now cost her a week's wages, by leaving the Hotel," informed Bill.

He actually looked like he was enjoying himself, with this bit of haggling over Ben's Sister.

"Well, I suppose I could make sure she gets her greengages, and a bonus into the bargain. How does two grand sound, by Friday. Whaddayasay? Generous enough for services rendered surely. Dont'chafink?"

Ben agreed that this would be acceptable.

Frankie had bagged the Rolls for two grand of his own money, but this certainly had to be the start of things turning around in his favour. He was grateful, but not too brown nosed towards Bill and Ben, and suggested one more drink in the Bar before he made his way to the Coast.

Neither was interested in socialising any further, and simply told him, not to stray off the beaten track. He was still under watchful eyes, 24/7.

"Fair enough," agreed Frankie, "Have no fear, gotcha loud and clear. See you both sometime in the week. If not, you can contact me at The Kensington to make arrangements for the big sale on Thursday."

They gave the now all too familiar shrug of their shoulders and left. Bill looking back, then throwing the car keys at Frankie, with a wry smile on his face,

"Don't worry sunshine, we'll be in touch," he added.

*

34. A Weekend To Remember.

He took a, ten-minute, brisk walk round to the Barclays Bank, and was greeted by Sylvia in the usual professional manner.
He told her he would be able to pick her up straight after work, and she could show him where she lived, then he would check into The Kensington. She was very excited, but alas would not be able to see him later in the evening as she and her parents regularly played cards on a Friday night, with other Family members.
"No worries," said the disappointed Frankie, "On the journey we can discuss what the next few days may bring. I am at your convenience, but I do have a couple of appointments next week, in London. I was hoping you might be able to join me?"
"We'll see," she replied, "See you at five fifteen," then gave him a quick peck on the cheek.

*

Sylvia was duly impressed when Frankie was waiting for her in the Bank Car Park, the sun had just come out so it was a nice afternoon. Who wouldn't be happy to be picked up in a Rolls Royce Convertible on a Friday evening after work?
A couple of girls from the Bank giggled and pointed as she got in the Car, Sylvia simply turned her sexy nose up at them both.
The journey went smoothly with Frankie outlining his plans for the forthcoming week. A couple of trips to London were necessary and he hoped she might be able to join him. He was made up when Sylvia told him she had booked the Tuesday, Wednesday and Thursday off as annual leave. He tried to get in on the card game, but she advised the following Friday would be more appropriate.
"Oh well," he consigned, "I suppose I can get the feel of Great Yarmouth, on my own for the time being. See you for Breakfast then?" as he dropped her off at her home.

"Of course darling," she replied. Then he got his second peck on the cheek. As he watched her walk up the garden path, Frankie felt a sense of belonging with this delightful little thing that had come into his life under such strange circumstances.

'Funny old thing, this life we live in', he said to himself.

Checking into The Kensington was a simple procedure. They were well aware of his imminent arrival, as Sylvia had made the Reservation for him. His large and airy room, with an extra large en-suite bathroom, was at the rear of the building, which at first caught him off guard, as he was expecting a nice sea-view. He realised when inspecting closer, that the fire escape door, just a few yards down the hall, enabled exit and entry to his room, could go undetected. This most certainly indicated Sylvia's intentions, so he was more than happy with the situation.

He could also keep an eye on his Rolls that was now discreetly parked for free at the rear of the building, bonus.

He wandered down to The Bar after a shower, not yet deciding where he might dine alone on his first night in Town. As he took the first sip of his Pint of Lager a familiar face sidled up next to him. None other than Vernon, the guy tailing him in Brighton,

"Well fancy seeing you Mr Slimtone, what a pleasant surprise," he said smiling, like a long lost relative.

"Surprise, sur-fucking-prise indeed," said Frankie under his breath, "I take it you have been assigned another job by Reggie and Ronnie, my newly acquired concerned guardians?"

"Yeah, that's about it, but my room has shared facilities, right up in the attic. I don't suppose you could have a word with someone to get me an upgrade could you? It looks like we are going to be here all week, and who knows what next weekend may bring. There's not much point trying to deny the situation is there?"

Frankie gave the matter quick consideration and made his mind up to give the guy the benefit of the doubt. After all, Vernon certainly seemed to be the one solitary voice of reason in all this mess so far, how much worse could it get. This turned out to be one of the best decisions Frankie ever made in his life.

A Lovely Pair of Knockers

"I might be able to help. I have contacts. Give it a day or so. Right then, how well do you know this place? I have company for the weekend, but I am at a loose end this evening, do you have any suggestions? I don't mind spending a couple of bob, but don't start taking liberties. You can still pay your own way, within reason. Whaddayasay?"

"Sounds good to me Frankie. Let me get you another pint and we can have a little chat," answered a relieved Vernon.

Once seated in a sea-view window in the Bar, he explained to Frankie how he had been dreading this second confrontation. He was not exactly Dick Tracy, and knew Frankie would be on to him at an early stage. They began a bit of idle chit-chat, then Frankie asked the inevitable question: How the hell had he got involved with the two gorillas he was now running these sort of errands for?

"Well," began Vernon, "I made it to Lance Corporal in the Army, when I did my National Service. My pal, who was also from Southend by the way, made Sergeant. We both signed up for a couple of extra years when our time was up, but neither of us enjoyed it in the same way, once our mates went back to civvy street. Anyway we had a couple of failed promises, when we came out, so were a bit despondent."

"One night we got a bit pissed and decided to chase up a couple of Cockney lads we had met in service. Bob was the brains and Barney was the brawn, fucking massive he was. We had got quite friendly and they mentioned they were into some decent money getting schemes. It went really well for quite a few years and we all got on like brothers, really good stuff. We called ourselves Purveyors of Fine Art and Antiquities, Mostly Antique Thievers rather than Antique Dealers."

"Me and Sarge were well chuffed back in 66' when the two bosses invited us both to Wembley for the World Cup Final. What a lovely day that was, and what a privilege too."

"Anyway, I obviously got to know a few more dodgy characters in London, but generally it was all good fun. There were never any scream ups and we always got our money."

Frankie interrupted at this point;

"Well I wasn't expecting to get your life story Vern, but carry on. Why don't we just order some food here tonight, they have a special on Fish and Chips, seeing as it's Friday. Whaddayasay?" he was intrigued by the bloke's outgoing manner and obvious forthright honesty.

"Great idea Frankie," replied Vernon, "Now where was I? It's funny, ain't it, how you can get a good feeling about someone? I knew I'd like you. Not in a funny way of course."

"Course not," agreed Frankie.

"Yeah the problem occurred just before Christmas 1969. We had started another little venture in Tottenham, a boozer on The High Road. Anyway I got asked to go on a job with a couple of geezers, they were promising some decent money. I had a few jars and agreed to do something I shouldn't. Tried to get out of it but the old pride kicked in."

"We did the job alright, but one of the boys shot one of the guards during the raid. The shit hit the fan, 'cause it turned out it was John McVicar. He had escaped from Durham Prison in October 1968 and had been on the run ever since, had stayed active and so was a bit of a desperado at the time. The press were having a field day with it all."

"I had it on my toes and went down to Brighton. I thought I had plenty of contacts, but nobody wanted to know. I got by, don't get me wrong, but I never really got back into the right sort of company. I rue the rotten day I got involved in that poxy job."

"Word had got about amongst the Bethnal Green Berets, as we liked to call ourselves, and I was ostracised from the crew. With no chance to explain myself or any chance of parole. We were a tight knit mob and basically I let the side down. If we had still been in the Army it would have been akin to desertion."

"Ready for another pint?" he continued, "That's it really, I suppose I just drifted from one wrong 'un to another after that. Then of course I hit the drink, which led to me drink driving, which led to me hitting a copper, which led to me getting nicked and going to Jail. Trouble is I didn't have Georgie Best's reputation, so my time was not so easy. Especially being blacklisted by me mates. It was like being on

A Lovely Pair of Knockers

a leper colony all on your own. That's when I came across the two herberts that seem to have you by the short and curlies at the moment. What's it all about Frankie? Oh that sounds like the title of a song or something."

*

Frankie was stunned. The Bethnal Green Berets were legendary, but he had never met one before. They were like a secret society, but much darker than something akin to the Freemasons. He was well aware Vince Nearly had had dealings with them. But he never imagined that he would meet someone like Vernon, who had obviously been involved at such a high pecking order. There was undoubtedly more to this fellah, than following someone about for a bit of wages. He must surely be much more useful than Frankie could have hoped for, when first giving him the benefit of the doubt.

He then recollected back to the time in 1970 when Tommy Barnes warned of something afoot. Maybe word was about then, about connaughts coming to town, and to be sure you knew exactly who it was you were dealing with. That would coincide with the time Vernon had got out of the nick.

Their dinner arrived, with Frankie taking this time to ponder the situation. It genuinely didn't seem like it was so bad after all. If he could persuade Vernon to convince Bill and Ben that everything was going to be alright he might get a bit of privacy next week. This, however, should not distract him from his main goal, keeping the pair of Dick Dastardly's sweet.

During the meal Frankie explained his position and expectations. Sylvia would be joining him for Breakfast and Vernon would hopefully keep at a safe distance, till Frankie had time to explain his presence. This was devised as Vernon being a third party to the dealings that would be finalised later in the week.

It would include an overnight trip to London on Tuesday, and they would all spend the night at The Royal Garden Hotel in Kensington. Vernon's employers would surely cover his travel expenses and modest accommodation. Frankie was willing to cover any extras. They both agreed that the pair would not be keen to pay the exorbitant rates charged for a room at such an establishment.

Vernon was up for it, so Frankie now had carte blanche to do what he did best. Convince people what was best for everyone, but of course it was always up to them, and it was their decision.

Frankie and Vernon got on like a house on fire after all these revelations. The Bar started to get quite busy, evidently a local Community Club enjoyed a Pub Quiz at the Hotel, so it just made sense to seek another venue.

They wandered along to The Imperial Hotel, a couple of hundred yards along the front, a bit more upmarket, but also more intimate and private for the conversation they had planned. Both agreed that anything discussed between them should be for their ears only, no need to concern Sylvia, and certainly not involve the 'Two Honey Monsters'. They gained confidence in each other every time one or the other came up with another nickname for the horrible pair. Frankie never asked and Vernon never offered their true identities, for both their safety and well-being.

Some things are best left unsaid.

The problems of the world were solved between the pair of them that night. Vernon would be Frankie's best man if it worked out with Sylvia, and Frankie guaranteed Vernon would meet the love of his life within six months if he stuck with him.

They staggered back to The Kensington well bladdered at about twelvish, but both feeling that they had met someone who would change each other's life for the good and the better. Fuck the bad and the ugly!

*

Frankie was slightly hung-over the following morning, but fortunately had the foresight the night before to request a wake-up call for 8:00 am. He was refreshed and excited to greet Sylvia in the foyer at 8:30 am, and they enjoyed a light breakfast. He knew instantly that she recognised he had had a few, and for some strange reason this comforted him.

During breakfast he explained about the strange awkward circumstances, which meant they had to put up with a kind of chaperone of sorts, nodding towards Vernon, who acknowledged accordingly. He advised this was Government business and trusted Sylvia would be sympathetic to their cause, she concurred.

The situation was soon discarded when Sylvia suggested that maybe 'The Observer' and they themselves, might feel a bit more comfortable if they joined forces and enjoyed the proposed schedule of the day together. This was music to Frankie's ears, the relevant introductions proceeded, so all three of them were now happy and relaxed. Her credentials as a personal Banker had never been questioned but was now confirmed.

Her hair was kept in place with an exaggerated large white headband, and minimal make-up. Orange lippy and she had a matching orange Artist style tunic with three-quarter length sleeves; navy culottes and espadrilles which gave her a continental aura about her, a Parisian look.

Her plans for the day were simple, a quick polite visit to her Synagogue, it would only take an hour, but would shave years off of any proposals that Frankie might have in mind. She was sharp, and had her eye on the ball. Or balls in Frankie's case. Vernon made his excuses and decided to go elsewhere. Good job.

After that it was down to the front and enjoy some of the sporting activities on offer. Crazy Golf can be a killer for the untrained eye, but Frankie shone.

Her favourite Café provided lunch, then a stroll along the prom, which included another bit of sport, this time on the Putting Green. Somehow or other Frankie managed to lose this time. At that point Vernon excused himself and arranged to meet later for Afternoon Tea, at the prestigious Imperial Hotel. Neither Frankie nor Vern mentioned or offered the information that they had already visited this establishment. She was showing them the town after all.

During Tea, Vernon was able to let them know that the coast was clear for the rest of the day and evening, adding that he had spent one of the nicest days for ages, in their company.

A Lovely Pair of Knockers

They agreed to meet mid-morning next day and then drive a few miles out of town to enjoy a nice Sunday Roast Dinner, at a country Pub that Sylvia held in high esteem.

The rest of the day was idyllic for both Frankie and Sylvia. Both nervous and excited at the same time, anxious even, about what was inevitably soon to happen. They went straight to the room and consummated their relationship. It was a bit quick, but then they enjoyed a bath together for more fun, then at it again, this time much more relaxed with each other's bodies.

They had dinner at The Imperial Hotel, enjoying each other's company during the delightful walk there and back. A quick nightcap then Frankie ordered a Taxi to take her home. Walking her to the door then paying the cabbie off with a fiver and a wink. Sylvia was dropped straight round the corner, up the metal staircase and Frankie let her in the Fire Exit door as planned. The night brought forth more blissful exercise, they felt and slept like Romeo and Juliet in each other's arms.

They woke simultaneously in the morning and enjoyed one another once more. Then again in the shower before joining Vernon in the Bar for Coffee, he'd had his Breakfast and looked at the pair with loving eyes that only a friend would. They were both glowing like star-crossed lovers and it was plain for everyone to see.

During the drive things looked familiar to Frankie, so then Sylvia made a confession. She had not been totally honest, although the Pub they were going to did in fact do the best Sunday Lunch in the area. She was hoping that Vern wouldn't mind dining alone, as she and her parents lived just around the corner and were expecting Sylvia to lunch with a new Gentleman friend. Vernon was not put out at all, and wished them all the best. Frankie in true Slimtone style bought the first round of drinks and paid for Vern's Lunch at the same time.

*

Frankie was greeted like a member of the family, and felt at home within minutes. Leonard and Leona were perfect hosts, and

A Lovely Pair of Knockers

apologised for not having pork on the menu. A little Jewish joke that did not go unnoticed, similarly to the token visit made to the Synagogue. It was all quite simple really, Sylvia's parents like all good Jewish families wished to see her settled down and start her own family. Frankie had forgotten how influential pulling into someone's driveway in a Rolls Royce Convertible could be. They were only too pleased that the glint in their daughter's eyes since the first time she had mentioned the customer from Brighton, should be so apparently affluent.

Chicken Soup was all served with fresh bread rolls.

The Roast Lamb dinner was absolutely scrumptious, accompanied with Homemade Yorkshire Puddings, and all the vegetables you could imagine.

The wine did not live up to expectations though. Absolutely diabolical, and should not even be given the privilege of being decanted. Still, like we say so often, you can't have everything.

They managed to converse quite well, with Mr Cohen telling Frankie of his interest in pocket watches, and that Sylvia had spoken out of turn when telling her parents that Frankie was into Fine Arts and Antiques. Confidentiality and all that.

"What do you think of this one then Leonard?" asked Frankie whilst producing from his jacket pocket, the quickly grabbed Grande Sonnerie from just four days ago.

"Nice piece," commented the head of the household, "Let me get my eyeglass, and then I shall give you my expert opinion. Just one moment please."

He returned to the table with his tools of the trade, and examined it thoroughly.

"I must admit that this watch is one of the finest examples I have ever had the pleasure to hold in my hand. It must be worth at least four thousand pounds in my humble opinion. If that was why you showed it to me. Do you have any idea, Frankie, how much it should be insured for?" asked Leonard.

"Well, when I sell it on, later next week, to a friend of mine in Hatton Garden, I'll be adding a nought to your valuation, and that will still leave room for him to make five to ten thousand pounds profit.

Then I shall be getting a right good deal on the engagement ring I intend to put on your daughter's finger. If, of course, that is okay by you Sir?"

The room went eerily silent. Sylvia was thrilled but said nothing. Her mother went stiff. Then Leonard smiled.

"You certainly don't hang about young man, do you? I know we have only just met, but I see no reason at this time to raise any objections to your proposal. What have you to say for yourself Sylvia? Have you something to add?" asked her Father.

"I am in favour of the suggestion, but I thought a chap should go down on one knee and ask the intended the appropriate question at an appropriate time. Don't you Mother?" came Sylvia's answer.

"Well don't look at me young lady, it is Frankie you should be asking," was all Leona could think to say. It was all so sudden.

Frankie was already down on his knee, and took Sylvia's hand in his, saying in a tender tone,

"Sylvia Slimtone, it has a nice ring to it dont'chafink? You stay with me my little treasure and we shall pick out a nice diamond to make it official, in just a couple of days time. Well whaddayasay?"

Her beaming smile was all the answer he needed, so he simply kissed her on the cheek, then smiled at her parents.

They picked up Vernon and he was chuffed to bits for them. He then held Frankie to his promise as best man.

To say they were all thrilled on the drive home would be an understatement. Sylvia arranged an upgrade for Vernon when they arrived back at the Kensington, and all three enjoyed a bottle of Champagne before retiring to their rooms. It no longer seemed appropriate for Sylvia to sneak in and out. She had brought an overnight bag and Frankie was more than happy to drive her to work in the morning. This had been clarified by Vernon and he didn't feel the need to join them.

Needless to say, Frankie and Sylvia enjoyed each other's bodies further that night. But this is no smutty Jackie Collins novel that reverts to sexual endeavours at every opportunity for cheap thrills, and extra pages.

A Lovely Pair of Knockers

*

35. All in a Weeks Work.

Frankie delivered Sylvia to work the following morning and still managed to make it back for last orders at Breakfast in the Hotel. Vernon was still in the Dining Room and indicated they might have a little chat. No worries.

He advised that he had conferred with 'The Twins', and that everything was okay for the intended foray into London the next day. They had agreed to pay £30 towards his room and a tenner towards petrol. He added that he felt they were being cheapskates on the ex's, but 'hey ho, and away we go'. Things were set.

It seemed an unlikely match, but Frankie and Vern had a nice day together. Frankie got well poggered at Crib by the old timer. Vernon pegged his way to victory, with the final score at eleven games to five. A resounding win that could not be put down to just luck. Frankie was a fair player, but a good cheat nearly always gets the edge at Cribbage. Vernon was a tried and tested card cheat from his time in the nick. This was how he had come into the debt of the two monsters that still seemed to hold all the cards, in the immediate future and probable eventual outcome of the next few days.

They strolled along to The Imperial for lunch, and then took a look in the Town Centre. Neither were shoppers, so this was a waste of time and they ended up in the Bookies, trying to outdo one another, on the races at The Glorious Goodwood meeting.

Frankie made his way into Norwich to pick up Sylvia from work, then a quick detour to her home and pick up the few bits and pieces she needed for the trip to London.

All three enjoyed the walk along to The Imperial for Dinner and Vernon insisted on paying. This was in gratitude of the room upgrade Sylvia had arranged, a sea view with en-suite.

*

The Tuesday saw them take the drive to London. A quick survey of the gear Frankie had in the auction then lunch at Quaglimo's in Jermyn Street. The rest was a little bit of sightseeing which included The Tower of London, Sylvia had never been given the proper tour of London, and they even managed to get down to The Blind Beggar in Mile End Road for a couple of drinks before going back to Kensington.

Vernon just gave a wink and left them to their own devices for the night. Three's a crowd and all that.

They had breakfast together; Vernon then explained he had other arrangements to attend to. Frankie took Sylvia to Harrods, then to the Bank Building next to St Paul's Cathedral, where they sat on the steps and fed the birds in the same manner as Mary Poppins. This was something Sylvia had always dreamed of doing, and Frankie loved making it happen. The breadcrumbs came courtesy of one of the waiters at the Hotel. Five quid to feed the birds, Mary P. only paid tuppence a bag.

Was it really worth that much? Of course it bloody well was.

Sartoria's, Italian restaurant, provided a lovely lunch in Saville Row, then onto Strawberry Fields, one of his favourite Bars in the same street, just behind Regent Street.

The West End was a revelation to Sylvia and she really didn't want to go back to the hotel. Frankie though, still had plans. They took the tube to Farringdon and walked to Hatton Garden where he met Jimmy the Jew as pre-arranged. The watch was exchanged for £40,000. Then a quick whisper in the ear, and a small box was placed into Frankie's hand.

He then presented to her, when bended down on one knee, the most fantastic three-carat princess cut diamond ring, and asked her to marry him. She did not even answer. Even Jimmy had a tear in his eye, probably because he knew he had just sold a six grand ring for four bags. Still, like they say, you can't have everything all of the time. He didn't cry for long, he had a punter for the watch who gave him £52,000, forty-five minutes later.

Back at the Bar in The Royal Garden Hotel and Vernon marvelled at the beautiful ring on her finger. They decided to take

A Lovely Pair of Knockers

dinner in the Restaurant and agreed to meet at eight o'clock after making the reservation.

The evening went well and they agreed to meet for Breakfast before deciding what to do the next day. Frankie couldn't help himself and decided to go for drinks in a few Bars just along the road with his new fiancée, Vern declined the invite and wished them goodnight.

He had a word with Frankie whilst Sylvia was in the powder room, that the two other interested parties were satisfied everything was on schedule for the Thursday sale. They would not be making their presence felt, and fingers crossed, by the middle of next week they would not be in Frankie's life ever again. Frankie felt reassured, so that was why he decided to hit the town. After all he still had thirty-five grand in his sky, so why not. He and Sylvia went for it and got quite drunk on the old Dom Perignon, this was their first but not to be the last time it would occur.

They were both feeling groggy next morning and left word with reception to inform Mr Vernon they would be taking Breakfast in their room. Would he please meet at 11:30 am, for coffee before they checked out? A nervous Vern called at 8:30, just to make sure everything was okay, extremely relieved when Frankie answered, after all Bill and Ben would still hold him solely responsible if anything went pear-shaped at this late stage.

They had coffee and while Frankie paid the bill, Vernon collected the Car, and confirmed he would drive to New Bond Street for the next stage of this experience.

*

Sylvia was excited about the Auction; she had never attended one before. Everything went according to plan. Bill and Ben were incognito, but their attendance still put Frankie on edge. He'd actually forgotten how foreboding they could be. Still it's not like he had given them much thought, with everything else going on.

Steve the driver was there, but said nothing.

The total came to a princely sum. Desk made £85,000, Matching Cabinet £42,000, something fishy there, as they would surely have made more if sold as a matching pair. The Bergeres Lord Mayor's £68,000 and the Queen Anne mirror made top of estimate at £43,000, this totalled £238,000, leaving £214.200 after 10% deduction for auctioneer fees.

Frankie excused himself for five minutes and left Sylvia after introducing her to an old friend Steve, from Brighton who was there. He whispered something into Steve's ear then departed. Whilst he conversed with his business partner Vernon, and some other associates that had just turned up. This would be the first time he had spoken with Bill and Ben for a few days and the cold sweat was already running down the back of his neck.

He first spoke with Vernon, hurriedly, whilst passing him an envelope, advising he would join them outside in five.

"Right then Vernon. Now is your moment of truth my old son. In that envelope is twenty-five grand. They have already had sixty-five, and have just witnessed that I shall be picking up cheques for two hundred and fourteen large later today."

"Most of which can be cashed in Norwich tomorrow. The rest will be payable on Monday. They wanted three hundred, then another bottle for services rendered. You should be up for a decent tip, but that's up to them."

"Anyway we already have our own arrangement, and you know I am a man of my word. Do your stuff mate and don't let me down."

They were surprisingly civil, when he saw them outside a few minutes later, Frankie was well aware this was down to Vernon.

"Well Frankie boy," began Ben, "It seems you have come through with flying colours. My skin and blister sends her regards and I thank you on her behalf for the due payment as agreed. Vernon here tells us you have behaved as should be expected. It has been interesting and we both," nodding towards Bill, "Are satisfied that you will continue to keep to our arrangement. It seems that congratulations are in order also, it's not been so bad after all has it matey?"

Knowing he could still mess it all up if he wasn't careful, Frankie just nodded in a humble fashion and replied,

"No comment. Don't be expecting a Wedding Invitation eh?"

A Lovely Pair of Knockers

Bill added, "Yeah well, at least you pay your bills, I'll say that for you. We know you still have to hang about for the cheques and all that, so we will leave you with Vern and see you first thing in the morning at the usual place in Norwich. Cheers."

Then came the all too familiar shrug of the shoulders and they both turned and walked away.

"That went well Frankie, didn't it?" asked Vernon.

"I suppose so," replied Frankie, "Now let's get back in there and see what my favourite bid of the day comes to."

The circular Louis XVIII ormolu gueridon was indeed the star of the show. Steve had already mentioned that the Cain had raised a few eyebrows and attracted a lot of attention. There were two interested parties in the room who were going head to head, which always raised the stakes. It was at £125,000 and then out of the blue a telephone bidder came into the fray, it eventually fetched £160,000 so there would be yet another cheque later for a further £144,000. Steve the driver came over and congratulated Frankie on the sale. Then declared he would be happy to accept £50,000 as his share. Frankie was on cloud nine, but was quick enough to agree to whatever he wished, promising to meet by Wednesday the following week with full payment. Steve drove home a very happy bloke, but as with Barry 'The Buzz' Bubball, years earlier, was left wondering how Frankie had managed to convince him it was in the best interest for everyone concerned, that a true honest and fair deal was acceptable to all those involved.

*

Sylvia was unexpectedly curious as to where all the stuff had come from, how much it cost and how much was Frankie's share. This was all discarded in the usual fashion, with Frankie adding,

"Just because I have put that rock on your pretty little finger Sylvie baby, does not entitle you to know all the ins and outs of my previous life and business. I have already told you, that some of these dealings are classified and I am not at liberty to discuss them with you. It's for your own safety. You do understand don't you? I had to get special clearance after Sunday's performance to even go through with it all."

This seemed to placate her for the time being, and Vernon sitting in the back smiled to himself, fully aware that this little pantomime, would soon all end in tears.

She insisted being dropped off home first to show off her ring, but was seriously disappointed when Frankie insisted she could not stay with him at The Laughing Cavalier. Business was of paramount importance and he would see her at the Bank first thing in the morning.

He was as upset as she was, but now was no time to have any snide comments about his previous shenanigans at The Hotel.

Kissing her goodbye he promised they would have a great weekend and that they may as well book into The Imperial for the weekend. They no longer needed to hide their feelings and all business would be sorted by Monday afternoon. Then they could make plans for their future together. This did the trick and she happily skipped up her garden path once more.

Vernon joined Frankie at the Hotel and suggested going somewhere else for dinner. Frankie advised there was a decent Chinese just up the road, The New Lotus, and the Sizzling Platter was a speciality. Vern agreed and they had a few beers with it, and just a couple back at the Cavalier along with an early night. Vern was okay, but Frankie was surprised how much he missed Sylvia.

*

The usual procedure was followed next day and Sylvia was a gem. She had already paid in the cheques for Frankie and express clearance had already been verified. It just took a while for the clerks to count all the cash. Frankie withdrew one hundred and seventy five thousand pounds. Handing over one-sixty to Bill once back at The Hotel.

Bill and Ben advised they would rendezvous at The Laughing Cavalier same time on Monday morning, to conclude their business. Bill then announced that they now wished Vernon to join them elsewhere on other important business at the weekend. Vernon did not look at all comfortable about the new schedule.

It was at this point that Frankie understood that although they may have some semblance of respect for his opinion or judgement, they still called all the shots. This made Frankie slightly curious as to what they had over poor Vern, or were they just bullying bastards to everyone. He would endeavour to find out.

No one in their right mind would be foolish enough to try and wriggle out of the last detail, so they were now confident enough to let Frankie go on his own. After all he had already parted with a quarter of a million so far and the balance was only fifty-two grand. This suited Frankie down to the ground. What was in store for Vernon was another matter?

They then departed and left Frankie to his own devices. Lunchtime soon came around and he met Sylvia for a Pub lunch, telling her they had the whole weekend to themselves, a bout of heavy snogging ensued. After all they were engaged.

The journey to Great Yarmouth was smooth and uneventful. Once checked in, Frankie announced he had actually done a decent week's collar.

*

36. Settling The Score.

The weekend had gone well, with another brief visit to the Synagogue on the Saturday morning, with best wishes all round from all the family. They certainly all came out of the woodwork when it looked like there might be a wedding on the cards.

The rest we shall leave as personal, but needless to say they enjoyed each other's company in more ways than one.

The journey to Norwich on the Monday though, became slightly tetchy and Sylvia was obviously uncomfortable.

"What's up wiv you this morning my luv?" enquired Frankie.

Sylvia revealed that she suddenly felt that she may have been used as a pawn, and was scared she may never see Frankie again.

"Don't be such a soppy cow Sylvie. You are the reason this has all gone so well. The opposition will all be sorted by eleven o'clock today, and you have made it all happen." Then as he dropped her off outside the Barclays Bank, said to her,

"You just make sure all that last lump of money is ready, and you won't ever have to go back to work at this branch again. We'll get you transferred to Brighton and then you and me, my little treasure, can be togever forever. Whaddayassay?"

"Oh Frankie, I love you so much." She then kissed and squeezed him and went into work.

Bill and Ben were both waiting outside as he pulled into The Laughing Cavalier car park at 8:45 am, both looking very sombre, but no surprise there.

"Bit of bad news Frankie," ventured Ben, "Old Vernon met with a nasty accident at the weekend, so won't be able to join us for our farewell dealings. It's all still in place I take it?"

"Yeah, of course it is. What happened? Come on give me the Babe now."

"It's quite simple Frankie," said Bill, "We run things around 'ere and we don't take kindly to anyone trying to tell us what we should and shouldn't do. Even if it does make sense, it's just the way we are, you get that don't'cha?"

"Well let's be fair fellahs, I haven't had much choice, but yes of course I understand, I wouldn't still be standing here if I didn't, now would I?" was Frankie's easy reply.

"Well Vernon started to get a bit above his station and needed a little reminder of the consequences of being on the wrong side of us. Now we don't know what kind of deal, or bribe, or stone-bonking bit of bullshit you have sold him, over the last few days. But we felt he had forgotten where he stood in our firm, and where his loyalties lie. He still owes big time, and unless he comes up with some kind of payment in the near future, we will have no further need of his services. Not only will his non-existent contract be terminated, he will be an' all."

Frankie could never recall which one of the two divulged this information, but assessed the situation quickly and acted on his tried and tested knocker boy instinct.

"Well, seeing as he seems to have done me no harm, and only enhanced my chances of survival. In fact during our forced shared vacation, I feel it is my duty, or even honour, as to enquire how much indebted he is to your company. I must add, that services rendered don't come into it, I can only help in matters of finance, within reason of course. Whaddayassay?"

Bill spoke first, "Well as we mentioned, Vernon met with a nasty accident and at the present time is in Hospital with a couple of broken legs. Still it couldn't be three could it, that's the old Brucie coming out of me again, can't resist a joke me. Anyway good game, good game, that chasing around in a car park, well it's always advantageous to be in the car rather than on foot don'tchafink?"

"He won't be about for a while but if you wanna make sure he is no longer tied to us, and doesn't meet with any more unfortunate accidents, ten grand will get him out of trouble, and that's being generous. Still we are confident that if you take on the debt you will pay up lively. You always seem to bring out the best in us me old sunshine. So what's it to beee Frankeeee?"

Frankie was suddenly slightly dizzy in the head. It was reminiscent of the time in The Waggon and Horses when Jackie Wadman asked what he wanted to drink. Still, he soon shook it off, and answered, as quick on his feet that any knocker boy would be proud of,

"Right then, here is what I propose. I still have some funds available after all my worldly goods have been disposed of, but what I am prepared to do is this. Once I have got all the readies from the J. Arthur, I will settle our bill. Last standing at £302,000, now with an added ten, and pay you a further £13,000, taking the total to £325,000 when all is said and done. I do, however, have an extra added clause, which is this…"

Bill and Ben were impressed with the little bugger for having such big balls, but tried their best not to show it. Frankie though, knew he had finally got their respect and attention.

"If at some time in the future, and hopefully never at all. If I should be in need of some strong-arm tactics, I can call on you two, to help out. That means I have paid in advance thirteen bags for services yet to be rendered. Do I have your word on it Gentlemen?"

He then held out his hand and waited for their reaction. They both looked at each other, bewildered. Nobody had ever had the bottle or balls, to actually set the rules in front of them, for many years. But they both equally admired his courage. The familiar shrug of the shoulders came as expected, and they both held out their hands at the same time. The choice of whose hand to shake first was impossible, so Frankie just closed his eyes and waited. The shake never came, but the deal was done.

*

The civilised walk to the Barclays branch took twelve minutes. The business inside took exactly the same time. Bill requested Frankie to join them in a local Restaurant just around the corner. It was open for their convenience only, family friends and all that. This was to discreetly hand over the final agreed settlement. Surprise, surprise, it happened to be the Vamos Ala Playa, so the staff were already well familiar with all the faces in attendance. Frankie though, was suddenly in a state of nervous disposition, or was he just getting paranoid again.

Due diligence was followed as expected, the cash was handed over and hands were shook. Bill and Ben confirmed that there was no more outstanding business to be attended to between either Frankie or Vernon and that probably their paths would never cross again. This was music to Frankie's ears, but was there more to the plot than meets the eye he thought to himself. Que sera, sera!

Anyway, that was it.

Frankie collected his bags from The Laughing Cavalier and never went back. He had lunch with Sylvia at the same Restaurant and picked her up after work. She never went back to that Branch.

They visited Vernon in hospital and Frankie assured him everything was cleared with the heavy mob, so when he was feeling better he could start life anew down in Brighton.

*

A Lovely Pair of Knockers

Epilogue.

This really and truly should have been entitled the 'What happened next Chapter?' But by way of true definition this Epilogue summarises all the events covered and poses questions of the future without giving it all away.

Vernon would later marry Shirley, Georgie Balcock's Missus. Frankie was the best man.
Vern was the best man when Frankie married Sylvia and they are all still very happy.

*

On one occasion though, I was lunching in Church Road with Frankie, Sylvia, Vernon and Grace. She had been reluctant at first to meet someone but surrendered to my protestations that she still had a life of her own to live. I assured her that the twins and myself would always need her so any other relationship she may develop would never interfere with our bond. Purely by chance my Dad drove past the Restaurant in the Bentley. He came in looking concerned and beckoned to me with the old pointy finger.
"What's up Dad?" I innocently enquired.
"How well do you know them people?" he asked abruptly.
"Frankie is a lovely bloke, just recently married Sylvia and the other fellah Vernon was his best man. Don't you agree that Grace need not be a lonely widow all her life? Why?"
"Well that Vernon is a wrong'un. Here's fifty quid towards the bill, you and Grace are leaving with me right now young lady."
This was no request, there was nobody in the whole world I trusted more than my Dad. So I did as I was told. I decided to make an excuse about being needed urgently at Scarlett's school.

When I got back to the table Vernon was indeed looking quite pale and very sheepish. He obviously recognised my Dad, but said nothing. Frankie refused the money of course and wished me all the best.

Grace said nothing but followed my lead without uttering a single word, not even acknowledging our lunch companions. Old school and all that, coming into play, not for the first time.

That afternoon Dad explained his reasons to us both, and so I was compelled to refuse any further social invitations that may involve Vernon.

It's a shame but let's be fair, blood is thicker than water.

*

So, everything was going good back in 1987, but now let's fast forward to 1993. The twins were both at private schools. My Dad's advice back in the day to move out to Hove, where better schooling was available was indeed correct. Will went to St Christopher's, just around the corner in New Church Road which was without doubt the best place for him, he even came home for lunch when I was not too busy at work. Whilst Scarlett attended Deepdene School for Girls, also close enough to come home for lunch when the opportunity arose.

My personal circumstances were now about to be tried and tested and come under scrutiny. I heard Steve Martin was back in town, but had it on good authority he was not the same person that we had all known of six years ago.

Completely by chance, Tracey had bumped into him at a wedding reception at The Grand Hotel, and although he was quite polite when enquiring as to my whereabouts, he was acquainting with a more notorious type of character. He was for sure in the company of people dabbling in the old nose candy and was perfectly at ease with it all, unlike years before.

Lo and behold a couple of days after hearing this news, at about 7:30 am there was a knock on my door, to which I did not answer. He was back and not ignoring me. I peeked behind my curtains and watched him saunter along the end of the road with just the one off chance glance over his shoulder. Reminiscent of our very first meeting at The Waggon and Horses, many years ago.

It was not a school day so I popped into the twin's room and just stared at them both for a good ten minutes. Recognising those all too familiar characteristics of their Father, who didn't have a hullabaloo about their existence. Or did he?

It was then that I decided that the only fair thing to do was let them all know, but would I tell him or them first? Things would have to be planned carefully, and the one person I knew who could help me do this properly would be Grace, or Trace or Poppy or my Dad. At this time I realised how lucky I was to have so many trusted people in my life. So lucky I was to even have the choice.

Anyway it was Grace that I first approached, and told her that Steve was back and asked her view.

Her answer was so easy and simple, I wondered why I had not figured this out myself, she began to explain her view in earnest,

"Well," she said, "If the situation of Man and Woman was reversed, i.e. after sex, the man was pregnant and not the woman. How would you feel if he had not told you that he had raised two beautiful children for five years and they had no idea who their Mother was? Surely at some time there would be some curiosity, so how would you feel?"

Obviously when explained in such simple terms, this information hit me like a tidal wave smack in the face, and I knew at that precise moment I had to do the right thing.

From my limited information though, I had no idea what his personal plans for the future might be, and I was not about to unhinge my children's routine and security.

Evidently he had just been released from Long Bay Jail, a maximum-security prison in Sydney, Australia. After serving a year for being the head of a ring of International Jewel thieves, that had attempted to smuggle £250,000 worth of jewellery into Oz from Hawaii.

A random check at Kingsford Smith Airport had foiled their plans. Nationwide T.V. coverage ensued, so anybody and everybody that had emigrated to Australia in the last ten years was fully aware of the culprit, and conveyed the information to all and sundry in Brighton. This also appertained that his biological Mother found out the information via Television as well, all her friends also. Slightly embarrassing, to say the least.

Not my Stevie surely? Was he back to stay? Just passing through? Or perhaps he had other plans afoot.

From my intimate knowledge of the man, whatever he did have in mind he would stick to it. I realised that I now had to get to know the Steve of 1993 and try to erase the thoughts of the Steve Martin of 1986, to the best of my ability.

Dad advised that the chance was worth taking and would do anything and everything to help. My position in the family business would not be hindered, and any time off for reconciliation was of no consequence. We were mainly involved in high-end rental properties now. With other interests dealt with by overseas companies. I owned half the company by now anyway, and certainly had enough resources at my fingertips to avoid any financial concerns or money worries.

*

I put my plan into action and saw him for the first time in Browns Wine Bar in Duke Street. He was with a mutual friend Dave Day, but immediately excused himself when he recognised me, that all too familiar smile that reminded me a bit of Frankie,

"Hello Steph. How are you doing darling?" he said at first.

We chatted for a while, during which time I told him I had twins. He was totally oblivious to the fact they might be his, and showed not the slightest interest when I showed him their pictures, that were always in my purse. He didn't flinch and could not see for himself that they were the spitting image of him. Unbelievable!

I had imagined that he would realise what I was doing, but it simply did not work out as I had planned. During our conversation I explained that Scarlett had a not so rare but incurable hearing defection, that the best Doctor's in the country had no answer for, just a name.

The medical terminology was very longwinded but I just couldn't quite manage to remember at that precise time the exact description of the condition and it's official title.

It was a form of deterioration that was contributory to her lack of concentration at times. Then the most fantastic miracle moment happened, that still to this day, I cannot fully comprehend, or come to terms with.

"Well would you Adam and Eve it," he said, "I met a lovely Lithuanian couple one time, in Adelaide. Whose daughter had exactly the same symptoms. I believe the condition is referred to as Sensorineural, if my memory serves me well. From time to time they get a lot of ringing in the ears."

He was spot on with this symptom, but how the hell did he manage to remember the exact name of the condition.

"They didn't have much money but their faith was humungous and they took her to a faith healer in a place called Coober Pedy in South Australia. I helped raise some money for the trip by organising a charity Pool competition, not swimming, the Pub game. They're quite keen on the game over there in Oz, so it was easy really."

At this moment in time I was absolutely flabbergasted, speechless and could not believe my ears.

He continued in a knowledgeable fashion,

"It's an underground kind of mining town that harvests some of the best Opals in the world. They're not crazy or anything it's just easier to live that way, what with the extremely hot weather. Anyway this woman worked miracles and the little girl got the all clear from the Doctor's after just three months of herbal remedies and prayer. Whaddayafink?"

Imagine my reaction. I threw my arms around him and whispered softly in his ear, "She yours too y'know."

He went as white as a sheet, stood up and just blurted out,

"I can give you all the details later, but unfortunately, I can never go back to Australia. Just so's y'know."

With that he left, scratching the back of his head in a very confused state of mind.

*

Tracey had met a nice bloke called Leon and was all loved up.

Grace, not deterred from her recent disastrous attempt at meeting someone, Vernon. Had now once again ventured into the world of dating and was seeing a lovely character called Neil Wellcape, a bit of a face with a shady past. Still this did not seem to worry her; after all, Barney had been a top tea-leaf himself.

Life is not always easy, but we have to do the best of what we get dealt with. The rest of my story and further tales of Brighton's Knocker Boys can be read at a later date.

> What will become of Willoughby Manor?
> Which charities will be our beneficiaries?
> What happened to the Coin Collection?
> Did The Faberge Egg come to light?
> What became of Frankie's properties?
> How did I dispose of all Dads' ill-gotten gains?

Do I get back with the twins Dad?

Well, not all the questions can be answered in one book.
So till next time...

Cheers everyone and I sincerely hope you have enjoyed reading these tales. Love always SM.

P.S. A quick thank-you to Grace and Trace for everything. Phil and Dale at The Brighton Print Centre as always, have been invaluable.

*

A Lovely Pair of Knockers

The Glossary.

This is not to condescend anyone who has decided to give this Publication a chance. Thank-You So very much, I really mean it. But some of you may not be familiar with all the tiny idiosyncrasies that bring the whole thing together, and by just taking five minutes to browse through some of these unfamiliar terms you will feel more 'involved' and don't be for one second deterred from referring back to this page to understand exactly what is going on. This also, hopefully, makes sure you do not get fed up by reading something that you don't quite understand, and put the book away, till another day.

It's just a couple of pages, so stick a bookmarker in the back for quick and easy reference. Please, just relax and enjoy!

Treacle as in Treacle Tart	= Sweetheart
Rattley	= Female companion
Danny as in Danny La Rue	= Clue
Jack	= On their own / Singular
Whistle as in Whistle & Flute	= Suit
Karked / Karking	= Dead / Dying
Poggered	= Beaten / Bashed Up
J. Arthur as in J. Arthur Rank	= Bank
Frog as in Frog and Toad	= Road
Holy Ghost	= Toast
Vera as in Vera Lynn	= Chin
Boat as in Boat Race	= Face
Gaff / Kenna / Kennel	= House / Dwelling
Battle as in Battle Cruiser	= Boozer
Sherbet/Shant	= Alcoholic beverage
Jubilee	= E as in Ecstasy
Hurry Up	= Speed / Amphetamine
Liquid Gold	= Poppers / Amyl Nitrate
Ricket	= Mistake
Haggerty	= House Clearance
Scoombers	= Moulsecoomb Council Estate
Hawkers	= Whitehawk Council Estate

A Lovely Pair of Knockers

Chored / Chogged	= Stolen
Pony as in Pony & Trap	= Crap / Bad
Mars Bar	= Scar
Goonered	= Sacked
Naused	= Messed Up
Cattled	= Flabbergasted
Schtum	= Mouth Shut / Keep Quiet
Mivvi	= Ice-cream Filled Lolly
Smudge/Frame	= Painting/Picture
Mullered	= Killed / Murdered
Lord Mayor	= Chair
Cain as in Cain & Abel	= Table
Peter as in Peter Pan / Can	= Safe
Connaught as in Connaught Ranger	= Stranger
Drum as in Drum and Bass	= Place
Mincers as in Mince Pies	= Eyes
Crust as in Crust of Bread	= Head / Skull
Tom as in Tom Foolery	= Jewellery
Muddy as in Muddy Water	= Daughter
Norman as in Norman Hunter	= Punter / Customer
Currant as in Currant Bun	= Son
Dustbin as in Dustbin Lid	= Kid /Kids
Hubble Bubble	= Trouble
Tick	= Credit
Rita as in Rita Hayworth	= Worth/Value
Babe as in Babe Ruth	= Truth
T.M.I.	= Too Much Information
Bish Bosh as in Dosh	= Money
Cherry as in Cherry Picker	= Nicker = £1
Bottle = £2 Carpet = £3	Rouf = £4
Dinar = Shilling (5p)	Cows Half = 10/- (50p)
Stripe = £1	Ching = £5
Cockle = £10	Score = £20
Half a Spot/Bull's-eye = £50	Spot / Ton = £100
Monkey = £500	Bag as in Bag of Sand = £1,000